Joseph Grego

Rowlandson the Caricaturist

A Selection From His Works: First Volume

Joseph Grego

Rowlandson the Caricaturist
A Selection From His Works: First Volume

ISBN/EAN: 9783337013943

Printed in Europe, USA, Canada, Australia, Japan

Cover: Foto ©Andreas Hilbeck / pixelio.de

More available books at **www.hansebooks.com**

Tho.s Rowlandson

ROWLANDSON THE CARICATURIST

A SELECTION FROM HIS WORKS

WITH ANECDOTAL DESCRIPTIONS OF HIS
FAMOUS CARICATURES

AND

A Sketch of his Life, Times, and Contemporaries

BY

JOSEPH GREGO

AUTHOR OF 'JAMES GILLRAY, THE CARICATURIST; HIS LIFE, WORKS, AND TIMES'

WITH ABOUT FOUR HUNDRED ILLUSTRATIONS

IN TWO VOLUMES — VOL. I.

London

CHATTO AND WINDUS, PICCADILLY
1880

DEDICATED

ALL LOVERS OF HUMOUR

PREFACE.

'Tuà nobis est gratiâ.'—Cic.
We have need of your favour.

THE EDITOR recognises that the admirers of Rowlandson's peculiar graphic productions, and those fortunate amateurs who are able to indulge their taste for collecting caricatures and works embellished with humorous illustrations, will not expect any excuse for the preparation and appearance of the present work : he anticipates that—in spite of much that he would improve—the two volumes devoted to a *résumé* of the great Caricaturist, with the multifarious, ludicrous, and grotesque creations which emanated from his fertile fancy, will be accepted as, in some degree, supplying that which, without being absolutely indispensable, has frequently been instanced as a compilation likely to be acceptable to the appreciators of graphic and literal satire.

To the initiated few this sketch of a famous delineator of whimsicalities, with the review of his works, times, and contemporaries, is offered with the conviction that the intentions of the Author are not liable to be misconstrued by them ; nor has he any grounds to dread that the subjects represented run the risk of being questioned at their hands on the grounds of propriety.

Fuller consideration is due to the many to whom the name of Rowlandson conveys no more than a perception of 'oddity' or of license of treatment which approaches vulgarity, to whom the innumerable inventions of the artist represent foreign ground—a novel, strange land, populated with daring absurdities, according to their theories.

It is felt that some justification is needed for the writer's temerity in volunteering as a pioneer to conduct the unsophisticated through the devious and eccentric intricacies which characterise the progress of pictorial satire, as demonstrated in the subject of the work now submitted to the public with all due deference.

The neophyte, it is anticipated, will be somewhat startled at the first glance of the surroundings amidst which he will wander ; but it is believed that, in the course of his journey through an anomalous past, he will alight on discoveries, more or less interesting in themselves, which provide abundant food for the student of humanity.

The writer deprecates a hasty conclusion, with the assurance that those who have the moderation to reserve their opinions until they have fully acquainted themselves with the materials, may possibly suffer their critical instincts to be modified in the process.

We have taken the liberty of scrutinising somewhat closely—with a view to the portrayal of its salient features—a generation which was marked with a colouring more intensified than those who live in our time are prepared to adopt. Of this age, diversified with much which has been discarded, we accept Rowlandson as the fitting exponent. His works epitomise a state of being comparatively recent in actual fact, but, from the circumstances of change, so distantly removed in appearance, as to constitute a curious experience to the majority.

With every qualification to ensure success, Rowlandson, as his story indicates, deliberately threw away the serious chances of life, to settle down as the delineator of the transitory impressions of the hour. 'There is wisdom in laughter,' says the sage ; and—without precisely regarding life as a 'stale jest'—our artist drew mirth from every situation, and illustrated from his own fecund resources that, while nearly every circumstance has its grotesque as well as its sinister aspect, the ludicrous elements of any given event are often more enduring than the serious ones.

Good-natured pleasantry, we may remind the reader, is held to be wholesome. Rowlandson's shafts, so far as our judgment serves, were never pointed with gall : while he possessed the faculty of seizing the weak or ridiculous side of his subject, he seems, unlike Gillray, his best-known contemporary, to have been an utter stranger to acrimonious instigations. A fuller acquaintanceship reveals the Caricaturist—as he was described in his day—'an inexhaustible folio of amusement, every page of which was replete with fun'—perhaps the most genial travelling companion who could be selected in traversing the ways of life led by our ancestors, for the half-century which witnessed the gradual extinction of the quaint, old-fashioned Georgian era, and inaugurated the less picturesque generation to which our immediate predecessors belong.

Be it recorded, concerning the part played in the world by the satirists, pictorial and literal—'the less they deserve, the more merit in your bounty.' We would modestly suggest the sapient axiom embodied by the great master, 'Fancy's favourite child,' relative to the transient jesters whose lot it has been 'to hold, as 't were, the mirror up to nature' upon the mimic stage : 'Let them be well used ; for they are the abstracts and brief chronicles of the time : after your death you were better have a bad epitaph, than their ill report while you live.'

CONTENTS

OF

THE FIRST VOLUME.

(1774—1799.)

BIOGRAPHICAL SKETCH.

The prevalent taste for pictorial satires—Contributions to the literature and history of caricature—Collections of caricatures in national museums—Rowlandson's publishers—Scarcity of his works and
the avidity of collectors—Difficulties in the way of forming a collection of Rowlandson's engraved
plates—Rowlandson regarded as an artist in water-colours—Examples of his productions to be
found in picture galleries—Establishes himself as a serious artist, 1777 to 1781—His contributions
to the Royal Academy as a portrait-painter in oils—His female likenesses—His versatile acquirements and imitative fidelity—Rowlandson considered as a landscape artist—As a painter of marine
subjects—George Cruikshank's estimation of Thomas Rowlandson— General review of Rowlandson's caricatures : Gambling, the Westminster Election, 1784; political struggles between the Whigs
and Tories, Pitt and Fox, the King and the Prince, fashions, the clergy, the Bar, usures, doctors,
quackery, John Bull, foreigners, cockneys, countrymen, the Universities, collegians, the military,
the navy, seaport sketches, amusements of the *bon-ton*, Vauxhall, the Opera, theatres, card-playing,
sharpers, drinking, feasting, sport, fox-hunting, horse-racing, prize-fighting, rural sports, masquer-
ading, picnic revels, fortune-hunters, elopements, Gretna Green, travesties, parodies, and burlesques, trials, scandals, housebreaking, highway robberies, the passions, the Royal Family—Imitations of the old masters : Female studies, *croquis* taken in France, Holland, Belgium, Germany,
England and Wales, the metropolis—The Regency struggle—Admiral Lord Nelson—The miseries
of human life—The Great French Revolution—Napoleon Buonaparte—The Delicate Investigation—
The Royal Academy, &c., &c.—Manifold production of drawings—Contributions to book illustration—Portraits of the caricaturist—The artist and his relatives—His schoolfellows—A student in
Paris—At the Academy schools—His early friends Bannister and Angelo—Tricks on the Royal
Academicians—His friends Pyne and John Thomas Smith—Studies of Continental character—
Between London and Paris—Is left a fortune—His passion for the gambling-table—The integrity
of his conduct—Successive exhibits at the Royal Academy—Portraits in oil—His travels at home
and abroad ; the companions of his excursions ; Mitchell the banker and Henry Wigstead the magis-
trate—Congenial spirits—Vauxhall Gardens—Lord Barrymore—Nocturnal frolics—Play—Succes-
sive drawings of social satires, contributed to the Royal Academy Exhibitions—Rowlandson robbed
—Identifies a thief—Lord Howe's victory—French prisoners—Sketches of the embarkation of the
expedition for La Vendée—Sojourns in Paris with Angelo, John Raphael Smith, Westmacott, and
Chasemore—Sketching in the Netherlands and Germany with Mitchell—John Bull on his travels
—Night auctions of pictures, drawings, and prints—Old Parsons, 'Antiquity' Smith, Edwin,
Greenwood, Hutchins, Heywood—Relaxations of the period—Nights at Mitchell's—Wigstead
and 'Peter Pindar'—Wolcot's stories—Dinners with Weltjé at Hammersmith—The Prince of
Wales—Theatrical worthies, Munden, Palmer and Madame Banti—Convivialities—The Prince's
Maître d'Hôtel : his cooking and anecdotes—Excursions in England : views in Cumberland, Corn-

1785.

PAGE

1790.

1791.

1792.

1793.

1794.

1795.

1796.

1797.

1798.

1799.

ROWLANDSON THE CARICATURIST.

Buyers and readers of books, all admirers of pictures, drawings, and engravings—
in a word, the intelligent, and, let us hope, larger proportion of the community—
are well aware, if they are inclined to search for information
in respect to the celebrities of art, or would inquire into
the personal careers of the renowned pioneers and practitioners of the serious branches of the profession, of whatever
period, school, or nationality, that numerous sources of
reference, tolerably easy of access, are open to the seeker
without being driven far abroad in his quest.

There exist, as we are all thoroughly aware, abundant
lives of artists, dictionaries of painters, and other prolific
sources of information upon the practisers of the sober walks of pictorial art, with
rich collections of engravings from their works, in fact, a complete library of
delightful literature, which goes far towards proving that the world at least
acknowledges a slight interest in individuals as well as works, and that people
care to learn some particulars of the men who spent their industrious existences,
and devoted the gifts of their admitted genius and application to the humanising
walks of life, and to the fitting illustration of the world's universal passions and
history, or to the delineation of the ever-varying beauties of nature under
picturesque aspects.

Wealthy collectors, the cultivated patrons of material refinement, frequenters
of picture galleries, those who love pictures by instinct, art amateurs, and the
hopeful and fervent student, have alike a provision prepared for them in this
regard, which happily leaves little to be desired. The memoirs of artists—men
whose domestic and inner lives in so many instances teach lessons of gentleness,
simplicity, and singleness of purpose, of perseverance under difficulties ; making
manifest to a world which is often slow to give them credit for the gifts that are
in them, the strong impulses of talent under untoward conditions—are, for the

most part, tender memorials, labours of love, cherished productions of biographers, whose own natural qualifications and trained appreciation of the subtler attractions of art have brought them into more intimate communion with the memorable subjects of their studies.

It has ever been a source of regret to the writer, since his youthful fancies were first won by the marvels of grotesque art, and the pleasant creations of the graphic humourists, that while the names of the designers, familiarly known as *caricaturists*—who have enriched the more playful branches of the profession—are household words, no fitting memorials are to be found of the careers of these draughtsmen of true genius ; they knew their generation, as is instanced in the inexhaustible memorials they have bequeathed their descendants in their works, and while they were themselves thoroughly familiar with the varied aspects and workings of the social life with which they were surrounded, their generation knew them not, and took no care to preserve any record of the capricious wits

whose pleasant inventions had often afforded them enjoyment. The humourists, who did so much to contribute towards the amusement of others, have been suffered to pass away, in too many cases, as impersonalities. The works of their fanciful and fertile imaginations have been accepted on all hands and allotted their recognised position among the other agreeable accessories of life, while the gifted professors have, with one or two notable exceptions, which make the reverse the more marked, been pretty generally passed over, if they are thought of at all under the relationship of realistic characters, as mythical beings, less tangible—as regards their connection with the living people of their generations, of whose persons, habits, and follies they have bequeathed animated instances to posterity —than the most weird and fantastic creations of their own pencils or etching-points, emanations of the mind, whose utmost substance amounts to paper, and printing-ink, and ideas.

The whimsical conceptions which owe their origin to Gillray, Rowlandson, Bunbury, Ramberg, Woodward, Dighton, Nixon, Newton, Boyne, Collings, Kingsbury, Isaac Cruikshank, his son, ' the glorious George,' the veteran calcographist, who has just passed away full of years and reputation, Lane, Heath, Seymour, and a bevy of their contemporaries, were in their day tolerably familiar, their etchings and sketches were in the hands of the print-buying public of the period, and they enjoy, as far as these relics of the past are concerned, a posthumous reputation which varies according to the merits of their productions, a generation or two having assigned them their just relative positions on the ladder of fame ; all the inimitable amusing travesties which reproduce the manners, and even the sentiments of past celebrities and perished generations, owe their creation to artists who were suffered to labour in partial obscurity ; while the creatures of their brains were in the hands of every one, their contemporaries, for the most part, did not trouble themselves sufficiently to reflect whether the designers had any real existence, possibly classing the actual, practical, living, and working men under the category of abstract ideas in their own minds, impalpable atomies, less substantial than their tangible satirical pictures, which enjoyed a popular circulation.

The late Thomas Wright, F.S.A. (with the collaboration of an earnest worker in the same field, the late F. W. Fairholt, F.S.A., who contributed the valuable aid of his pencil), has done a great deal for the subject in his 'History of the Grotesque in Literature and Art,' and still more in his 'Caricature History of the Three Georges.' 'The Caricature History of the Fourth George,' which offers a still wider field of selection, as regards political and pictorial squibs and satires, has yet to appear.

A preliminary contribution to the history of caricature, as an attempt to repair in some measure the oversight of indifferent contemporaries, 'The Works of James Gillray the Caricaturist, with the Story of his Life and Times,' published under the auspices of Messrs. Chatto and Windus, has already met with a favourable reception at the hands of the press and the public ; the present writer devoted several years to the completion of the volume, with the solitary end in view of associating the artist more intimately with his works, in the estimation of the public, before it was too late. Mr. Thomas Wright, as an indefatigable pioneer in a comparatively unbeaten track, deserved personal recognition on the strength of his important contributions, bearing on the political history of the House of Hanover, as duly set forth in the present writer's introduction, and to his name was offered such repute as was conferred by the editorship.

The writer, from his gleanings in the same direction, has been able to offer the public a sketch of the ' Life of Henry Bunbury the Caricaturist,' with slighter *croquis* of his contemporaries. During the interval since the first intention of compiling the present volume as a further contribution to the literature of caricature assumed a definite form, some ten years back, the preparation of the work, imperfect and incomplete as it confessedly must remain—a mere *ébauche* at best—has been proceeding by slow and toilsome stages, the self-imposed task being rendered a more difficult one than in the instance of James Gillray,[1] from the disheartening circumstance that it is utterly impossible to arrive at anything approaching a comprehensive view of the works of Rowlandson ; no adequate collection being in existence, as far as the writer has discovered, with the possible exception of an accumulation in the hands of Mr. Harvey of St. James's Street, the advantages of which gathering (it has been going on steadily for years) have hitherto remained inaccessible to the editor, the possessor's time having been too occupied by the requirements of his other engagements to permit him to arrange the prints as he wishes. This circumstance is to be regretted, since Mr. Harvey admits the

personal interest he feels in caricature, upon which, when communicatively inclined, he is able to furnish very valuable information, in part the results of his own wide experience as a purchaser, and still more, perhaps, of painstaking investigations conducted for his private delectation; as his position and opportunities enable him to gratify his tastes in this direction to the fullest extent, it is hinted that on occasions he may feel disposed to furnish the critic with certain valuable facts of a special nature, drawn from the results of his own practical investigations in directions not generally available. This gentleman is, undoubtedly, an authority, and as, it is believed, he possesses unrivalled opportunities for forming a unique collection of prints by any master whose works he may fancy, the writer has, from season to season for the past six years, deferred the completion of his volume on the faith of a generous-sounding promise that he should be allowed to consult Mr. Harvey's collection of prints by Rowlandson, which, according to his knowledge, must be both interesting and valuable, and may possibly contain a great deal that has escaped his previous researches, however zealously they may have been instituted.

The sacrifice of time, labour, and patience involved in attempting to compile

---

[1] The preparation of *The Works of James Gillray, the Caricaturist, with a Story of his Life and Times* (376 pp. quarto), was in itself no bagatelle ; and three working years of steady application were invested in its pages and illustrations.

anything approaching a fairly compendious summary of Rowlandson's etchings is simply incredible. The desire to furnish a complete catalogue, though seemingly reasonable in itself at the first glance, is discovered upon experience to be practically impossible, and hence out of the question as regards arrangement; the productions of the artist, multiplied by pen, graver, and etching-point, as supplied by the hand of the master, or reproduced by other engravers, are legion, and where the examples are scattered no amount of application can adequately ascertain.

As far as kindly assistance is concerned, the writer has to acknowledge, with sincere gratitude, that where his previous experience has taught him to anticipate courtesies, he has been gratified in the highest degree, and he is proud to record that he once more finds himself indebted for cordial sympathy to the best qualified experts of the day.

Mr. G. W. Reid,[1] the respected keeper of the prints and drawings in the British Museum, with Messrs. Fagan and Donaghue, urbane members of his staff, have at all times made his access easy to the invaluable collection of social and political caricatures in his department; Mr. George Bullen (whose affability and scholarly acquirements are proverbial), the respected keeper of the printed books in the same magnificent national institution, has been able to facilitate the writer's quest of illustrations and caricatures by Rowlandson, so far as they come within

the scope of the important department which that gentleman so efficiently administers; the obliging and accomplished custodian of the superb collection belonging to the *Bibliothèque Nationale* of France has most readily allowed the writer to avail himself of the select and valuable gathering of caricatures by Rowlandson, which are to be found under his charge. It must be mentioned that the caricature resources of the royal collection in the museum at Brussels were as courteously placed at his service by the well-informed custodian, who, it may be added, takes a considerable individual interest in this branch as illustrative of men and manners under special aspects. The writer has pursued his perquisitions as far as the national state collection of engravings contained in the Trippenhuizen Museum, Amsterdam. These magnificent national institutions are all, more or less, rich in caricatures of an historical description, but unfortu-

---

[1] The Editor, among other special subjects, of a descriptive catalogue of the works of George Cruikshank. 3 volumes quarto. Published by Messrs. Bell and Sons, 1871. (Only 130 copies printed.)

nately, as regards the success of the present undertaking, the works of Rowlandson, numerous as they are, happen to be the reverse of the strong features of their collections of satirical prints, either political or social. The writer has accordingly been thrown back, to a dispiriting extent, on his own necessarily restricted resources; and the numerous illustrations which accompany this volume are for the most part unavoidably drawn from his own folios.

The principal source from whence it was hoped the best information could be detached proved utterly and exceptionally valueless; the writer refers to the important publishing establishments (and the successors who carry on the firms at the present day), whence the far-famed caricatures were originally issued. The firms of the Humphries, Hollands, Jackson, J. R. Smith, and others under whose auspices the artist's earliest, and in several instances most finished and ambitious works, first secured their lasting reputation, have long become extinct, as far as the editor is informed. But three leading print-publishing houses, established by Rowlandson's principal patrons, to whom the publication of the major part of his works was due, are still flourishing, under conditions modified to harmonise

with the requirements of the present age, by descendants and successors of the well-known founders. These resources have proved, however, a disappointing failure, as far as assistance towards the compilation of a catalogue of the artist's productions is concerned. To Mr. Rudolph Ackermann, the respected inaugurator of the 'Repository of Arts,' a truly liberal and enterprising gentleman, who will be referred to at greater length in the course of this volume, Rowlandson (with many other professional artists and authors) was deeply indebted both for business-like co-operation, for the pains he took to sell the artist's countless original drawings, for personal encouragement, untiring friendship, and pecuniary accommodation. Messrs. Ackermann have unfortunately preserved no account of the numerous publications due to the hand of the caricaturist, and issued for half-a-century by their respected firm, nor have they any collection of impressions from the plates they gave to the public.

The same observation applies to Mr. William Tegg, whose father, the indefatigable and well-known Thomas Tegg of Cheapside, published hundreds of the satirist's later and cruder caricatures, which were more generally familiar in the windows of printsellers, &c., since copies were multiplied to a larger extent than was practicable in the case of delicately finished aquatints, which gave fewer impressions, and commanded higher prices. Consequently, Rowlandson is better known to the public by his least desirable prints, and under his most common-place aspect. Mr. S. W. Fores seems to have issued an important proportion of Rowlandson's larger and more valuable plates, with the addition of an immense number of small subjects etched by Rowlandson, and finished by clever aquatinters, published in a more costly form than was generally the custom of the time. The successors of this gentleman have mentioned that the firm has not preserved any list of the publications issued under its original and well-recognised standing, in respect to satirical production, as *Fores' Caricature Museum*, but it is understood that, at the present writing, there still remains in the house a collection, in huge volumes, of early impressions from the multitudinous plates issued from the establishment under its earlier auspices —a publisher's summary, in short, such  as, it is to be regretted, is rarely preserved for any length of time. Unfortunately, owing to the exigencies of their modern print business, the writer has not been permitted to consult this highly interesting collection; he has, however, been informed, as an equivocal sort of consolation for his discomfiture, by the member of the firm to whom his application was addressed, that the major part of the prints, as far as the works of Rowlandson are concerned, are of a political character, and that the interesting and valuable social engravings are wanting; he also learns that nothing of importance by Rowlandson is to be found in this collection.

It is worthy of note, that the majority of the caricatures described in the present work, as published by S. W. Fores, belong almost entirely to the more attractive order of social satires, and pictorial skits at home and abroad, or cartoons levelled at the leaders of fashion, holding up the prevalent follies of the hour to legitimate ridicule. The writer confesses that he is inclined to feel a deeper regret at his inability to describe these political prints, presuming his informant, who certainly ought to know, is correct in this conclusion, since he is unable to account for their existence, as amongst the immense number of carica-  tures published by S. W. Fores, he has not hitherto lighted upon the series in question. Rowlandson's political prints —which, as the reader will realise in the progress of this compilation, are numerous enough in all conscience—were mostly published, as regards the early examples, by Humphries (a few of the somewhat hackneyed Westminster Election set, 1784, were due to S. W. Fores, it is acknowledged); while his later productions in this field, such as the succession of plates attacking Buonaparte, were issued from Ackermann's Repository of Arts, or circulated by Thomas Tegg (like the series treating of that *Delicate Investigation*, the Clarke scandal), according to the circumstances of the artist's employment or the cost of the plates. Popular prices being a requisition in the case of the sets published from the City, a coarser method of execution, with unmistakable instances of haste, detract in an unqualified degree from the interest of these prints, as instances of the artist's ability, which is exhibited to greater advantage in productions where his skill was allowed a more liberal exercise, as is evidenced in the capitally executed plates published by the West End print-selling firms.

The hopeful chances of aid from fountain-heads, upon experience, diminished to zero; and, while obstacles multiplied, the writer found it necessary to redouble his energy. As it proved that his own collection must, in the end, serve as the main source of reliance, fresh efforts were made to increase his gathering, and valuable additions were gradually secured. The process was somewhat tedious and costly withal, but it was the only course left open, unless the intention was renounced after the work had been adver-tised in progress.

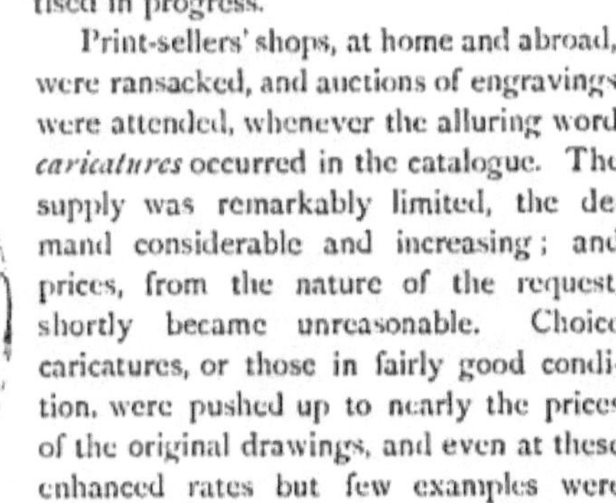

Print-sellers' shops, at home and abroad, were ransacked, and auctions of engravings were attended, whenever the alluring word *caricatures* occurred in the catalogue. The supply was remarkably limited, the de-mand considerable and increasing; and prices, from the nature of the request, shortly became unreasonable. Choice caricatures, or those in fairly good condi-tion, were pushed up to nearly the prices of the original drawings, and even at these enhanced rates but few examples were forthcoming. In Paris, Brussels, and London, a five-pound note became about a fair equivalent for a moderately fine impression after Rowlandson, if the plate were large and the subject important or curious, while for certain of the more sought-after examples, this rate was doubled; for such plates as *Vauxhall Gardens*, dealers expect a still larger price—indeed, five-and-twenty pounds have been demanded in many instances. The chances of fresh examples by Row-landson coming into the market have decreased, and possibly the competition will relax when there is no longer a chance of exciting it.

The writer has necessarily made the acquaintance of several gentlemen who are fervent collectors of Rowlandson's works, and he by no means ignores his obligations to those happy possessors of rarer specimens, who have frequently carried them off with an air of conquest from discomfited rival amateurs, the condition of their purses, and the artistic enthusiasm aroused at the moment, rendering similar triumphs comparatively facile, when incidental questions as to actual worth are too insignificant to engage the attention.

Certain collectors of eminence, who are discriminating selectors of caricatures, well qualified to judge of their technical merits, and who, further, are well posted up in curious and-out of-the-way points of the political and social histories of the times thus illustrated, have volunteered the results of their researches ; these good-natured offers have arrived too late to be available, but the writer is not the less indebted to the kindness which prompted the action ; in an earlier and preparatory stage, these advances would have been of considerable value and assistance.

So much for the materials ; perhaps too much stress has been laid, as far as the reader's patience is concerned, on the preliminary difficulties which have hindered and weakened the execution of the writer's desire to reproduce, by pencil and pen, a fair gathering of the works of our greatest humorous designers, an idea long cherished, and tardily carried out, as regards the first part of his task, *James Gillray*; and beset, as he has recounted, in respect to THOMAS ROWLANDSON, the concluding portion, by unforeseen impediments and technical difficulties which it would be tedious to enumerate ; they may, however, in a minor degree, be taken into consideration as a plea for the obvious shortcomings of this laborious compilation, and, while inclining rigid specialists to be less exacting, induce critics to regard the unavoidable faults of the performance with lenient forbearance.

For the space of a century, Rowlandson's caricatures, which are more properly *croquis* of the life which surrounded him, have continued to afford delight to the appreciators of graphic humour, from the date, 1775, when he sent his first contribution to the Royal Academy. It was only this year (1878) that a pair of his remarkably spirited drawings, *Faro Table at Devonshire House*, and *A Gaming Table*, attracted considerable praise and attention on the walls of the Grosvenor Gallery. Although the artist was master of the most elegant refinement, both of delineation and colouring, and produced the most delicious female heads with that lightness and daintiness of touch which was his peculiar gift, bringing all the graces, sparkle and animation of the French school to bear upon the models of winsome female beauty our own favoured isles produced for the exercise of his pencil, we are constrained to admit, thus early in our summary, that too many of his productions are strongly tinctured by that coarseness of subject and sentiment which has been held to disfigure the works of contemporary humorists ; his wit, it must be remembered, was of the jocose school of Smollett and Fielding, and in justice it must be taken into consideration that his designs, even in their most uncompromising and grosser aspects, simply reflect the colour of a period which was the reverse of squeamish, and, as has been pertinently observed by the late Thomas Wright, ' of a generation celebrated for anything rather than delicacy.'

The artist was pretty generally recognised as the famous illustrator of *Doctor Syntax* and *The Dance of Death*, and in this relation he is fairly acknowledged by posterity; this limited view, as the present volume is designed to demonstrate, being far indeed from an adequate acknowledgment of his proper artistic standing. Rowlandson's higher qualifications, as a draughtsman in water-colours of remarkable merit, a portrait-painter of felicitous promise, and the originator of countless witty and pointed conceptions, were discovered more tardily. His surprising facility for representing the human figure, with knowledge and freedom of execution, his marvellous power of combining groups and crowds of figures in active movement, his grasp of expression, and fluency of colour and handling, were more particularly admitted (though in a sense they have since been lost sight of) after the Exhibition of 1862, where two of his truly characteristic subjects, of considerable size, made their appearance on the walls, to the amazement and delight of the spectators, who had no previous acquaintance with his whimsical genius.   These two drawings, which opened the eyes of the world to his gifts for a little season, are entitled *An English Review* and *A French Review*; they originally formed a very noticeable feature on the walls of the Royal Academy in 1786 ; it is believed that eventually they came into the possession of the Prince of Wales, and, with the rest of George IV.'s collection, have remained in keeping of the royal family ever since, her gracious Majesty, the Queen, being pleased to lend them, with other fine representative examples of art, to the Exhibition Commissioners of 1862.

The *English Review*, and its companion drawing, a *French Review*, hang at Windsor Castle, where we are informed there is a very large accumulation of caricatures, drawings and prints, put away in a closet, in the order of their appearance; which, it is likely, have remained undisturbed for generations. It is not impossible that, hidden away in this mass of satirical productions, may be found the series of drawings, notoriously of a free tendency as regards subject, which Rowlandson is understood to have produced for the delectation of George IV. A collection of a similar description was, as we learn from the same authority, destroyed by a nobleman well known for his princely liberality, on the death of the patron who had selected the subjects.

In the unrivalled collection of water-colour drawings of the English school, which are found on the walls of the sumptuous permanent Museum of Art at South Kensington, are exhibited three characteristic examples of Rowlandson's talents in the caricature direction. *The Parish Vestry*, 1784, a humorous and spirited drawing, belonging to the artist's best time, formed part of the munificent gift made by Mr. William Smith to the nation; as did the second example, entitled *Brook Green Fair*, which we should assign to about the year 1800. The third drawing, representing *The old Elephant and Castle Inn, Newington*, is also due to a liberal donor, being the gift of G. W. Atkinson, Esq.

As has been related, the caricaturist produced thousands of capital drawings, delicately tinted, excelling in all styles; and from these original designs, he executed in turn thousands of spirited etchings with his own hand, which were frequently coloured to reproduce the first sketches, or aquatinted by engravers (sometimes by himself), in imitation of drawings tenderly shaded in Indian ink, to which, in some instances, the resemblance is sufficiently faithful to deceive the eye of anyone who is not familiar with this method of reproduction.

It must be borne in mind—and we insist the more earnestly on this point, as, from some incomprehensible wilfulness, it has seemingly been suffered to sink out of sight for a time—in treating of Rowlandson, that the man was essentially an artist; it is undoubtedly true that he was gifted (perhaps we might consider fatally as far as his proper estimation is concerned) with the faculty known as *caricature*, and he excelled in burlesque, but his successes were sufficiently high in other branches of the artist's profession to indicate that he was equally qualified by original talents, by academic training which he might have turned to the best advantage, by a sense of the beautiful unusually keen, and a happy power of expressing his first impressions, to take a foremost place amongst the best recognised masters of the early English school, to whose body he might have been an ornament, if he had not preferred his chosen calling of ' a free-lance ' with a roving commission to work mischief. His remarkable gifts of originality, ever fertile, and apparently exhaustless, and facile powers of invention, either pleasant or terrific, which seemed spontaneous, were in his case insurmountable hindrances, instead of promoting his advancement and reputation as a painter of acknowledged value and eminence. He had the calamity—so fatal, in his and many other instances, to serious application—to succeed without sensible effort ; from the very first his progress was a series of triumphs ; none of the students of the Academy could draw such ludicrous and yet life-like figures, and thus his popularity with his fellow-labourers was assured ; his studies from the nude, both in London and

in Paris, were wonderful for the rapid ease and talent with which they were executed, and hence arose another source of glorification, and although personal vanity has never been mentioned in connection with the artist (he being thoroughly blind to everything but his own particular hobbies), the professors at home and abroad, and the members of the Academy themselves, were proud to patronise in their classes such precocious ability, which could accomplish the most difficult delineations without effort, and thus reflected credit on their schools ; and the prodigy who drew from the life, in his youth, as vigorously and well as the most painstaking adepts in their maturity, could not fail to receive a dangerous amount of admiration, which tempted him to depend upon trifling exertions, and left his ambition without a spur.

While yet in his boyhood he was recognised as a genius, and was unhappily flattered into becoming a wayward one ; the very fluency of his pencil, and the fidelity of his memory towards the grotesque side of things proved his stumbling-blocks. It is with more than a passing shade of regret that we reflect, with his far-seeing colleagues at the Academy and elsewhere, how eminent a painter was lost in the development of a *caricaturist*, admirable and unsurpassed in his own branch as Rowlandson must admittedly remain. The gifts which were in the man were marvellous, and beyond this he possessed nerve to persevere, and manly resolution to sustain his exertions, as he proved in his youth, and subsequently demonstrated when past life's meridian, times then being less prosperous, since fortun s and legacies had long ceased to fall in adventitiously, but the very excitement of setting the little world wondering, and making the public smile, while his tickled audience accorded him the cheapest popularity by crowding in admiration round his travesties, turned the wilful artist away from serious application, where no immediate fun was to be secured for either the limner or his following.

Rowlandson's sense of feminine loveliness, of irresistible graces of face, expression, and attitude, was unequalled in its way; several of his female portraits have been mistaken for sketches by Gainsborough or Moreland, and as such, it is possible, since the caricaturist is so little known in this branch, that many continue to pass current. From 1777 to 1781, five years of Rowlandson's residence in Wardour Street, with all the freshness of his academic studies, and the laurels unfaded he had won in the schools, with golden opinions, as a youth of paramount promise, indulged by the most eminent of the Royal Academicians and the French professors, the artist practised the more laborious and prosaic, but surer branch of portrait-painting with success, and his pictures  were duly received by his patrons and well-wishers amongst the omnipotent Forty, and found their place on the walls of the Royal Academy Exhibition without a break—no barren compliment when it is remembered that his compeers were Reynolds, Gainsborough, and Hoppner, and that of the two or three hundred works selected for the gallery at the period referred to, the superb canvases of the artists named constituted an average of over ten per cent. of the entire exhibits.

If we but think for a passing instant over the winsome portraitures of fair women, whose faces live, for the delectation of all time, on the canvases of Sir Joshua Reynolds, Gainsborough, Romney, and a few lesser luminaries, it is cruel to realise that Rowlandson, from sheer wantonness (promoted by what seemed a happy hit in 1784),[1] neglected his opportunities in the direction of portraiture,

[1] *Vauxhall Gardens* (503), *An Italian Family* (462), *The Serpentine River* (511); *vid* Catalogue of the Royal Academy (1784), Fourteenth Exhibition.

with an indifference which, while proving his disinterestedness and superiority to mere profit, is the more exasperating when we are frequently told, as every one of Rowlandson's contemporaries who has mentioned the caricaturist never fails to reiterate, that the successive presidents of the Royal Academy, the great Reynolds, the royally patronised West, the courtly and fashionable Lawrence, the very men we have mentioned who were, it must be conceded, the most competent judges on the point, pronounced their conviction that his abilities entitled to acceptance, as one of themselves, a brother artist whose addition to their ranks they would have gloried to acknowledge, since he had the undoubted genius to reflect a lustre on the Academy, if he had exerted his talents in the recognised channels, and withstood the impulse of his notoriety for producing irresistibly droll novelties, which, as they foresaw, must infallibly prove pernicious to the practice of sober portraiture.

The versatile acquirements of our artist may, in a sense, be looked upon as an infirmity, a theory which had been thoroughly established while the subject of it remained in the flesh, and enjoyed a certain perverse gratification in contributing to support its soundness and perspicacity.

In landscape art we discover Rowlandson successfully rivalling the most respected practitioners in water-colours amongst his contemporaries, and helping the younger professional generation, that carried the art to perfection, to discard the obsolete theories of blackness for clear translucid colouring. His studies after nature are much esteemed, and are to be occasionally recognised in galleries and collections. It is a sufficiently capricious circumstance which has come within our experience—we have heard it asserted confidently more than once—that Rowlandson, the simple harmonious colourist and ready draughtsman, whose brush with limpid tints so deftly translated on paper the charms of sylvan scenes; the truthful artist who pictured the forest, fall, and glade, the distant hamlets amidst the foliage, the picturesque windings of the silver stream, the rustic cottages, the cattle wending leisurely through the fertile pastures, the mellow atmosphere, and the far-extending horizon, is often held a distinct individual from that other universally known Rowlandson—of equivocal reputation, it is hinted—whose daring reed-pen produced grotesques which perhaps were inimitable, but which, it is certain, were often indefensibly vulgar.

The artist's facility was so considerable that, had he been less scrupulous (his horror of fraud and imposition, especially in their pecuniary reference, was implacable, in spite of, or perhaps in contradistinction to, his other levities), he could have allowed his own productions, in the manner of his reputable contemporaries, and even of deceased celebrities, whose subjects and method he chose to imitate as a question of pure ingenuity—(while his own style is above all difficult to reproduce)—to pass current as veritable originals by the masters. A book of etchings consisting entirely of these imitations is described in the course of this work, and he has managed to assume, without copying any particular picture, the *modus operandi* of the artists, and has varied his own manner of execution and disguised his salient individualities with such subtlety, that, even to the etching-point, slight trace of Rowlandson remains to betray the acknowledged imposition.

In his sketches after nature, as we have ventured to advance in respect to his female portraits and delicious studies from life, in many instances it is difficult to distinguish between the artless rustic groupings and charming pastoral drawings

by George Moreland and Thomas Gainsborough, let alone those of Barrett, Hills, Howitt, Pugh, and other of his associates (who executed pictures lightly outlined with a reed-pen, shaded with a warm tint and delicately washed with transparent water-colours, as was then the process),[1] and the acknowledged contributions of our versatile genius to this department, in the earlier stages of the captivating art of water-colour drawing.

The writer, in the course of his preparation for this work, has been at the pains to consult more than one well-recognised artist of reputation and authority ; seeking for hints from professors whose celebrity extended well back towards the beginning of the nineteenth century ; these respected ancients, who are now nearly all gathered to the shades to join the subject of this volume, being from their age, knowledge, and experience, as well as from the traditions of their earlier masters, most likely to know and remember circumstances of a special character bearing upon the subject. Some of these worthies were actually

---

[1] In the early Exhibition Catalogues, studies in water-colours, where the primitive sepia or Indian ink was supplemented by other tints, are described as STAINED DRAWINGS.

working as contemporaries of the caricaturist who departed fifty years ago.   The last time the writer met George Cruikshank, a few months before that truly splendid old gentleman passed away, full of years and honour, to his well-earned repose, he took occasion to allude to the veteran's acknowledged admiration for the works of his extraordinarily endowed predecessor, James Gillray, in whose footsteps he had very literally commenced his career, being selected during the lifetime of the gifted caricaturist (when Gillray's genius had proved too exacting for the tension of his faculties, and his reason had unhappily departed, never to be restored beyond an occasional lucid flitter) to complete several plates which the attacks of his malady had suspended.   George Cruikshank, the most deservedly popular of the name, was not a little proud of having been thought worthy, while still a very young man (Gillray's faculties were deranged in 1811), to take up the plates of the first genius that has adorned his art.   With the earnestness of his disposition, and perhaps with characteristic partiality, he regarded the unfortunate Gillray as the greatest man, in his eyes, who ever lived, indisputably 'the prince of caricaturists,' as he has appropriately christened him, and this title,

won from a loving disciple, who, in his turn, became still more famous, is likely to last as long as the great caricaturist is remembered.

George Cruikshank voluntarily called on the writer to express the interest he good-naturedly felt in certain slight records of past caricaturists then publishing, and to communicate some valuable facts about the works of his father, a meritorious artist whose reputation would be widely increased if his pictures, exhibited at the Royal Academy, were better known. On a subsequent occasion the cheery veteran imparted various anecdotes on the subject within his knowledge, but confessed that he had never been admitted to terms of personal familiarity with either Gillray or Rowlandson in the flesh. It was his father, Isaac Cruikshank—for whose graphic powers in the same walk he expressed the best deserved and truest filial respect—who enjoyed their intimacy, and it was he who related (with a genial force happily done justice to by his descendant) to his deeply interested son the circumstances with which George was acquainted.

The writer was naturally eager to gather, while there was yet time, any facts which might be of importance for the furtherance of his contemplated sketch of Rowlandson's career, which was then occupying all his energies, from the last representative of the famous caricaturists, who formed, in himself, so desirable a link with the generation of the Georgian epoch, which had been dissolved into

the thinnest elements for three-fourths of a century back.   Cruikshank expressed
the most cordial interest in the undertaking, and genially declared, by way of an
encouragement, which is the writer's most appreciated reward, that he should
look forward to its successful completion, and further promised that if, in revising
his notes, and the personal memoirs, touching upon such kindred topics (which,
as he imparted, had long employed his leisure), he could discover any allusions of

an interesting description to his gifted contemporary Rowlandson, or any similar
memoranda left by his father, he would communicate them for the benefit of the
present volume.   His death has unfortunately prevented the accomplishment of
this valued service, which was volunteered spontaneously with his well-known
readiness to confer favours.

The point about Rowlandson which had most impressed George Cruikshank
is somewhat original, and properly belongs to this part of our subject ; hence we

have been glad to have an opportunity of quoting the trustworthy authority of
the aged caricaturist. ' Rowlandson,' said George, ' was a remarkable man in
most respects ; ' the waywardness of his youth and the notoriety of his gambling
days seemed to have rather prejudicially influenced the mind of his simpler
successor, who had taken his place in 1827, as he had, almost of right, succeeded
to the working-table and unfinished plates of James Gillray, many years before.

Cruikshank, moreover, considered that Rowlandson's academical successes, his successful rivalry of Mortimer in depicting the nude, the knowledge of his art and the fluency he had acquired, were altogether exceptional features in the profession of a caricaturist, to his English views; but, according to his kindly creed, mellowed by age—his steel a trifle tempered since his own youth, when his shafts too were not without poignancy—' Rolley ' was somewhat unreflecting, and reckless in exposing the infirmities of others, having but scant regard for his own reputation or the feelings of society, and further he had suffered himself to be led away from the exercise of his legitimate subjects, to produce works of a reprehensible tendency, which respectable dictum will probably find numerous subscribers.

A SHIPPING SCENE.

Strangely as it may sound, it was not as a caricaturist that Rowlandson had gained Cruikshank's admiration ; he appreciated the artist enthusiastically as an accomplished water-colour painter, the equal in his opinion of most of the founders of our special school. Rowlandson's masterly power over the delineation of the figure, and his happy gift, amounting almost to inspiration, of portraying female charms of face and person, deserved high regard in Cruikshank's estimation ; his peculiarly felicitous pictures of quaint Continental life, and the examples his free and scholarly handling held out, as admirable models of style to the French caricaturists of his day; the social sketches produced in Paris at the beginning of the century, though remarkable for neatness and delicacy, being laborious, formal, timid, and wanting in that racy comicality, and dashing power of expression, characterising the drawings under consideration, to which George accorded unqualified praise.

It was chiefly for his skill in landscape delineation that Cruikshank respected the artist under discussion, and more especially, as he declared, warming with his reminiscences of the drawings he called to mind, he had never seen anything superior, in his estimation, to Rowlandson's water-side and maritime sketches, for their clear freshness and simple air of fidelity to nature; the banks of the river, the 'pool' filled with vessels, wharves, landing-places, ports, and naval stations, with the noble men-of-war lying off; and the bustling craft, travelling 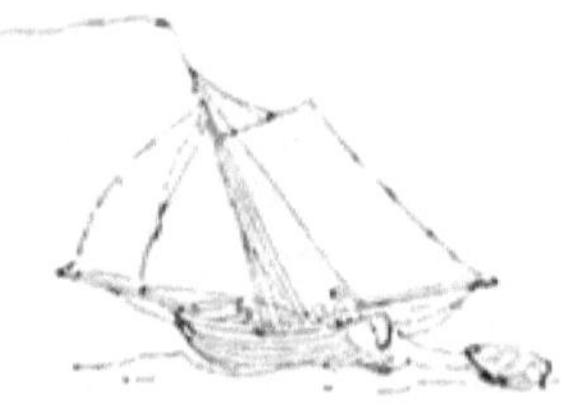 between the fleet and the shore; the groups of busy figures, far and near, happily introduced in a state of seeming activity; the shipping, which he drew with picturesque ease and dexterity, his far-spreading landscapes and distant horizons, the treatment of the water, the movement of his skies, and the general sense of expanse and atmosphere, were beautiful in the extreme, all noted down, as they were, without apparently a second thought, with the slightest possible labour, recalling in a forcible degree the drawings of William Vandevelde, who was, in Cruikshank's opinion, the only artist whose marine studies could be quoted in comparison with those of Rowlandson.

We are necessarily anxious to avoid the suspicion of attempting to prove too much, and it must be admitted that we do not pronounce Rowlandson a Rubens, a William Vandevelde, a Reynolds, and a Moreland, all at once; any more than we can be deluded into the belief that his landscape drawings might be claimed by Turner, Girtin, De Wint, Fielding, or David Cox. In treating of our artist in relation to the truly great  names which have been frequently put into contrast with his own, it must not be forgotten that his works are spoken of, as they exist, under their modest condition of sketches manipulated in the very slightest manner possible, and, if considered at all in juxtaposition with those of the higher luminaries,

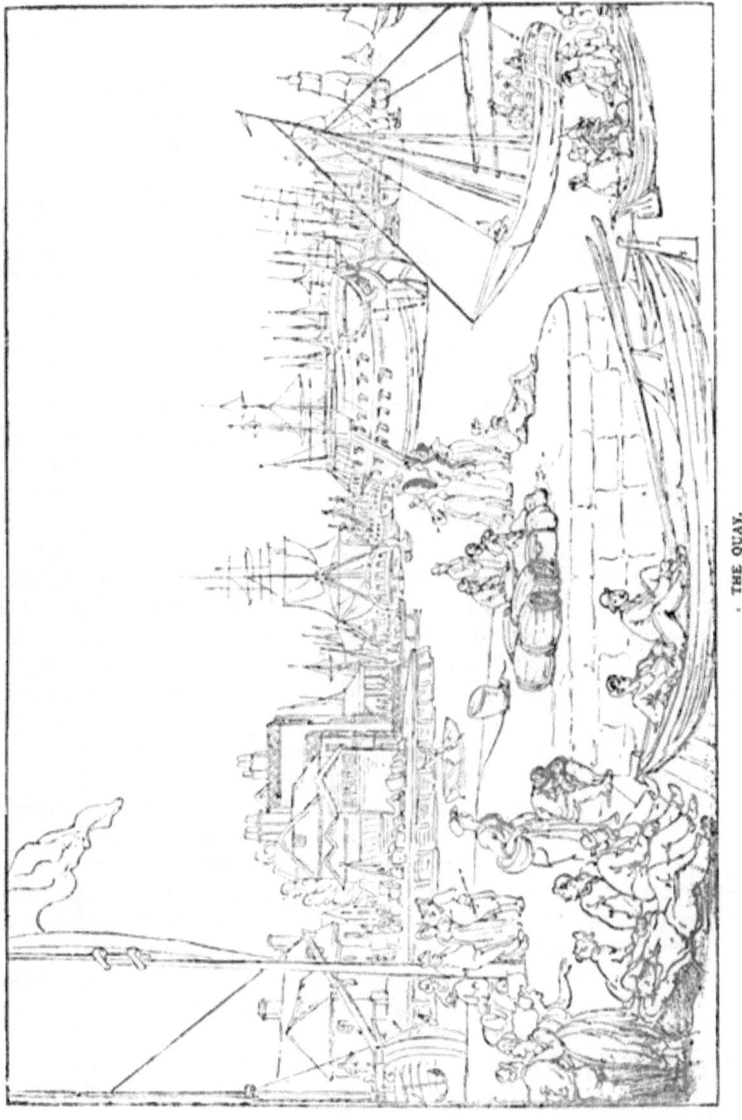

THE QUAY.

it is only by the side of studies executed under similar circumstances; it would be a piece of pretension, entirely out of character on our part, to even suggest submitting Rowlandson's attempts in the most respectable exercise of his talents in competition with the more substantial finished and ambitious pictures bequeathed us by the select few of really eminent painters, whose unrivalled works cannot fail to afford the most unqualified delight to all cultivated lovers of art of whatever school. *Their* productions are admitted to stand alone, even though there exist diversities of opinion, schisms, and heresies in regard to the generality of the profession.

*　.　*

In resuming our summary of Rowlandson's conceptions in the *caricature* branch, we must notice, while contemplating his strongly characterised works, that, while the rest of his competitors in the grotesque walk have in most examples left no record of their prints beyond the plates on which they were executed, for every subject he has produced of his own designing, at least one corresponding drawing has existed, and frequently three or four variations of leading ideas are worked out as completed pictures, without, however, any appearance of experimentalising under difficulties of execution—technical points never puzzled his skill; and such daring flights as Rubens ventured with the brush, in the way of foreshortened and difficult attitudes, Rowlandson's reed-pen accomplished right merrily. as if by its own volition, and without a thought on the part of its highly-trained wielder, about such common-place requirements as the posing of living models or preparatory sketches. The original notions of Rowlandson's whimsical inventions are in the generality of instances far worthier of attention than the most spirited etchings he thought fit to circulate after them ; and it is well to keep in mind that the artist has produced some thousands of humorous conceptions (placing his more serious studies out of the question), of which no engraving has ever appeared ; and amongst these unpublished delineations may be included several of the most ingenious and attractive pictures executed by his hand, especially from the year 1790, that is to say, for more than two-thirds of his professional life—a circumstance with which every collector of original drawings by this artist is thoroughly conversant.

The career of Rowlandson may be divided into periods ; the work belonging properly to the several stages is tolerably distinctive as to general characteristics. An adept can positively determine, within a year or two, the particular section to which his designs, when the date happens to be wanting, may be justly assigned, and, as his manifold sketches and etchings extend over the space of half a century, this circumstance is a trifle remarkable in itself.

The first period, as far as his published plates are concerned, includes his smaller social and political satires; the execution, though free and fluent, as his productions uniformly were, exhibits indications of care which is not so traceable as his method grew mellower, and practice confirmed the facility which came to him as a gift. These juvenile etchings bear more affinity to Gillray's manner of manipulation than is traceable in his subsequent cartoons. A view of *A Hazard Table* and its frequenters (*E.O. or the fashionable Vowels*, October 28, 1781) offers perhaps the best indications of his growing powers, between 1774 and 1783. His publishers were Humphrey, Holland, Jackson, and a few others; and he further appears, in conjunction with J. Jones, to have gone into the publishing way himself, at 103 Wardour Street.

In 1784 the excitement of the famous Westminster Election seems to have

carried him more thoroughly into political satires, and, as we observe, his humour discovered an unflagging source of impulse round the parliamentary candidates, Fox, Wray, and Hood; the fair Duchess of Devonshire, Lady Duncannon, and honest Sam House, the Whig canvassers, and their opponents on the ministerial side, the Hon. Mrs. Hobart (Lady Buckinghamshire), and the Duchess of Gordon; together with the whimsicalities of the polling-booth. If we were asked to select his most noticeable social and satirical effusions, we should incline to particularise *English Curiosity, or the Foreigner stared out of countenance*; *1784, or the Fashions of the Day*; and *A Sketch from Nature* (January 24, 1784).

In 1784, Rowlandson realised the full extent both of his powers of fancy and his mastery of the art of water-colour delineation. He discontinued the practice of sending portraits to the Exhibition of the Royal Academy, in which he had persevered for five years, and contributed in their places three mirth-provoking drawings, which must have produced no little sensation amongst the visitors, who were unaccustomed to such works. These were the inimitable *Vauxhall Gardens*, which reveals his talents at their best, *An Italian Family*, and *The Serpentine River*.

In 1785 appeared some of John Raphael Smith's graceful publications after Rowlandson's more refined originals, notably *Vauxhall, Opera Boxes, Toying and Trifling, An Italian Family, A French Family, Grog on Board, Tea on*

Shore ; Filial Affection, or a Trip to Gretna Green ; Reconciliation ; Intrusion on Study, or the Painter disturbed ; Comfort in the Gout ; and several other excellent subjects in his most finished manner, besides an animated scene after Henry Wigstead, *John Gilpin's Return to London.*

Rowlandson sent five important and highly humorous drawings, displaying advanced qualities in the direction of execution, to the Royal Academy in 1786 ; those of the first consequence were *An English Review, A French Review,* the pair exhibited at the International Exhibition 1862 ; *Opera House Gallery,* under which designation, as we suspect, we recognise his *Box Lobby Loungers,* published the very same year ; *A French Family* (published the year previous) ; and *A Coffee House,* of which we can discover no further record.

Among the engraved works for the same year we must refer to the print of *Box Lobby Loungers,* already mentioned, and *Covent Garden Theatre,* as the most noticeable as to size, subject, and the numerous figures introduced.

Rowlandson sent four known works to the Royal Academy, the season following (1787). They were *French Barracks,* a superlative drawing, *Grog on Board a Ship, Countrymen and Sharpers* (engraved by Sherwin as *Smithfield Sharpers*), and *The Morning Dram, or Huntsman rising,* engraved as *Four o'clock in the Country,* S. W. Fores (October 20, 1790). All Rowlandson's con-

tributions for this year have been published ; indeed, it is very possible, from the popularity of the caricaturist's novel exhibits, that all the pictures he sent to the Royal Academy were straightway issued on copper. There are two exceptions, *The Serpentine* and *A Coffee House,* of which the writer has never succeeded in meeting impressions, but it by no means follows that sooner or later they may not come to light, and it does not seem unlikely that the first named, *The Serpentine River,* may be another version of *Cold Broth and Calamity* (published in 1792).

Amongst the engraved works of 1787, the writer instances *Baron Ron's Dental Surgery, or Transplanting of Teeth,* and a series of five *Hunting Scenes, The Morning, The Meet, The Run, The Death,* and *The Dinner,* published in a folio size, and now somewhat rarely met with as a set.

In the two succeeding years Rowlandson again threw his etching-point into party conflicts, and came out with a shower of political squibs on the amenities of the *Regency Struggle*. Nothing very ambitious in the way of social satires appeared in 1788. Among minor subjects we may allude to *Housebreakers, A Cart Race, The School for Scandal, A Fencing Match, A Print Sale, Lust and Avarice*, and *Luxury and Desire*, as being slightly above the average. In 1789 and 1790 but few works of exceptional character were issued to gratify Rowlandson's devoted admirers or the general public. *She don't deserve it ! Don't he deserve it ? A Racing Series, The Course, The Betting Post, The Mount, The Start*, and *A Fresh Breeze*, take the lead. *La Place des Victoires à Paris* belongs to 1789, and, in the writer's estimation, it is perhaps one of the most attractive subjects due to the artist's pencil, exhibiting, as it does, the quaint surroundings of Parisian life, as noted by the caricaturist before the Revolutionary era—delineations of feminine beauty, and studies of real character, such as no effort of the imagination could fabricate, unless assisted by travel, a familiar

acquaintance with the locality, and keen observation. A fitting companion is given to this delightful subject in another important drawing, crowded with diversified life and animated groups, produced in 1800; *The Thuilleries in Paris*, a reminiscence of previous studies in the French metropolis, of manners noted anterior to the destruction of antiquated fashions ; the dainty *belles* of *ton*, and the picturesque society which might be discovered flourishing under the reign of Louis XVI., before the inauguration of the all-devouring Republic, which worked more change in a few feverish months of turbulence, in which all the recognised phases of the past were lost, than many sober decades had effected in their better regulated courses.

The best of Rowlandson's publications for 1790 were *A Kick-up at a Hazard Table*, in which, as may be supposed, he was perfectly at home ; *Four o'clock in the Morning in Town*, which was also in the artist's way, and its companion, *Four o'clock in the Morning in the Country; Frog-hunting* (Gallic *gourmets fins*), and *Tythe Pig*, a fine old English equivalent.

The year 1791 was richer in those more ambitious plates, which the writer is seeking to identify, and several of the caricaturist's choicer subjects appeared, etched by his hand, and finished in aquatint, to facsimile the meritorious original drawings. *A Squall in Hyde Park* is one of the score or two of delineations of the highest type, which adequately demonstrate the exceptional qualifications of the artist ; and these, we have no hesitation in averring, have never been excelled in their walk, as far as executive ability, sense of loveliness, grouping, movement, grasp of character, powers of observation, and diverting qualities are concerned. Another remarkable subject of extraordinary ability, founded on Rowlandson's Continental studies, entitled *French Barracks* (exhibited in 1787), and its pendant, *English Barracks*, were issued this year. *An Inn Yard on Fire*, belonging to the same important series ; *The Attack ; The Prospect before us ; The Pantheon ; Chaos is Come Again*, in allusion to the dilapidated state of Drury Lane theatre condemned by the surveyors ; *Toxophilites ; House breakers ; Damp ; Sheets* and *Slugs in a Saw Pit*, among the numerous lesser subjects, bring up the total of the truly estimable works which gratified the public in 1791.

Cold Broth and Calamity, a skating scene representing disasters in the park, from a ludicrous point of view ; *A Dutch Academy*, drawn from the caricaturist's experiences in the Netherlands ; and *Studious Gluttons* were the leading plates published in 1792.

New Shoes, a small, but delicate subject, belongs to 1793.

In 1797 appeared the admirable plates published after Rowlandson's studies in the Netherlands ; we cannot too highly commend such inimitable originals as *Fyge Dam, Amsterdam ; Stadt House, Amsterdam ; Companion View, Amsterdam ;* and *Place de Mer, Antwerp.*

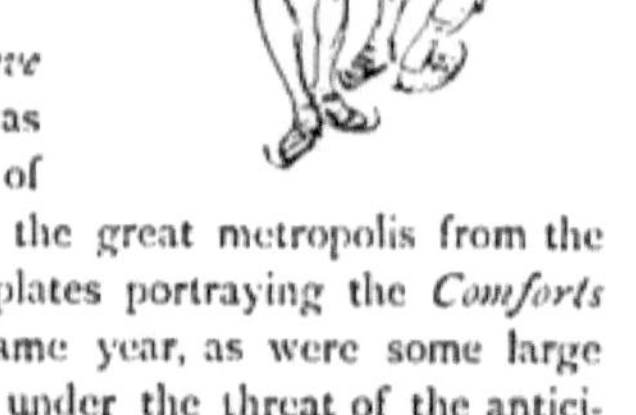

Admiral Nelson Recruiting with his Brave Tars after the Glorious Battle of the Nile, was published in 1798 ; a series of *London Views*, of considerable merit and importance, entrances to the great metropolis from the four leading turnpikes ; and a series of twelve plates portraying the *Comforts of Bath*, are most worthy of attention in the same year, as were some large studies of reviews of the Volunteer Forces, held under the threat of the anticipated French invasion.

Distress, from a large picture, indicating the horrors of shipwreck with tragic impressiveness, is assigned to 1799.

Summer Amusement, a Game at Bowls ; Doctor Botherum, the Mountebank ; Preparations for the Academy ; and A French Ordinary, were among the noticeable features of the artist's publications in 1800 ; the peculiarly interesting panorama of the Parisian world anterior to the French Revolution, entitled *The Thuilleries in Paris* was also produced this year.

Rowlandson's skill as an etcher had further, about this time, provided him with abundance of work in executing the humorous conceptions of Woodward and Bunbury after his own characteristic fashion.

Rowlandson's plate of *The Brilliants*, and a long series of subjects designed by Woodward, with many originals of his own, sufficiently excellent in their order, but not of the first consequence, found their way to the public in 1801. The leading print-publishers at the West End, Rudolph Ackermann, S. W. Fores, Williamson, and Rowlandson himself,[1] at his residence, 1 James Street, Adelphi, issued an inexhaustible collection of highly ludicrous social satires, and numerous patriotic and political subjects, during intervening years; and in 1807 the name of Thomas Tegg of Cheapside was added to the print-publishers who employed the remunerative talents of the indefatigable caricaturist. Rowlandson also continued to execute the whimsical conceptions of less qualified draughtsmen, and swarms of comicalities—by Woodward, Bunbury, Wigstead, Nixon, and other fashionable amateurs, who possessed the humorous vein, but lacked the skill to give their ideas a fitting form for presentation to the public—were put into acceptable shape, and etched by our artist at this period.

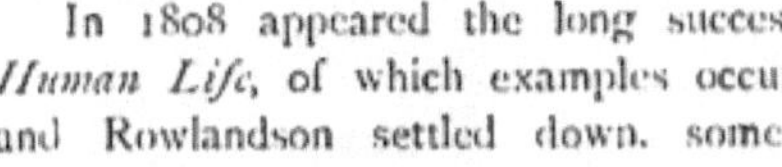

In 1808 appeared the long succession of *Miseries of Human Life*, of which examples occur in previous years; and Rowlandson settled down, somewhat grimly, under worthy Mr. Ackermann's auspices, to take up the gauntlet against the dreaded Buonaparte, the great little Corsican, against whom Gillray had waged such savage warfare until his powers dwindled into vacancy, and George Cruikshank stepped valiantly into the place of the colossus of caricaturists, and carried on the combat with unflagging zeal and whimsicality on his own account. Rowlandson's ludicrous attacks upon the ambitious 'disturber of the peace of Europe' were duly appreciated by his audience, and the demand for these blood-and-thunder caricatures increased monthly, to the extreme delectation of the great British public, whose antipathies to the conquering general were, at least, founded on sound and excusable principles, and if the overflowing excess of their detestation sometimes blinded the people to points of detail, and wilful misrepresentations passed current, and rather swamped their more generous sentiments—which were put out of sight for awhile—it must be remembered that this patriotic zeal was well directed against the man who had announced his august intention of subjugating England, and was, by accord, considered as the common enemy, and anyone who had indulged the temerity of openly acknowledging the grander elements of his character, since pretty tolerably established, would have been flouted by

---

[1] The artist's name frequently occurs upon his plates as his own publisher, and, as might be anticipated, the prints produced under this sponsorship are invariably of his most popular description.

acclamation, and we are not sure but the national scorn would have fittingly signalised such an unpatriotic enormity.

It is certain that the caricaturist's travesties of the little emperor, his burlesques of his great actions, and grandiose declarations (which, in themselves, occasionally overdid the heroic, and trenched hazardously on the ludicrous), his figurative displays of the mean origin of the imperial family, with the cowardice and depravity of its members, won the popular applause; as did the satirist's representations of the hollowness of Boney's vaunted victories, and the treachery of his designs in the days of his success; and, when disasters began to cloud the career of the mighty Napoleon, and cherished projects were met with sickening failures—as army after army, collected for the slaughter by schemes, lies, fraud, and force, melted away, and the prostrate powers of the Continent plucked up courage, singly at first and finally in legions, until the end of the Corsican's glory

arrived—the artist lent his skill to celebrate the delight of the public, and the rejoicings over the discomfiture of the traditional bugbear; glib cartoons were hurried off by Ackermann and often by Tegg—the City competing with the West End in the loyal contest of proving the national enmity to Buonaparte, by buying every caricature—the more extravagant the better relished —that the artists, who toiled like Trojans while the harvest lasted, could contrive to furnish in season for the demand.

A suspicion crosses our mind that, in too many cases, the incentive was to gratify the hatred of the Corsican, rather than any remarkable inherent merit that could be discovered in the satires; the best of which were but feeble vehicles for the exhibition of the jovial abilities of the designers; who, we dare venture to hint, found themselves a little out of their element, plunged, as it were, in the 'blood and iron' theory, striking out with their etching points with the most approved pantomimic vengeance! Very few of these mock-heroic sallies imprint themselves on the recollection by the sheer force of their own brilliancy, as was the case in the single instance of James Gillray, in the past, and as happened—an undeniable test of the veritable fire of genius—frequently with the cartoons of John Tenniel within our own experience, when the magnitude of the occasion has conjured up the inspiration, and rekindled the latent flame.

Our reflections upon the bellicose creations of Rowlandson and Cruikshank, while their hostile vapourings continue irresistibly droll, never stir the more

passionate emotions or reach impulses which lie below the surface ; being risible,
it is true, but the reverse of inspired ; and although many a hearty laugh may be
enjoyed over the ludicrous turn the twain caricaturists have, in spite of themselves, given to situations of an avowedly tragic tendency, their very fury seems
an unctuous jest, their simulated earnestness takes a farcical turn, and the result
of a careful review, as the writer has made quite recently, of their prolific
slaughterous sallies, is the conviction that, often unconsciously to themselves,
they have chiefly succeeded, from the inevitable bent of their innate humoristic
impulses, in burlesquing the fiery feeling abroad, which the public were contented
to gratify in pictorial guise.

It is certain that those discriminating critics best qualified to appreciate the
talents of Rowlandson and Cruikshank, who worked up the anti-Corsican crusade
contemporaneously, are continually disposed to regret that the wondrous inventive abilities of these fertile designers were not exercised in a more congenial
field.

Our caricaturist worked away, fierce and implacable, following every turn of

Boney's fortunes with a show of savage ardour, until the idol
fell in 1815. Rowlandson, in addition to the immense mass
of caricatures which he fabricated with unflagging energy,
came out brilliantly with several large transparencies, painted
for public exhibition, outside Ackermann's Repository, on
the occasion of the general illuminations, which fittingly
signalised the successes of the allied armies after Leipsig,
the final downfall of the Emperor after Waterloo, and the
subsequent peace rejoicings.

A fresh subject for the exercise of Rowlandson's caricature capabilities was
furnished in 1809 by the scandalous revelations which were disclosed, as evidence
at the bar of the House of Commons, during the 'inquiry into the corrupt practices of the Commander-in-Chief, in the administration of the army.' With
ill-advised weakness the popular Duke of York seems to have transferred the
exercise of the patronage legitimately invested in his department, to Mrs. M. A.
Clarke, a clever and unscrupulous mistress, whose extravagances he had for
awhile contributed to support at Gloucester Place. The demand for this exciting pabulum was sufficiently eager to induce the caricaturist to bring out a
fresh pictorial satire almost daily, and sometimes two or more appeared on the
same day, while the 'delicate investigation' was proceeding, and the public
interest in the circumstances remained at a boiling heat. We are not inclined to
argue that any of these ephemeral compositions, superior as they were to the
ruck of contemporaneous productions, were worthy, in any degree, of the artist's
graphic powers, or were likely to contribute to his celebrity. For some time

Rowlandson's ambition seemed to cool down, and although he was working hard, and producing a fair average of results, he appeared satisfied to turn his skill to the most prosaic account, as the means of earning a livelihood. He made no fresh efforts to astonish his admirers, or to sustain his fame by novel efforts of genius, such as we have particularised as appearing before the commencement of the nineteenth century.

Among the countless caricatures, good, bad, and indifferent, according to the circumstances of their publication, produced between 1809 and the close of the designer's career, nearly twenty years later, we cannot direct the reader's attention to many subjects above the generality of similar productions by Rowlandson's hand. It must be borne in mind that the artist's opportunities for graceful delineation had been considerably curtailed; the fair leaders of the old picturesque generation, whose effigies beam so charmingly on Reynolds's canvases, and the days of powder, flowing locks, silk coats, laces, lappels, and their accompaniments, had gradually disappeared, and left a prosier people, of sober exterior, in their stead. The difference between the exteriors of Rowlandson's lively personages, at the earlier part of the career, is so distinct from the outward appearance of his surroundings, and of the world which continued to exercise his pencil, at the close of his years, that it is extremely difficult, with the evidence before our eyes, to credit that such extreme changes could take place within the lifetime of one individual. The wanton cruelty of time in dealing thus harshly with the delicious models,

which at one period seemed expressly constituted for the exercise of Rowlandson's pencil, may have discouraged the artist, and given him a distaste for exertions of ambition in which his heart had no part, while his fancy still hovered round his retrospects of the brilliant scenes, at home and abroad, that had met his sight in his gallant youth.

A few of Rowlandson's plates in 1811 recall his best days, but we are not too confident that the originals veritably belong to the year which is engraved upon the plates; indeed, in two cases at least, *Exhibition Stare Case, Somerset House*, and *Royal Academy, Somerset House*, the caricatures are most probably reprints, with the dates altered. This practice, common enough in his day, is productive of no slight confusion; all Rowlandson's most popular conceptions, 'the palpable hits' which held their own in the public favour, and were eagerly secured, were republished from year to year, to meet the demand, and, in most cases, the plate was freshly dated, as if the print had only then appeared for the first time. This principle has complicated our task, as it is most difficult to secure even a solitary impression of the finer works, and but scant means exist of tracing them back to the actual date, in the absence of any considerable collections to which the student may apply for purposes of reference and comparison. If the reader will be at the pains to consult the 'Appendix,' containing the nearest approach to an arrangement of Rowlandson's works, under the years of publication, the writer could arrive at under existing circumstances, it will be seen that the same caricatures frequently reappear, with altered dates, for successive years.

In the latter part of the artist's career, although he executed a great many works of interest in themselves, and his inexhaustible social satires are often meritorious, and always ingenious, his best talents were devoted to the production of original drawings for immediate sale. They were chiefly disposed of through the assistance of Rudolph Ackermann, 101 Strand ; and S. W. Fores, Piccadilly. Both these steady patrons of the declining years of a genius, who must, in a sense, have found the close of his life exposed to somewhat chilling influences, are reported, on good authority, to have held hundreds of Rowlandson's original drawings, scrap-books, and portfolios, filled with his admirable sketches at the time of his death ; but these collections have of course been since dispersed.

In addition to the immense gathering of water-colour drawings left by Row-

landson, which had accumulated in the possession of those re-spected gentlemen with whom he held business relations, there were several fine collections, formed about the same period, to be found in the possession of his intimates. Mitchell the banker, his constant friend in town, with whom Rowlandson frequently travelled on the Continent, had secured the most remarkable gallery of the artist's diversified views abroad, and particularly his sketches of life and character in France and the Netherlands, the latter being the most remarkable for broad humour. Henry Angelo, the fencing-master, and Bannister, the comedian, ancient school-fellows of the caricaturist, and, as will be seen, faithful comrades through life, were also steady collectors of his picturesque eccentricities, and many noblemen, and celebrities of the day—among them is mentioned the name of the dashing, and somewhat irrepressible, Lord Barrymore—took a pride in filling their folios with his works, which, as we are told, they justly esteemed ' an inexhaustible fund of amusement.'

A few later collections, with the names of the owners, and the titles of the leading subjects, are mentioned at the end of this volume, with a view to completing the interest of the subject, and affording a slight indication of the whereabouts of many of his productions.

It appears from the statements of Rudolph Ackermann, Rowlandson's industry was such that the considerate owner of the fashionable Repository—favourite lounge of the dilettanti as it was—at last found it difficult, as regards the selling department, to keep pace with his friend's creative abilities. In short, the artist produced drawings faster than the public, as it seems evident, felt inclined to purchase them for the time being, and it became a perplexing problem how to increase the demand proportionately to the supply ; for the multiplication of the sketches for awhile—probably under the spur of some emergency, or the pressure of apprehensions for the future—became so overwhelming that the worthy publisher, in his relation as a practical man of business, fancied he foresaw the approaching depreciation of the value of Rowlandson's drawings making such strides, on the strength of an overstocked market, he was afraid, in the end, the artist's remuneration would be so seriously diminished, that it would not be worth his while to persevere, unless a new line could be successfully struck out.

These anticipations were probably well founded, and we cannot but acknowledge that our artist had discarded prudence, and become thoroughly reckless—at least, as far as we can judge by appearances, for possibly he had more confidence in the ultimate request for his studies than was entertained by his friendly employers, and time has proved the soundness of his judgment. If the story we are told of his novel method of multiplying his drawings is serious, it will strike the reader that Mr. Acker-

mann had reason to feel anxious, on his *protégé's* account. It is related that Rowlandson would saunter from his neighbouring lodgings in the Adelphi, round to the *Repository of Arts*, and, as the title of Mr. Ackermann's establishment was no misnomer, every possible appliance was therein found ready to hand. The artist would then order a saucer of vermillion, and another of Indian ink, ready ground, from the colourist's room, with reed pens, and several sheets of drawing-paper ; he would then combine his inks in the proportions he thought proper, in the flesh lines vermillion predominated, in draperies Indian ink, shadows were a warm mixture of the two, and distant objects were faintly rendered in Indian ink alone. The outline was filled in on this principle, but, as the designer's own manual and dexterous rapidity had ceased to satisfy him, he had ingeniously discovered an expeditious method of multiplication sufficient for his purpose, without resorting to the sister art of engraving. The drawing was made on the principle essential in any engraving which has to give impressions, that is, the subject was reversed, right being changed to left—the only extra care required ; the outline was somewhat stronger, and the reed-pen more fully charged than was the usual practice, and when the design was completed it formed the *matrix* from which, before the ink became fixed, by means of a press, and paper damped to the proper consistency, it was easy to print off duplicates as long as the ink held out. We are rather inclined to speculate that, ingenious as the process seems, in description, it would by no means turn out a perennial flowing fountain, and two or three decent replicas would exhaust the original, however judiciously manipulated. The copies obtained by this manifold contrivance were corrected and strengthened, according to their requirements ; the series of impressions were then shaded with Indian ink, so as to lend the figures contour and solidity, and express the lighter distance ; and then came the final tinting, in delicate washes of colour, and the completed works were ready for introduction to the public. The writer does not believe that this *modus operandi* was ever followed up systematically ; that it has been

resorted to on occasions, his own observations have demonstrated ; and he confesses to a passing acquaintance with a collection of drawings by the artist (belonging to a gentleman of distinction, who is quite satisfied as to their merits), which are for the most part the results of this system, and he has more than once, in the course of his peregrinations, come across the *matrix* design, very spread and mysterious as to outline, having been exhausted in the working, but shaded with spirit, coloured, and sent into the world, a shameless left-handed production, craftily smuggled into circulation to confuse collectors, and throw discredit on its dexter counterparts. This accounts for a certain proportion of the duplicates after Rowlandson, which are of frequent occurrence ; and often have purchasers felt their self-esteem lowered, when another possessor of the same design in a firmer outline has assured them that they have been deceived into buying a mere copy, oblivious that the guilty pair are both due to the hand of the master, and that possibly other members of the same illicit family are lurking in the folios of rival amateurs. A grand central gathering of works by Rowlandson, presuming a person of sufficient enterprise could be found to prosecute the scheme of a comprehensive exhibition of the artist's works, would reveal some curiosities in the way of reproductive capability.

For the credit of our artist, and the comfort of collectors, we can record our assurance that this crafty method was never persevered in, the replicas issued under this illegitimate contrivance are confined to a brief period, the temptation to flood the market was kept within restricted limits, and Mr. Ackermann's business aptitude quickly discovered a method of enhancing the caricaturist's reputation and augmenting his means, without the necessity of resorting to tricks of ill-advised ingenuity. The successful projection of a series of monthly publications allowed the indefatigable projector—who exercised a princely liberality in his dealings, as publishers go—to pay his friend, the artist, so handsomely, that he was relieved from the necessity of multiplying his sketches in any inordinate profusion, and enabled him to take more time and pains, both in seeking his subjects, and working them out at his ease. The results of this happy conception, *The Poetical Magazine*, the three *Tours of Doctor Syntax*, and *The Dance of Death*, enjoyed unqualified popularity. They were followed by other works of a corresponding description, which were also well received. The

publisher had his reward; we have every reason to believe that Rowlandson enjoyed his fair share of these successful ventures; and continued to furnish book-illustrations, steadily following up the new branch he had discovered for the exercise of his abilities. Mr. Ackermann's enterprise provided him ample occupation. These octavo prints were produced on the same principle as the superior plates after his *chefs-d'œuvre* of the Academy period: a neat and carefully finished drawing of the original design was first prepared (these studies were afterwards purchased by Mr. Ackermann), and Rowlandson etched the outline sharply and clearly on the copper plate, an impression from the 'bitten-in' outline was printed on drawing-paper, and the artist put in his shadows, modelling of forms and sketchy distance, with Indian ink, in the most delicate handling possible; the shadows were then copied in aquatint on the outlined plate, sometimes by the designer, but in most cases by an engraver who practised this particular branch, which a few experts were able to manipulate with considerable dexterity and nicety. Rowlandson next completed the colouring of his own Indian ink shaded impression in delicate tints, harmoniously selected; his sense of colour being of a refined order as regarded the disposal of tender shades agreeable to the eye. His aptitude in this respect is quite as remarkable as his ease of delineation ; and, if his outlines can be copied with any approach to deceiving the eye of a connoisseur, an attempt to imitate his colouring, simple as it remained in its characteristics, is tolerably certain to betray the fraud.

The tinted impression, which was intentionally finished with greater delicacy and elaboration than the artist generally displayed, served as a copy for imitation, which was handed to Mr. Ackermann's trained staff of colourists, the publisher finding constant employment for a number of clever persons whom he had educated expressly for this skilled employment. These artists had worked under his auspices and personal supervision for years, until, by constant practice, and the pains which were taken by the publisher to improve their abilities, they attained a degree of perfection and neatness never arrived at before, and almost beyond belief in the present day, when the system has fallen into comparative disuse. The assistants did their best to reproduce the effect of the original drawings, and the number of impressions required to satisfy the public must have kept them

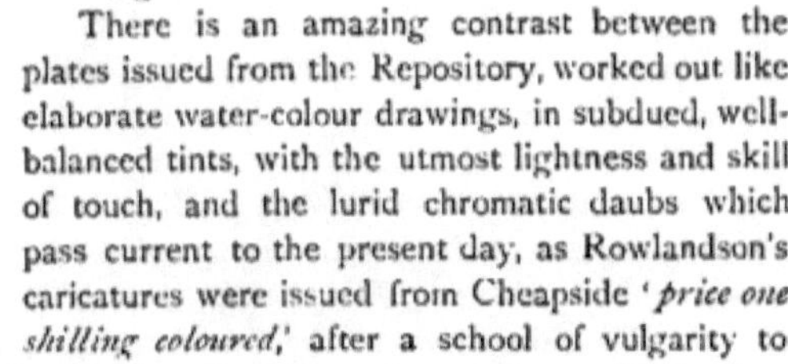

constantly at work, and occasionally jeopardised their high finish.

There is an amazing contrast between the plates issued from the Repository, worked out like elaborate water-colour drawings, in subdued, well-balanced tints, with the utmost lightness and skill of touch, and the lurid chromatic daubs which pass current to the present day, as Rowlandson's caricatures were issued from Cheapside '*price one shilling coloured*,' after a school of vulgarity to which the panorama of the Lord Mayor's Show *at one penny*, with its four yards of florid tenuity, is quite a refined work of art.

We are not inclined to offer uncharitable reflections on Rowlandson's City publisher ; the caricatures—excepting always certain rougher specimens, loosely executed enormities after designs by some of the amateurs of the period, which indubitably belong to the slip-shod order—are fair enough in their way, when one is lucky enough to meet with uncoloured copies ; it is the bad taste of his customers, the respectable dealer evidently stooped to flatter, with which we are inclined to disagree, and we think justifiably ; for although it was very good of the gentleman in question to issue so many copies of his plates, with a providential eye to the future, that impressions are sufficiently numerous to this day, all print-buyers must deplore the waste of staring colour expended in making his publications abominable to the sight of modern purchasers, and ruinous to the fair fame of the designer, by the uncompromising use of three positive pigments, red, blue, and yellow, to which, with an occasional brown, the colour-box seemed restricted, in most cases liberally plastered over the etchings—figures, sky, buildings and background being treated to the same smart hues in undiluted garishness, which utterly confuses the mind as to the meritorious qualities of the subjects so bespattered, and has the sinister effect, deplorable in itself, of compelling persons of chaste dispositions to dread caricatures as being on the surface something worse than scarlet abominations, fiendishly aggravated with additional lurid iniquities of a depraving tendency.

We have introduced Rowlandson in his later relation to the arts, as a skilful and popular contributor of book illustrations; we cannot leave this portion of our subject without offering a cursory review of his various labours in this capacity, since the wider circulation of printed publications has made his name more familiar to the great world than the finest masterpieces already alluded to, which seem doomed to remain unknown and inaccessible to the bulk of the public.

The first independent publication we have to notice was simply a gathering of subjects, extending over three or four years, collected in 1788, and issued as *Rowlandson's Imitations of Modern Drawings*, folio; including imitations of the styles of Gainsborough, Wheatley, Mortimer, Barrett, Gilpin, Bartolozzi, Zucchi, Cipriani, &c.

In 1786, Rowlandson supplied G. Kearsley, the publisher of those well-known satirical effusions of Dr. Wolcot, *The Poems of Peter Pindar*, with illustrations to the first volume of the quarto edition of these familiar works. This publication was continued the next year. In a burlesque strain, Rowlandson also came out with twenty illustrations, the drawings suggested by Collings,[1] caricaturing passages in Boswell's *Journal of a Tour in the Hebrides*, published by E. Jackson, small folio (1786). Our artist further supplied certain plates in parody of incidents in the *Sorrows of Werther*, also from suggestions by Collings, who designed a capital series of drolleries in travesty of passages literally extracted from Lord Chesterfield's *Polite Letters*.

G. and J. Robinson, in 1790, published the results of a trip to Brighton, which the artist had enjoyed in company with his friend, the frequent companion of his wanderings and frolics, Henry Wigstead, Esq., the sitting magistrate at Bow Street—*An Excursion to Brighthelmstone made in the year* 1782, by Henry

---

[1] The original sketches of this series were recently bequeathed to the South Kensington Museum, where they are attributed to Bunbury : a contemporary advertisement (1786) announces the designs to the forthcoming *Journal of a Tour in the Hebrides* to be furnished by Collings and Rowlandson.

Wigstead and Thomas Rowlandson, with eight engravings by Thomas Rowlandson, oblong folio.

There also appeared, in this and the following years, a series of *Miniature Groups and Scenes*, published by M. L., Brighthelmstone, and H. Brookes, Coventry Street, London; and a series of *Sheets of Picturesque Etchings*, published by S. W. Fores. Rowlandson also furnished numerous book-plates, octavo, to the series of novels published by I. Siebbald, Edinburgh; among the works thus illustrated we must particularise the novels of Fielding and Smollett.

The succeeding year (1792) our artist also contributed illustrations, in large size folding plates, designed after suggestions by Henry Woodward, to a quarto edition of Smollett's Novels. *Cupid's Magic Lantern*, with illustrations, etched by Rowlandson, also after designs by Henry Woodward, was published in 1797.

The Comforts of Bath, and the folio *Views of London*, belong to 1798. The same year the name of W. Wigstead, Charing Cross, appears as the publisher of the following works :—

Annals of Horsemanship, with seventeen copperplates by Henry Bunbury, Esq. Engraved by Thomas Rowlandson.

The Academy for Grown Horsemen, with twelve copperplates, by Henry Bunbury, Esq. Engraved by Thomas Rowlandson.

Love in Caricature, with eleven plates by Thomas Rowlandson.

The handsome and expensively got-up publications inaugurated by Mr. Ackermann, began to occupy our artist in 1799. The first of this well-executed series, with which Rowlandson was connected, was a set of plates, accurately coloured in *fac-simile* of the original drawings, in square folio, described as,

The Loyal Volunteers of London and Environs, with eighty-seven plates, designed and etched by Thomas Rowlandson.

Martial ardour being the key-note this year, when foreign invasion menaced our shores, Henry Angelo and Son, who were appointed fencing-masters to the Light Horse Volunteers of London and Westminster, collected a series of subjects which the artist had prepared under their direction, and issued the results of their joint ingenuity as a supplement to the elder Angelo's *Treatise on Fencing*, under the title of, *Hungarian and Highland Broadsword Exercise*, with twenty-four plates designed and etched by Thomas Rowlandson, oblong folio.

Another publication, issued by Ackermann in 1799, appeared as *Delineations of Nautical Characters*, in ten plates by Thomas Rowlandson.

In 1800, the results of an excursion to North and South Wales, undertaken in concert by the author and artist, were given to the public under the following description: *Remarks on a Tour to North and South Wales in the year* 1797, by Henry Wigstead, with plates by Thomas Rowlandson, Pugh, Howitt, &c. Published by W. Wigstead, Charing Cross.

Rowlandson also supplied some illustrations to *The Beauties of Sterne*, a selection of choice passages from the works of that author.

A series of *Views in Cornwall, Dorset, &c.*, appeared as a separate publication in 1805. The artist contributed serious book-plates to an edition of the *Sorrows of Werther*, in 1806. A smaller edition of the witty *Annals of Horsemanship* and *Academy for Grown Horsemen* (portions of which are attributed to the pen of the convivial Captain Grose, the well-known antiquary, author of *The Military Antiquities*, etc.—the original design of the work with the illustrations belonged to Henry Bunbury) was issued in a cheap form by Thomas Tegg in 1800, the etchings being executed in a reduced form by Thomas Rowlandson, and published under the title of *An Academy for Grown Horsemen and Annals of Horsemanship, by Geoffry Gambado*, octavo. A collection of plates portraying *The Miseries of Human Life*, consisting of fifty etchings by Thomas Rowlandson, small folio, was published in a reduced form the same year.

The principal work, however, which appeared in 1808, was, and must remain, a fitting instance of the enterprise and good taste of Rudolph Ackermann, his liberal employment of artists whose abilities were of the first order; while demonstrating the popularity of his publications, which could guarantee the most considerable outlays, with a successful return of the capital invested.

We refer to the splendid *Microcosm of London, or London in Miniature*, with 105 illustrations by Pugin and Rowlandson, in three volumes, quarto. A more extended notice of this valuable series is given in its proper place in this volume, under the description of works for 1808; although we believe the actual preparation of the plates extended over some years.

We have also to notice :—

The Caricature Magazine, or Hudibrastic Mirror, published by Thomas Tegg, and continued to 1810, 386 plates, in five volumes, oblong folio.

The Art of Ingeniously Tormenting, with illustrations by Rowlandson and Woodward, octavo ; published by Thomas Tegg, Cheapside, 1808.

A Lecture on Heads, by George Alexander Stevens, with twenty-five illustrations by Rowlandson and Woodward, octavo, published by Thomas Tegg, Cheapside, 1808.

Chesterfield Travestie: or School for Modern Manners, with ten caricatures engraved by Rowlandson from drawings by H. Woodward (who supplied the letterpress), duodecimo, was also published by Thomas Tegg, Cheapside. 1808.

In 1809, appeared numerous book-plates supplied by the artist to publishers. Thomas Tegg issued an edition of *Sterne's Sentimental Journey,* and *The Beauties of Sterne,* in a separate volume; both *embellished with caricatures by T. Rowlandson.* This gentleman also published an edition of *The Surprising Adventures of the renowned Baron Munchausen,* with numerous original engravings by Thomas Rowlandson; *The Annals of Sporting by Caleb Quizem,* with illustrations by Rowlandson and Woodward; *Advice to Sportsmen, selected from the Notes of Marmaduke Markwell;* with sixteen illustrations by Rowlandson; *The Trial of the Duke of York,* with Rowlandson's collected caricatures on the subject, in two volumes; *Investigation of the Charges brought against H.R.H. the Duke of York, &c.,* with fourteen portraits by Rowlandson, two volumes; and Butler's *Hudibras,* with five illustrations by William Hogarth, engraved by Thomas Rowlandson.

Beresford's *Antidote to the Miseries of Human Life,* octavo, is also advertised in 1809.

The Pleasures of Human Life, by Hilari Benevolus & Co., with five plates by Thomas Rowlandson, &c., was published by Longmans, 1809.

It was in 1809 that Ackermann projected his *Poetical Magazine,* royal octavo, which, it was arranged, should appear in consecutive monthly parts, as a means of affording his friend, the artist, substantial and progressive employment. The generous thought which prompted this enterprise was fittingly rewarded by the successful reception this venture secured at the hands of the public, and the patrons of Ackermann's 'Repository of Arts.' *The Poetical Magazine* was quite a feature amongst novel publications; the famous plates supplied by Rowlandson (two monthly), and the verses felicitously written up to the caricaturist's designs by William Coombe, under the title of *The Schoolmasters' Tour,* and introducing the highly popular *Doctor Syntax,* formed the only important contributions to the Magazine, which came to a conclusion (at the fourth volume), with the end of the first *Picturesque Tour.*

The success which attended the appearance of the familiar *Tour* was altogether beyond the expectations of either publisher, artist, or author. The etchings on the plates to *The Poetical Magazine* were worked fairly away and renewed. In 1812, *The Tour of Doctor Syntax in Search of the Picturesque,* with thirty-one illustrations by Thomas Rowlandson, was published in a separate form in royal octavo, a fresh set of the much-admired plates, with but the

slightest variations, being prepared expressly, and these in turn proved insufficient to supply the number of copies demanded by the delighted public. The
Tour had a still larger success in its independent form, and several editions
appeared in one season; the request continued for years, and was sufficiently
encouraging to induce the projectors to follow it up with a new series, *The
Second Tour of Doctor Syntax, in Search of Consolation*, with twenty-four illustrations by Thomas Rowlandson, which also appeared in monthly parts, and was
issued in a collected form in one volume, royal octavo, in 1820. A third tour,
in *Search of a Wife*, was ventured in 1822, but this was evidently intended to
be the final sequel, as the hero, ' Doctor Syntax,' is removed from life's scene at
the close.

Returning to Rowlandson's successive contributions of book-illustrations,
we find a satirical work, *Munchausen at Walcheren* issued in 1811 ; and a *Tale
of the Castle* (Dublin), published by Stockdale in 1812, as *Petticoat Loose, a
Fragmentary Poem*, illustrated with four plates by Thomas Rowlandson, quarto.

The artist also issued a series of
Views of Cornwall in the form of an
independent volume the same year.

Mr. Ackermann had introduced,
some years before, an illustrated
Miscellany to his subscribers, which
ran a long and highly successful
career, under the title, borrowed from
the circumstances of its publication,

of *Ackermann's Repository of Arts, Literature, Fashion, and Manufactures*.

In the pages of this admirable magazine were given many continuous contributions of a valuable and interesting character, the contents being as diversified
as the description of the undertaking. Among the serials were numerous es-
says of merit, which, in the projector's opinion, were entitled to the distinction of separate publication, and, at intervals, the discriminating proprietor of the
Repository selected various series of articles by his best qualified and most
respected colleagues in the work, and re-issued their contributions, with the
enhanced attraction of fresh pictorial embellishments, as separate publications.
In this manner a succession of *Letters from Italy*, which had appeared in the
Repository, between 1809 and 1813, furnished by Lewis Engelbach (who supplied reviews of music ; it has been said his criticisms may be usefully studied
by the most successful living contributors to the press), were republished in 1815
in one volume, royal octavo, as *Letters from Naples and the Campana Felice*,
with seventeen illustrations by Thomas Rowlandson.

Another deserving work, published by R. Ackermann, in the same finished style, with coloured engravings in aquatint, delicately completed by hand to resemble water-colour drawings, as were the major part of the illustrations to this series, appeared under the title of *Poetical Sketches of Scarborough*, with twenty-one illustrations by J. Green ; etched by Thomas Rowlandson, 1813.

In 1815 was published *The Military Adventures of Johnny Newcome*, with fifteen illustrations by Thomas Rowlandson, royal octavo, printed for Patrick Martin, 198 Oxford Street. This work is written in Hudibrastic metre, by 'An Officer' in imitation of the flowing lines supplied by Coombe to the *Tours of Doctor Syntax.* Another volume (1815 and 1816) was published by Thomas Tegg, Cheapside, also composed after the model of the same easy versification, under the description of *The Grand Master, or Adventures of Qui Hi in Hindostan, a Hudibrastic poem in eight cantos, by Quiz*, illustrated with twenty-eight engravings by Thomas Rowlandson.

The principal triumph of our artist's later years appeared in 1815 and 1816, Rowlandson inventing the subjects, and Coombe supplying the descriptive versification, as was their usual method of proceeding in the entire succession of publications, undertaken under this artistic and literary co-partnership, and issued by R. Ackermann.

We refer to the *Dance of Death*, which had first been offered the public in monthly parts under the old and highly successful system, between 1814 and 1816. This production, which repays the most careful consideration, received a flattering reception, and, in spite of the grim nature of the subject, enjoyed surprising popularity, and added considerably to the reputation of those concerned in its appearance. We have no hesitation in recording our impression that the ingenuity and invention displayed in the seventy-two plates illustrative of the *Dance of Death* are considerably in advance, in point of invention, of the pictures supplied to its more genial and popular rival *Doctor Syntax.* Both artist and author had arrived at a period of mature experience, which qualified and disposed them to bring their finest faculties to the treatment of this melodramatic theme, in which they must have discovered morbid fascinations ; since it has enabled them to rise above their average efforts. As we have noticed, although the conception is monumental, not to say sepulchral, in its characteristics, and on occasions, ghastly in its humour, the result is a masterpiece to the memories of Rowlandson and Coombe ; the fires of their early inspirations were rekindled from their decline ; and the *Dance of Death* has always impressed us as the last flicker of expiring genius ; a fitting memorial of the vast and almost forgotten faculties of the projectors.

A fuller account of this impressive and truly remarkable work, will be found under the year 1810, where we have endeavoured to do justice to the exceptional qualities of a performance which, in our modest conviction, surpasses any previous treatment of the same subject.

In 1816 Rowlandson commenced a series of charming little pictures designed in outline, avowedly intended as an assistance to landscape-artists in the direction of suggesting, and supplying animated groups of figures, suitable for introduction into drawings. The etchings were executed with exceptional neatness, ease, and spirit, and the entire collection is highly interesting; it appeared under the title of *The World in Miniature, figure subjects for Landscapes, Groups, and Views,* and was published by Mr. Ackermann at 'The Repository.' A series of a similar description was commenced under the same designation by Rowlandson in 1821, and finished by W. H. Pyne in 1826; the set was somewhat diffusive, if it extended to 637 parts, as we are told.

Our artist's illustrations to the *Beauties of Tom Brown* belong to 1809.

Rowlandson also contributed a frontispiece to another of Tegg's publications in 1816, *The Relics of a Saint, by Ferdinand Farquhar.*

Rowlandson found a congenial exercise for his skill, taste, and mirth-imparting qualities in the illustration of Oliver Goldsmith's *Vicar of Wakefield,* in 1817, when the famous tale re-appeared, embellished with twenty-four designs by the artist. Mr. Ackermann was induced to republish this delightful story as a vehicle for the display of the delicate humoristic, and more refined qualifications of the caricaturist (who, by the way, had almost ceased to deserve this epithet).

Nothing could be more artless than the pathos of this fiction, its simple humour is ever fresh, and Rowlandson has executed his portion of the undertaking in a congenial spirit, indeed the happy impulses of the author seem spontaneously embodied in the picturesque designs.

The success of the *Dance of Death* was so considerable that the publisher endeavoured to share its popularity with a successor. The two volumes constituting the first work were, however, executed in a superior manner; and more pains were taken to bring the plates to the utmost perfection, as reproductions of the original drawings, than was the case with later publications. *The Dance of Life,* illustrated with twenty-eight coloured engravings by Thomas Rowlandson, published by R. Ackermann, royal octavo, appeared in 1817, and although fairly executed, neither the conceptions of Rowlandson, nor the verses of Coombe, rose above the commonplace; it is evident that the sentiment which had inspired their gifted faculties in the former subject found no revival in the present volume, which is somewhat disappointing after the talent which is manifested in its predecessor.

A pendant to the *Military Adventures of Johnny Newcome* was issued in 1818 as *The Adventures of Johnny Newcome in the Navy*, a poem in four cantos, with sixteen plates by Rowlandson from the author's designs, by Alfred Burton, published by Simpkin and Marshall, Stationers' Hall Court, Ludgate Hill. More attention was paid to the artistic preparation of the succeeding portion of *The Second Tour of Doctor Syntax in Search of Consolation*, with twenty-four illustrations by Thomas Rowlandson, royal octavo, which Mr. Ackermann introduced to the public in a collected form as the companion to the popular first volume in 1820.

Rowlandson also furnished illustrations to certain pamphlets or chapbooks in 1819; we may particularise one under the title of *Who killed Cock Robin?*—a tract on the Manchester Massacre, published by John Cahnac. We have also to notice his contribution to a chapbook which appeared the same year, as, *Female Intrepidity, or the Heroic Maiden.*

The same year appeared *Rowlandson's Characteristic Sketches of the Lower Orders; intended as a Companion to the New Picture of London* containing fifty-four coloured plates, printed by S. Leigh, 18 Strand, 1820.

Another contribution, *A Tour in the South of France*, drawn from the excellent serial publication, 'Ackermann's Repository of Arts, Literature, Fashion, and Manufactures,' originally supplied to its pages in instalments between the years 1817 and 1820, was republished in a completed form in 1821, with additional attractions, in the way of fresh embellishments, by the unflagging hand of our artist, under the title of *A Journal of Sentimental Travels in the Southern Provinces of France*, illustrated with eighteen coloured engravings from designs by Thomas Rowlandson, royal octavo, published by R. Ackermann, 101 Strand.

A French version of 'Doctor Syntax's Tour in Search of the Picturesque,' *Le Don Quichotte Romantique, ou Voyage du Docteur Syntaxe à la Recherche du Pittoresque et du Romantique*, also appeared in Paris this year, with twenty-eight illustrations, drawn on stone, after the original designs of Rowlandson, by Malapeau, lithographed by G. Engelmann.

The final complement of 'The Tours,' prepared under the same auspices as the earlier peregrinations, reached completion as an additional volume in 1822, and the monthly instalments were then reissued in a collected form to join the two predecessors as *The Third Tour of Doctor Syntax in Search of a Wife*, with twenty-five illustrations by Thomas Rowlandson, royal octavo, published by R. Ackermann.

A further instance of the universal popularity enjoyed by *The First Tour of Doctor Syntax in Search of the Picturesque* was afforded, in 1822, by the appearance of an edition translated into German and freely adapted as *Die Reise des Doktor Syntax um das Malerische au Frusuchen* with Rowlandson's famous illustrations imitated on stone and lithographed by F. E. Rademacher, Berlin.

The interest which it was found, on experience, still surrounded the grotesque prototype *Dr. Syntax*, induced the energetic projectors—publisher, artist, and author—under their old, well-defined relations, to venture on a farther extension of the familiar framework, and a fresh volume, which had, like the preceding publications, found its way to the public in monthly instalments, was inaugurated in 1822 under the description of *The History of Johnny Quæ Genus: The Little Foundling of the late Doctor Syntax—a poem by the author of The Three Tours* (William Coombe)—embellished with twenty-four coloured engravings by Thomas Rowlandson.

The same year our artist issued another distinct volume of landscape subjects of his execution under the title of *Rowlandson's Sketches from Nature*; a collection of seventeen plates, drawn and etched by the artist and aquatinted by Stradler. *Crimes of the Clergy*, an octavo volume, with two plates by our artist, also appeared in 1822.

As a further proof that the numerous editions in royal octavo of the illustrious schoolmaster's wanderings were insufficient to satisfy the requirements of his patrons, Mr. Ackermann offered the public a fresh copy, in three volumes 16mo. of *The Three Tours of Dr. Syntax, Pocket Edition,* with all Rowlandson's plates, executed on a smaller scale to suit the convenience of enthusiasts, who might require to carry the volumes about with them ready for immediate reference, or for perusal on their travels and at odd moments, if such an opportunity should be in request.

In 1825 Charles Molloy Westmacott, an intimate friend of the caricaturist, in whose company we learn he visited Paris, thought proper to edit a publication under his pseudonym of 'Bernard Blackmantle,' a collection of whimsical extracts from the press, which had appeared in print in the previous season. The description of his production is as follows: *The Spirit of the Public Journals for the year 1824, with Explanatory Notes.* Illustrations on wood by T. Rowlandson, R. and G. Cruikshank, Lane, and Findlay. London; published by Sherwood, Jones, and Co., Paternoster Row, 1825. Our artist contributed eleven highly humorous cuts to this publication, his drawings being engraved on wood—a novel process as far as the designs usually supplied by Rowlandson are concerned.

A notable plate was furnished by the caricaturist in 1825 to *The English*

Spy, a work also produced under the auspices of 'Bernard Blackmantle,' after the description of the better-known *Life in London*. The major part of the plates are due to the hand of Robert Cruikshank. Rowlandson's name is given on the title-page as having contributed a portion of the illustrations on wood, but the only example of his skill we have been able to identify is an adaptation of his drawing (now the property of Mr. Capron), *The Life School at the Royal Academy*, which he originally presented to his old friend John Thomas Smith, of the British Museum. Plate 32.—*R. A—ys of Genius Reflecting on the True Line of Beauty at the Life Academy, Somerset House*, by Thomas Rowlandson ; and this illustration is undeniably the most interesting to be found in the entire contents of the two octavo volumes of which Mr. Westmacott's *English Spy* is composed ; further particulars of this subject are given under the year 1825.

After the caricaturist's death in 1827 the admirable publications, of which his coloured plates formed the principal attractions, were discontinued ; the taste of the public had changed. Wood blocks and steel plates came into fashion.

Cheap annuals illustrated with woodcuts came into favour for a season, until the appearance of the more elaborately prepared 'Gift Books,' with fine steel engravings, 'Keepsakes,' 'Gems,' &c., subsequently took their place. The folios of Mr. Ackermann were still sufficiently rich in studies by Rowlandson to furnish the framework for a fresh publication. A choice was made from the large collection of original drawings, published and unpublished, which still remained, after the artist's decease, in the possession of the indefatigable proprietor of the 'Repository' ; and these sketches, which of necessity, for the most part, are assignable to Rowlandson's declining period, when his drawings became looser in execution and less picturesque in point of subject, were selected as the materials for a new venture, with a departure from the old popular style of reproduction in facsimile of the artist's pictures coloured by hand.

The subjects culled from Mr. Ackermann's portfolios were redrawn on a reduced scale, either as a whole, or striking portions of caricatures, and prominent figures or groups were adapted, transferred to wood-blocks, and put into the hands of an engraver. In cutting the designs a considerable amount of the original spirit, with the individuality of execution peculiar to the master, have unfortunately been sacrificed; the engravings are heavy and poor; however, they offer a rough idea of the nature of the studies which happened to remain in the hands of the publisher, and some interest attaches to this circumstance, as the major part of these designs have never been issued on copper.

Mr. W. H. Harrison was engaged to write up to the pictorial sketches, and he has constructed various small fictions founded on the suggestions offered by the engravings; but the entire work is somewhat clumsy in contrivance, both as respects the illustrations and the literary setting intended to assist their interest in the eyes of the public; the editor's inventions are neither original nor brilliant. The title of the annual produced on this compound principle was *The Humourist, a Companion for the Christmas Fireside, embellished with fifty engravings, exclusive of numerous vignettes after designs by the late Thomas Rowlandson:* published by R. Ackermann, 96 Strand, and sold by R. Ackermann, junior, 191 Regent Street, 1831. *The Humourist* contained sixty-seven illustrations in all; the titles of these, and a brief description of the various subjects, will be found at the close of the present volume, under the year 1831.

Although Rowlandson was so well known as an artist, no fitting memorials of his career are extant; and while, as we have related, the task of discovering a collection of works by the artist, worthy of illustrating his exceptional abilities, is surrounded by unforeseen difficulties, the operation of culling personal traits, or records of the life and adventures of the caricaturist, demands even greater extensions of patience. Nothing short of sincere appreciation for the vast talents of the man, and of a lasting conviction of the original qualities of his works, could have encouraged the writer to prolong his researches, the chances in this case of alighting on any discoveries of note being so problematical.

The person of Rowlandson was familiarly recognised amongst his contemporaries from his youth, when he was first admitted as a student at the schools of the Royal Academy (about 1770), through his diversified fortunes, till his death, which occurred on April 22, 1827.

His figure, we learn, was large, well-set-up, muscular, and above the average height—in fact, his person was a noticeable one; his features were regular and defined, his eye remarkably full and fearless, his glance being described as penetrating, and suggestive of command; his mouth and chin expressed firm-

SMITHFIELD SHARPERS ; OR THE COUNTRYMAN DEFRAUDED.

Old Trusty, with his Town-made Friends,
To gentle sleep himself commends,
    With Tray upon his knees ;
Whilst Tom, his son, all eager, gaping,
Expects each moment he'll be scraping
    The treasure up he sees.

Meanwhile the Harpy Tribe are plotting,
By forcing liquor, winking, nodding,
    To cheat the youth unlearn'd ;
Who, to his cost, will quickly find
Nor watch, nor money, left behind,
    And Friends to Sharpers turn'd.

ness and resolution ; the general impression conveyed to a stranger by his countenance, which was undeniably fine and striking in its characteristics, was that of the inflexibility of the owner.

Two or three portraits of the caricaturist are traceable, besides numerous burlesque transfers of his own effigy to his imaginary personages. In common with Cruikshank, Thackeray, and many other humorists of the brush and etching-needle, he was prone to introduce the presentment of his own lineaments in whimsical juxtapositions. The most generally recognised likeness, from which a separate plate has been published by Mr. Parker, occurs in a clever eccentric drawing, exhibited by the artist at the Royal Academy Exhibition in 1787, under the title of *Countrymen and Sharpers* (No. 555).

This subject was subsequently engraved by J. K. Sherwin, whose portrait also figures therein, in the person of the pigeon, while Rowlandson has chosen to represent himself as the leading sharper, he who, with blustering front, is fleecing the simple youth at cards, in defiance of his well-accepted reputation for rigid integrity ; for although the gaming table long held the caricaturist an enslaved votary, ready to make the most reckless sacrifices to tempt the fickle favours of the gambler's fortune, it is recorded by those of his acquaintances who have mentioned this disastrous failing (which by the way he shared with all the wealthy, distinguished, and witty celebrities of his day), and deplored the havoc it made with his means, and professional pursuits, that his sense of honour was ever of the keenest, his word was always regarded as sufficient security, and he possessed a delicacy of feeling, and a sense of independence, which would not allow him to remain under a debt or an obligation.

At the time Rowlandson sent his drawing of *Countrymen and Sharpers*[1] for exhibition, he was 31 years of age, and according to the portrait, looks manhood personified, with a fine comely figure, and a face that imprints itself on the recol-

---

[1] A somewhat different version of the origin of this caricature is given in the *Memoirs of John Bannister, Comedian*, by John Adolphus (8vo., 1839) : ' His friend and fellow-student Rowlandson was, unhappily, much addicted to games of chance, and Bannister used to remonstrate with him on the subject with amiable but ineffectual perseverance. On one of these occasions John Raffaelle Smith, the engraver, admonished Bannister on the inutility of his efforts. "You may spare your sympathy and advice also," he said ; "for that Tom Rowlandson was, is, and ever will be incurable." The artist, in merry revenge, brought out a print called *Hawks and a Pigeon*, in which Smith, endowed for the occasion with a most villanous aspect, the very personation of a sharper and a knave, exhibited conspicuously.

' By way of reprisal, Smith produced a well-known and popular engraving, in which Rowlandson and some others are represented as confederates in fleecing an innocent. Bannister lent his aid in forming the group, and, putting on for the occasion a face from which all appearance of sense was effectually banished, sat for the young dupe. Parsons on seeing the production said : " Why, Jack ! you are the last of your fraternity that I should have selected for the model of a flat. Why, when you were a little Cupid in the green-room, Kitty Clive, who was not apt to mince matters, used to say you looked as innocent as a little sucking devil." '

lection, his hair in a profusion of wavy tresses, worn long, and 'clubbed' as was the fashion of the period. His bold and piercing eyes set under massive and somewhat prominent brows.

The next attributed portrait belongs to 1799, when Rowlandson was 43 years of age. In the design, *An Artist travelling in Wales,* the result of a journey he made with his friend, the convivial Henry Wigstead, he has represented himself, with a due allowance for burlesque, looking older than his years ; the long hair is still there, but its curls are thinned, time and a struggle with seasons less rosy than his youth of many fortunes, are telling on the outward man, but the brows, eyes, mouth and chin have diminished nothing of their resolute characteristics— indeed, they are more marked—and the strong nervous figure is beginning to look gaunt.

The Chamber of Genius appeared in 1812 with the appropriate quotation :—

> Want is the scorn of every wealthy fool ;
> And genius in rags is turned to ridicule.—Juv. *Sat.*

The head of the caricaturist is strongly defined on the shoulders of the gifted occupant of a garret, and the likeness is just what might be supposed from the countenance, as given in 1787, viewed through the intervening quarter of a century of struggles, and disenchantments, when cares of the hour, and incidental anxieties, touching provision for the future, had commenced to take the place of the artist's original careless hardihood.

The last portrait to which we shall at present refer is by another hand ; and was sketched when the health of the caricaturist was a grave source of apprehension, since we learn that during the last two years of his life he was a severe sufferer. It represents the figure of a large and powerful-looking old gentleman, of impressive presence ; the main characteristics, and the marked profile have gathered force with increasing years, the brows are even firmer, and the features more defined ; this *croquis* of the veteran was drawn by his old friend, and erst fellow-pupil, John Thomas Smith, the keeper of the drawings and prints in the British Museum, and the study was taken while the caricaturist was looking over some prints, on one of his visits to the treasures in his friend's department. The sketcher, who has written the circumstances under which it was taken, below the portrait, has given Rowlandson's age at seventy,—within a year, in fact, of his death. The caricaturist's flowing locks are considerably shorn by the hand of the inevitable mower, and his penetrating eyes do not disdain the assistance afforded by a pair of huge tortoiseshell-rimmed spectacles, in which they are framed ; but as far as the visible flight of time goes, regarding the outward man, he might be assumed to possess powers of vitality sufficient to carry him over another score years.

If our memory does not deceive us, a sketch of the caricaturist's figure, from the life, and drawn in chalks, was exhibited some time ago at Bethnal Green, in the Loan Collection, formed under the auspices of the Science and Art Department.

*   *   *

We learn that our artist, who is perhaps the most popularly recognised practitioner of the caricature branch, was born in the Old Jewry, in July 1756, that is to say, just a year before his remarkable compeer James Gillray. The members of the Rowlandson family, according to the little we can trace of their personal history, seem to have been highly respectable people of the middle class in life. The name is not of common occurrence. There is a tract relating certain misfortunes which attended two bearers of this cognomen; a pious and worthy couple who in the seventeenth century went evangelising to New England, where they suffered incredible persecutions, and escaped all sorts of dismal tortures amongst the aboriginal Indians, in whose hands they had the mischance to fall; the succession of hardships which they encountered, and their final miraculous deliverance, are duly recorded for the encouragement of the faithful. The narrative, which is simple and circumstantial, forms an item of ' improving reading ' not without its interest in the present age. There is nothing to prove the relationship of this faithful and much-enduring pair to our caricaturist, beyond the circumstance of the similarity of name. Rowlandson the elder was assuredly at one time a man of fair substance, as we are informed—' some say a city merchant,' but his disposition, like that of his son, seems to have been tinctured with recklessness. Mention is made of an uncle Thomas Rowlandson, who was godfather to the subject of our notice ; also, as far as we can discover, connected with mercantile pursuits. This relationship was destined to serve the caricaturist in good stead, if he had only exercised the commonest prudence in husbanding the resources which he derived from this connection. We discover that, before Rowlandson had arrived at man's estate, his chances of inheriting a provision to help him on his way, together with the prospect of any future support, so far as the paternal resources were concerned, had melted away ; the elder Rowlandson's ' speculative turn ' had taken a sinister bent, considerable sums had been sunk, and still more portentous liabilities had been incurred, ' by experimenting on various branches of manufacture,' which were attempted on too extensive a scale for the means at his command ; and, his resources becoming exhausted, before the fruition of his schemes, pecuniary embarrassments involved his career, and he failed to realise the considerable fortune which his sanguine temperament had anticipated. The natural talents of the son, and the professional training which had cultivated his gifts, were the only contributions he received, on attaining manhood, towards his future maintenance, as far as the help he could derive from his father was concerned. Other adventitious aids came to the artist's assistance, indeed, in spite of the untoward direction which the previous prosperity of the elder had taken, Rowlandson was to a large degree the spoiled child of fortune throughout his early career.

HOW TO TREAT A REFRACTORY MEMBER.

We are not informed whether the paternal estate was restored to solvency. Among the various 'valuable legacies' which, it is related, fell to the caricaturist's share (only to be scattered broadcast), it is very possible that, in some sort, an inheritance from his father formed part of these unexpected 'good gifts.' It seems, although we have no direct records of the remaining relatives, that Rowlandson had a sister, since we learn that his brother-in-law was Howitt, famous as an artist for his delineation of animals, for his spirited hunting subjects, being eminent as a sportsman, rider, and angler ; and, like the caricaturist, somewhat of a spoiled child—a wayward genius—of a congenial soul, and vivacious impulses, a trifle too given to yield to careless convivial company, or the allurements which the hour might hold forth, oblivious of sober consequences to follow.

Thomas Rowlandson, the uncle, had married a certain Mademoiselle Chattelier, who was, it is evident, a lady with some command of wealth; and from the partiality and indulgence of this aunt, our artist, we are told, 'derived that assistance which his father's reverse of fortune had withheld.'

Another reference to the family name further occurs amongst the announcements of marriages for September 1800 (*Gentleman's Magazine*, vol. 70, p. 898), where we find that Thomas Rowlandson, Esq., of Watling Street, espoused Miss Stuart, daughter of George Stuart, Esq., of the Grove, Camberwell, Surrey. It is obvious that Rowlandson senior intended to give his son a sound training. As a school-boy, the future celebrity wandered into the precincts of that Soho district to which he afterwards clung in his varying fortunes with the persistence developed by habit.

The caricaturist began to draw his first instalments from the fount of knowledge at the scholastic symposium of Doctor Barvis in Soho Square, 'at that time, and subsequently, an academy of some celebrity.' We are told this estab-

lishment was kept by Doctor Barrow when young Rowlandson was pursuing his studies. The respectability of the school, and its soundness as an educational institution, is satisfactorily demonstrated to our mind from the circumstance that the great Edmund Burke had elected to confide his beloved son, with whose training, it is well known, the philosopher took especial pains, to the charge of Doctor Barrow; and Richard Burke, the gentle gifted youth whose untimely death hastened the decease of his patriotic father, was a school-fellow of our artist. J. G. Holman, who was destined to acquire reputation as a dramatic writer and performer, was another school-fellow. It appears that, within the walls of this academy, Rowlandson made the acquaintance of John Bannister, whose inimitable talents were afterwards to delight the town, and whose name is a lasting ornament to the histrionic profession; it was, further, in Soho Square that young Rowlandson and young Angelo, the son of the well-known Henry Angelo (one of the best recognised and most respected foreigners domiciled in London of his day), fencing-master to the Royal Family, became fast and firm friends. The intimacy existing between this worthy trio, dating from these early days, continued steadfastly through life. All these lads were, in different degrees, enthusiasts of the graphic art; Angelo and Bannister had strong predilections for the arts, and both drew as amateurs in their subsequent careers, although, with Rowlandson, they originally meditated following up the artist's profession seriously. As to our friend Rolley, like all beginners gifted with the pictorial vein, he could make sketches intuitively before he had learnt to do anything else, as seems the rule with youths who possess the artistic faculty and an imaginative temperament; his powers of fancy directed his hand at a precociously juvenile age to the practice of exercising his abilities with pencil and pen. 'From the early period of his childhood,' it is recorded, 'Rowlandson gave presage of his future talent;' he could make sketches before he learned to write, and, according to the usual course, 'he drew humorous characters of his master and many of his scholars, before he was ten years old. The margins of his school-books were covered with these his handiworks.'

Rowlandson's genius was of the rapid order, his powers were matured before the average of students have sounded the direction of their inclinations. Young Henry Angelo left Doctor Barrow's and Soho Square, for Eton, while Bannister and Rowlandson quitted the seminary of polite learning to follow the arts at the Schools of the Royal Academy; here our artist made rapid strides, and gave

convincing proofs of his ability, dexterity, and quickness of parts, during the short interval his name was entered as a probationer.

In his sixteenth year, somewhere about 1771, Rowlandson had the advantage of being sent to Paris to continue his education; we learn that he 'spoke French like a native.' It was his aunt, *née* Mademoiselle Chattelier, residing in the French metropolis, a widow with what would have then been considered, in that capital, a handsome fortune, who invited her hopeful nephew over to the very centre of gaiety, dissipation, and luxurious refinement—Paris in the latter days of Louis the Fifteenth's reign being a very Capua for a youth of light and picturesque disposition such as our artist possessed. The impulse for purposeless frivolities, so deleteriously nourished amidst the gaieties of Parisian life, seems to have been kept in tolerable subjection by his earnest intentions to work hard at his adopted profession, which certainly must have sustained Master Rolley during his earlier residence on the Continent, until the cup of pleasure was raised to his lips by an unexpected accession of means. The student did a wonderful deal of real solid work and thoroughly steadfast application, before, like Moreland, he allowed himself to be whirled into the eddy of fashionable distractions; in Paris he was inscribed as a student in one of the drawing academies there, and his natural abilities, aided by the excellence of the methods practised around him, to which his gifts moulded themselves quite naturally, enabled the probationer to make rapid advances in the study of the human figure, and laid the foundation for his future excellences. During his first sojourn, which lasted for nearly two years, Rowlandson became a perfect French buck, with a decided leaning, however, towards the fine-art section of the condition, and a pride in his professional calling; he learned to draw with fidelity to nature, with the graceful ease, and *abandon*, and the sparkle of style which marks French pictorial art of the period immediately antecedent to the reign of Louis the Sixteenth, the very ideal of luxury and refinement. It is related that, during his abode in Paris, 'he occasionally permitted his satiric talents the indulgence of portraying the characteristics of that fantastic people, whose *outré* habits perhaps scarcely demanded the exaggerations of caricature.'

Rowlandson returned to London for a season; and, while still a youth in years, his studies at the Academy were resumed; his progress was now so marked that he was set up as a friendly rival to Mortimer, another talented student, who had won the admiration of professors and pupils alike, by his skilful drawings after the nude figure. Our artist seems to have been highly popular with the two sections of academicians and students; the former appreciated his masterly endowments, the latter were won by his whimsicalities, his spirit of mischief, and the marvellous gift he possessed of turning every situation to comical account in the production of exhaustless graphic satires, which seemed to flow from his pen of their own sweet wilfulness.

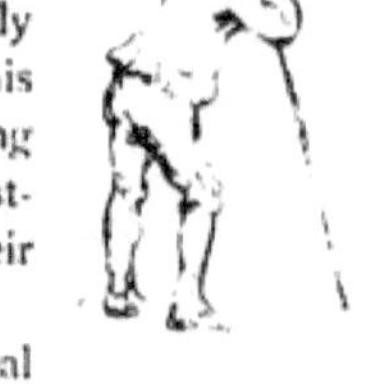

John Bannister, who, as we have seen, had evinced an equal predilection for the graphic art, with powers, however, of lesser brilliancy, was then studying in the antique school, their old friendship was renewed, and a fresh alliance for fun and frolic was straightway entered into.

These hopeful aspirants were a great acquisition to the mirth of the schools, but both these eccentric geniuses must have sorely tried the patience of their venerated pastors and masters. The nature of their drolleries, which were incessant, is exposed in an extract from the *Reminiscences* of Henry Angelo, who formed the third person of this waggish trio.

'At the period when Wilson held the appointment of Librarian to the Royal Academy, the students were accustomed to assemble in the library; Bannister and Rowlandson were students, and both being sprightly wights, Wilson kept a watchful eye upon their pranks. The one was apt to engage the attention of his fellow-disciples by caricaturing the surly librarian, never forgetting to exaggerate his mulberry nose; whilst the other, born to figure in the histrionic art, a mimic by nature, used to divert them, in his turn, by playing off the irritable 'Old Dick.'

Michael Moser was keeper at Somerset House while Bannister and Rowlandson were students of the Royal Academy, at which period the drawing-school was held in a part of the old palace, Somerset House, just behind the site of the present institution. Moser, in virtue of his office as keeper, had apartments there, which included accommodations for a housekeeper, and other female domestics.

'Bannister and Rowlandson, as before observed, were prankish youths. The latter once gave great offence by carrying a pea-shooter into the life academy, and, whilst old Moser was adjusting the female model, and had just directed her contour, Rowlandson let fly a pea, which, making her start, she threw herself entirely out of position, and interrupted the gravity of the study for the whole evening. For this offence, Master Rowlandson went near getting himself expelled.

'Bannister, who at this time drew in the plaster academy, not having gained the step that admitted to the drawing from the life, used to amuse Moser with his mimicry, and he was, indeed, a pet of the worthy keeper.

'One evening, observing that the student had vacated his seat at his desk, the keeper went to seek him, and, hearing an unusual giggling and confusion in the basement storey he descended to learn the cause; when he discovered the young artist romping with the servant-maids.

'What are you doing, sir, hey?' inquired the keeper, taking him gently by the ear; 'why are you not at the *cast?* You are an idler, sir.' Bannister met his reproof with an arch smile, and whispered, 'No, kind sir, I only came down to study from the *life!*'

In dealing with this part of the subject, every scrap of information has its interest, the resources in this direction being unfortunately most restricted. The task of writing on Gillray, and that within the lifetime of the subject, was likened to the toil 'of bondsmen commanded to make bricks without straw,' a comparison with which we have a lively sympathy, as we have realised to the fullest extent the difficulties which surrounded that undertaking. The obstacles to be surmounted in the instance of the first caricaturist are found to be rather more vexatious in the case of the companion volume, taken up under similar auspices. to elucidate the works of Rowlandson, and to trace the artist's career as far as lies within the writer's capabilities. Sixty years ago it was declared while treating of the first-named genius, in reference to contemporaneous indifference: 'It is a scandal upon all the cold-hearted scribblers in the land to allow such a genius as Gillray to go to the grave unnoticed; and a burning shame that so many of his works should have become ambiguous for want of a commentator. The political squibs have lost half of their point for want of a glossary, and many of the humorous traits of private life, so characteristic of men and manners, are becoming oblivious to ninety-nine hundredths of those who perambulate the streets of this mighty town.' This remark, so appropriately applied to Gillray (before Thomas Wright, and successive elucidators, had contributed to render the reading of these pictorial fables fairly clear, and the solutions easy of access), is equally striking as respects its undoubted truth in its application to Rowlandson—in his instance the pioneering remained to be accomplished— although his works are less complex in themselves, a description of them has hitherto proved too perplexing an attempt, since, how were the subjects to be collected ?

We feel a glow of gratitude to that worthiest old authority, *The Gentle- man's Magazine*, which contained a capital obituary notice on the caricaturist's decease, April 22, 1827, written by 'one who had known him for more than forty years ;' this article has been copied literally in all subsequent notices of Rowland- son.

W. H. Pyne, the artist, who, under a pseudonym as *Ephraim Hardcastle*, con- ducted the earliest of English fine-art reviews, *The Somerset House Gazette*, 1824, was one of the intimates of the caricaturist, and he has left slight allusions to Rowlandson, both in his  *Gazette* and in another publication of his enterprising, *Wine and Walnuts, or After Dinner Chat*, by Ephraim Hardcastle, 1823.

John Thomas Smith, as we have shown elsewhere, was on terms of personal friendship with Rowlandson throughout his life; but strangely enough, in his *Nollekens and his Times*, and his second volume, *Memoirs of several Contem- porary Artists from the time of Roubiliac, Hogarth and Reynolds, to that of Fuseli, Flaxman, and Blake*, no mention is made of his much-esteemed as- sociate. A passing allusion to his 'friend and fellow-pupil' Rowlandson, occurs in 'Antiquity' Smith's *Book for a Rainy Day*.

Henry Angelo, the early schoolfellow and constant comrade of our artist, a gentleman of varied accomplishments, obliged the reading public with his *Reminiscences* in 1830, a chatty, interesting, and in some respects highly valuable book, of which we wish there were more, since the two volumes are, as described by the title, filled with *memoirs of his friends, including numerous original anecdotes and curious traits of the most celebrated characters that have flourished during the last eighty years*. Unlike the author of *Nollekens and his Times*,

Angelo has given due prominence to his recollections of the caricaturist's works and career, and his terms of familiar intimacy have supplied him with many entertaining details, trivial or unimportant in themselves perhaps, but very much to the purpose from a biographical point of view, as aids to the effort of reproducing the subject in his wonted aspect, as he struck the men amongst whom he passed his life. The spirit of Angelo's *Reminiscences* will not bear dilution, and so we think it better to offer his memoirs of the artist as they were published.

'Thomas Rowlandson, John Bannister, and myself, having early in life evinced a predilection for the study of drawing, we became acquainted whilst boys, and were inseparable companions.

'Everyone at all acquainted with the arts must well know the caricature works of that very eccentric genius, Rowlandson ; the extent of his talent, however, as a draughtsman is not so generally known. His studies from the human figure at the Royal Academy were made in so masterly a style that he was set up as a rival to Mortimer, whom he certainly would have excelled, had his subsequent study kept pace with the fecundity of his invention. His powers, indeed, were so versatile, and his fancy so rich, that every species of

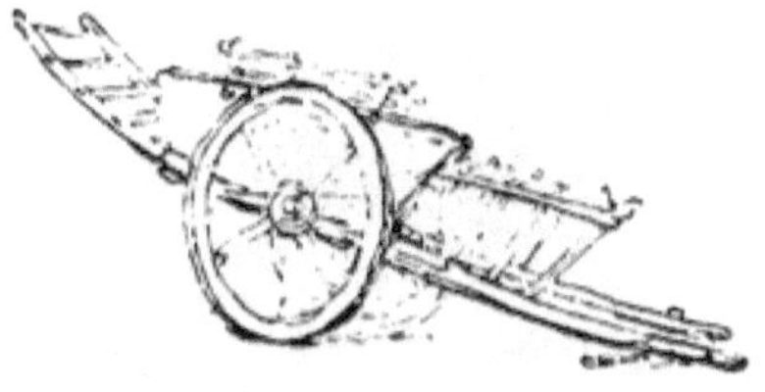

composition flowed from his pen with equal facility. His misfortune, indeed, was, as I have been assured by capable authorities who noticed his juvenile progress, that of possessing too ready an invention ; this rare faculty, strange as it may seem, however desirable to the poet, often proves the bane of the painter. "The poet," as Milton says, "can build the lofty rhyme," even with a dash of his pen. The painter, however easily he may conceive the structure of a mighty building—be it a temple, or be it a ship—must describe the subject perfectly with all its parts ; he must set to work *doggedly*, as the great lexicographer, Johnson, said, and labour at the thing with the patience of the philosopher. Rowlandson was no philosopher, and so his uncontrollable spirit, sweeping over the prescribed pale, took its excursive flights and caught its thema on the wing. Hence I think it may safely be averred that he has sketched or executed more subjects of real scenes in his original rapid manner, than any ten artists his contemporaries, and etched more plates than any artist, ancient or modern.

'Few persons—judging from the careless style of drawing and etching which he so fatally indulged in, too soon, after acquiring the first rudiments of his art— would believe the possibility of his being the author of some of his earlier designs ; for although all are too slight, yet there are certain subjects of his composition carried through with a compatibility of style so truly original, and so replete with painter-like feeling, that Sir Joshua Reynolds and Sir Benjamin West pronounced them wonders of art.'

On this same head we have the testimony of Ephraim Hardcastle in the *Somerset House Gazette.* A certain weight, beyond the mere evidence of partiality, is due to the opinions of such authorities as Henry Angelo and W. H. Pyne, who at least deserve the credit of understanding the subject ; both were familiar with the best works of their day, and in the case of the latter we respect the opinion of an artist of wide experience and well-known repute.

'Thomas Rowlandson, the merry wag, he who has covered with his never-flagging pencil enough of *charta pura* to placard the whole walls of China, and etched as much copper as would sheathe the British navy. Of his graphic fun and frolic we have seen, Heaven knows, full many a ponderous folio.

'Master Roley, so friendly dubbed by many an old *connère*, would have taken higher flights of art had he so willed, for he could draw with elegance and grace ; for the design, no mind was ever better stored with thought—no genius more prolific. Nothing, even allowing for caricature, could exceed in spirit and intelligence some of the off-hand compositions of this worthy.

'Predilections for outline and the pen have ruined many a genius who would have done honour to the arts. Mortimer, Porter, and many other artists have sacrificed their talents and their fame to the indulgence of doing that with the pen (confound both goose-quill, crow-quill, and the reed !) that should have occupied that fitter instrument the pencil, aforetime called the painting-brush.'

Angelo affords us occasional glimpses of Rowlandson in Paris, and frequently alludes to the artist's travels on the Continent. It seems, at various stages of his career, he roved about sometimes in search of subjects, at others, on parties of pleasure. We have seen the young student sent to Paris to pursue art ; later on Angelo finds him there, at nineteen, still earnest and hard-working.

'The subjects of his humorous designs were not sought in England alone. He travelled early in life to France, Flanders, and Holland; and stored his portfolios with sketches highly characteristic of the habits and manners of the people, at every town through which he passed. Paris, as viewed under the old *régime*, opened a prolific source for his imitative powers. Nothing can exceed the fun and frolic which his subjects display, picked up among every class, from the court down to the *cabaret*. He mixed in all societies, and speaking French fluently, made himself acquainted with the habits of thinking, as well as those of acting, in that city, where everything to an English eye bore the appearance of burlesque.

'Hogarth had already pronounced Paris "all begilt and befouled." Rowlandson found it so; and taking that as a sort of maxim which governed all things, physical as well as moral, in the polite city, he burlesqued even the burlesque.

'His drawings of *The Italian* and *The French Family*, from which John Raffael Smith made engravings, had great merit. My friend John Bannister had one of the originals. I remember the last time I saw poor Edwin the comedian (I mean the elder), was on occasion of his wishing me to procure for him these originals. He was too late in his application, and was obliged to solace himself with the coloured prints, which were touched upon by the hand of Rowlandson. They were handsomely framed and hung in his dining-room on the first floor of one of the houses on the north-east piazza, Covent Garden. They subsequently became the property of Lord Barrymore.

'It would be difficult to enumerate the many choice subjects which he depicted even in these first tours to the Continent. Those descriptive of Parisian manners would now be viewed with tenfold interest, as the general external appearance of things was infinitely more original and amusing before the period of the commencement of the Revolution than since. Indeed, I can speak of these changes from my own observation, whilst two years in that city, and in the midst of its ever-varying gaieties, more than half a century ago.[1]

'During my residence there, Rowlandson came over in company with an Englishman of the name of Higginson, whom he got acquainted with at Dover; a pleasant companion, but, as it fell out, one who seemed to live on his wits.

'Their arrival in Paris was immediately after the death of Louis the Fifteenth at the moment of the putting on public mourning (1774). Mr. Higginson had letters of introduction (like Sylvester Daggerwood) to several persons of distinction, and resided at an hotel adjacent to my quarters. He sent the *valet de place* with a civil note to request the loan of my black suit, which he knew would fit him to a T. On the written assurance that it would be returned in time for me

---

[1] This was written in 1835.

to pay a promised visit in the evening, I readily consented. Rowlandson lost sight of him for two days and nights ; on the morning of the third day he returned, and I went, not over well pleased, to demand restitution, when on entering his apartment, he received me with, " Ah ! *mon ami*, is it you ?" seated under the frosting powder-puff of a French *friseur*, having his hair frizzled and powdered *à la mode*, in my mourning suit. Rowlandson sketched the group, and subjoined a motto, " Free and Easy." I had many of the drawings made by my friend Roly at this time.'

It is most likely that our artist's first contribution to the Royal Academy (it was the seventh exhibition) arrived from Paris ; in 1775 there appeared, under the catalogue Number 253, a certain drawing entitled *Delilah payeth Sampson a visit while in prison at Gaza*, by Thomas Rowlandson ; the exhibitor's address is given '*at* No. 4 Church Street, St. Ann's.'

This, no doubt, like his contributions up to 1784, was of a serious character.[1]

From 1777 we find Rowlandson settled down to portrait-painting, his address being given at Wardour Street ; his contributions to the Academy were as follow :—

1777.	No. 302.	A Drawing.
1778.	,, 259.	Portrait of a Young Gentleman, whole length.
1779.	,, 275.	An Officer, small, whole length.
,,	,, 276.	A Gentleman, ,,
1780.	,, 373.	Landscape and Figures.
1781.	,, 334.	Portrait of a Lady in a fancy dress.
,,	,, 339.	Portrait of a Gentleman.

It is improbable, however, that the artist's disposition for change would allow him to vegetate in one spot for any length of time, and we are not surprised to discover that his tours to the Continent became frequent ; as far as we can judge of his extended travels, it appears it was in 1778—while his youthful ardour was still fresh, when his sprightly faculties had not been jaded by the allurements of fashionable life, and his hand had not been betrayed into the careless execution which determined some time after his decisive rejection of serious art for the indulgence of uncompromising caricature—that he went very earnestly to work ; travelling in Flanders and through the cities of Germany ; making clever studies and finished pictures of the incidents of his journeys ; noting the travellers he encountered, their mode of conveyance, the foreign nobility and their equipages,

<hr>

[1] A correspondent to *Notes and Queries*, who signs S. R. (4th Series, IV., September 11, 1869, p. 224), while alluding to this drawing, also mentions having seen a portrait of George III. by Rowlandson, which possessed great art merit ; and adds : 'I possess early drawings by him, executed with a fine quill pen, and most tenderly tinted, which are highly refined in style, excellent in drawing, and in elegance and grace may be classed with the productions of Stothard.'

the townsfolks and the country people, coaches, waggons, and, above all, horses
(which he then drew with great fidelity and spirit from life), as far as the figure
subjects which enlivened his pictures were concerned ; while his views were
faithful representations of the places he visited, worked out with the completeness
of landscape art.

The drawings of this period evince the excellence of his talents. There is
sufficient spice of character introduced into the groups, and incidents which
give action to his pictures, to raise his subjects above the average treatment,
but the comic element is subordinated to the general harmony of the whole
conception ; and we have every opportunity of forming our opinion, from the
numerous interesting series of studies which have come under our attention,
that it was not until about 1782 that our artist began to cut himself adrift
from the more legitimate occupation of his vast abilities in the regions of serious
art, for the allurements which the readier exercise of his talents as a caricaturist
held out for the indulgence of his eccentric and wayward tendencies. As

we have seen, his early bias was
undoubtedly towards the simply
ludicrous ; then intervened his
academic training in London and
Paris, the maturing of his powers
necessitating an immense, and
indeed almost incredible amount
of sterling hard work, such as
fitted him to excel in any branch
of his calling he elected to pursue ; followed by an attempt towards his establishment as a serious artist and portrait-painter, and then a relapse in the direction
of his early impulses. This inclination was fostered by the encouragement of
his friends, and the influence of their example. His cronies were, as was most
natural, the humorous designers. There was the great and gifted Gillray, the
prince of caricaturists, whose works created an impression on the public justified
by their remarkable qualities. The friendship of this man, whose reputation
was so wide, and whose mastery of the situation appeared extraordinary,
encouraged Rowlandson to strike out a pathway in the same direction ; bringing
original qualifications to bear on this impetus, which in no degree clashed with
the strongly marked intentions of Gillray's scathing inventions. There was
his constant friend Henry Wigstead, a man of social standing, profusely liberal
in his house, a jovial companion out of doors ; who, richly endowed with the
vein of humorous invention allied to powers of observation, and a refined sense
of the beautiful, as well as a ready knack of seizing the comic features of a
situation, entrusted his sketches to Rowlandson, that they might be produced in

fitting form ; and to the proper execution of these whimsicalities Rowlandson willingly lent the full force of his own trained skill.   Another amateur of distinction, whose example and influence must have had considerable weight with our artist, was Henry Bunbury, the caricaturist, a man of family, of means, and, above all, of high culture.   The celebrated Bunbury seemed formed expressly to be courted by the most eminent of his contemporaries ; he had married one of the beautiful Miss Horneeks; the Duke and Duchess of York were delighted with his company ; amongst the brilliant assemblies at Wynnstay, Bunbury's society was the most relished ; Walpole, Garrick, Reynolds, and Goldsmith were constantly laying adulation at his feet, or exchanging gallant little pleasantries with this favoured child of fortune ; West and Reynolds were respectfully solicitous that he should send his contributions to the Royal Academy ; the writers of the day were given to deplore that the occupations of town and country life, the court, the hunting-field, and the ceremony of receiving

company at his country-house or paying visits to the seats of his noble friends, sadly interfered with the exercise of his artistic abilities.

The instance of Bunbury, who was Rowlandson's senior by six years, no doubt had considerable influence upon our artist's career; the praise and adulation lavished upon the amateur sketches of the man of fashion, and the prophecies which writers were in the habit of recording, that, if Bunbury had not, from his birth and station, been indifferent to mere monetary advantages, the pursuit of his talents must have infallibly produced him a large access of fortune (which he did not need, by the way, since his means were ample) possibly helped to turn Rowlandson from quietly persevering in the less congenial study of portraiture, and induced him to show the public what could be done in the grotesque walk.   Nor must we forget Mitchell the banker, whose friendship was always at our caricaturist's service, his travelling companion to the Continent, where Rowlandson and his patron passed for the veritable representatives of John Bull.   There was 'the facetious Nixon,' the pleasant and witty John, 'a choice member of the celebrated Old British Beef-Steak Club, honorary secretary, and sometime providore to that society of native gourmands ;' further, like his friend Bunbury, distinguished as a man of talent and taste, possessed of original gifts in the humorous department of graphic art, he was an honorary exhibitor at Somerset House for many years : this gentleman, who had perfected the study of how to get the largest possible amount of enjoyment out of existence, also came to Rowlandson to put his drawings into acceptable shape, and to introduce his eccentric pleasantries to the public. Nor must the well-known amateurs and choice spirits, Woodward and Collings, be omitted from the list of those familiars of the artist who, by precept and example, encouraged him to devote his accomplishments to the comic branch. It is not surprising that the tendency of this influence, allied to the strong original bias natural to our artist, drew him farther away from the steady pursuit of art, and plunged him into the tempting career of a caricaturist, a pursuit which held out peculiar attractions to an artist gifted with his whimsical inclinations. We must do Rowlandson the credit to admit that, at the outset, he distinguished himself marvellously. His first contributions, under his changed profession, were by no means discreditable to his great qualifications; indeed these drawings, from the successful impression they produced on the public, appeared to justify the resolution the artist had taken, and to prove that he was evidently more at home in the fanciful branch than any of his predecessors or contemporaries. In 1784 Rowlandson contributed three somewhat ambitious subjects to the Royal Academy Exhibition; according to the Catalogue No. 462, *An Italian Family*; No. 503, *Vauxhall*; No. 511, *The Serpentine River.*

Vauxhall Gardens, which is possibly the best recognised of Rowlandson's more aspiring compositions, was engraved by R. Pollard, aquatinted, to resemble the drawing, by F. Jukes, and published under the auspices of John Raphael Smith, also a convivial companion, a leading spirit amongst the careless souls who formed Rowlandson's social surroundings; the well-known printseller, who was 'a jack-of-all-trades' according to his own admission, was celebrated for his liberality to artists; he personally practised the arts both of engraving and painting, and he excelled in executing spirited portrait sketches, in crayons, 'miniatures in large' as they were called, of the fashionable personages of his day.

The Study of *Vauxhall* is replete with character; the persons of the principal frequenters are, it is believed, portraits of numerous celebrities of the period.

Angelo, in his *Reminiscences*, which touch upon every topic of the time, among other interesting allusions, recounts the partiality which he and Rowlandson entertained for the popular resort of the past, and the attractions which, according to his admission, its diversions held out to the pair.

, ' *Vauxhall.*—I remember the time when Vauxhall (in 1776, the price of admission being then only one shilling) was more like a bear garden than a rational place of resort, and most particularly on Sunday mornings.

' It was then crowded from four to six with gentry, demireps, apprentices, shopboys, &c. Crowds of citizens were to be seen trudging home with their wives and children.   Rowlandson the artist and myself have often been there, and he has found plenty of employment for his pencil.

'The *chef-d'œuvre* of his caricatures, which is still in print, is his drawing of Vauxhall, in which he has introduced a variety of characters known at the time, particularly that of my old schoolfellow at Eton, Major Topham, the macaroni of the day.   One curious scene he sketched on the spot purposely for me.   It was this :—A citizen and his family are seen all seated in a box eating supper, when one of the riffraff in the gardens throws a bottle in the middle of the table, breaking the dishes and the glasses.   The old man swearing, the wife fainting, and the children screaming, afforded full scope for his humorous pencil.

'Such night scenes as were then tolerated are now become obsolete.   Rings were made in every part of the gardens to decide quarrels ; it no sooner took place in one quarter, than by a contrivance of the light-fingered gentry, another row was created in another quarter to attract the crowd away.'

Before taking leave of Rowlandson and Angelo, the most agreeable of companions, at Vauxhall, we must add a further note of another of their holiday jaunts, once more borrowed from the *Reminiscences.*

'Mrs. Weichsel (Mrs. Billington's mother) was the favourite singer at Vauxhall; upon one occasion she had her benefit at the little theatre in the Haymarket. Her daughter and son added considerably to the entertainment that night; though the former could not have been fourteen years old, her execution on the pianoforte surprised everyone.   The son, then a little boy, played a solo on the fiddle in such peculiarly fine style that the audience were both astonished and delighted.   Exhibiting his early abilities standing on a stool, I was present that night with Rowlandson the artist, who made a sketch of him playing, which he afterwards finished for me, and which, within these few years, was within my collection.'

We will leave Rowlandson rejoicing in the popular impression his drawings had produced in the Exhibition of the Royal Academy for 1784, where, as his friends were inclined to prophesy, his fame and fortune were both assured, and turn to the subject of another fortune which seems to have come into his possession about this period.   We have said that the artist was a spoiled child of prosperity ; his contemporaries record their impression that the indulgences of his aunt, the ex-Mademoiselle Chattelier already referred to, as the kindly patroness of her wayward nephew's budding talents, who supplied him incautiously with money, when he would have been better without it, paved the foundation of those careless habits which attended his manhood ; and to her injudicious generosity his biographer affects to trace that improvidence for which, says our authority, poor Rowlandson was remarkable through life. After this aunt's decease, she left him seven thousand pounds, much plate, trinkets, and other valuable property. He then indulged his predilections for a joyous life, and mixed himself with the gayest of the gay. Whilst at Paris, being of a social spirit, he sought the company of dashing young men ; and among other evils, imbibed a love for play. He was known in London at many of the fashionable gaming houses, alternately won and lost, without emotion, till at length he was minus several thousand pounds. He thus dissipated the amount of more than one valuable legacy. It was said to his honour, however, that he always played with the feelings of a gentleman, and his word passed current even when with an empty purse. Rowlandson assured the writer of the memoir which appeared, on his death, in the obituary of *The Gentleman's Magazine* for June 1827, that he had frequently played throughout a night and the next day ; and that once, such was his infatuation for the dice, he continued at the gaming table nearly thirty-six hours, with the intervention only of the time for refreshment, which was supplied by a cold collation, presumably consumed on the spot and during the intervals of play.

This uncontrollable passion for gambling, strange to say, did not pervert his principles. He was scrupulously upright in all his pecuniary transactions, and ever avoided getting into debt. He has been known, after having lost all he possessed, to return home to his professional studies, sit down coolly to produce a series of new designs, and to exclaim, with stoical philosophy, ' I have played the fool ; but,' holding up his pencils or the reed pen with which he traced his flowing outlines, ' here is my resource.' Such was his dexterity of hand, combined with the richest fertility of imagination, and graphic mastery over the movements of the human figure, that in a few hours he produced inimitable pictures, replete with his best qualities of humour, form, and colour, with incredible rapidity ; and these ingenious productions, invented in endless variety, were at once put into circulation, and excited the competition of collectors of drawings and caricatures, who eagerly accumulated every sketch which his facile hand designed, too often under the pressure of the actual necessities of the hour, or the careless effusions of the intervals in his pleasures or dissipations.

Rowlandson's contributions to the Academy in the succeeding years were as follows :—

1786.   No. 560. A French Family.

   ,,   ,,   566. Opera House Gallery.

   ,,   ,,   575. An English Review.

   ,,   ,,   583. A French Review.

   ,,   ,,   599. Coffee House.

It was about this time that our caricaturist met with a somewhat disagreeable adventure, which is thus related by his friend Angelo :—

'*Rowlandson robbed.*—Having walked one night with Rowlandson towards his house, when he lived in Poland Street,[1] we parted at the corner. It was then about twelve o'clock, and before he got to his door a man knocked him down, and, placing his knees on his breast, rifled him of his watch and money. The next day he proposed that we should be accompanied by a thief-taker, to try to find him out, as he was certain he should know him again. We first repaired to St. Giles's, Dyot Street, and Seven Dials, but to no purpose. In one of the night-houses, four ill-looking fellows, *des coupes-jarrets*, so attracted our attention, that whilst we sat over our noggin of spirits, as he always carried his sketch-book with him, he made an excellent caricature group of them for me, introducing a prison in the background. An idea may be formed from the caricature, of the different gradations which lead to the gallows—petty larceny, house-breaking, foot-pad and highway robbery ; and he afterwards finished it for me in his best style, superior to the greater part of his works ; this was about 1790. The coloured drawing once was included in my

collection, in a room crowded with various subjects, the greatest part caricatures by my old friend Rowly—his general appellation among his friends.

'Our first interview originated in Paris (about 1775) ; he was then studying in the French school. Lately, having to dispose of my collection (I may say unique), my friend Bannister purchased it of me, and it was added to his many choice and valuable drawings of the first masters, which were so very superior that the four thieves ought to have esteemed it an honour to be placed in such good company.[1]

'The next night a gentleman was robbed in Soho Square in like manner. Soon afterwards several suspicious characters were taken to an office then in Litchfield Street, Soho, suspected of street robberies, and Rowlandson and

---

[1] According to the Royal Academy Catalogue, Rowlandson removed from 133 Wardour Street to 50 Poland Street, Pantheon, between 1786 and 1787.

myself went there out of curiosity, accompanied by many others who had been robbed. They were all placed before us, but none were identified. Rowlandson was particularly called upon to look around him, but to no purpose. One man in particular made himself more conspicuous than all the others, treating his curiosity with contempt, saying, "I defies the gemman to say as how I ever stopped him any *vare*." "No; but you are very like the description of the ruffian," answered Rowlandson, "who robbed a gentleman last Wednesday night in Soho Square." This was a thunderbolt to the man, who instantly looked pale and trembled. The gentleman was immediately sent for, and as soon as he entered the room, though there were several for examination, he fixed directly on the man that had been suspected. At the sessions following he was found guilty of robbery, and hanged. This pleased my friend mightily; "for, though I

got knocked down," said he, "and lost my watch and money, and did not find the thief, I have been the means of hanging *one* man. Come, that's doing something." '

We incidentally learn a few particulars of subjects which found their way into Angelo's gallery, the collection which subsequently came into the possession of his excellent friend Bannister.

'*Black and White.*—Being fond of the arts and particularly of caricatures, I had by me a great number of Rowlandson's, to one of which I was puzzled to give a name. The subject was an old man, at breakfast, seated near the fire, his gouty leg on a stool, and the kettle boiling over; the water is falling on his leg, and he is ringing the bell. The room door is open behind him, and a black servant is kissing the maid, who is bringing in the toast. I

<hr>

[1] The drawing of the four ruffians is now, we understand, in the possession of Mr. William Bates, B.A., &c., and forms one of an interesting collection of caricatures by Rowlandson held by that admirer of his works. *See Account of Original Drawings in the Appendix.*

requested Theodore Hook to write a title to it, and he put, "*Chacun à son goût.*"[1]

We are further afforded an opportunity of recording Rowlandson's enthusiasm for his profession. The details of a certain visit he paid, with Angelo, to Portsmouth, and the unflinching nerve he exhibited under circumstances which were calculated to distress a less robust constitution, are thus recounted by his friend and travelling companion :—

'The general rumour, after Lord Howe's action on June 1, 1794, was that he would return to Portsmouth. I was anxious to see the sight, for it was expected he would bring the French prizes with him.

'The evening after my arrival, according to promise, Rowlandson the artist came to join me.

'The morning following we saw, on the Gosport side, the landing of the French prisoners, numbers of different divisions filing off to the different stations allotted them. As for the wounded, previous to their quitting the boats, carts were placed alongside, and when filled, on the smack of the whip, were ordered to proceed. The sudden jolting made their groans appalling, and must have occasioned the wounds of many to produce an immediate hemorrhage. The sight was dreadful to behold : numbers were boys, mutilated, some not more than twelve years old, who had lost both legs. In the evening we went to Forton Prison. Those who were not in the last engagement were in high spirits in their shops, selling all sorts of toys and devices, made from shin-bones, &c. In one of the sick-wards we saw one of the prisoners, who, an officer told us had been a tall, handsome man, previous to the battle ; but, having received a shot that had lacerated his side, a mortification had taken place. He was then making his will ; his comrades were standing by, consoling him, some grasping his hand, shedding tears.

'This scene was too much for me, and made such an impression on my mind that I hastened away ; but I could not persuade Rowlandson to follow me, his inclination to make a sketch of the dying moment getting the better of his feelings. After waiting some time below for my friend, he produced a rough sketch of what he had seen :—a ghastly figure sitting up in bed, a priest holding a crucifix before him, with a group standing around. The interior exhibited the contrivance of the French to make their prison habitable. When finished, it was added to my collection, a memento of the shocking sight I beheld at Forton Prison.

'Our curiosity not stopping here, we entered another sick-ward, but the stench and closeness of the place, crowded as it was, prevented our remaining there

---

[1] The main characteristics of this subject belong to *Careless Attention*, 1789 : a dashing son of Mars taking the place of the black flunkey.

more than a very short time. The next day, having seen quite enough, I returned to town. Rowlandson went to Southampton, where he made a number of sketches of Lord Moira's embarkation for *La Vendée*. I saw them afterwards, and was delighted, for it appeared he had taken more pains than usual, and he must have portrayed them well, from having been on the spot himself at the time. The shipping and the various boats filled with soldiers were so accurately delineated, that I have often since regretted that I did not at that time purchase them. Mr. Fores of Piccadilly, who had by him many of the very finest drawings executed by Rowlandson in his best days (for latterly they were inferior), fortunately purchased them. He was one of his first and best patrons ; and I understand he had twenty-five folio volumes of the most choice caricatures of the last and present centuries, which must have been an invaluable *recueil*, showing not only what we have been, but the age we lived in. Had Rowlandson gone with the expedition then landing in *La Vendée* as a draughtsman, the attack at Fort Penthièvre, and the incident that followed, would have furnished us with many eventful scenes of that fatal expedition.'

As we have related, Rowlandson was no stranger to the Continent; in the early part of his career he was constantly abroad. We have shown how he studied in Paris ; afterwards we find him wandering farther afield, and taking in Germany and the Netherlands. Then we are introduced to him as a man of fashion, bowling through the legacies which had fallen to his lot, both in the French metropolis and in London, calmly sitting down to gamble away his fortune by the shortest route with the best will in the world. Anon he accompanies his friend Mitchell the banker on a wider tour. Then we hear of his sojourning in Paris with other congenial spirits, and making the most of the passing season with his friends John Raphael Smith, Westmacott, and Chasemore : on all these occasions he produced drawings innumerable ; his most frequent travelling companion seems, however, to have been his steadfast patron the banker, and it was this liberal collector who rejoiced in the opportunity of securing the artist's most desirable Continental studies. Our oft-quoted authority Angelo, who, happily for those who entertain an interest in the caricaturist, never tires of telling little anecdotes of his chum Roley, in his own familiar manner relates a few particulars of the figure these worthies made in the eyes of the *Monsieurs*, amongst whom their visits were favourably received.

' Mr. Mitchell, however, possessed the best collection of Rowlandson's French and Dutch scenes. Among those were many in his most humorous style, particularly a *Dutch Life Academy*, which represents the interior of a school of artists, studying from a living model, all with their portfolios and crayons, drawing a Dutch Venus (a *vrow*) of the make, though not of the colour, of that choice specimen of female proportion, the *Hottentot Venus*, so celebrated as a public sight in London, a few years since.

'This friend and patron of Rowlandson, Mr. Mitchell the quondam banker, of the firm of Hodsol and Co., was a facetious, fat gentleman—one of those pet children of fortune, who, wonderful as it may appear, seem to have proceeded through all the seven ages (excepting that of the *lean* and slippered pantaloon), without a single visit from that intruder upon the rest of mankind, yclept *Care*. In him centred, or rather around him the Fates piled up, the wealth of a whole family. He was ever the great gathering *nucleus* to a large fortune. He was good-humoured and enjoyed life. Many a cheerful day have I, in company with Bannister and Rowlandson, passed at Master Mitchell's.'

Under the auspices of this great banker, Rowlandson subsequently made a tour to France, and other parts of the Continent. 'His mighty stature astonished the many, but none more than the innkeepers' wives, who, on his arrival, as he travelled in style, looked at the larder, and then again at the guest. All regarded him as that reported being, of whom they had heard, the veritable Mister Bull. His orders for the supplies of the table, ever his first concern, strengthened this opinion, and his operations at his meals confirmed the fact.

'Wherever he went he made good for the house.

'On this tour, Rowlandson made many topographical drawings, in general views of cities and towns ; amongst others, the High Street at Antwerp, and the Stadt House at Amsterdam, with crowds of figures, grouped with great spirit, though his characters were caricatures.

'The most amusing studies, however, which filled the portfolio of his patron were those that portrayed the habits and customs of the Dutch and Flemish, in the interior scenes, which they witnessed in their nocturnal rambles in the inferior streets at Antwerp and Amsterdam. Some of these compositions, drawn from low life, were replete with character and wit. One of the most spirited and amusing of these represented the interior of a *Treischuit*, or public passage-boat, which was crowded with incident and humour.'[1]

Another reminiscence of Rowlandson and Mitchell is found in the *Somerset-house Gazette*, edited by Ephraim Hardcastle (W. H. Pyne), an intimate associate of the caricaturist and a member of the artist's circle of friends.

'I look back with pleasure to former days, when old Mr. Greenwood used

---

[1] Mr. Henry G. Bohn, the well-known publisher, informed the writer that at one period he had a collection of drawings by Rowlandson, chiefly fine Continental views, such as the Series in Holland and Flanders, made for the artist's patron Mitchell the banker, numbering nearly a hundred.

to hold the print auctions by candle-light, and have a perfect recollection of his good-humour and upright dealing. I well remember, too, a number of artists and amateurs who constantly attended his room, to purchase etchings of the old masters for themselves and friends.

'Old Parsons, as he was called, and young Bannister, the celebrated comedians, were both collectors and amateur artists : the latter was considered an excellent judge of prints. Rowlandson, the humorous draughtsman, and his friend and patron Mr. Mitchell the banker, of the firm of Hodsols, were also frequently of this evening rendezvous of artists, amateurs, and connoisseurs.'

John Thomas Smith, the whilom pupil of Nollekens the sculptor (with whose life he favoured the public), and one of Mr. Reid's predecessors as Keeper of the Print Room of the British Museum, in his loquacious *Book for a Rainy Day* rambles into the subject of picture sale-rooms, and notes the eccentric characters, collectors, and their individualities, to be met with thereat in his time. On this subject 'Antiquity Smith's' account tallies with that given by Angelo. We have confined our extract to the paragraph which introduces the caricaturist as a crony and erst fellow-pupil of the versatile chronicler.

'I must not omit to mention another singular but most honourable character, of the name of Heywood, nick-named "Old Iron-wig." His dress was precise, and manner of walking rather stiff. He was an extensive purchaser of every kind of article in art, particularly Rowlandson's drawings ; for this purpose he employed the merry and friendly Mr. Seguier, the picture-dealer, a school-fellow of my father's, to bid for him.

'I shall now close this list by observing that my friend and fellow-pupil, Rowlandson, who has frequently made drawings of Hutchins and his print auctions, has produced a most spirited etching, in which not only many of the above described characters are introduced, but also most of the print-sellers of his day.'

The editor of this work has seen a drawing by Rowlandson of this very auction, the *cognoscenti* gathered round the long tables lighted with flickering candles, and peering over the engravings, glasses on nose, while the auctioneer was endeavouring to excite the interest of the company in the prints brought to his rostrum.

Before we pass on to other contemporaries of the caricaturist, we think it advisable to introduce the reader to the society which Rowlandson shared round the hospitable mahogany of the banker, who, like Wigstead, Nixon, Weltjé, and certain other generous hosts of our artist's acquaintance, appears to have kept open house for the entertainment of choice friends, where the enjoyments of social intercourse were prolonged to the verge of dissipation, and the fun, which en-livened their hours of relaxation, was frequently kept up until the next day was well advanced; the associates being loth to interrupt the pleasures of their sitting, protracted as their gaieties might be considered according to the more staid usages of a better regulated age, such as we have been taught to regard our own.

'Mr. Mitchell resided for many years in Beaufort Buildings, Strand, and occupied the house tenanted by the father of Dr. Kitchiner, of eccentric memory. Here, after the closing of the banking-house, he was wont to retire, and pass a social evening, surrounded by a few chosen associates whose amusements were congenial, and whose talent well paid the host for his hot supper and generous wine. Often, even beyond the protracted darkness of a winter's night, he and his *convives* have sat it out till dawn of day, and seen the sun, struggling through the fog, from the back windows, shed its lurid ray on the rippling waters of the murky Thames.

'Well do I remember sitting in this comfortable apartment, listening to the stories of my old friend Peter Pindar, whose wit seemed not to kindle until after midnight, at the period of about his fifth or sixth glass of brandy and water. Rowlandson, too, having nearly accomplished his twelfth glass of punch, and replenishing his pipe with choice *oro-nooko*, would chime in. The tales of these two gossips, told in one of these nights, each delectable to hear, would make a modern *Boccaccio.*'

Angelo, in his capital chatty *Memoirs*, relates an anecdote of one of Wigstead's pranks played off on the satirist Peter Pindar, whose trenchant wit spared 'nor friend nor foe;' but, in his turn, Dr. Wolcot did not relish ridicule, especially when it happened to be excited at his own expense. It was discovered that, eminently satirical as was the bard with his pen, he was not emulous to shine as a wit in colloquial intercourse with strangers, or even amongst his most intimate associates. It was asserted, with some fidelity, that 'Dr. Wolcot's wit seemed to lie in the bowl of a teaspoon.' 'I could not guess the riddle,' writes the discursive and cheerful author of the *Reminiscences*, 'until one evening, seated at Mitchell's, I observed that each time Peter replenished his glass goblet with cognac and water, that, in breaking the sugar, the corners of his lips were curled into a satisfactory smile, and he began some quaint story—as if, indeed, the new libation begot a new thought.

'Determined to prove the truth of the discovery which I fancied I had made, one night after supper, at my own residence in Bolton Row, he being one among a few social guests, I made my promised experiment. One of the party, who delighted in a little practical joke, namely Wigstead, of merry memory, being in the secret, he came provided with some small square pieces of alabaster.

Peter Pindar's glass waning fast, Wigstead contrived to slip the fragments of spurious sweetness into a sugar-basin provided for the purpose, when the Doctor reaching the hot water, and pouring in the brandy, Wigstead handed him the sugar-tongs, and then advanced the basin of alabaster. "Thank you, boy," said Peter, putting in five or six pieces, and taking his tea-spoon, began stirring as he commenced his story.

'Unsuspicious of the trick, he proceeded: "Well, sirs,—and so, the old parish-priest.—What I tell you (then his spoon went to work) happened when I was in that infernally hot place, Jamaica (then another stir). Sir, he was the fattest man on the island (then he pressed the alabaster); yes, damme, sir; and when the thermometer, at ninety-five, was dissolving every other man, this old slouching, drawling, son of the Church got fatter and fatter, until, sir—curse the sugar! some devil-black enchanter has bewitched it. By —— sir, this sugar is part and parcel of that old pot-bellied parson—it will never melt;" and he threw the contents of the tumbler under the grate. We burst into laughter, and our joke lost us the conclusion of the story. Wigstead skilfully slipped the mock sugar out of the way, and the Doctor, taking another glass, never suspected the frolic.'

Let us take a further glimpse of the social meetings which Rowlandson shared in company with Angelo, who duly set down the outlines of the evenings' diversions in his *Memoirs*. As this anecdote introduces a personage who figures somewhat prominently amidst the more lively records of the period, we must be allowed to say a word or two about the giver of the feast, where we are admitted by favour and enabled to watch the proceedings from a distance.

Another excellent friend, occasional host, and boon companion of our caricaturist was, as we have mentioned, Weltjé, the Prince of Wales' cook and steward, a German of eccentric proclivities, who was pretty universally recognised as a character in his generation. The huge person of this worthy is frequently introduced into the social satires of the period; the artistic and literary wags alike delighted to make the figure of the old *bon-vivant* conspicuous; it seems that Weltjé was in no wise offended at this popularity, however unflattering might be the intentions of the wicked wights; he was a calm humoristic philosopher, whose composure was not easily deranged, and in return for their mischievous sallies, which only amused him, he made the wits, who grew waggish at his expense, his guests at his residence Hammersmith Mall; where he kept such a table as attracted all classes of society, and to which his friends were ever welcome. Weltjé's culinary accomplishments, united with his hospitable proclivities, rendered him a truly remarkable host; his good humour was imperturbable, his store of anecdotes inexhaustible, and his German bluntness rather added to the charm of his pleasantries; even that superfine Sybarite and highly sensitive exquisite, the Heir Apparent, Mr. Weltjé's patron and employer, was glad to dissemble his offended dignity when his precious and immovable cook was the assailant. Angelo, who declares he owed many a convivial day to the kindness of this rough diamond, assures us in his *Reminiscences*: 'Whether at Carlton House or his own, Weltjé was always remarkable for singularity. I have been told that when Alderman Newnham was one day dining at Carlton House, the Prince said to him, "Newnham, don't you think there is a strange taste in the soup?" "It appears so to me, your highness." "Send for Weltjé." When Weltjé made his appearance, the Prince observed that the soup had a strange taste. Weltjé called to one of the pages, "Give me de *spoone*," and putting it in the tureen, after tasting it several times, said, "Boh! boh! tish very goote," and immediately left the room, leaving the spoon on the table, without taking further notice of the complaint.'

It is not, however, with the worthy Weltjé at Carlton House, but at his own villa, that we have to deal. An-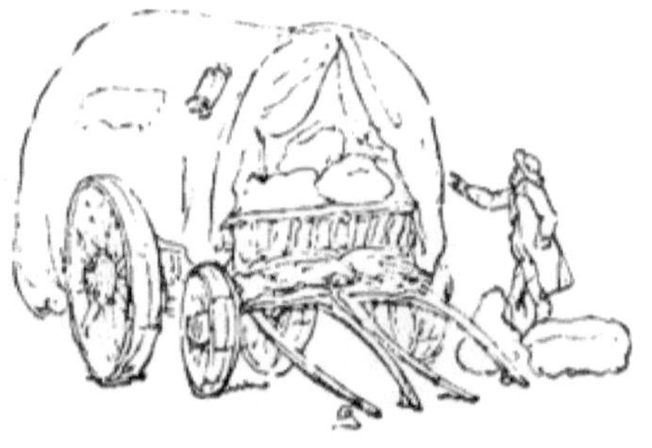
gelo introduces us to a capital dinner-party which took place at Hammersmith Mall, when the old associates, Rowlandson, Bannister, and Munden, were among the guests; Madame Banti the opera-singer, and Taylor, also of the Opera House, with Mr. Palmer of Bath, contributed to make up a tolerably festive party. The dinner was long and *bien recherché*; the dishes choice, and cooked in superior style; the sprightly conversation, in which the company delighted, had been somewhat suspended during the discussion of a great variety of *entremets*, which were duly appreciated by all the guests, and especially by Madame Banti, who not only tasted of every dish, but, in addition to a quantity of strong ale, drank a bottle of champagne. The guests were preparing for that flow of wine and conversation which were the *agrémens* of social intercourse at the period. The repast was concluded as everyone imagined, and nobody felt disposed to touch another morsel, when Weltjé's grand piece of the entertainment made its appearance—a huge boar's head, at which delicacy everyone stared in consternation.

Weltjé plunged into his element, mixing up *sauces piquantes* at table, of such ingredients as oil, lemon, cayenne, and different concomitants.

The guests, already lavishly regaled, were inclined to expostulate. 'Indeed, Weltjé, we have had more than enough.' 'Boh!' responds the entertainer, 'I vill make you all hungry again ; two heads gomed to dis gontry, von for me, toder for de Queen, dat de Prince of Bronsvick sent ; ' and away proceeded the compounding of sauces.   The long interval occupied in Weltjé's culinary preparations was shortened by droll anecdotes, peculiar to his own description, introduced for the purpose of distracting the attention.   Such was his account of his adventure on his return home to Hammersmith, in his carriage, from Carlton House. ' Fon I gote to de fost dumbpike beyond Kensington, from town, de goach stobed some time, fon me say, " Godam, ged on : " fon de dumbike say, " Sir, dere be nobody on de bokes."   I was very much fraightened, so I did ged up myself.   The next day gome de goachman : " Pray, sir, fon am I to ged the carriage ready ? "   " Tartifle, what become of you last night ? " '   The coachman, it appears, had fallen off the box in a drunken stupor ; unhurt, he had, never troubling himself about his charge, taken a nap all night under a hedge, and attended on his master the next morning to receive orders as coolly as if nothing unusual had happened.   The *sauce piquante* is ready by the time the host has raised a few laughs ; clean plates are handed round ; a large dish is filled with slices of the boar's head, swimming in provocative mixtures ; and the guests fall to again ; verifying, as Angelo relates, the French proverb that, *l'appétit vient en mangeant*, or, as Hamlet says, ' As if increase of appetite had grown with what it fed on.' The second repast proved so excellent that the plates were continually replenished.   The poets, painters, actors, musicians, and others, who crowded Weltjé's liberal entertainments, with ' those whose superior station was more suited to a palace,' then gave themselves up to unrestrained mirthfulness.   The dinner Angelo describes will serve as a type of the many similar entertainments at which our caricaturist assisted.   With the dessert Madame Banti became somewhat lively, from her repeated libations of champagne, being, as Angelo informs us, ' in higher spirits than any French woman I had ever seen.   With the enthusiasm of a true John Bull, she sang "God save the King," that she might have been heard on the other side of the river.   Munden, whom she had never seen before, sang the " Old Woman of Eighty ; " and to give effect to the song, tied his pocket-handkerchief round his head, though his superior humour needed no addition.   When he had finished his song, Banti left her seat in ecstasy, and went to the other side of the table, where he and I were sitting, and was so pleased with his mummery (it could be nothing else, for Joe never was an Adonis), that she came behind his chair and kissed him ; which, however, did not excite a blush, but an agreeable surprise.   What with the songs, the choice wines, the delicious fruits (from Weltjé's hothouse), and the zest given to the entertainment by Banti, it formed such a delightful treat, that the evening passed too quickly, and it was time to depart long before we were sated with " the feast of reason and the flow of soul." '

To return to the working life of our caricaturist : it must be borne in mind that Rowlandson's journeys were not confined to the Continent ; from drawings which have come under our attention, we find he must have seen the Lakes : it is highly probable that he paid a visit to Henry Bunbury, who, towards the close of his life, settled at Keswick, where he died in 1811. We also know, from his works, that our artist was familiar with England and Wales : his tours, with his friend Henry Wigstead, have produced many interesting *souvenirs* ; we have described how they travelled to Wales, and how, too, they saw Cheshire, Cornwall, Devon, and Somerset ; we find them scampering off to the newly established Brighthelmstone, and to the more old-fashioned watering-places on the coast of Kent. It was at Margate that Rowlandson lost his most congenial associate, who having gone there, in the autumn of 1800, for the benefit of his health, did not live to return ; the death of Henry Wigstead was a serious bereavement to the caricaturist, the earliest of those losses of his cherished associates which influenced his spirits considerably.

We can also catch glimpses of Rowlandson on the Scarborough coast, and in Norfolk. Yarmouth seems to have been a favourite spot with him. We find him studying at seaports along the south coast ; with Plymouth, Portsmouth, and Southampton he was thoroughly familiar. Of the Thames and the Medway, and the shipping to be encountered thereon in war-time, he has left sketches innumerable ; he has visited the fishing spots on the former, and

drawn the pretty towns which mark the valley of the river. With London, and its diversified spots of interest, from east to west, and north to south—the centre, and the outskirts alike—he had the most intimate acquaintance. We have already spoken of the drawings he made in the two University cities, and his series of views of the noble colleges.

An Historical Sketch of the Art of Caricaturing was written by the well-known antiquarian J. P. Malcolm, F.S.A., and published in 1813. This book, which might, had the author so willed, have supplied the curious with valuable hints, drawn from personal acquaintance, concerning professors of the art then living, is confined to the briefest recapitulation, as far as concerns contemporary works, the book being retrospective in principle ; and it is difficult to discover any allusions of value to those Caricaturists lately deceased or who were still alive. Malcolm's appreciation of grotesque art was somewhat catholic, but he does not seem as familiar as might reasonably be supposed the case, with the masterpieces of the men who were flourishing in his time, or perhaps their *chefs d'œuvre* were then so generally familiar as to need no further recognition. The

compiler of the Historical Sketch was evidently an amateur of humorous productions, and could describe the progress of grotesques, but he does not seem to
have completely carried out the scheme of his treatise.

We have borrowed a paragraph from this excellent antiquarian, as an instance
of his criticisms on the subject of the present volume.

'*Rowlandson's Views in Oxford and Cambridge*, 1810, deserve notice for the
slight and pleasing manner with which he has characterised the architecture of
the places mentioned ; but it is impossible to surpass the originality of his figures ;
the dance of students and *filles de joie* before Christ Church College is highly
humorous, and the enraged tutors grin with anger peculiar to this artist's pencil.
The professors, in the view of the Observatory at Oxford, are made as ugly as
baboons, and yet the profundity of knowledge they possess is conspicuous at the
first glance ; and we should know them to be Masters of Arts without the aid
of the background.   The scene in Emanuel College Garden, Cambridge,
exhibits the learned in a state of relaxation ; several handsome lasses remove

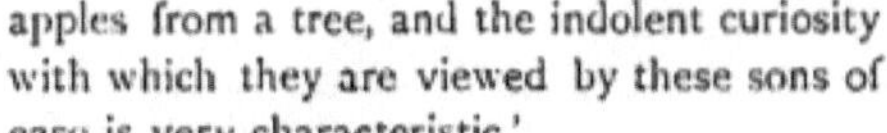

apples from a tree, and the indolent curiosity
with which they are viewed by these sons of
ease is very characteristic.'

While considering Rowlandson in relation
to his contemporaries, we have chiefly to deal
with those gifted gentlemen who were, like
himself, generally spoken of in their generation as *caricaturists*, and to whose works our
artist was able, from his more considerable
acquirements, to give a presentable form, and
put into circulation through the medium of his proficiency with the etching-
needle.

Foremost among these we must speak of Henry Bunbury, so many of whose
felicitous conceptions have derived additional force and popularity alike through
the agency of our artist.

In speaking of the caricaturist's treatment of these amateur works, we are
glad to be able to offer our readers the respectable testimony of Thomas Wright
in support of our own modest opinion, with which intention we quote a few
paragraphs from our late friend's *History of Caricature and Grotesque in Literature and Art.*

'At various periods certain of Bunbury's designs were engraved by Rowlandson, who always transferred his own style to the drawings he copied. A
remarkable instance of this is furnished by a print of a party of anglers of both
sexes in a punt, entitled *Anglers of* 1811 (the year of Bunbury's death). But
for the name, " H. Bunbury, del.," very distinctly inscribed upon it, we should

take this to be a genuine design by Rowlandson; and in 1803 Rowlandson engraved some copies of Bunbury's prints on horsemanship for Ackermann, of the Strand, in which all traces of Bunbury's style are lost.

'There was much of Bunbury's style in that of Woodward, who had a taste for the same broad caricatures on society, which he executed in a similar spirit. Some of the *suites* of subjects of this description that he published, such as the series of the *Symptoms of the Shop*, those of *Everybody out of Town*, and *Everybody in Town*, and the specimens of *Domestic Phrensy*, are extremely clever and amusing. Woodward's designs were also not unfrequently engraved by Rowlandson, who, as usual, imprinted his own style upon them. A very good example of this practice is seen in the print entitled *Desire*, in which the passion is exemplified in the case of a hungry school-boy, watching through a window a jolly cook carrying by a tempting plum pudding. We are told in an inscription underneath : " Various are the ways this passion might be depicted ; in this

delineation the subjects chosen are simple—a hungry boy and a plum pudding." The design of this print is stated to be Woodward's ; but the style is altogether that of Rowlandson, whose name appears on it as the etcher. It was published by R. Ackermann on January 20, 1800.'

In transferring the works of other caricaturists to the copper, Rowlandson was in the habit of giving his own style to them in such a degree that nobody would suspect they were not his own if the name of the designer were not attached to them.

We cannot take leave of the Caricaturists without offering a few slight particulars concerning the respective careers of the most eminent and appreciated practitioners of the graphic art in its grotesque bearings.

The fecundity of invention displayed in the works of Henry Bunbury entitles him to rank among the first in this class of designers. The happy faculty which he possessed of 'reading character at sight,' and the rare felicity with which he could embody whatever his observation or fancy suggested, with that scrambling style which was entirely his own, evince that he was born with a genius to make a figure in this pursuit. This gentleman may be instanced as a proof, too, that where there is an original faculty for any peculiar art, it will develop itself, though the possessor may be entirely unacquainted with the scientific principles of art. Nothing could be farther removed from legitimate art than the style exhibited in the drawings of Bunbury; yet no one has hit off the peculiarities of character, or expressed with less exaggeration those traits which constitute the burlesque. Bunbury, indeed, may be said to have steered his humorous course between sterling character and caricature. When he appears to outrage nature by representing distortion of figure or form, the fault is not intentional. Those who have not properly studied the drawing of the human figure, must occasionally, in spite of themselves, render their objects preternatural.

It should be added, in honour to the memory of this gentleman, that he never used his pencil at the expense of personal feeling. His satire upon the French people was not individual, but national; and the characters which he introduced in his humorous designs at home, were characteristic of a class, but never the individuals of a species.

Henry William Bunbury, the caricaturist, was born in 1750. He was educated at Westminster, whence he was removed to St. Catherine's Hall, Cambridge. On leaving the university he devoted himself, with some enthusiasm,

to the fine arts. He was passionately fond of out-door sports, and, as in the instance of Leech in our own days, the saddle held out attractions superior even to the pleasure of exercising his fancy. His contemporaries were much given to deplore that he preferred the excitement of risking his neck in the hunting field to the cultivation of the profession his skill should have adorned. His taste and invention were admired not only by the most gifted and elevated persons of his time, but artists and critics alike lavished their encomiums on the favoured designer. Horace Walpole coveted the sketches which Bunbury exhibited on the walls of the Academy, while Sir Joshua Reynolds and Sir Benjamin West combined to pay their finest compliments to the artist, and to publish abroad their flattering sense of his merits. Bunbury appears to have spent the greater part of his time on the estates belonging to his family, varied by trips to the Continent and visits to his patrons the Duke and Duchess of York, at Richmond and other residences, with occasional sojourns in Wales, the scenery of which had considerable attractions for his sense of the picturesque. He was a frequent guest of Sir W. W. Wynne, and his pencil has celebrated the theatrical gatherings at Wynnstay. We also meet him in town, surrounded by illustrious friends, and we find Goldsmith, Garrick, and other notabilities corresponding with the kindly and generous caricaturist during his sojourns at his country seat.

Henry Bunbury was married, August 26, 1771, to Catherine, daughter of Kane William Horneck, Esq., lieutenant-colonel of the army of Sicily. This lady bore him two sons, and one of them, Sir Henry Bunbury, we believe, represented the county of Suffolk in Parliament, after the decease of his uncle Sir Thomas Charles Bunbury, who had previously enjoyed the distinction. Bunbury, the artist, was elected lieutenant-colonel of the West Suffolk regiment of militia. His manners were most popular, and it was remarked that he carried his cheerful and vivacious spirit into every society he frequented. He died at Keswick, in Cumberland, where he had settled towards the close of his life, and his sketches of the mountain scenery in his vicinity are said to have displayed the hand of a master, and to have gained universal appreciation for their effect and truthfulness.

As a delineator of character, it is stated 'that his sketches approached nearest to Hogarth of any painter of his period, in the representation of life and manners ; his pencil never transgresses the limits of good taste and delicacy, and had he been under the necessity of pursuing art for profit, instead of amusement and pleasure only, he would probably have made a great fortune by the produce of his genius, which the print-sellers have found a lucrative source of gain, engravings and etchings after his works having always been eagerly demanded.'

The high estimation in which the caricaturist was personally held is confirmed by the obituary notice which appeared on his decease in the *Gentleman's Magazine;* the praise seems to be spontaneous, and its object, from all we can gather, richly merited the friendly testimony.

'May 7, 1811.—At Keswick, Henry William Bunbury, Esq., second son of the Rev. Sir William Bunbury, Bart., of Mildenhall, and of Great Barton, in the county of Suffolk, and brother to the present Sir Thomas Bunbury, Bart. He was distinguished at a very early age by a most extraordinary degree of taste and knowledge in the fine arts. The productions of his own pencil have, from his childhood, been the admiration and delight of the public. The exquisite humour of some of his drawings, and the grace and elegance of the rest, were unrivalled ; and he is, perhaps, the only instance in which excellences of such various and almost opposite character have been united in the same subject in an equal degree. But though he possessed in this respect a peculiar genius, he neglected no branch of polite literature. He was a good classical scholar, and " endowed with the love of sacred song." The Muses were to him *dulces ante omnia.* He was an excellent judge of poetry ; and the specimens remaining of his own composition put it beyond a doubt that he would have been as eminent with his pen as with his pencil, if his natural modesty, underrating his own powers, had not prevented him from pursuing it with more application. These accomplishments were conspicuous, and obtained for him universal esteem. His social and moral qualities, while any of those remain who shared his friendship, will continue the objects of fond admiration and regret. No ribaldry, no profaneness, no ill-natured censure, ever flowed from his lips, but his conversation abounded in humour and pleasantry; it was charming to persons of all descriptions. No one was ever in his company without being pleased with him; none ever knew him without loving him. His feelings were the most benevolent, his affections the most delicate, his heart the most sincere. He was void of all affectation, alive to praise, but not obtrusively courting it. Conscious, but not ostentatious of merit; of unblemished honour; full of that piety and liberal-handed charity which influences the heart, and seeks the witness, not of the world, but of his Maker.'

The writer of the obituary notice expressed a conviction, confirmed, as he stated, by an intimacy of fifty years' standing :—

'All who had,' concludes the memorial, 'the slightest acquaintance with him, will bear witness to the extraordinary tenderness of his disposition, to his kind

and active friendship, to his universal benevolence, practically displayed through his entire career.'

The name of Woodward occurs so frequently in caricatures to which *Rowlandson sculpsit* is added, that our readers will probably not consider the following sketch of this eccentric gifted celebrity either out of place, or entirely superfluous.

Recapitulating his recollections of humorous artists, Angelo informs us that— 'The inventive genius of one burlesque designer was exhaustless—George Moutard Woodward, commonly designated by his merry associates, Mustard George. This original genius was the son of the steward of a certain wealthy landholder, and resided with his father in a provincial town, where *nothing* was less known than *everything* pertaining to the arts. He was, as his neighbours said, a "*nateral geni* ;" for he drew all the comical *gaffers* and *gammers* of the country round; and having, to use his own words, "*taken off* the bench of justices, wigs and all, *shown up* the mayor and corporation, *dumb-foundered* the parson of the parish, silenced the clerk, and made the sexton laugh at his own *grave* occupation," he thought it expedient to beat up for new game in the metropolitan city.

'"A caricaturist in a country town," said George, "like a mad bull in a china-shop, cannot step without noise; so, having made a little noise in my native place, I persuaded my father to let me seek my fortune in town."

' It appears that the caricaturist came not to London, like many another wit, pennyless ; his father allowed him an annuity of first fifty, and augmented the sum to a hundred pounds. With this income, and what he obtained by working for the publishers, he was enabled to enjoy life in his own way ; and might be *met*, with a tankard of Burton ale before him, seated behind his pipe, nightly at Offley's : or, if not there, smoking the fragrant weed, at the *Cider Cellar*, the *Blue Posts*, or *The Hole in the Wall*. Latterly, his rendezvous was transferred to *The Brown Bear* at Bow Street, where he studied those peculiar species of low characters, the inhabitants of the round-house, and the myrmidons of the police. Enamoured with the society of these able physiognomists, he ultimately took up his quarters at the *Brown Bear*, and there, to the lively grief of these tender-hearted associates, one night died in character, suddenly, with a glass of brandy in his hand.

' The wit and invention of this artist places him above all others in the personification of low scenes of humour. Among his earliest productions were those series of groups entitled *Effects of Flattery, Effects of Hope, &c.*, which were illustrated by scenes of truly dramatic excellence, and upon which might well be built farces for the stage which could not fail to delight the town. His *Babes in the Wood, Raffling for a Coffin, The Club of Quidnuncs*, as pieces of original humour, have never, perhaps, been equalled. Had this low humourist studied drawing and been temperate in his habits, such was the fecundity of his imagination and perception of character, that he might have rivalled even Hogarth. His style, always sufficiently careless, latterly even outraged the *outré*. Yet there were those, and men of taste too, who insisted that the humour of his pieces was augmented by the extravagance of this defect.'

The name of Henry Wigstead will be met with pretty constantly in the course of this volume ; his designs approach the nearest to those of Rowlandson as far as regards humorous qualities, a cultivated sense of beauty and grace, and a decided grasp of character, without that violent divergence from the semblance of humanity as ordinarily recognised, to which failing the old-fashioned caricaturists were somewhat over-addicted, as we are inclined to suspect ; but, like many worthy amateurs of his period, his own hand lacked the skill to express all that his eye saw and his taste appreciated. In the guise of a skilled translator of crude ideas, our Caricaturist, with ready ease, and that dexterity which was peculiarly his own, came to the rescue most efficiently, and his etchings and scrapings have preserved many a capital design, due to the esteemed Wigstead, which otherwise would have been lost ; the sterling excellence to be detected in many of these pictorial scenes and satires, renders the action meritorious, which has enabled posterity to judge how far those praises which partial contemporaries lavished upon all these non-professional humourists, were justified by the actual merits of their subjects. We have already recounted certain jocose and whimsical traits in the disposition and career of this genial son of merriment; we have nothing to add but the brief notice from the obituary of *The Gentleman's Magazine* for October 1800, which informed many a congenial friend of the loss society had sustained, and made many a heart feel saddened by the stroke which had fallen on the kindliest and best of comrades.

'At Margate, where he went for the benefit of his health, Henry Wigstead, Esq., of Kensington, an active magistrate for the county of Middlesex.[1] He was a man of considerable talent, and contributed to the celebrity of the Brandenburgh theatre, both by his pen and his pencil. He was a good caricaturist, which naturally made him more enemies than friends. He was hospitable and generous to a degree of extravagance. He married the daughter of Mr. Bagnal, of Gerard Street, with whom he had a good fortune, and by whom he leaves two children, a son and a daughter.'

Another eminent humourist, in whose praise contemporaries were enthusiastic, but whose biography no one has taken the pains to collect, was John Nixon, *the facetious Nixon,* as he is generally entitled in the memoirs and scribblings of the period; beyond the kindly appreciative anecdotes of this worthy, set down by Angelo, barely any record exists. Pleasant John Nixon was an Irish factor, and resided for many years in Basinghall Street, where, over his dark warehouses, he and his brother Richard kept 'bachelors' court.' The elder brother, John, however, was the principal mover in all the convivialities and Bacchanalian revels celebrated in this old-fashioned dwelling; 'which was not too large for comfort, and yet sufficiently spacious in the first floor, at least, to spread a table for twelve. Who that were witty, or highly talented of the days that are gone, who, loving a social gossip, over a *magnum bonum* of capital wine, had not been invited to his hospitable board?' The Nixons were wealthy, and had the felicity to be well enabled to enjoy life according to their own liking.

John Nixon, besides possessing a well-deserved reputation for social qualifications of no ordinary calibre, was a man of taste and talent, and an amateur performer in various arts, his accomplishments being multifarious.

As a man of business he was highly respected, as a man of pleasure universally sought, and as generally esteemed. Sedulous in his commercial pursuits, in the counting-house his maxim was that there is time for all things, and he found leisure daily, when the ledger was closed, to open his heart to the enjoyments of friendly intercourse. 'I have no objection to placing my knees under

[1] Sitting magistrate at Bow Street.

another man's table,' the social *convive* would say, 'but I had rather seat him at my own.'

Nixon was at home at the Beef-steak Club, where he was made honorary secretary and providore, a well-bestowed distinction, since he was a first-rate connoisseur of wines, and a capital judge of a rump of beef. ' My lord duke,' he would say to the noble president, ' he who would invite Jupiter to a feast on a steak, should select a prime cut of little more than half-an-inch thick, from a Norfolk-fed Scot,' and this, says Angelo, became statute law in that glorious club.

Among other pursuits for which Nixon obtained notoriety among the *haut ton*, he was known for his fondness for the stage. An excellent amateur performer, he shone as one of the stars of the celebrated private theatricals held at Brandenburgh House, when in the possession of the Margrave and Margravine of Anspach. It was under the splendid roof of these entertainers, on an occasion when all the amateurs were celebrating their host's anniversary, that Nixon was honoured with his cognomen of 'the well-bred man.' On his late arrival in a piebald uniform, his blue dress-coat, with the gold buttons of the Beef-steak Club, being considerably powdered, the wearer, who was not in the least disconcerted or embarrassed, related, on taking his seat at the table, a droll tale of adventures on the road, to the hearty amusement of the company, while the servants were in convulsions of laughter, as Nixon described how the post-horses were knocked up, and he was  obliged to complete his journey and his engagement in the cart of a baker, where he got completely dusted with flour ; whence the Margravine facetiously dubbed him the ' well-bread man.'

John Nixon's original talent for the humorous department of the graphic art was well known ; as an honorary exhibitor at the Royal Academy for many years, his grotesque scenes such as *Bartholomew Fair*, and village fêtes, abounding with character, diverted the public. Angelo, in recording the comical celebrity of his friend, mentions, 'Nixon had the reputation of introducing, through his inventive faculty, that most amusing species of caricature, the converting spades, hearts, clubs, and diamonds into grotesque figures and groups, which he designed with a whimsicality of appropriateness, that Gillray, or even George Cruikshank himself, might have envied.'

The list of amateur artists, who enjoyed Rowlandson's friendship, and whose designs received the advantages which his assistance was able to lend them, will not be complete without the name of Collings, well known in the regions of

Covent Garden, and some time editor of the *Public Ledger*, who was a lively satirist, both with his pencil and his pen. 'When Boswell's *Tour to the Hebrides* was ushered forth, it was celebrated by as many crackers and squibs as the *Burning of the Boot* (Lord Bute). Among other assailants, the impenetrable Bozzy had to expose his front to this lampooner's shafts. A whole series of designs were published by this witty wag, the heroes of which, or rather the knight and the esquire of his drama, were Johnson and Boswell. The knight, it is likely, never saw them ; and, as for the squire, his love of notoriety rendered him, if not vain of, at least not vulnerable to, these successive attacks.[1]

'The Laird of Auchinleck, indeed, had a large collection of these satires upon "self and company," as he used facetiously to inscribe them, and boasted at the judge's table that his *History* would be more copiously illustrated than even the Lord High Chancellor, Clarendon's.'

Caleb Whiteford, another crony of the caricaturist, was an excellent judge of paintings (especially works by the old masters) and was generally known as a fervent admirer of George Moreland's pictures ; he was the reputed discoverer of 'cross readings,'[2] and a dabbler in verse. It was he who, as everyone will remember, received such a complimentary notice in the postscript to the mock epitaphs known as Goldsmith's *Retaliation*, that there were not wanting those who contributed to the flattery by suspecting that the additional epitaph was due to Caleb's own pen.

Old Caleb Whiteford, the witty wine-merchant and 'connoisseur in old masters,' knew everyone of any reputation, and was well-received at the various hospitable boards to which allusions have been made in the course of these discursive notes ; he was a welcome guest at numerous convivial gatherings of the artistic and literary coteries of the period, whose jovial meetings and good cheer have been suffered to pass into oblivion, unrecorded by the scribes who shared 'the cakes and ale,' in the palmy days of sociable festivities and kindly familiar intercourse.

'Mr. Ephraim Hardcastle, citizen and drysalter,' as he whimsically elected to style himself—in sober fact, W. H. Pyne, the artist to whose literary ventures we have already referred—has on occasions come to the rescue in his *Wine and*

[1] See Boswell (the Elder). *Twenty Caricatures by Collings and Rowlandson in Illustration of Boswell's ' Journal of a Tour in the Hebrides, 1786.'*

[2] These cross-readings obtained such celebrity that the inventor was tempted to distribute amongst his friends specimens, which 'he had been at the expense of printing upon small single sheets.' We quote a couple of examples from a slip, which was in the possession of J. T. (*Antiquity*) Smith's family, and, being considered something of a curiosity, is given in the pages of *Nollekens and his Times.*

> Sunday night many noble families were alarmed—
> By the constable of the watch, who apprehended them at cards.

> Wanted, to take care of an elderly gentlewoman—
> An active young man, just come from the country.

Walnuts, or after-dinner Chit-Chat. Here is the report of a conversation concerning Rowlandson, which is supposed to have taken place between Whiteford and the caricaturist's jolly friend Mitchell, culled from the *Chit-Chat* in question, which was published in 1823.

'Well, Master Caleb Whiteford [1] was on his way up the hill in the Adelphi to his post at the Society of Arts, and who should he stumble upon at the corner of James Street, just turning round from Rowlandson's, but Master Mitchell, the quondam banker of old Hodsoll's house. He had, as usual, been foraging among the multitudinous sketches of that original artist, and held a portfolio under his arm, and as he was preparing to step into his chariot, Caleb accosted him: "Well, worthy sir ; what! more choice bits—more graphic whimsies to add to the collection at Enfield, eh ? Well, how fares it with our friend Roly ?" (a familiar term by which the artist was known to his ancient cronies).

' "Why, yes, Master Caleb Whiteford, I go collecting on, though I begin to think I have enough already, for I have some hundreds of his spirited works ; but somehow there is a sort of fascination in these matters, and—heigh—ha—ho —hoo!" (gaping) " I never go up—up—bless the man, why will he live so high ? It kills me to climb his stairs "—holding his ponderous sides—" I never go up, Mister Caleb, but I find something new, and am tempted to pull my purse-strings. His invention, his humour, his— his oddity is exhaustless." " Yes," said Whiteford, " Master Roly is never at a loss for a sub-ject, and I should not be surprised if he is taking a bird's-eye view of you and me at this moment, and marking us down for game. But it is not his drawings alone ; why, he says he has etched as much copper as would sheathe a first-rate man-of-war ; and I should think he is not far from the mark in his assertion.'

' "Yes," replied the banker, "he ought to be rich, for his genius is certainly the most exhaustless, the most—the most—no, Mister Caleb, there is no end to him ; he manufactures his humorous ware with such increasing vigour, that I know not what to compare his prolific fancy to, unless it be to the increasing population. . . .

' " Roly has promised to come down. I would have taken the rogue with me, only that he is about some new scheme for his old friend Ackermann, there, and he says he must complete it within an hour. You know Roly's expedition." '

James Heath, also a caricaturist, and a delineator of sporting sketches, was another of Rowlandson's intimates; a Good-Friday jaunt, or an Easter excursion,

---

[1] Caleb Whiteford was Vice-President of the Society for the Encouragement of Arts, Manufactures, and Commerce.

was for many years indulged by these worthies, who with genial Bannister, the comedian, and their faithful chronicler, Henry Angelo, the fencing-master, annually kept up the practice of proceeding on a jovial expedition at this season, some distance from town, Staines, Windsor, or some similar starting-point, being the rendezvous selected by these congenial spirits.

The list of Rowlandson's friends would be incomplete without the name of George Moreland, who, with all his eccentricities and shortcomings, was another favoured child of fortune, whose inheritance was natural genius; and though the fairy gift was turned to the very worst account, dragged through the mire of dissipation, and sordidly made to supply the means of that social degradation, which lowered the possessor beneath his worst associates, the power remained in the poor shattered wreck, and did not forsake him until, in a state of premature decay, he perished miserably before his easel.

A sketch of Moreland's career is by no means called for in this place. His erratic disposition was not without its whimsical traits; sufficient anecdotes exist of the wayward painter to prove that, beyond his happy qualifications for his art, there was found in his composition a spice of pleasantry that did not always degenerate into buffoonery or horse-play, with occasional flashes of wit and sprightly allusions which, to say the least of them, were remarkably apposite. Perhaps too much stress has been laid upon Moreland's deficiencies, while his more agreeable traits have been somewhat slighted. Putting aside the numerous anecdotal sketches of the painter, we have only to record, in this place at least, that a friendship existed between the subject of this volume and the man to whose sketches those of our caricaturist frequently offer a suggestive resemblance, it being actually difficult to distinguish between the unsigned etchings and drawings of the two artists, in the walk practised by Moreland. The similarity of their talent is more evident perhaps in the larger hunting scenes, and the studies of female heads, tinted in colours, than in any other direction; although, with the pencil or the chalk, their rustic landscapes, from the freedom of their respective handlings, are remarkably alike, both in the choice of subjects and the spirit of the execution.

As we have already noticed, the most characteristic portrait of Moreland, and the one which appears to offer us the most life-like representation of the capricious painter, is due to the skill of Rowlandson. We are informed, in a note which we gather from Angelo, that Moreland, in his various flittings round the metropolis in dread of creditors, when he took sanctuary with any intimate whose residence he happened to remember, gave his colleague the caricaturist the opportunity of exhibiting his friendship by harbouring him in his lodgings under one of these emergencies, which were of tolerably frequent occurrence. ' Rowlandson, the artist, lodged at Mrs. Lay's printshop, a few doors from

Carlton House, Pall Mall. One morning when I called upon him, we heard a loud knock at the street door, and looking out of the window, he said, "There's Colonel Thornton——knock again! He may be at this fun three months longer ; he is come for his picture, but Moreland, having touched fifty pounds in advance, is never at home to him now. He's in the next room, which he has for painting. You had better go and do the same with him, and drink gin and water ; he'll like your company, and make you a drawing for nothing." This was in the middle of the day.'

We are inclined to think that the most memorable of the caricaturist's associates was James Gillray, whose age was within a year of that of Rowlandson ; it is a coincidence that two unrivalled geniuses, and in such eccentric walks, should have been both contemporaries, and steady-going friends, never clashing in the course of their respective careers. In this work various allusions will be noticed to the intimacy which subsisted between these remarkably gifted men, each perfectly original in his fashion, and both possessing singular points of resemblance in their characters.

We content ourselves with mentioning that they occasionally entered into friendly alliances, but that, when pitted against each other, they had more regard for friendship than for party warfare, which they utterly despised, except as an opening for the exercise of their skill.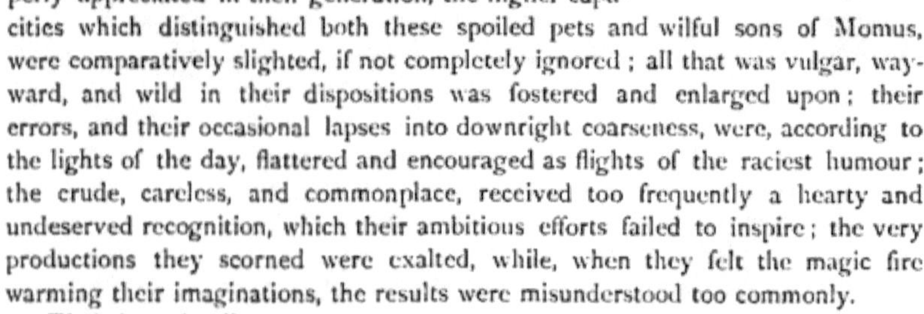

Gillray and Rowlandson were, perhaps, never properly appreciated in their generation, the higher capacities which distinguished both these spoiled pets and wilful sons of Momus, were comparatively slighted, if not completely ignored ; all that was vulgar, wayward, and wild in their dispositions was fostered and enlarged upon ; their errors, and their occasional lapses into downright coarseness, were, according to the lights of the day, flattered and encouraged as flights of the raciest humour ; the crude, careless, and commonplace, received too frequently a hearty and undeserved recognition, which their ambitious efforts failed to inspire ; the very productions they scorned were exalted, while, when they felt the magic fire warming their imaginations, the results were misunderstood too commonly.

Their keen intellects, and their satiric sense of the almost constant unfitness of things as they found them, the gnawing of the vanity of vanities, ever present, must have made their temperaments peculiarly sensitive to such slights as the want of discrimination in their admirers which occasionally shocked and continually disheartened them—evils which the want of culture, or consideration on the part of their audience, continually brought in their train.

It is no matter of surprise that the enchantments which they saw before them at the opening of their careers, vanished all too soon, and left them chilled, and

inclined to become misanthropes ; the very genius, which promised to be a delight
to themselves and to mankind, proving a bitter curse.

When the satirists, who felt alike and were sympathetic on most points, met,
it seems their intercourse was the reverse of boisterous—in fact, they were rather
inclined to be depressed, or, at least, they shrunk within themselves with a more
marked contrast to the conduct which should, it was supposed, distinguish
notorious pictorial humourists, and became, perhaps, a trifle more retired and
undemonstrative than ordinary—possibly to the disappointment of the less-in-
formed *habitués*, who evidently thought they were defrauded of a diversion, and
had a right to anticipate, these gentlemen being in a sort graphic jesters by profession, that in private life they would feel themselves impelled to play off a little
whimsical jugglery for the entertainment of the company. These professional
tricks belonged to the lesser lights, and we warrant that Woodward, Collings,
Newton, and the smaller following of the eccentric art, were infinitely more
amusing to the taste of their auditors.

It is certain Gillray was grave and self-contained, and Rowlandson, in his
degree, participated in his friend's humour, slightly at first, perhaps, as a passing
depression, and, later in life, with an intensified and growing grimness, and a
gathering gloom, as friends dropped off, and age crept on, and the caricaturist's
world was materially altered for him, as his work seemed over.

' For years Gillray occasionally smoked his pipe at *The Bell, The Coal-Hole,*
or *The Coach and Horses* ; and, although the *convives*, whom he met at such dingy
rendezvous, knew that he was that Gillray who fabricated those comical cuts, the
very moral of Farmer George and Boneyparty, of Billy Pitt and Black Charley,
he never sought, like that low coxcomb Moreland, to become king of the company.
He neither exacted, nor were they inclined to pay him, any particular homage.
In truth, with his associates, neighbouring shopkeepers and master manufac-
turers, he passed for no greater wit than his neighbours. Rowlandson, his ingenious compeer, and he, sometimes met. They would, perhaps, exchange half-
a-dozen questions and answers upon the affairs of copper and aquafortis ; swear
all the world was one vast masquerade, and then enter into the common chat of
the room, smoke their cigars, drink their punch, and sometimes early, sometimes
late, shake hands at the door, look up at the stars, say " It is a frosty night," and
depart, one for the Adelphi, the other to St. James's Street, each to his bachelor's
bed.' [1]

Our friend Angelo, a bright chirpy spirit, who retained his liveliness unim-
paired, let us hope, to the last of his long days, not having any pretensions to
be a genius, was exempt from the sinister tendencies which too frequently attend

[1] *Somerset House Gazette and Literary Museum,* No. 26. By Ephraim Hardcastle (W. H. Pyne).
1824.

its possession. Although, as he confesses in his *Memoirs*, not precisely the 'rose' himself, he had lived near it, and his association with men of an admittedly high type, as far as gifts of fancy and versatile talents were concerned, had taught him to observe the drawbacks not unusually allied to distinguishing attainments; and he records a few sober axioms for the enlightenment of those who have been excluded from his privileges.

'Those who at a distance contemplate characters like these, so professedly eminent for invention, wit, and satirical humour, naturally suppose their society must be universally sought; and that such must, of necessity, be the life and soul of the convivial board. Men, however, who see much and speculate but little, know better. Among the dullest in company could be pointed out those who are "wondrous witty" by themselves; and this not from pride of their superior faculty to please, but from a constitutional shyness or modest desire to avoid notice or applause—or from indolence, or actually from conscious dulness when absent from the study and the desk, when without the pencil and the pen.

'Peter Pindar was witless, even over his bottle, with his most intimate cronies. Anthony Pasquin was sour, and not prone to converse. Churchill was a sulky sot. Butler was lively neither drunk nor sober—a choice companion only when "half gone;" hence, as the witty Duke of Buckingham observed, "he was to be compared to a skittle, little at both ends, but great in the middle!" Burton, who had no less humour than Cervantes, and the learning of a whole university to boot, was neither a cheerful companion, nor endurable to himself. A hundred more could be named, whose aptitude and promptness to discover the ridiculous side of human action, has astonished the grave; and yet, these men who have thus exposed folly to the laughter of mankind, have been themselves the dullest dogs alive. Gillray was always "hipped," and at last sunk into that deplorable state of mental aberration which verifies the couplet, so often quoted, wherein the consanguinity of wit to madness is so eminently proved, to the comfort of those who thank God for their own stupidity.'

Perhaps the most constant friend, and certainly the best adviser, our caricaturist retained to the grave was his principal publisher, Mr. Rudolph Ackermann. We have mentioned this gentleman last among the personal associates of Rowlandson, as his untiring services only ended with the life of the artist.

The name of Rudolph Ackermann, who died March 30, 1834, is worthy of more than a passing mention; he has been cited as one of the first natives of Germany who, by far-sighted and active occupation, accompanied by philanthropic exertions for the benefit of his fellow-creatures, raised the character of his nationality to a high point of esteem in other countries. An account of his energetic and charitable career appeared in the *Didaskalia*, Frankfurt-am-Main, No. 103,

April 13, 1864, and was adopted by the writer (W. P.) of an excellent notice upon the well-known publisher, in the pages of *Notes and Queries*, (4th S. iv., August 7 and 14, 1869). The son of a coach-builder, Rudolph Ackermann was born April 20, 1764, at Stolberg, in the Saxon Hartz. We are told 'his sympathies with the misfortunes of others were so warmly excited by the misery seen around him in the famine of 1772–73, that he frequently in later years excused the zeal which he showed on other occasions, by pictures of the distress that he experienced when he, at the age of eight years, was employed for hours daily in distributing food and money.' In 1775 his father removed to Schneeberg. Rudolph received his education in the local school till he was fifteen years old, and showed a decided predilection for literary pursuits ; but his father's pecuniary position precluding the choice of a profession to more than one of his sons, he entered the paternal factory. An elder brother, Frederick, instructed Rudolph in the use of the drawing instruments, and he busied himself more willingly in the offices than in the workshops, gaining an acquaintance with details, which proved subsequently as important to his advancement as were his visits to Dresden, the towns of the Rhine, and Hueningen near Basle. He afterwards went to reside in Paris, where he became the friend of Carrossi, the most esteemed designer of equipages of his time, and Rudolph, who proved his best pupil, acquired sufficient knowledge as a practical draughtsman to push his way in the world. From Paris he proceeded to London in pursuit of fortune, and to turn his talents to account : he was delighted to find that, in the metropolis, carriage-building was one of the most successful occupations, and that the exercise of his acquirements would be handsomely rewarded ; so for several years, until 1795, he was employed in furnishing the principal coachmakers with designs and models for new and improved carriages. The models of the state coach, built at the cost of nearly 7,000*l.*, for the Lord-Lieutenant of Ireland in 1790,[1] and that for the Lord Mayor of Dublin in 1791, exhibited his taste and skill. In 1805, the preparation of the car that served as a hearse at the funeral of Lord Nelson was entrusted to him ; and during the years 1818–20 the patent for a moveable axle for carriages engaged much of his attention.

It is not, however, in this connection that we have to consider Ackermann, but rather in his relation to the arts as a print-seller and publisher. On his marriage with an English lady, with commendable prudence, he became desirous of establishing a business which would, in case of his own premature decease, prove a suitable provision for his family. He commenced the print trade at 96 Strand,

---

[1] The reader may observe a similar chariot in the Museum at South Kensington ; it might readily be mistaken for the one referred to above, and is of the most elaborate character. It is described as 'built for the Lord Chancellor of Ireland (1780), the panels painted by W. Hamilton, R.A.'

and soon after he secured a large apartment, 65 feet long, 30 feet wide, and 24 feet high, at 101 Strand (erected upon the courtyard of Beaufort House), which had been the drawing academy of William Shipley; it had then passed to Henry Pars, and later passed into the hands of the Radicals, and became notorious as the British Forum, when it was used by John Thelwall for his oratorical lectures. These meetings exceeding the bounds of reasonable political discussion, the Government instituted prosecutions, and the Forum ceased to exist. On the ministerial interference, October 1794, Mr. Ackermann was enabled to secure the lease of the premises, and the room was again used as a school for drawing. In 1796 the entire business was removed to 101 Strand. The drawing academy seems to have flourished; and in 1806 there were three masters engaged for figures, landscape, and architecture, and some eighty pupils were resorting to the school, when the requirements of the founder's business, as a publisher, print-seller, and dealer in fancy articles, papers, medallions, and artist's materials, had so increased, that the convenience of this room as a warehouse became of more consideration than the continuance of the school.

During the revolutionary era, and when French emigrants were numerous in this country, Mr. Ackermann was one of the first to find a liberal employment for the refugees; it is said that he had seldom less than fifty nobles, priests, and ladies engaged upon screens, card-racks, flower-stands, and other ornamental work.

His inventive faculties and his disposition to take up with new ideas were marked by many improvements he introduced. At the beginning of the century he was one of the first who arrived at a method of waterproofing paper, leather, woollen stuffs, and felted fabrics, in which he obtained for some time considerable traffic; this branch was conducted in a factory he established at Chelsea for the purpose.

He further contrived an apparatus which was at least ingenious, both in theory and intention. To counteract Napoleon's endeavours, by bridling the news-papers, to keep the French nation in complete ignorance, as was actually the case, of events that were disastrous to him, Mr. Ackermann bethought himself of reviving, for the annoyance of the enemy, the use made by the French in 1794–96 of aërostation in *L'Entreprenant* and the *Télémaque*; and he contrived a simple mechanism which would, every minute, detach thirty printed placards from a packet of three thousand. Three such parcels were attached to balloons thirty-six inches in diameter, made of gold-beater's skin, and committed to the air in the summer of 1807. The success of the experiment was proved at Woolwich in the presence of a Government commission. With a southerly wind the balloons passed over Salisbury and Exeter, and several of the placards, as a proof of the practical working of the machinery, were returned to London from various parts of the country.

Mr. Ackermann was one of the first inhabitants of London who adopted the use of gas as a means of artificial light to his premises.

The establishment of lithography in England was another example of his patient and persevering expenditure of money and time in the introduction and improvement of a novelty. 'He was not content with translating Alois Sene felder's treatise in 1819, but made a journey to the residence of that inventor, in order to exchange the results of their theory and practice before producing in 1822 a *Complete Course.* The business relations between leading artists and Mr. Ackermann enabled him to induce them to touch the lithographic chalk; so in 1817, through Prout and others, the process became an acceptable, or rather a fashionable mode of multiplying drawings; lithography, for want of such advantages, when introduced into this country by Mr. Andrée, of Offenbach, in its original and rude state, had failed to make its way, and all its subsequent success may be attributed to Mr. Ackermann's personal emulation of the advancement it made in Munich.'

In 1813, upon receiving an authentic account from Count Schönfeld of the misery produced in Germany by Napoleon's wars, particularly in Saxony, culminating in engagements at Leipzig (during the 'five days' October 15–19, 1813), 'Mr. Ackermann temporarily abandoned the oversight of his own multifarious occupations, in order to exert all his strength in procuring aid for the sufferers. With the help of the Duke of Sussex, he formed a committee in Westminster and in the City; the first obtained a Parliamentary grant of 100,000*l.*, and the second furnished a larger sum in private contributions. This was the occasion on which the use of Whitehall Chapel was granted for a musical performance in aid of the subscription. For two years, Mr. Ackermann undertook the task of corresponding with the German committees for distributing these sums, examining into the urgency of the appeals for help, and apportioning the fund. The members of " The Westminster Association for the further relief of the sufferers by the war in Germany," were anxious to commemorate their sense of the pains, prudence, and probity Mr. Ackermann had displayed, by presenting him with a testimonial in silver; this costly acknowledgment, together with a vote of thanks proposed to be inscribed on parchment in gold, he had the modesty to decline, begging that all thanks for his services might be comprised in a few autograph lines from the Archbishop of Canterbury.'

In his business relations we are told, 'the discretion which he exercised in choosing his subordinates, and the liberal manner in which he repaid their services, enabled him to produce several books which deserve the notice of all those who know how to appreciate the merit of these illustrated works in colour, relatively to others of similar pretension, both of that time and of the present day.

'A long list might be formed by enumerating the literary, musical, and scientific men of more or less eminence, who appeared as his coadjutors, and who enjoyed his intimacy. Several of them owed to him a helping hand, either in their first efforts or in their declining fortunes. To the end of his days he retained a strongly-marked German pronunciation of the English language, which gave additional flavour to the banters and jests uttered in his fine bass voice; but he wrote in English with great purity on matters of affection and business long before middle life.

'From early in 1813, every Wednesday evening in March and April was given to a reception, half a conversazione and half a family party, in his large room, which then, as at other times, served as an exhibition of English and foreign books, maps, prints, woodcuts, lithographs, drawings, paintings, and other works of art and ornament, besides the leading Continental periodicals. There on those evenings, by annual invitation,[1] amateurs, artists, and authors were sure to find people whom they knew, or wanted to know. Many an introduction grew to an acquaintance; and the value of such evenings to foreigners was often gratefully acknowledged by travellers, who, with any distinction in art or literature, were welcome without any other introduction.

'His active assiduity and his spirited enterprise were suspended by a weakness of sight, commencing from his charitable exertions in 1814, which made his repose at Camberwell, and afterwards at Ivy Lodge in the Fulham Road, first a matter of prudence, and later on of necessity. In the spring of 1830 he experienced an attack of paralysis, and never recovered sufficiently to exert his intelligence in business. He removed for a change of air to Finchley, but a second stroke produced a gradual decline of strength in the honourable old man; and March 30, 1834, saw an end put to the hearty kindness, constant hospitality, and warm beneficence which had been inseparable from his unquestioned integrity. He was interred on April 9 in the family grave, in the burial-ground of St. Clement Danes.'[2]

The little that remains to be recorded of the Caricaturist is best ex-

---

[1] According to Mr. Jerdan, the first *missive printed on stone* (drawings having been printed by this process some while before), was an invitation to one of Ackermann's conversaziones: 'Mr. Ackermann has the honour to inclose a card of invitation to a Literary Meeting at his Library, on Tuesday, the 20th February, at seven o'clock in the evening; and on the same evening in each week, until the 10th day of April inclusive.

[2] *Notes and Queries*, August 1869. See article signed W. P.

pressed by the kindly writer, a friend of nearly half a century's standing, who contributed an obituary notice of the artist to the *Gentleman's Magazine* (June 1827).

It is not generally known that, although a considerable proportion of Rowlandson's humorous political and social etchings are in many instances strongly tinctured by an absence of refinement in taste, and are roughly executed—the means simply of tiding over some pressing necessity, or providing funds for further relaxations—his early works were characterised by painstaking and conscientious application ; and his studies from the human figure at the Royal Academy were scarcely inferior to the productions of Mortimer, then the most admired and proficient among the Academic professors.

From the versatility of his talent, the fecundity of his imagination, his command of composition, in which he equalled the greatest masters, the grace and elegance with which he could design his groups, added to the almost miraculous despatch with which he supplied his patrons with perfectly original compositions upon every subject, it was a theme of regret at his decease, that he had not sufficiently valued his reputation, to which it has been suspected he was thoroughly indifferent. It was universally admitted in his own days that, had he pursued the course of art steadily, he might have become one of the foremost and most celebrated historical painters of the English school. His style, which was purely his own, was unquestionably original. His bold, fluent, and spiritedly turned outlines were thrown off with easy dexterity, with his famous reed-pen, in a tint composed of vermilion and Indian-ink, the general effect was rapidly washed in, so as to produce an effective *chiaro-oscuro*, and the whole was coloured in tender tints with a most harmonious arrangement of colour.

His manner, though slight in almost every instance, is highly effective ; and it is known on indubitable authority that the presidents of the Royal Academy, Sir Joshua Reynolds and Sir Benjamin West, whose manners were most foreign to those of the Caricaturist, individually asserted their conviction that many of his drawings would have done honour to Rubens, or to the most esteemed masters of design of the old schools.

For many years he was too indolent to seek new employment, and his kind friend, and it may be added with justice, his best adviser, Mr. Ackermann, the respected and leading publisher of Rowlandson's period, supplied him with ample subjects for the exercise of his talent. The many works which his pencil illustrated are existing evidence of this, and books containing impressions from Rowlandson's etchings continue to fetch high prices, and are industriously sought after. Many suggestions for plates to enliven new editions of *The Travels of Dr. Syntax, The Dance of Death, The Dance of Life,* and other well-known productions of the pen of the prolific Coombe, the Defoe of the eighteenth century, will remain esteemed and lasting mementoes of his graphic humour.

It should be repeated that his reputation had never reached its full maturity in the life-time of Mr. Ackermann, his friend, patron, and publisher. The inimitable water-colour drawings of Rowlandson, of which he had a large collection, were justly appreciated by connoisseurs, and his folios have often been viewed with admiration and delight by the many professional artists and amateurs who frequented Mr. Ackermann's conversazioni at his library at the old house in the Strand. No artist of the past or present school, perhaps, ever expressed so much as Rowlandson, with so little effort, or with so evident an appearance of the absence of labour.

The artist's remains were followed to the grave by the two friends of his youth, John Bannister and Henry Angelo, and his constant friend and liberal employer, Rudolph Ackermann.

June 8, 1774. *A Rotation Office.*—A chief magistrate is seated at a table, and three justices, with their hats on, and sticks in their hands, are seated beside

THE VILLAGE DOCTOR.

him. To the left of the chief is the justice's clerk ; and behind the bench is a placard, 'Robbery and Murder. Reward of Justice.'

June 8, 1774. *The Village Doctor.* Published by H. Humphrey, Bond Street.—This print appears to have been about the earliest recognised specimen

of Rowlandson's handiwork.   The plate has a wash of aquatint, all over it, and
the etching is free and bold.   As an early work it evinces certain carefulness and
discrimination, which promised well for the artist's future if he persevered in
the same direction.   The suggestion of the subject, according to the initials, is
due to Henry Wigstead, whose name appears on numerous fine examples of
Rowlandson's skill.   The village practitioner, outside whose cottage is the sign
of a gilt pestle, has evidently been disturbed under false pretences on previous
occasions, and now a real client has knocked him up, for the benefit of his professional services, his indignation is bursting forth on the wrong object.

1780.   *Scene at Streatham.   Bozzy and Piozzi.*

BOZZY.

Who, mad'ning with an anecdotic itch,
Hath said that Johnson called his mother, witch?

MADAME PIOZZI.

Who, from Macdonald's rage to save his snout,
Cut twenty lines of defamation out?

The scene of this animated dispute is the Library at the house lately inhabited
by the departed Thrale.   Mrs. Piozzi (late Mrs. Thrale) and Boswell are in
high dudgeon over their respective memoirs of their idol, the defunct Doctor
Johnson.   In both of their 'Lives' the trifling weaknesses of the great Lexicographer are made ridiculous, under the misguiding impulse of the 'anecdotic itch.'
The rival biographers are bouncing and stamping about the study, in a fine rage,
ready to pull one another to pieces.   The learned lady's second husband, the
stout musician, Piozzi, with his violoncello by his side, is seated in an easy chair,
regarding the disputants with consternation, while deprecating violence.

Peter Pindar's lines on the subject are appended to the plate ; an additional
couplet or two are worth borrowing :—

BOZZY.

How could your folly tell, so void of truth,
That miserable story of the youth
Who, in your book, of Dr. Johnson begs,
Most seriously, to know if *cats laid eggs* ?

MADAME PIOZZI.

Who told of Mrs. Montague the lie—
So palpable a falsehood?   Bozzy, fy!

.   .   .   .   .

BOZZY.

Who would have said a word about Sam's wig :
Or told the story of the *peas* and *pig* ?

MADAME PIOZZI.

Now for a *saint* upon us you would palm him ;
First *murder* the poor man, and then *embalm him* !

BOZZY.

His character so shockingly you handle—
You've sunk your *comet* to a *farthing candle.*

March 1780. *Special Pleading.* Published by A. McKenzie, 101 Berwick
Street, Soho.

Lovely Nymph, assuage my anguish,
At your feet behold a swain,
Begs you will not let him languish ;
One kind word will ease his pain.

A stout knight (possibly a lineal descendant of Sir John Falstaff) is the
Pleader ; he is lounging on an elegant sofa of the early Georgian period, making
inane love to a pretty girl placed by his side, dressed in a picturesque Watteau-
like costume, with a quilted petticoat and a quaint mob-cap added ; the amorous
old trifler's hand is on the slim waist of the beauty ; the damsel is standing up in
a negligently easy pose, while she is toying with her antiquated admirer and
waving his enormous and elaborately curled double-tailed wig in the air.   A dog
is at her side.   The drawing of this picture is unusually graceful and easy, even
for Rowlandson ; this is most noticeable in respect to the pretty coquette.   The
etching is spirited and brilliant, and the background and accessories are delicately aquatinted, to bear out the resemblance to a sketch in Indian ink.

July 18, 1780. *The School of Eloquence.*—The interior of a fashionable
debating society of the period ; the members are the quality of both sexes.
The design was doubtless admirably worked out in the original drawing ; but it
has suffered at the hands of an unknown etcher.   Published by Archibald
Robertson, Savile Passage.

September 1, 1780. *Italian Affectation. Pacchierolti.*—The figures of two
distinguished foreigners, as imported into this country over a century ago, for
the delectation of the *cognoscendi* and the leaders of high taste.   A pair of overdressed Italian artists, extravagantly posturing to one another in some operatic
scena.   A spindle-shanked signor, hat in hand, is pouring out his ardour to an
affected and modish *prima donna* in a love-making situation, outrageously
burlesqued.

September 18, 1780. *Sir Samuel House.*—The full-length portrait of 'Honest
Sam House,' famous in his day for his zeal and patriotism, the enthusiastic
supporter of Fox, a character familiar to all the electors of Westminster, as

an indefatigable canvasser on behalf of the 'Friend of the People;' during the contests for Westminster, Sam kept open house for the friends of the Whig chief, and entertained all the notabilities of the Whig party. Summer and winter, Sam dressed in a clean nankeen jacket and breeches, and brightly polished shoes and buckles; he wore no covering, neither hat nor wig, on a perfectly bald head; his waistcoat was constantly open in all seasons, and he wore remarkably white linen; his legs were generally bare, but when covered, it was always in stockings of the finest silk.

In Rowlandson's spirited portrait old Sam is standing in his sturdy fashion, clean, shaven, and bright, in his eccentric costume, with his shining round poll, a pot with his cipher in one hand, and his pipe in the other. In the rear is shown his public-house, with smokers and customers indicated at the windows. This portrait, which seems to have been deservedly popular, was published with variations. In one impression (printed in sepia), is a barrel inscribed '*No Pope*,' and in another, '*Fox for ever! Huzza!*' The second plate is crossed with very fine stipple, and an old man is introduced in the background with his hand on his bald head.

The prints are signed with the initials T. R. and J. J., and were published by Thomas Rowlandson and J. Jones at 103 Wardour Street. Under some impressions is the inscription, 'The first man who jumped off Westminster Bridge.'

SAM HOUSE.

Not more the great Sam House, with horror, star'd,
By mob affronted to the very beard;
Whose impudence (enough to damn a jail)
Snatch'd from his waving hand his fox's tail,
And stuff'd it, 'midst his thunders of applause,
Full in the centre of Sam's gaping jaws;
That, forcing down his patriotic throat,
Of 'Fox and freedom!' stopp'd the glorious note.

November 13, 1780. *Naval Triumph, or Favours Conferred.*—Admiral Keppel is riding in triumph through the gates of Greenwich Hospital, mounted on the shoulders of a veteran salt, on crutches, who has lost both an eye and his legs in the service of his country. The Admiral, with his riband and star, is condescending to give a helping hand to another naval commander, who is dancing in merrily by his side.

The shake of the hand with such goodness and grace
Shows who is in favour, and who is in place.
At Greenwich the invalids poor will proclaim
What at present we do not think proper to name.

Poor disabled sailors are limping off on their crutches, disgusted with the results of their sacrifices and the miserable rewards for their services ; while a drummer is drubbing in their favoured and well-requited commanders.

THE POWER OF REFLECTION.

The composition of this subject is particularly good, and it is worthy of remark that, in the coloured impressions of this print, the tinting is arranged with considerable success ; and although, as is the general practice with caricatures, none but the most vivid colours are employed, the arrangement is so good and delicate that the general effect is as harmonious and artistic as in the original drawings by Rowlandson's own hand.

June 30, 1781.   *The Power of Reflection.*   Published by J. Harris, Sweeting's Alley, Cornhill.—This print is executed in mezzotint by J. Jones, whose name appears several times in connection with that of Rowlandson, on the series of plates which we shall particularise in the progress of this work. The contrast is very marked between the Duenna, the lines of whose face have fallen in under the assaults of time, and the demoiselle, in all the pride of youth and attractiveness, aided by the bravery of a fashionable and *piquante* toilette. *The Power of Reflection* is probably intended to suggest a pictorial pun. While the maiden is absorbed in the pleasing reflection of her own figure as thrown back in the mirror, her senior, with a ponderous and probably serious volume before her, is employing her thoughts on contemplations of a more philosophical description.

October 28, 1781.   *E O, or the Fashionable Vowels.*—It may be noticed, respecting the earlier works of Rowlandson, that his efforts, soon after he left the Academy, were marked with more care and elaboration than his later etchings ; while the effects of his training were still fresh in his mind, he evidently took more pains in the direction of finish, and it is particularly in his management of *chiaro-oscuro* that we detect the superiority of the artistic productions of his first period ; although experience alone could give him that special freedom and facility which render his best-known productions remarkable.

In the early and clear impressions of the *E O Table*, and its surroundings, the artist's skill is even more conspicuous than usual in the spirited grouping ; the attitudes and expressions of the several gamblers are distinct with individuality and strongly-marked traits of character. Every variety of emotion—cunning, credulity, confidence, anxiety, stolid indifference, scheming, craft, stupidity, hectoring, exaltation, and despair—we find pictured with an ability which surprises us, contrasting as it does with the indifferent caricatures and the dearth of humorous talent in the years which intervened between the death of Hogarth and the appearance of the more ambitious subjects by Gillray and Rowlandson, works executed while the talents of these masters were at their best, and before they had grown careless of their reputation.

The *E O Table*[1] was republished at various dates : in January 1786 it re-

----

[1] From Malcolm's *Manners and Customs of London during the Eighteenth Century* (1810). 'Mr. Carlton, Deputy Clerk of the Peace, and Clerk to the Justices of Westminster, stated to a Committee of the House of Commons, in 1782, that E O Tables were very numerous ; that one house in the parish of St. Anne, Soho, contained five, and that there were more than three hundred in the above parish of St. James's : those were used every day of the week, and servants enticed to them by cards of direction thrown down the areas.'

appeared with a new title, as *Private Amusement*, and from time to time it was reissued, the date of publication being altered to suit the several occasions.

E O Tables.—'In the year 1781 there were swarms of E O Tables in different parts of the town, where a poor man with a shilling only might try his luck. They were open to everybody, till at last the Bow Street police began to interfere.'

An attempt was made, at the commencement of 1731, to suppress some of the most considerable gaming-houses in London and the suburbs, particularly one, behind Gray's Inn Walks. The editor of the *St. James's Evening Post* observed upon this occasion: 'It may be matter of instruction as well as amusement to present our readers with the following list of officers which are established in the most notorious gaming-houses :—

' A *Commissioner*, always a proprietor, who looks in of a night; the week's account is audited by him and two others of the proprietors.

' A *Director*, who superintends the room.

' An *Operator*, who deals the cards at a cheating game called *Faro*.

' Two *Croupees*, who watch the cards and gather the money for the bank.

' Two *Puffs*, who have money given them to decoy others to play.

' A *Clerk*, who is a check upon the *Puffs*, to see that they sink none of the money given them to play with.

' A *Squib* is a *Puff* of a lower rank, who serves at half-salary while he is learning to deal.

' A *Flasher*, to swear how often the bank has been stripped.

' A *Dunner*, who goes about to recover money lost at play.

' A *Waiter*, to fill out wine, snuff candles, and attend in the gaming-room.

' An *Attorney*, a Newgate solicitor.

' A *Captain*, who is to fight any gentleman that is peevish for losing his money.

' An *Usher*, who lights gentlemen up and down stairs, and gives the word to the porter.

' A *Porter*, who is generally a soldier of the Foot Guards.

' An *Orderly-man*, who walks up and down the outside of the door, to give notice to the porter and alarm the house at the approach of constables.

' A *Runner*, who is to get intelligence of the Justices meeting.

' Link-boys, watchmen, chairmen, drawers, or others, who bring the first intelligence of the Justices' meetings, or of the constables being out—*half-a-guinea* reward.

' Common-bail, affidavit-men, ruffians, bravoes, *cum multis aliis.*'

November 27, 1781. *Brothers of the Whip.* A. Grant, del. : published by H. Humphrey.—In this engraving a good deal of Rowlandson's manner is traceable, and the etching is at least due to his hand. The subject represents a group of four *brothers of the whip*, whose persons and features are marked with that discrimination for character and faculty for grasping individual peculiarities distinctive of the caricaturist. In the background are figured coach-horses, carriages, saddle-horses, grooms, &c., all depicted in his own marked style.

CHARITY COVERETH A MULTITUDE OF SINS.

November 27, 1781. Charity Covereth a Multitude of Sins, published by H. Humphrey.—A dashing young officer is roving, in pursuit of pleasure, in a dangerous vicinity. With a generous hand he is dropping a gold-piece into the hat of a reduced sailor. Two Savoyards, a man with an organ, and a girl with a hurdygurdy are soliciting the contributions of the charitable.

BOB DERRY, OF NEWMARKET.

December 10, 1781. The State Watchman Discovered by the Genius of Great Britain Studying Plans for the Reduction of America, published by J. Jones.—This subject is engraved within a circle, and, in point of execution, it bears more resemblance to Rowlandson's later style; it is not unlike Gillray's work of the same date.

The somnolent Lord North is fast asleep on his sofa, dreaming, according to the caricaturist, of new theories for the recovery of America.

The figure of *Britannia*, with her staff and cap of Liberty, is well designed ;
she is crying, ' Am I thus protected ? '   A miniature figure is introduced, who is
endeavouring to arrest the sleeper's attention—' Hallo, neighbour ! what, are you
asleep ? '   This officious person is, it is believed, intended to represent ' *Sir
Grey Parole.*'[1]

   No date.   Bob Derry, of Newmarket.
   No date.   Luxury.

LUXURY.

[1] Lord North's Administration, which had the onus of conducting the American War, was daily
growing weaker and losing popularity ; it resigned in March of the year following, and the Rocking-
ham Ministry came into office.   The first condition of this more liberal Administration had obtained,
through the negotiations of Lord Shelburne, the consent of the King to ' peace with the Americans, and
the acknowledgment of their independence.'   In a later caricature by Gillray, which appeared on the
resignation of Lord North—*Banco to the Knave*, April 12, 1782—the figure of Sir Grey Cooper, one
of the Treasury Secretaries, is introduced, exclaiming, ' I want a new master.'   On this gentleman's
chair is the name ' *Sir Grey Parole*,' because, it is understood, he usually sat on the left of Lord North
on the Treasury Bench ; and when that statesman, who trusted to his memory for the principal points
elicited in the debates, had been overcome by the constitutional somnolency which was a favourite
subject of ridicule with the satirists, the Secretary aroused his chief, and supplied the deficiency of
notes by suggesting the thread of argument, or *parole*, as required.

February 1783. *Long Sermons and Long Stories are apt to lull the Senses.*
Published by W. Humphrey.

1783. *Amputation.* Republished by S. W. Fores, October 17, 1793.

AMPUTATION.

1783 (?). *The Rhedarium, for the Sale of all sorts of Carriages, by Gregory Gigg.*—The auctioneer is in his pulpit, employed in knocking down an assortment of vehicles to a small but sufficiently eccentric-looking audience. A gouty individual, propped on crutches, is making a bid for an antiquated kind of cabriolet, which the groom is trotting up for inspection ; around are curricles, travelling carriages, and a general assemblage of the machines on wheels representative of the past.

1783.   *The Discovery.*—A small political print, a parody on Shakespeare's
'Macbeth.' Lord North, who is the principal agent of the 'Witches' Incantation,'
is crying :—

Call Fiends and Spectres from the yawning deep.

BURKE
(*who is among the witches*).

Cast in your mite, each midnight hag ;
Fill the Protector's poisoned Bag.

MOTHER WILSON.

Here's old Nick's nose.

JEFFREY.

Here's Devil's dung.

DUNSTAN.

The wind of Boreas,
Belial's tongue,
A Traitor's heart.

SAM HOUSE.

And Gibbets' blocks.
But hold, ye hags, for here comes Fox.

Fox

(who has suddenly entered, and is standing in his ordinary declamatory attitude).

And set the ministers of Hell to work.

December 22, 1783. Great Cry and Little Wool. Published by Humphrey, Strand.—Somewhat in Sayer's style, the principal figures giving indications of

INTERIOR OF A CLOCKMAKER'S SHOP.

his manner. The personification of Evil, with his horns, hoofs, pointed claws, and forked tail, has a firm hold of Fox, and is shearing the 'Protector's' chest and clawing at his profuse locks. The India Bill, under the Evil One's arm, indicates the source of the satire. The surroundings are more especially in Rowlandson's free handling; the India House is in the background, and the members of the

East India Corporation are performing a gleeful dance around a memorable pile—the funeral pyre in effigy of their arch-enemy, treated as a fox roasting on a gibbet.

1783 (?). *The Times.*—This caricature represents the situation, from a popular point of view, at the period of the struggle for the Regency which occurred on the first illness of the King. According to Rowlandson's print, right is prevailing and everything is to be settled for the future happiness of the kingdom by the Prince of Wales's accession to the throne; as will be remembered, it was for a short period doubtful whether the King's health would ever be sufficiently restored to enable him to resume the control of the State.

The heir-apparent is shown as the virtuous prince we read of in fairy tales, endowed with all the graces both of mind and person. The Prince is supported, at the foot of the throne, by such protection as *Liberty* and *Justice* are placing at his disposal; his foot is on the first step, the *Voice of the People*; the other steps are *Public Safety, Patriotism,* and *Virtue*; the crown remains suspended over his head, his right hand is on his heart, and *Britannia* is leading him to his place, while she is waving back the party which opposed his assumption of an *ad interim* Regency. The symbolical *Ruler of the Waves* is declaring : ' I have long been deceived by hypocrisy, but have at last discovered an intention of sacrificing the rights of my people to satisfy a private ambition.' The Queen and her German friends, Madame Schwellenberg and others, are represented as disconcerted Furies, waving hissing snakes, and begirt with *Falsehood, Envy,* &c.

Queen Charlotte combined with Pitt to oppose, by every stratagem within their power, the assumption of the Regency by her eldest son. The Queen is brandishing the torch of *Rebellion*; Pitt is thrown into despair, and he is 'bidding a long farewell to all his greatness,' before his retirement from public life, as reasonably might have been his case, if the Prince's party had come into power. *Commerce,* allegorically represented as a fair female, is applauding the elevation of the Prince to the vacant throne, and a deputation from the Corporation of the City is expressing these encouraging sentiments through the Lord Mayor :— ' Whilst we mourn the occasion, we must feel ourselves happy in reflecting that we are blessed by a prince whose wisdom will protect our liberties, whose virtues will afford stability to our empire.'

1784.

POLITICAL CARICATURES.

A few examples of the caricatures published by Rowlandson during the famous contested election for Westminster in 1784 were included by the present writer in his account of the works of *James Gillray the Caricaturist*, as certain prints issued on this occasion were doubtless due to a combination on the part of the two caricaturists; however, those plates which bear special indications of Rowlandson's style were set down to their proper author.

January 1, 1784. *The Pit of Acheron, or the Birth of the Plagues of England.*—This plate bears the initials *F. N.*, 1784, in the right-hand corner, but there is no doubt, judging from the evidence of the style of execution, that the chief merit is due to Rowlandson. During the progress of the struggle, in 1784, plates innumerable were published anonymously, or with varying initials. Collectors who have devoted time and observation to the subject, and such well-qualified writers as the compiler of *The History of Caricature and Grotesque in Art, The Caricature History of the Georges, &c.*, seem agreed upon the proportion of prints which are due to the skill of our artist, whose handiwork is very prominent amongst the series of electioneering and political satires which appeared on the occasion of Fox's renowned campaign at the Westminster hustings, when the *Champion of the People* contended successfully against the second Ministerial candidate, Sir Cecil Wray, although the latter received all the assistance which Pitt, with the influence of the King as well, unscrupulously exercised as it was, could bring into play, legitimately or otherwise, to defeat the popular Whig chief, and to inflict the mortification of a lost election upon 'the party' and on their leader, who was at that time the pet aversion of George the Third and idol of the people.

It will be remembered that Rowlandson was by no means a party satirist; unlike Sayer, who was notoriously in the Ministerial pay, he lavished his satire on both sides alternately, utterly regardless of partisanship, and, often at the expense of consistency, we find his cartoons alternately espousing and ridiculing the same section, Whig or Tory, Ministerialist or Opposition, in plates of whimsically opposite tendencies, which not infrequently bear the same date.

The Pit of Acheron, if we may trust the satirist, is not situated at any considerable distance from Westminster; the precincts of that city appear through the smoke of the incantations which are carried on in the Pit. Three weird sisters, like the Witches in ' Macbeth,' are working the famous charm; a monstrous cauldron is supported by death's-heads and harpies ; the ingredients of the broth are various ; a crucifix, a rosary, *Deceit, Loans, Lotteries*, and *Pride*, together with a fox's head, cards, dice, daggers, and an executioner's axe, &c., form portions of the accessories employed in these uncanny rites. Three heads are rising from the flames—the good-natured face of Lord North, the spectacled and incisive outline of Burke, and Fox's 'gunpowder jowl,' which is drifting Westminsterwards. One hag, who is dropping *Rebellion* into the brew, is demanding, 'Well, sister, what hast thou got for the ingredients of our charm'd pot?' To this her fellow-witch, who is turning out certain mischievous ingredients which she has collected in her bag, is responding, ' A beast from Scotland called an Erskine, famous for duplicity, low art, and cunning ; the other a monster who'd spurn even at Charter's Rights.' Erskine is shot out of the bag, crying, ' I am like a Proteus, can turn to any shape, from a sailor to a lawyer, and always lean to the strongest side !' The other member, whose tail is that of a serpent, is singing, ' Over the water and over the lee, thro' hell I would follow my Charlie.'

January 4, 1784. *The Fall of Dagon, or Rare News for Leadenhall Street.* Published by William Humphrey, 227 Strand.

> And behold Dagon was fallen upon his face to the ground before the ark of the Lord, and the head of Dagon and both the palms of his hands were cut off upon the threshold.

The image of Dagon, which in this case is borrowed to typify the Coalition Ministers, has fallen from the overset *Broad Bottom* pedestal, and is in the posture described by the quotation ; its double-faced head wears the profiles of North and Fox. Tower Hill is represented in the background ; a scaffold is erected, and the public executioner is just bringing down his axe on the neck of a traitor—a delicate compliment to the heads of the late Administration. John Bull has changed the sign of his house to *The Axe*, and he is composedly enjoying his pipe under its shadow.

January 7, 1784. *The Loves of the Fox and the Badger, or the Coalition Wedding.* Published by W. Humphrey, 227 Strand.—Nine small compartments, very neatly executed upon one plate, are employed to portray the unpopular Coalition Ministry between Fox and North. (1) *The Fox beats the Badger in the Bear Garden.* The unwieldy form of the Badger (Lord North) lies, apparently asleep, on the floor of ' the House ;' the Fox, with his brush erect in triumph, is in command of the situation. (2) The *Fox* has been throwing dice on Hounslow

Heath, and he has a *dream*; the vision seems to indicate a choice between a prison or a traitor's head on a spike. (3) The *Badger*, with his riband, tucked up comfortably on a sofa, also indulges in a *dream*; the objects offered for his selection are seemingly the gallows or an executioner's block. (4) *Satan unites them*; the arch-fiend, in person, is joining their paws and pronouncing the magic spell, '*Necessity.*' (5) *They quarter their arms.* Their new escutcheon is symbolical; above a scroll marked '*Money*' the twin supporters are holding up a well-filled Treasury-bag, borne by John Bull, above whose head flourishes a pair of donkey's ears. (6) *The priest advertises the wedding.* The Devil, presiding at the pay-table, is enlisting the advocacy of the press, and three editors, in return for substantial considerations, are respectively promising: 'I'll *Chronicle* the Coalition,' 'We will *Post* them,' 'Harry will take both sides.' (7) *The Honeymoon or Eddystone Lighthouse*; the pair are making up a flaming beacon. (8) *The New Orator Henley, or the Churching.* The happy pair are now in their glory, seated on a throne in the '*Bear Garden,*' and surrounded at a respectful distance by the heads (stuck on poles) of the members of their new Parliament, and described as a '*Mopstick majority.*' The churching is proceeding; the original pastor is still present, and is prompting Orator Henley, whose tub stands on a block, labelled, '*Honest Jack Lee*;' the Orator is holding forth a parchment, and declaring, 'A charter is nothing but a piece of parchment with a great seal dangling to it;' to which pious deduction his clerk mounted on 'A Seat for Portsmouth,' is crying, '*Necessity. Amen.*' (9.) *The Wedding Dance and Song.* The pair, now led by the nose by their Satanic friend, are perforce compelled to execute a pretty lively dance, as their conductor wills. They are singing this appropriate *epithalamium*:—

> Come, we're all Rogues together;
>   The people must pay for the play:
> Then let us make Hay in fine weather,
>   And keep the cold winter away!

It seemed, at the beginning of 1784, as if Fox were completely master of the political situation, and indeed he approached much nearer to an absolute control of the Administration than he was ever destined to reach again during the lifetime of his great opponent. The bold manœuvres of Pitt, backed by the royal favour —the King and his friends condescending to dissimulation and subterfuge where honest policy would not suffice their turn—were crowned with unexpected success, and the Cromwell of the hour fell suddenly from his influential eminence. Up to the famous Westminster Election, Fox was paramount, both in Parliament and out of doors; for although Pitt was actually Crown-Minister, both he and his party were almost powerless when arrayed against the members of the ex-Coalition

Ministry, their opponents, led by Fox, and his strong following, who were the real masters of the situation ; thus we find a very characteristic portrait of the *Friend of Liberty and of the People* introduced, with an allusion to Cromwell.

January 19, 1784. *His Highness the Protector.*—The supplies are kept with a tight hand ; and Fox, taking advantage of his power, has put a huge padlock on the door of the Treasury, the key of which he seems determined to retain in his own keeping; a small dagger, held in the popular champion's right hand, indicates that he is prepared to stand on the defensive. His colleague Lord North, with his star round his neck, appears as a bulldog, who is supporting his leader in keeping the supplies inviolate.

The apprehensions of the Pittites (whose chances of retaining the reins of administration in defiance of an Opposition too strong for their policy, now seemed desperate), pictured forth the total subversion of Throne and State ; and it was under this influence that the King—whose stubborn will was strengthened by contradiction—indulged his threat of retiring to his German possessions, if he could not secure the return to office of his particular friends, whose hopes of recovering their lost control of the State were somewhat forlorn previous to the election ; while Fox, on the other hand, was endeavouring to force the King to accede to the measures he had introduced for the restriction of the royal prerogative. A very complete, but necessarily over-coloured, view of the anticipations of ' the party ' is thus pictured forth by Rowlandson.

January 23, 1784. *The Times, or a View of the Old House in Little Britain,—with Nobody going to Hanover.* Published by W. Humphrey, 227 Strand.—The Old House is seemingly in a bad way ; the foundation is *Public Credit* ; the Funds, represented as a grilled gate, are secured with a huge padlock ; the Royal Crown and Sceptre are placed on a block, and marked *for sale*; seated on another block, labelled *Protector*, sits the fox, guarding the Treasury ; round his waist is a chain secured to the *Coalition-pillar*, which is depicted as rather a twisted support. Lord North has perched his unwieldy person upon a turnstile, and is crying, indifferent to consequences, ' Give me my ease, and do as you please.' The upper part of the *Old House* is raising more cause for mistrust, since the old building is overweighted and crushed with a mass of *Taxes*, piled on the roof, the accumulated pressure of ' the accursed ten years' American war, fomented by the Opposition and misconducted by a timid Minister.' A light balcony has been thrown out, and therein things are proceeding in true show-man style. Burke is officiating as exhibitor, and blowing through a trumpet ; another statesman is doing the harlequin-business ; merry-andrew ' Sherry ' is flourishing his bottle and dancing round the corner of the balcony, on which is a placard announcing a wonderful combination of attractions : ' The Scarlet Woman of Babylon, the Devil, and the Pope.' ' The Man of the People ' is pictured as a feather,—on the flag of the party. The sign of the *Old House, Magna Charta*, has fallen to tatters, and the board is dropping down ; two lawyers, who appear at the window, are repairing the edifice according to their theories ; one of the props of the edifice, *the Lords*, is spared, but the other, *prerogative of the Crown*, is being lopped off by one of the legal magnates. The King is turning his back on the place, and starting in a state coach on his way to Hanover, deaf and blind to the prayers of some of his subjects, who are imploring the royal compassion on their knees. *The Sun of England's Glory* is setting in the distance, and an eye of light, piercing through the clouds, is warning the retiring monarch to 'Turn out these robbers and repair the House.'

February 3. *The Infant Hercules.*—Another caricature was directed against the ex-Coalition Ministers, representing them as twin serpents whose tails ('American War' and 'East India Bill') are entwined ; the heads of Fox and North appear on the shoulders of the monster. Pitt is figured as the infant Hercules ; he has taken his seat on the 'Shield of Chatham,' and has grasped the throats of the serpents, the tails of which are already lopped off. 'These,' he cries, 'were your Ministers.'

> Lord North, for twelve years, with his war and contracts,
> The people he nearly had laid on their backs ;
> Yet stoutly he swore he sure was a villain
> If e'er he had bettered his fortune a shilling.
>
> > Derry down, down ; down, derry down.
>
> Against him Charles Fox was a sure bitter foe,
> And cried that the empire he'd soon overthrow ;
> Before him all honour and conscience had fled ;
> And vowed that the axe it should cut off his head.
>
> > Derry down, down ; down, derry down.
>
> Edmund Burke, too, was in a mighty great rage,
> And declared Lord North the disgrace of the age ;
> His plans and his conduct he treated with scorn,
> And thought it a curse that he'd ever been born.
>
> > Derry down, down ; down, derry down.
>
> So hated he was, Fox and Burke they both swore,
> They infamous were if they enter'd his door ;
> But, prithee, good neighbour, now think on the end—
> Both Burke and Fox call him their very good friend !
>
> > Derry down, down ; down, derry down.
>
> Now Fox, North, and Burke, each one is a brother,
> So honest, they swear there is not such another ;
> No longer they tell us we're going to ruin,
> The people they *serve* in whatever they're doing.
>
> > Derry down, down ; down, derry down.

But Chatham, thank heaven ! has left us a son ;
When *he* takes the helm, we are sure not undone ;
The glory his father revived of the land,
And Britannia has taken Bill Pitt by the hand.
                    Derry down, down ; down, derry down.

BRITANNIA ROUSED, OR THE COALITION MONSTERS DESTROYED.

February 3, 1784. *Britannia Roused, or the Coalition Monsters Destroyed.*—
Britannia, the symbolical goddess, is fairly aroused, and her greatness and power
are effectually asserted on the persons of the late Ministers.   Her strong arm is
throttling the lethargic Lord North, and she has seized the body of Fox, whose
person she is dashing over her head, in a manner which threatens the extinction
of the popular idol.

The East India Company and its Corporation became, for a time, the chief bone of contention. Fox had gone out of office on the rejection of his provisions for the proper regulation of our Eastern Empire,[1] and Pitt, on coming into power, introduced his own motion with the same object. The view of the public on this point was expressed by Rowlandson's satirical summary of the situation.

February 7, 1784. Billy Lackbeard and Charley Blackbeard Playing at Football.—Fox and Pitt are both kicking with a will; the football is the old House of John Company, Leadenhall Street; the edifice is turned upside down, and the rival players are succeeding in keeping the vast concern suspended in the air between them. *Billy Lackbeard* has just turned from the study of Blackstone, —an allusion to the youth of the Prime Minister. It is interesting to remember that Pitt had resigned his ambitious mind seriously to the study and practice of the law, in case the progress of events should deprive him of Parliamentary significance. The commencement of his career was somewhat troublous, especially during the 'Regency struggle,' when the state of the King's health rendered the accession of the Prince of Wales probable, in which case the governing power would have remained in the hands of his more experienced rival. Behind Fox is a dicebox, and at his feet lie packs of playing-cards, indicating that gambling was the only resource left him, if he could not succeed in regaining office.

The influence which was being brought to bear, through illegitimate channels, to strengthen the party of Pitt's followers, who found themselves in such a minority as to be powerless at first, was recognised and commented on out of doors. The satirists freely exposed the Ministerial manœuvres; it was evident that the Court party, and especially the King, would count no sacrifice too great, could they but contrive to prevent the return of the members of the late Coalition Ministry to power, this hostility being intensified by the prejudices borne in the royal mind against Fox.

So strongly did this influence work that we find in *The Morning Post and Daily Advertiser* for February 10, 1784, the names of twenty-two members who had fallen under the spell of Ministerial beguilements. The advertisement is quite simple, and appears without either comment or explanation; the heading is pictorial, and represents a string of rats—such as might preface an ordinary rat-catcher's advertisement—it is placed above the name of Jack Robinson, in capital letters. Then follow, in three short columns, the names of the twenty-two Parliamentary rats who had gone over to the good pickings which the King

---

[1] 'General Johnson reminded Mr. Fox that he had undertaken to bring in another East India Bill. Mr. Fox did not deny that he had said he could have his Bill ready within a day or two—he said so still; but, as there was not, at present, any Government—any strong, and efficient, and constitutional Government—he thought it would be absurd to enter on the discussion of any measure; since, whatever it might be, it would not be carried into execution.'—*Morning Post*, Feb. 9, 1784.

was able to hold forth as a temptation in return for the allegiance of these renegades.

This curious advertisement is repeated in a satirical print which Rowlandson prepared on the same subject.

March 1, 1784. *The Apostate Jack Robinson, the Political Rat-catcher. N.B. Rats taken alive.*—Before the door of the Treasury, from whence the converter of rats draws his supply of baits and lures, travelling cautiously on all-fours and feeling his way, the political rat-catcher is slily augmenting his captures. Round the apostate Jack's waist hangs the *cestus of corruption*, in his

THE APOSTATE JACK ROBINSON, THE POLITICAL RAT-CATCHER.

pocket is a little aide-de-camp, who is made to cry, ' We'll ferret them out ! ' On his back is a double trap, baited with miniature coronets, places, &c. ; one or two rats have been secured in this ; golden pieces strew the floor, and with these the rats to be captured are playing and coquetting. A large bait of pension is held to the nose of one grave old veteran, probably intended for Edmund Burke, and the other rats are watching the bait with longing looks. A placard is pinned on the wall, ' Jack Robinson, Rat-catcher to Great Britain. Vermin preserved.' Under the heading of ' Rats of Note ' is given the very list of apostates as published in the *Morning Post,* beneath Jack Robinson's patronymic.

Second Title.

Thus when Renegado sees a Rat
In the traps in the morning taken,
With pleasure he goes Master Pitt to pat,
And swears he will have his bacon.

March 3, 1784. A Peep into Friar Bacon's Study.—A spectacle of conjuration, which discloses matters of some historical moment. In the centre of the picture stands the brazen head which is giving forth its oracles. King George the Third, who has thrown a conjuror's cloak over his star and riband, is holding out two divining-rods, and questioning the head—'What is this?' To this the magic bust is giving forth these oracle-like phrases : 'Time is, Time was, Time is past ;' while three luminous circles, each bordered with the word *Constitution,* help to illuminate the obscurity of the revelation. The first view of the Constitution, 'Time is past,' displays the King on his throne, with a radiance like the sun ; the other bodies of the State barely come within the charmed circle ; the Houses of Lords and Commons appear mere 'air balloons.' 'Time is' offers another view of the Constitution ; the King's circle has diminished, that of the House of Peers is increasing in magnitude and becoming bound up with the royal circle ; the House of Commons, without infringing on either, has arrived within the circumference of the Constitution ; and in the third view we find the three circles assimilated in size and working one within the other—the Constitution in its perfected form, in fact. Behind the King the members of the late Ministry are appearing at a door. Fox, North, and Burke are in the front rank ; they bid the monarch 'Beware!' The King's friends, led by an imp of Satan, or, perhaps, by the Devil in person, are finding their way down the back-stairs. Foremost is a figure bearing a lantern, which is throwing a light on the movements of the Opposition. Lord Temple, and other influential supporters of the Ministry, are making their entry on the scene, and crying, 'We must destroy this coalition,' 'A fig for the resolutions,' &c.

March 8, 1784. Master Billy's Procession to Grocers' Hall.—Pitt has, according to the picture, supplemented his Parliamentary tactics by flattering the citizens, and bidding for the Corporation influence. He is drawn going to *Grocers' Hall* in state to receive the freedom of the City in a gold box, which is carried at the head of the procession. Great enthusiasm prevails, as a liberal gentleman, in the uniform of a naval officer, is distributing handfuls of coin amongst the mob. Banners are carried in the procession with the party watchwords, '*Pitt and prerogative,*' and '*Youth is a most enormous crime.*' The car of Sir Watney, drawn by satyrs comes first ; then, in the middle, perched up in a triumphal car, and with a feather in his hat, comes Master Billy, drawn, of course, by *King's men.* Sir Barney follows, drawn by his admirers, and shouting, 'Pitt and plum-pudding for ever!' The show is passing the shop of 'Tommy Plume, grocer to his Majesty;' this worthy, who is crying, 'O what a charming youth!' is seen at his window, surrounded by shouting spectators.   At the sign of the *Lord Chatham* is gathered another party of sightseers; they are enthusiastically declaring that 'Master Pitt is very like his father!'

March 11, 1784.   *The Champion of the People.*—The sturdy figure of Fox, clad in somewhat theatrical armour, and protected by the *Shield of Truth*, is resolutely combating the overgrown *Hydra* of patronage, whose growing and unconstitutional power—it was hinted—would shortly destroy the liberty of the

MASTER BILLY'S PROCESSION TO GROCERS' HALL.

subject.   The monster, a compound of the Pittite party and its royal supporter, is hissing and spitting venom with all its various heads, *Tyranny, Assumed Prerogative, Despotism, Oppression, Secret Influence,* and *Scotch Politics*; while three heads have been already lopped off by the champion's sword, *Duplicity* and *Corruption* are laid in the dust.   The foreign Powers are represented in alliance, and dancing round the *Standard of Sedition.*   Natives, of the subject East Indian races, are kneeling and blessing their champion; and a compact array of *English and Irish supporters* is drawn up under the standard of '*Britannia and Universal Liberty.*'   Fox's followers are respectively declaring, 'While he protects us, we will support him;' and 'He gave us a free trade, and all we asked; he shall have our firm support!'

March 26, 1784. *The State Auction.*—This print illustrates the pass to which, as it was assumed, the Constitution was coming under the evil effects of the undue extension of the royal prerogative. The 'State Auction' is held, under high patronage, in the '*Commission warehouse; money advanced on all sorts of useless valuables, by Pitt and Co., Auctioneers. N.B. Licensed by Royal Autho- rity.*' Pitt, seated on his rostrum, under the royal arms, is knocking down 'State property' in the capacity of auctioneer. The first lot is, it seems, the most interesting one in the sale : 'The Rights of the People, in 558 volumes.' Pitt's friend Dundas is acting as sale porter. 'Show the lot this way, Harry,' cries the auctioneer. 'Agoing, agoing ; speak quick, or it's gone. Hold up the lot, ye Dund ass !' To which invitation the Scot, Dundas, who has been doing his best to help Master Pitt, responds, 'I can hould it na higher, sir !' Pitt is favouring the biddings of the 'Hereditary Virtuosi,' a compact knot of Peers and 'the King's friends ;' at their head stands Lord Chancellor Thurlow, who is disparaging the Opposition. 'Mind not the nonsensical biddings of those com- mon fellows.' The 'chosen representatives' of the people are standing by them- selves, apart from the bidders ; their backs are turned upon the entire proceedings, and they are apparently leaving the sale-room *en masse*, by way of protest, at the same time exclaiming, 'Adieu to Liberty !' 'Despair not !' and 'Now or never !' Fox alone is making a resolute stand ; he cries, 'I am determined to bid with spirit for lot 1—he shall pay dear for it that outbids me.' The lots are of general interest. Lot 2 is *Magna Charta* ; lot 3 is '*Obsolete Public Acts* ;' lot 4, the Sword of Justice ; lot 5, the Mace : lots 6 and 7, legal wigs and gowns, &c. The sale-clerk, recording the biddings on the parchments of 'sundry Acts,' is declaring gleefully, 'We shall get the supplies by this sale !'

March 29, 1784. *The Drum-Major of Sedition.*—The portrait of Major John Cartright, one of the most energetic and disinterested Reformers, is given under this title. The Major is firmly grasping a pole of Liberty in his right hand, and is holding forth in front of the hustings erected for the election, round which are gathered numerous voters and a crowd of others, who are being addressed from the platform. Admiral Lord Hood is introduced, shouting, 'Two faces under a Hood !' The speech made by the Drum-Major of Sedition has a strong ironical tendency. 'All gentlemen and other electors for Westminster who are ready and willing to surrender their rights and those of their fellow- citizens to secret influence, and the *Lords of the Bedchamber*, let them repair to the prerogative standard, lately erected at the Cannon Coffee House, where they shall be kindly received—until their services are no longer wanted. This, gentle- men, is the last time of asking, as we are determined to abolish the power of the House of Commons, and in future be governed by Prerogative, as they are in France and Turkey. Gentlemen, the ambition of the enemy is now evident.

Has he not, within these few days past, stole the Great Seal of England, while the Chancellor [1] was taking a bottle with a female favourite, as all great men do? I am informed, gentlemen, that the enemy now assumes Regal Authority, and, by virtue of the Great Seal (which he stole), is creating of peers and granting of pensions. A most shameful abuse, gentlemen, of that instrument. If you assist us to pull down the House of Commons, every person who hears me has a chance of becoming a great man, if he is happy enough to hit the fancy of Lord Bute and of Mr. Jenkinson. Huzza! God save the King!'

March 30, 1784. *Sir Cecil's Budget for Paying the National Debt.*—Sir Cecil Wray, in spite of his Ministerial friends, does not seem to have been a popular candidate after he had deserted the Liberal party; indeed, he became the mere puppet of the hour, the Ministerial struggles of the '*King's friends*' being not so much directed to bringing in their nominee, as to inflict the mortification of a defeat on Fox. Two unfortunate projects, which Sir Cecil Wray had originated, were perpetually used against him by his opponents; these were his proposals to abolish Chelsea Hospital and to tax maid-servants. In the print '*Sir Cecil's Budget for paying the National Debt*' has been accepted, and Chelsea Hospital is brought to the ground, involving in its destruction all the disabled veterans for whom the country was bound to provide. Sir Cecil is shown in the distance, exposed to very humiliating treatment; a pensioner, who has escaped the downfall of the Hospital, is whipping him forward with his crutch, while a group of female servants, with pails and brooms, are visiting on his person, the injustices they anticipated. 'Tax servant-maids, you brute, and starve poor old soldiers—a fine Member of Parliament!' While in office Fox had proposed a tax upon receipts, which was loudly cried down by his Tory opponents; it was now written of Wray:—

> For though he opposes the stamping of notes,
> 'Tis in order to tax all your petticoats;
> Then how can *a woman* solicit your votes
>   For Sir Cecil Wray?
>
> For had he to women been ever a friend,
> Nor by taxing *them* tried our old taxes to mend,
> Yet so *stingy* he is, that none can contend
>   For Sir Cecil Wray.
>
> The gallant Lord Hood to his country is dear;
> His voters, like Charlie's, make excellent cheer;
> But who has been able to taste *the small beer*
>   Of Sir Cecil Wray?

---

[1] Lord Thurlow, whose private life, if we may believe the caricaturists, was not of the purest.

Then come, ev'ry free, ev'ry generous soul,
That loves a fine girl and a full flowing bowl,
Come here in a body, and all of you poll
　　　　　'Gainst Sir Cecil Wray!

In vain all the arts of the Court are let loose,
The electors of Westminster never will choose
To run down a Fox, and set up a *goose*
　　　　　Like Sir Cecil Wray.

March 31, 1784. The Hanoverian Horse and the British Lion. A scene in a new play, lately acted in Westminster with distinguished applause. Act ii.,

THE HANOVERIAN HORSE AND BRITISH LION.

scene last.—The faithful Commons are still suffering from the aggressive tendencies of the White Horse of Hanover, which is trampling on '*Magna Charta*,' '*Bill of Rights*,' and '*Constitution*,' kicking, rearing, and driving the members of the 'faithful Commons' forth with his heels. The brute is neighing out '*Pre-ro-ro-ro-ro-rogative*;' while Pitt, a remarkably light jockey, is encouraging the excitement of the brute : 'Bravo ! go it again ; I love to ride a mettle steed. Send the vagabonds packing.' The sturdy person of Fox is safely astride the British Lion ; the royal beast has quitted his place in the army of England, leaving the notice, '*We shall resume our situation here at pleasure.—Leo Rex.*' He is keeping a watchful eye on the Hanoverian Horse, and protesting, ' If this horse is not tamed he will soon be absolute king of our forest.' Fox has come on the scene prepared to render efficient assistance ; he is provided with a bit and bridle, and a stout riding-whip, to tame and control the high-mettled Hanoverian steed. 'Prithee, Billy,' he is crying to Pitt, 'dismount before ye get a fall—and let some abler jockey take your seat!'

April 3, 1784. *The Two Patriotic Duchesses on their Canvass ; requesting the favour of an early poll.*—The zealous canvassers for 'the Champion of the people' are enlisting the sympathies of possible voters. Their mode of procedure is shown at a butcher's stall, according to the satirist's view of their patriotic exertions. The Duchess of Devonshire, wearing the Prince of Wales's plume in her hat, above an immense favour *for Fox*, has placed one arm round the waist of a young butcher, and, with her left hand, is pushing a well-filled purse into his pocket ; at the same time she is cementing the compact with a chaste kiss. Farther on is seen the Duchess of Portland, who is attempting to beguile another butcher's apprentice ; but she is less successful, probably because her personal attractions will not bear comparison with the graces of the winning Georgiana.

April 4, 1784. *The Incurable.*—Fox, in a strait-jacket, with straw disposed in his hair, is represented as mad beyond recovery ; he is singing in forlorn despair :—

> My lodging is on the cold ground, and very hard is my case,
> But that which grieves me most is the losing of my place.

Doctor Munro, the King's physician, in his court-dress, is examining the patient through his eyeglass, and attesting, 'As I have not the least hope of his recovery, let him be removed amongst the *Incurables.*' Below the print the following lines occur :—

> Dazzled with hope he could not see the cheat
> Of aiming with impatience to be great.
> With wild ambition in his heart, we find,
> Farewell content and quiet of his mind ;
> For glittering clouds he left the solid shore,
> And wonted happiness returns no more.

The poll was opened on April 1, and continued without intermission until May 17.

April 8, 1784. *The Rival Candidates.*—The three candidates who were contesting the 'great fight' for the representation of Westminster are represented according to their supposititious characteristics. Fox, with his hand on his heart, and his arm held out in a declamatory attitude, stands for *Demosthenes* ; Hood is introduced as *Themistocles* ; and Wray is less flatteringly served up in the character of *Judas Iscariot.* It must be remembered that '*the Knight of the Back-*

stairs' had been nominated for the previous Parliament by Fox, with whom he had shared the representation of Westminster, but Wray thought fit to desert to the Tories and oppose his political leader, forsaking his friends and his principles for the sake of promised Ministerial patronage.

April 10, 1784. *The Parody, or Mother Cole and Loader.* (See Foote's 'Minor,' page 29.)—The broad-spread figure of Lord North, with a capacious hood round his head, is parodied as the sanctimonious *Mother Cole*; a bottle of 'Constitution Cordial,' to sustain her sinking spirits, is placed by her side. Fox, as *Loader*, with his dicebox thrown to the ground, is listening, handkerchief in

RIVAL CANDIDATES.

hand, to *Old Moll's* lamentations. 'Ay, I am going, a-wasting, and a-wasting. What will become of the House when I am gone Heaven knows. No, when people are missed, then they are mourned. Sixteen years have I lived in St. Stephen's Chapel comfortably and creditably; and, tho' I say it, could have got bail any hour of the day! No knock-me-down doings in my House—a set of regular, sedate, sober customers—no rioters. Sixteen did I say? Ay, eighteen years have I paid *Scot* and *Lot*, and during the whole time nobody has said, "Mrs. North, why do you say so?"—unless twice that I was threatened with impeachment, and three times with a halter!' Fox is moved to respond, 'May

I lose deal, with an honour at bottom, if Old Moll does not bring tears in my eyes.'

April 12, 1784.   *The Devonshire, or most approved method of securing votes.*—The Duchess of Devonshire has taken to her arms the person of a fat and greasy butcher, whom she is favouring with a salute in the zeal of patriotism; another fair canvasser (possibly the Duchess of Gordon), rejoicing in proportions more expanded than those of the beautiful Georgiana, is seconding the proceeding; while, shouting 'Huzza, Fox for ever!' a lusty butcher, with his tray under his arm, is cheering and hurrying up to share his possible reward.

THE DEVONSHIRE, OR MOST APPROVED MANNER OF SECURING VOTES.

April 12, 1784.   *The Westminster Watchman.*—Charles James Fox is represented as the trusty guardian, standing unmoved and at his ease amidst the 'Ministerial thunderbolts;' he wears on his head the *cap of Liberty*, and his support is the *staff of 'uprightness;'* his dog, the faithful companion of his rounds, is *Vigilance*; and his lamp, which sheds its light on everything around, is *Truth*. A pair of superannuated and useless watchmen are shuffling off—Hood 'for Greenwich,' and Wray 'for Chelsea.'

The plate is inscribed to Fox's supporters—' To the independent Electors of Westminster this print of their staunch old watchman, the guardian of their rights and privileges, is dedicated by a grateful Elector.   N.B. *Beware of counterfeits, as the Greenwich and Chelsea Watchmen are upon the look-out!*'

April 12, 1784.   *The Poll.*—The scene is still the polling-booth, Covent Garden ; the canvassers, committees, and mobs are giving their entire attention to the performance carried on for their entertainment between the fair rival advocates, who are balanced at either end of a plank laid across a stone post. The Duchess of Devonshire is sent up into the air ; her end of the poll is carried over Fox's head ; '*Duke and no Duke, a play,*' is placarded above her.

The opposite extreme of *the poll* is weighed down effectually by the weight of a corpulent lady, described in these election squibs as *Madame Blubber*, the

THE WESTMINSTER WATCHMAN.

Honourable Mrs. Hobart (Lady Buckinghamshire), of *Pic-Nic* notoriety.   Hood is cheating by kneeling down and clinging to the skirts of the Ministerial championess, he lends an additional weight to his side of the balance ; behind them is Wray, defying his opponent.   Over the heads of this group flutters a placard, ' *The Rival Candidates, a farce.*'

The Opposition party dwelt mainly upon Sir Cecil Wray's renegade want of principle in turning against his leader, Fox.   His liberality was severely called in question, and there was a satirical story of his keeping nothing in his cellar but small beer.   The old symbolism of slavery and France—wooden shoes—was revived for the occasion ; much stress was laid on the extensive polling of soldiers for Hood and Wray at the beginning of the election, when on one occasion two hundred and eighty of the Guards were sent in a body to give their votes as householders. This, Horace Walpole observes, *was* legal, 'but which my father (Sir Robert) in the most quiet sessions would not have dared to do.' All dependents on the Court were commanded to vote on the same side as the soldiers. The following placard, which was put out early in the canvass, is a fair example of the courtesies with which the Ministerial manœuvres were acknowledged by their opponents :—

'All *Horse Guards, Grenadier Guards, Foot Guards*, and *Black Guards* that

LORDS OF THE BEDCHAMBER.

have not polled for the destruction of *Chelsea Hospital* and the *tax on maid-servants* are desired to meet at the *Gutter Hole*, opposite the Horse Guards, where they will have a full bumper of *knock-me-down* and plenty of *soapsuds*, before they go to the poll for Sir Cecil Wray or cat.

'N.B. Those that have no shoes or stockings may come without, there *being a quantity of wooden shoes provided for them.'*

April 14, 1784. *Lords of the Bedchamber.*—The Duchess of Devonshire, in her morning gown and cap, is favouring two privileged visitors with a cup of tea in her boudoir.

The Duchess is attending to the tea urn ; above her head hangs the Reynolds portrait of her liege lord. Sam House, in his publican's jacket, is seated, stirring a cup of tea, on the sofa beside Fox, who is familiarly patting his friend and indefatigable ally on his bald head by way of friendly encouragement.

Sam House was one of the most popular figures of his day, and he came into especial prominence, as we have seen, during the Fox's canvass. He is said to have kept open house during the Westminster Election at his own expense, and was honoured by entertaining the great Whig nobility. He was an indefatigable supporter of Fox, and his assistance was, as may be supposed, of no trifling moment to the cause.

> See brave Sammy House, he's as still as a mouse,
>   And does canvass with prudence so clever ;
> See what shoals with him flocks to poll for brave Fox ;
>   Give thanks to Sam House, boys, for ever, for ever, for ever !
>   Give thanks to Sam House, boys, for ever !
>
> Brave bald-headed Sam, all must own, is the man
>   Who does canvass for brave Fox so clever ;
> His aversion, I say, is to *small beer and Wray !*
>   May his bald head be honour'd for ever, for ever, for ever !
>   May his bald head be honour'd for ever !

April 20, 1784. *The Covent Garden Nightmare.*—This subject is a parody on a painting by Fuseli. Rowlandson has taken the idea and fitted it to the purpose of an electioneering squib. Fox is represented stretched in an uneasy slumber, nightmare-ridden. An unearthly incubus oppresses his body and haunts his repose ; a corpulent imp is crouched on his hams pressing the great man's chest, while the head and shoulders of a supernatural mare are shown making their appearance through the bed-curtains. On a table by Fox's side are shown the dice and dicebox, the satirist's inevitable resource when dealing with the frailties of the ' man of the people,' who, it must be confessed, had in his day committed sufficient excesses in the way of gambling ; a vice he absolutely renounced in after-life, but not before it had ruined his purse, imperilled his reputation, and proved a fruitful source of recrimination in the mouths of his enemies.

April 22, 1784. *Madame Blubber on her Canvass.*—We find the Duchess of Devonshire and the Honourable Mrs. Hobart—the most prominent of the fair electioneering agents who threw the power of their personal charms into the political arena—scandalised alternately ; her Grace the fascinating Georgiana was represented as a softening influence by which the votes of the butchers were secured ; we find Pitt's fair champion, *Madame Blubber* (Lady Buckinghamshire), endeavouring to cajole the same classes in identical fashion. The lady, who, it must be acknowledged, was somewhat stout, is trying her hand amongst the rough sellers of meat; she is holding out a purse as a bait, saying, ' Hood and Wray, my dear butcher;' the butcher's dogs are regarding the canvasser suspiciously; their master, at ease in his armchair, without moving his pipe from his mouth, is puffing out bluntly, ' I'm engaged to the Duchess!' ' Pho! give her a glass,' suggests the butcher's friend, who is drinking punch with him from a bowl on which is the figure of a fox, the chopping-block serving as their table. *Madame Blubber* has a train of appreciative butcher's men in her wake; one is declaring that she is ' the fattest cattle he ever handled!' a drover is observing, ' Lincolnshire, dammee!' and a lad with a tray pronounces her a ' plumper!'

THE COURT CANVASS OF MADAME BLUBBER.

To the Tune of ' The First Time at the Looking-glass.'

A certain lady I won't name
  Must take an active part, sir,
To show that DEVON's beauteous dame
  Should not engage each heart, sir.
She canvass'd all, both great and small,
  And thunder'd at each door, sir;
She rummaged every shop and stall—
  The Duchess was still before her.

Sam Marrowbones had shut up shop,
  And just had lit his pipe, sir,
When in the lady needs must pop,
  Exceeding plump and ripe, sir.
' Good zounds,' says he, ' how late you be!
  For votes you come to bore me;
But let us feel are you beef or veal -
  The Duchess has been before you.'

A fishmonger she next address'd
  With many a soothing tale, sir,
And for his vote most warmly press'd,
  But all would not prevail, sir.
' The finest cod's-head sure in town,
  Of oysters send two score too.'
' Extremely, madame, like your own—
  The Duchess has been before you.'

A grocer next, to make amends,
  The dame with smiles accosted:
' You grocers all to PITT are friends,'
  Of her connection boasted!

' For plums and raisins, ma'am,' said he,
  ' I'm willing for to score you:
In politics we shan't agree—
  The Duchess was here before you.'

Sly Obadiah was at prayers
  With many pious folk, sir;
His pretty maid on the *back-stairs*
  She found, and thus bespoke her:
' This riband take, all interest make;
  Your master will adore you,
For Hood and Wray pray kiss and pray.'
  ' Now, Duchess, I'm once before you.'

A stable-keeper to engage
  She then her talents tried, sir;
He fell into a monstrous rage,
  And all her smiles defied, sir.
' Are you a full moon or Court balloon?
  Get out, you female Tory;
Tho' Courts prevail I'll not turn tail—
  The Duchess was here before you.'

However courtiers take offence,
  And cits and prudes may join, sir,
Beauty will ever influence
  The free and generous mind, sir.
Fair DEVON, like the rising sun,
  Proceeds in her full glory,
Whilst madame's duller orb must own
  The Duchess moves before her.

April 22, 1784. Wit's Last Stake, or the Cobbling Voter and Abject Canvassers. —Every stratagem which could secure the popular voice for either candidate was

freely put in practice ; but while the Pittites resorted to threats and force, Fox
and his adherents relied mainly on persuasion and good humour.   *Wit's last
Stake* shows the exertions made in the canvassing department.   Fox is in the
centre of the picture, giving his knee as a seat for his fair advocate, the Duchess
of Devonshire, who is resorting to a subterfuge commonly employed as a pre-
caution against actions for bribery at elections, by the stall of a cobbler, who
happens to be a voter : her Grace has discovered that her shoe requires a stitch ;
the cobbler, with his tongue thrust out at the side of his mouth, is working at
the supposititious repairs with pantomimic energy ; meanwhile his wife is receiving

WIT'S LAST STAKE, OR THE COBBLING VOTER AND ABJECT CANVASSERS.

in payment for the job a handful of sovereigns from her Grace's purse.   The
scene takes place in Peter Street, and the cobbler's board announces, ' *Shoes made
and mended by Bob Stichett, cobbler to her Grace the tramping Duchess.*' A fox's
brush is being waved overhead out of the first-floor window by a supporter,
who has been provided with pipe and pot at the Whig expense.   Fox is giving
his right hand to another voter, a tattered and stupified-looking scavenger, to
whom Sam House is also administering comfort in the shape of a pot of porter.
Among other followers of the ' Man of the People' Rowlandson has introduced a
chimney-sweeper and his boy.

Fox's canvass was enlivened by the rough humours of the various classes whose favour he required to enlist ; his own good-nature was equal to every emergency. One blunt tradesman, whose vote he solicited, replied, ' Mr. Fox, I cannot give you my support ; I admire your abilities, but d—— your principles !' To which the candidate smartly responded, ' My friend, I applaud you for your sincerity, but d—— your manners ! '

In another instance Fox's application to a saddler in the Haymarket for his interest was met with a practical joke—the man produced a *halter*, with which he expressed his willingness to oblige the statesman. Said Fox, ' I return you thanks, my friend, for your intended present; but I should be sorry to deprive you of it, as I presume it must be a *family piece.*'

April 22, 1784. King's Place, or a View of Monsieur Reynard's Best Friends. —Another gathering of Fox's fair adherents. The Prince of Wales, surrounded by fashionably-dressed nymphs, wearing one of Fox's favours below his plume, and with a fox-brush in his hand, is speaking in his friend's favour : ' He supported my cause !' A pleasingly-drawn female—probably intended to suggest Mrs. Robinson, the *Perdita* of the Prince's early love-story—is asserting, ' He is as generous as a prince, and a prince should not be limited !' A group of Lady Abbesses are also saying ' good things ' in their candidate's favour : ' He introduced his Royal Highness to my house !' ' I have taken many a pound of his money. Fox for ever. Huzza !'

April 22, 1784. Political Affection.—The Duchess of Devonshire is still slandered by the satirists ; according to the present unjust version her ' political affection ' is causing her to neglect her infant, the heir of the Cavendishes, to lavish her tenderness on a hybrid prodigy, a fox dressed up in the robes of an infant. By the side of a neglected cradle is seen a cat, forgetting her kitten to lick the face of a poodle.

This coarse hostility to the Duchess was probably popular in its day, as we find a long series of allusions conceived in the same spirit.

April 23, 1784. Reynard put to his Shifts.—The artists always took care to draw the Duchess of Devonshire as handsome and graceful as possible, even when their satires were most reckless and unsparing ; while they descended to outrage the lady's fair reputation by innuendoes which were utterly unwarrantable. The beauteous Devon is standing in the middle of the picture, filled, as usual, with animation for the Whig cause ; she is offering the shelter of her protection to a panting and frightened fox, whose pursuers are following fast on his brush. A huntsman is encouraging his hounds : ' Tally O ! my good dogs !' ' No Coalition,' ' No India Bill,' and other party utterances are put into the mouths of the pack.

April 29, 1784. The Case is Altered.—The election has gone against Sir Cecil Wray, and he has to turn elsewhere ; Fox, it will be remembered, in addition to his return for Westminster, was elected for Kirkwall (Scotland), and in the print he is shown driving his discomfited opponent to Lincoln.

The Ministerial candidate is not travelling with a flourish of trumpets, but is smuggled off in the 'Lincolnshire caravan for paupers;' the knight is reflecting over his reverses: 'I always was a poor dog, but now I am worse than ever.' Fox is acting as charioteer; he is saying, over his shoulder, 'I will drive you to Lincoln, where you may superintend the *small beer and brickdust.*'

Lord Hood, who has come upon this conveyance suddenly, is moved with pity for his late colleague; he cries, 'Alas! poor Wray.'

THE CASE IS ALTERED.

As the increasing number of votes gave fresh spirit to the Foxites, satirical squibs, and songs exulting over Wray's possible downfall and his future fate, were plentifully put forth by the wits of the Opposition. The following specimen will illustrate the nature of some of the placards which were scattered about towards the close of the election :—

Oh! help Judas, lest he fall into the PITT *of ingratitude ! ! !*

The prayers of all bad Christians, Heathens, Infidels, and Devil's agents are most earnestly requested for their dear friend,
JUDAS ISCARIOT, *Knight of the Back-stairs,*

April 29, 1784. *Madame Blubber's Last Shift, or the Ærostatic Dilly.*— This caricature pictures the hustings at Covent Garden, with a distant view of Richmond Hill. *Madame Blubber* has patriotically contrived to convert herself into an air-balloon, for the collection and conveyance of *outlying voters*, crying, 'This may save him,' an allusion to some incident in the canvass. A brace of voters have been secured in the parachute of this novel Ærostatic Dilly; these favoured gentlemen are enabled to take a flying view from their elevation of the hustings below. Wray and Hood are anxiously looking forward to the arrival of their balloon. According to the inscription given on the plate, in the artist's hand, the print represents 'The grand political Balloon, launched at Richmond Park, on the — March, 1784, and discharged by secret influence with great effect in Covent Garden at 12 o'clock on the same day.

'As it may be necessary to explain to the public upon what principles a body was conveyed twelve miles with so great velocity, it must be understood that the lady, though ponderous, being of a volatile disposition, out of decency sewed up her petticoats, which, being filled with gas, immediately raised her to a considerable height in the atmosphere, and, by the attraction of secret influence, was conveyed to her desired object—the support of Hood and Wray and the Constitution—and descended happily to the hustings with two outlying and dependent voters.'

Tho' in every street	Eight trips in this way,
All the voters you meet	For Hood and for Wray,
The Duchess knows best how to court them,	I'll make poll sixteen in one day.
Yet for outlying votes,	Dear Wray, don't despair,
In my petticoats,	My supplies by the air
I've found out a way to transport them!	Shall recover our losses on Monday!

April 30, 1784. *Procession to the Hustings after a Successful Canvass.* (No. 14.)—Fox's supporters, a body of highly respectable householders, wearing huge Fox favours in their hats, are walking in procession to the hustings, cheered by the mob, and preceded by a marrowbone-and-cleaver accompaniment. At the head of the train marches the famous Duchess, with a somewhat novel standard; the other fair canvassers, whose portraits occur in the previous prints, are following in the footsteps of their illustrious leader; one is carrying a placard, '*Fox and the Rights of the Commons;*' another has a mob-cap and an apron, borne fluttering on a pole, with the words, '*No tax on Maid-servants.*' Behind follows a monster key—*the key of the back-stairs*—carried to deride the defeated candidate and the Court influence which had vainly been brought into play for his support.

May 1, 1784.   *Every Man has his Hobby-horse.*—The successful candidate
is chaired in a novel and agreeable fashion ; his noble supporter, the Duchess of
Devonshire, has taken him 'pick-a-back,' and, with staff and scrip, is bearing
the victor on his triumphant progress ; she is pausing at the door of *Mungo's
Hotel, dealer in British spirits*, and soliciting the hospitality of the proprietor,
a black man : 'For the good of the Constitution, give me a glass of gin !'

Various bacchanalian revels are proceeding around, on the strength of Fox's
triumphant return ; the mob are huzzaing around two monster standards, which
are topped by the cap of Liberty, and inscribed, '*Rights of the Commons. No*

PROCESSION TO THE HUSTINGS AFTER A SUCCESSFUL CANVASS.

prerogative,' '*Fox and Liberty all over the world.*' An ensign is introduced, as appropriate to the occasion, significantly figuring forth a pair of executioner's axes,
bound with a wreath of laurel.

May 6, 1784.   *Wisdom Led by Virtue and Prudence to the Temple of Fame.*
—This print is ascribed to Rowlandson, and in various points it offers a close
resemblance to his style of execution.   *Wisdom* in the present case is personified
by the successful candidate for Westminster ; the Duchess of Devonshire and
Lady Duncannon, wearing *Fox* cockades in their head-dresses, are represented
as *Virtue* and *Prudence.*   The former lady is also carrying a fox's-brush ; she is
crying :—

> Let Envy rail and Disappointment rage,
> Still Fox shall prove the wonder of the age !

To which Lady Duncannon is adding :—

> Triumph and Fame shall every step attend
> His king's best subject and his country's friend !

Britannia is seated, in an attitude of expectation, at the portal of the *Temple of Fame;* she is bidding her patriotic son 'welcome to her arms.' Sir Cecil Wray, represented as a disappointed Fury, is seen in the distance ; he is soliloquising :—

> Now, by the ground that I am banish'd from,
> Well could I curse away a winter's night.

May 11, 1784. A Coat of Arms. Dedicated to the Newly-created Earl of Lonsdale.—There is no publisher's name to the plate, which offers a fanciful and by no means flattering design for an appropriate coat of arms and supporters, gratuitously presented for the use of Sir James Lowther, *the newly-created Earl of Lonsdale.* Two ragged and semi-clad Volunteers, the one minus his *culottes,* the other without shoes, with the initials W.M. on their crossbelts, form the supporters of a shield, above which figures the earl's coronet. There are six quarterings, each filled in with paper scrolls : 'False Musters,' 'False Certificates for Volunteer Companies,' 'False Returns,' 'Retention of Clothing,' 'Contract for building a man-of-war (cancelled and money returned),' and 'Retention of Bounty.' The motto of this suggestive escutcheon is, '*Who doubts it ?* '

Pitt had obtained his first seat in Parliament (1781) through the influence of Sir James Lowther, described by 'Junius' as 'the contemptuous tyrant of the North.' In 1784, when the King and his Prime Minister deemed it prudent to reward the adherents of their party, and at the same time strengthen the Court influence, by creating a new batch of peers, Pitt repaid his obligation to Lowther (the Duke of Rutland, Pitt's fellow-student at Cambridge, had enlisted Lowther's influence in his favour), by raising him to the House of Peers, under the title of the Earl of Lonsdale, thus overleaping the two inferior stages of the peerage. It might be supposed that this reward would have been commensurate with his pretensions, but Earl Lonsdale's name appearing at the bottom of the list of the newly-created earls published in the *Gazette,* he threatened to reject the earldom, and means were with difficulty found to appease his irritation.

The wits of the 'Rolliad' made the most of the circumstance : 'Hints from Dr. Prettyman to the Premier's Porter.—Let Lord Lonsdale have *my Lord* and *your Lordship* repeated in his ear as often as possible ; the apartment hung with garter blue is proper for his reception.'

My lords, my lords, a whisper I desire—
Dame Liberty grows stronger—some feet higher ;
   She will not be bamboozled as of late—
Aristocrate et la Lanterne
Are very often cheek by jowl, we learn,
   Within a certain neigh'b'ring bustling State :
I think your lordships and your graces
Would not much like to dangle with wry faces.

         PETER PINDAR'S *Ode to Lord Lonsdale.*

May 11, 1784. *The Westminster Mendicant.*—The rejected candidate for Westminster has been sent forth a wanderer. The figure of Sir Cecil Wray is represented as a blind beggar ; he is resting his head and shoulders on a long staff ; under his left arm is held a *Subscription Scrutiny Box*, in allusion to the vexatious scrutiny set on foot by his party ; and he holds a spaniel by a string ; a second begging-box is attached to the dog's collar. The mendicant is issuing a doleful appeal to the public :—

     Pity the weak and needy, pray ;
     Oh ! pity me ; I've lost the day.

Above the head of the blind man's dog is the following :—

     See here the dog, of all his kind
     The fittest for a beggar blind :
     The beast can bark, or growl as hog ;
     His name is Churchill,[1]—oh, the dog !

Below the title is engraved :—

     Ye Christians. charitable, good, and civil,
     Pray something give to this poor wandering devil.
     By men cast out, perhaps by God forgiven,
     Then may one Judas find a road to heaven.

The Irish chairmen—who had played such a conspicuous part in the early riots, where they routed the sailor-mob brought up by Hood to intimidate Fox's voters—had a fling at their discomfited enemy in a ' new ' ballad, ' *Paddy's Farewell to Sir Cecil* ' :—

     Sir Cecil be aisy, I won't be unshivil ;
      Now the Man of the Paple is chose in your stead :
     From swate Covent Garden you're flung to the Divil ;
      By Jasus, Sir Cecil, you've bodder'd your head.
         Fa-ra-lal, &c.

---

[1] In several of the caricatures directed against Wray the discomfited candidate is invoking the assistance of Churchill, who was, however, apparently unable to offer his patron any effectual aid.

> To be sure, much avail to you all your fine spaiches ;
>   'Tis nought but palaver, my honey, my dear ;
> While all Charlie's voters stick to him like laiches,
>   A friend to our liberties and our *small beer.*
>   Fa-ra-lal, &c.
>
> Ah, now ! pray let no jontleman prissent take this ill ;
>   By my truth, Pat shall nivir use unshivil werds ;
> But my varse sure must praise, which the name of Sir Cecil
>   Hands down to oblivion's latest records.
>   Fa-ra-lal, &c.
>
> If myshelf with the tongue of a prophet is gifted,
>   Oh ! I sees in a twinkling the knight's latter ind !
> Tow'rds the verge of his life div'lish high he'll be lifted,
>   And after his death, never fear, he'll discind.
>   Fa-ra-lal, &c.

May 18, 1784. The Westminster Deserter Drumm'd out of the Regiment.—
This caricature brings the election scenes in Covent Garden to an end ; the Court
party is defeated, and the Man of the People has triumphed.   Sir Cecil Wray is
handcuffed as a deserter, and is being drummed away from the hustings ; he is
exclaiming, ' Help, Churchill! Jackson, help! or I am lost for ever!'   It is worthy
of record that Sir Cecil Wray's figure disappears from the caricatures until
1791, when we meet him again with a barrel of small-beer under his arm, assisting
the members of the Opposition (whose ranks he rejoined) to carry out the ' *hopes
of the party,*' as set forth in a famous pictorial satire by Gillray (July 14, 1791).

In the *Westminster Deserter* ' honest Sam House ' is drumming away with
a will, and Wray is obliged to run the gauntlet of a line of exasperated Chelsea
Pensioners, who are expressing a wish that '*all public deserters may feel public
resentment ;*' a body of maid-servants are marching in the rear, with shovels,
mops, and brooms, brought out in readinesss to sweep forth their antagonist.
The electioneering mob is divided between hooting the ' Deserter' and applauding the success of the ' Champion of the People,' who is planting the standard of
Britannia and manfully acknowledging his gratitude to his supporters : ' Friends
and fellow-citizens, I cannot find words to express my feelings to you upon this
victory.'

Fox's difficulties, as regarded his seat for Westminster and the hostilities of
his opponents, the Court party, did not end with the election : the Ministerialists
had from the first declared their intention of demanding a scrutiny if Fox succeeded, because it was known that, under the circumstances, this would be a long,
tedious, and expensive affair.   The returning officer acted partially, and upon
Sir Cecil Wray's application for a scrutiny declined to make his return pending

THE WESTMINSTER DESERTER DRUMM'D OUT OF THE REGIMENT.

the investigation. Fox had secured a seat for Kirkwall, so that he was not hindered from taking his place in the House; and after some months' delay, and a great deal of fighting on both sides, the High Bailiff, Thomas Corbett, was ordered to duly return Charles James Fox as Member for Westminster, as is set forth in a caricature by Rowlandson (*see* March 1, 1785). Fox subsequently thought proper to bring an action against the High Bailiff, and that functionary in return for his perfidy was cast in heavy damages—a fresh triumph for the Opposition.

May 18, 1784. *Secret Influence Directing the New Parliament.*—King George III. is complacently seated on his throne; once more reassured on the subject of his Parliament, he is remarking, with self-congratulation, 'I trust we have got such a Parliament as we wanted.' *Secret Influence* is represented on one side by a huge serpent whispering secret counsel to the monarch. The head of the reptile is that of Lord Temple. Lord Thurlow, on the other side of the throne, still wearing his Chancellor's wig, his body represented as that of a monstrous bird of prey, is observing, with his usual overbearing roughness, 'Damn the Commons! the Lords shall rule,' while the Scotch influence, in the person of Lord Bute, partially concealed behind the throne, is echoing, 'Very gude, very gude; damn the Commons!'

Britannia, unconscious of her danger, is calmly reposing, with her elbow resting on her shield, while Fox, who has recognised the dangers which are threatening the liberty of the people, is trying to rouse the slumberer, and crying, 'Thieves, thieves! Zounds, awake, madam, or you'll have your throat cut!'

May 18, 1784. *Preceptor and Pupil.*

> Not Satan to the ear of Eve
> Did e'er such pious counsel give.—MILTON.

The Prince of Wales, wearing his plumed hat, has fallen asleep; Fox, now represented as a toad, with a fox's brush for a tail—who has crept from the concealment of some neighbouring sedges—is insinuating pernicious counsel into the ear of the slumberer—

> Abjure thy country and thy parents, and I will give thee dominion over
> Many powers. Better to rule in hell than serve on earth.

May 18, 1784. *The Departure.*—This affecting scene is taking place outside the Prince of Wales's residence; his Royal Highness is watching the departure of his friend from the window. Fox is mounted on a patient ass, ready to ride the road to 'Coventry;' the High Bailiff, having unlawfully refused to make his return until the conclusion of the scrutiny which Sir Cecil Wray thought proper to instigate, the caricaturist hints that, for the time, the Whig leader will be 'left out in the cold' until the question of his return is finally settled.   Fox has accordingly rolled up his India Bill, and is taking a doleful farewell of his fair champions, the Duchess of Devonshire and Lady Ducannon, on either side of his steed ; the sorrowing ladies are grasping his hand and crying—

> Farewell, my Charley !—let no fears assail.
> Ah, sister, sister, must he, then, depart ?
> To lose poor Reynard almost breaks my heart.

SECRET INFLUENCE DIRECTING THE NEW PARLIAMENT.

Fox is observing, before his departure—

> If that a Scrutiny at last takes place,
> I can't tell how 'twill be, and please your Grace !

Burke is standing, equipped as a postilion, in readiness to drive off his ally, with a *plan of economy* under his arm.

May 25, 1784. *Liberty and Fame Introducing Female Patriotism to Britannia.*

> She smiles—
> Infused with a fortitude from heaven.
>
> SHAKESPEARE'S *Tempest.*

This print has nothing of the caricature about it, excepting, perhaps, the unusual spirit, lightness, and ease of execution. All the figures are graceful and elegant, and the attitudes leave nothing to be desired. Britannia is on her throne, the British lion is at her feet, and the ocean, with her ships riding triumphant, is extending as far as can be seen; the figures of *Liberty* and *Fame*, with their respective attributes, are tripping up to the throne, leading the beautiful Georgiana forward to receive the laurels of victory.

May 20, 1784. For the Benefit of the Champion. A catch, to be performed at the New Theatre, Covent Garden. For admission apply to the Duchess. N.B. Gratis to those who wear large tails.

FOR THE BENEFIT OF THE CHAMPION.

The 'catch' is performed by the Duchess of Devonshire, Fox, and Lord North; the grief expressed by the singers is, of course, apocryphal. The Duchess is leading; she wears a Fox favour in her hat, which is further garnished with a fox's brush; she is pointing to a tombstone topped with the death's head and crossbones, and inscribed, 'Here lies poor Cecil Ray.' 'Look, neighbours, look! Here lies poor Cecil Wray.' 'Dead and turned to clay,' sings Fox; to which Lord North adds, 'What! old Cecil Wray?' The sharp profile of Burke is thrust through the door. The pictures hanging round the room are appropriate to the subject: a committee of foxes are wondering over 'The Fox who has lost his tail;' 'The Fox and the Crow,' in which sly Reynard is represented as gazing longingly at the cheese held in the crow's beak; 'Fox and the Grapes,' and 'Fox and Goose.'

May 28, 1784. *The Petitioning Candidate for Westminster.*—Designed according to a note on the plate, by Lord James Manners, and executed by Rowlandson. As we stated in an earlier caricature, due precautions were employed that Fox should not be left without a place in the newly-constituted Parliament, and accordingly in the present print—nearly the last of the series put forth on the Westminster Election for 1784—Fox, with a fox's head and brush, completely dressed in a suit of tartan, is speeding along, on a Highland pony, away from Kirkwall (for which he took his seat) back to London, flourishing his plaid, and crying, 'From the heath-covered mountains of Scotia I come.'

We can now take leave of the caricatures called forth on the Westminster Election and continue our review of the remainder of the satirical prints issued by Rowlandson in the course of 1784.

November 2, 1784. *The Minister's Ass.* Vide *Gazetteer*, November 11, 1784. Published by S. W. Fores, 3 Piccadilly.—Three mounted figures are shown crossing Wimbledon Common; one gentleman's donkey is speeding along briskly; a gallant lady, mounted on a grey horse, is riding between the two cavaliers and their donkeys; she is giving a friendly cut with her whip at the animal bestridden by her left-hand neighbour—the minister's ass, in fact, which is refusing to gallop forward; the rider is wearing his blue riband. A figure in the rear is endeavouring to reduce the refractory beast to reason with a scientifically administered kick.

December 10, 1784. *Anticipation of an intended Exhibition, with an excellent new ballad to be sung by a High Character, to the tune of ' The Vicar and Moses.'* Mark Lane, delin. and fecit. Published by T. Harris, High Street, Marylebone. —This caricature sets forth by anticipation the fate of Christopher Atkinson, M. P., who was sentenced on November 27, 1784, and pilloried November 25, 1785. A print by Gillray (August 12, 1782) gives a view of the trial under the title of ' *The Victualling Committee Framing a Report.*' Peter Pindar also makes a poetical allusion to the circumstances. Christopher Atkinson, M.P. for Heydon, Yorkshire, was convicted of peculation in his semi-official capacity as corn-factor to the Victualling Board. He was finally tried at the King's Bench for perjury, found guilty, and expelled from the House of Commons.

In Rowlandson's view of the novel situation of the contractor the pillory is raised on the Corn Exchange, and the criminal is standing with his head and hands enclosed in a board, with two dwarf corn-sheaves on either side; the Sheriffs, with a numerous crowd of citizens, are attending the exhibition, which Atkinson does not find to his taste. The sentiments of the pilloried contractor are expounded in a ballad :—

Here stand I, poor soul,
With my head in a hole,
To be gazed at by all passers by ;
And what's this about,
This racket and rout,
But for swearing a mercantile lie !

They say that for gain
I've a rogue been in grain
But what is all that to the point ?
If all were so serv'd
Who, like me, have deserv'd,
The State would be soon out of joint.

Many agents, I fear,
Would have their heads here,
And, like me, be expos'd to detractors ;
What would you do then,
For Parliament men,
Should any of them be contractors ?

For my part I rejoice,
And with loud, grateful voice
Proclaim it to all my beholders ;
Notwithstanding your scoff,
I think I'm well off,
That my head is still left on my shoulders.

I know it full well,
And for once truth will tell,
Tho' my speech in this d—d place may falter :
Not a session goes by
But much less rogues than I
Their last contract make with a halter.

But as I am quitting
I think it is fitting
My future pursuits you should know :
When I leave the King's Bench
I will live with the French ;
To the devil my country may go.

1784. *John Stockdale, the Bookselling Blacksmith, one of the King's New Friends.* (See *Intrepid Magazine.*)—Old Stockdale, the somewhat notorious publisher of his day, who, like the hero of the last picture, had the honour of standing in the pillory, is shown at his forge, surrounded by hammers and horseshoes, and with a tethered jackass waiting his attentions, as soon as the *Bookselling Blacksmith* shall have completed the work he has in hand, the somewhat incongruous occupation of hammering out folio volumes on an anvil.

January 24, 1784. *A Sketch from Nature.* Published by J. R. Smith, 83 Oxford Street.—This plate is apparently scarce, since the only impression the writer has seen is one in the French National Collection of Engravings, Paris, where the admirer of Rowlandson's works will be gratified to discover a very fair gathering of caricatures by this master, the collection containing certain scarce subjects which it is difficult to find elsewhere, besides several proofs of rare plates. The prints throughout are in capital preservation ; in several instances an impression from a rare plate, and a coloured print from the same, are mounted side by side.

A Sketch from Nature, which is the first and perhaps the best print of the Paris series, is rendered, like most of the plates published by J. R. Smith, exceptionally interesting from the care and delicacy bestowed on the engraving, and the success with which the tender expressions, which Rowlandson knew so well how to throw into the faces of his female beauties, are preserved and transferred to the copper. The subject is engraved in stipple, and, as a print after Rowlandson, it exhibits unusual quality and finish. The subject is somewhat hazardous : a situation borrowed from that inexhaustible epic the *Rake's Progress,* presenting all the license of debauchery, but expressed without coarseness. A mixed party of nymphs and roysterers are performing bacchanalian orgies ; the ' Lady Abbess ' has succumbed to her potations, and is slumbering heavily in her armchair. Punch and wine are flowing indiscriminately ; a poodle has come in for the contents of a punch-glass, which is overturned, and a man in tipsy wantonness is upsetting a punch-bowl over the dog's head. The arms of a sweetly pretty Bacchante are entwined round the neck of the maudlin reveller. Beside the well-filled table sits a youthful military ' blood ; ' another nymph, whose adolescent charms are liberally displayed, is seated on the knee of this son of Mars. The young lady is evidently disposed to be frolicsome, since she is flourishing in the air a full-bottomed wig, which she has snatched from the head of a corpulent Silenus, in whom age has failed to bring sober reason or to correct frivolity ; this ancient buck is deservedly getting his face scratched and clawed in an amorous struggle with a handsome maiden, dressed in a hat and feathers, who is forcibly repelling the advances of the elderly rake.

1784. *English Curiosity, or the Foreigner Stared out of Countenance.*—From this social caricature it seems that some distinguished foreigner was visiting this country in 1784, whose general appearance was exciting more public attention

than would be considered polite. The foreigner is dressed in a gay military
uniform, and has gone to enjoy himself at the theatre; but the eyes of the
audience do little else but stare at his uniform. The identity of this bird of
passage is not very positive at this date. The plate, as a whole, is as characteristic and well-drawn an example of Rowlandson's etchings as can be found;
the countenances of the spectators are capitally filled in, the various types of

COUNSELLOR AND CLIENT.

theatre-goers are hit off with spirit, and the female faces and figures are
rendered with remarkable sweetness.

1784. *Counsellor and Client.*—A simple citizen has waited on his lawyer
with a document; the client is seated, very ill at ease; we can see that he is
the person who will suffer; his face expresses perplexity and suspense. The
counsellor is, on the contrary, very much at his ease, and is looking over the

document confided to him, with a sly and satisfied expression, evidently seeing his way to some 'excellent practice.'

May 4, 1784. *La Politesse Française, or the English Ladies' Petition to His Excellency the Mushroom Ambassador.* Published by H. Humphrey, Bond Street.—The representative of Louis XVI. is all bows and smirks, lace ruffles and cravat, sword, bagwig, and shoe-buckles; he has turned his face away from a bevy of fair English beauties, bejewelled, prodigiously feathered, and wearing long court trains; the ambassador is obdurate to the entreaties of his petitioners. ' Parbleu, mesdames, *vous n'y viendrez pas.*'

> With clasped hands and bended knees,
> They humbly sought the Count to please,
> And begged admission to his house.
> Not that for him they cared a louse,
> But wished within his walls to shine,
> And show those charms they think divine.
> His Ex. beheld these belles unmov'd—
> His back their impudence reproved.

July 24, 1784. *1784, or the Fashions of the Day.* H. Repton inv., T. Rowlandson fecit.—The Park, with its mixed crowd of fashionable promenaders and pleasure-seekers, has afforded the designer ample scope for the delineation of both grotesque and graceful figures, modishly apparelled. In 1784, while the older generation still clung to the garments characteristic of the earlier Georges, the younger branches rushed into all the latest innovations—costumes which are generally received as distinctive of the end of the last and the beginning of the present century. Thus to the observer of the picturesque the fashions of 1784 offered the external habits of two distinct epochs. Among other features, indicative of the introduction of novelties, the artist has represented the parasol, or more properly the umbrella, then an object likely to occasion remark, as its general use was just coming into fashion.

August 8, 1784. *The Vicar and Moses.* Published by H. Humphrey, 18 New Bond Street.—A pictorial heading, in Rowlandson's characteristic style, to the famous old song of ' *The Vicar and Moses,*' by G. A. Stevens. The Vicar has been dragged unwillingly from his ale-cup, by his clerk, to assist at the burial of a child; the family mourners are waiting in the churchyard, as shown in the picture; Moses, the clerk, has put on his bands and found the parson's place in his book, and he is lighting the erratic footsteps of his patron with a broken candle placed in a horn lantern; as to the rotund dignitary of the Church, he is reeling along reluctantly; he wears his cassock and bands, as was the daily fashion at one time, and his hat is thrust well over his full-bottomed wig, which is somewhat awry; in one hand he retains his faithful pipe, and his tobacco-box is held in the other. The verses, which are tolerably well known, offer a whimsical description of how the Vicar, who happened to be *non si ipse* (*i.e.* 'the parson was tipsy'), having been disturbed at his meditations over a pot of ale, was informed that he was required to read the burial service over the body of one of his flock; the pastor felt strongly inclined to remain where he was, and proposed to postpone the ceremonial.

Then Moses reply'd :
'Sir, the parish will chide
For keeping them out in cold weather.'
'Then, Moses,' quoth he,
'Go and tell 'em from me
I'll bury them warm all together !'

'But, sir, it rains hard ;
Pray have some regard.'
'Regard ! ay, 'tis that makes me stay,
For no corpse, young or old,
In rain can catch cold ;
But faith, Moses, you and I may !'

Moses begg'd he'd be gone,
Saying, 'Sir, the rain's done ;
Arise, and I'll lend you my hand.'
'It's hard,' quoth the Vicar,
'To leave thus my liquor—
To go when I'm sure I can't stand.'

At length, tho' so troubled,
To the churchyard he hobbled,
Lamenting the length of the way.
Then 'Moses,' said he,
'Were I a Bishop, d'ye see,
I need neither walk, preach, or pray !'

The whole composition is more humorous than reverential, but it indicates the taste of the period, according to the last lines :—

'And thus we have carried the farce on :
The taste of the times
Will relish our rhymes,
When the ridicule runs on a parson.'

November 1, 1784. *New-Invented Elastic Breeches.* Designed by Nixon. Etched by Rowlandson. Published by W. Humphrey.

November 8, 1784. *Money-Lenders.*—A young nobleman is receiving the visits of certain usurers. One Hebrew gentleman, the principal, or 'capitalist,' is dressed with a certain attention to the fashion of the day, which proves that he is by no means an insignificant member of the money-lending fraternity. A deed or bond, the security on which the young spendthrift is expecting an advance, is being duly examined by a more miserly-looking Shylock—'a little Jew-broker,' in fact. As to the borrower, it is clearly indicated that he is quite at his ease in the transaction; it seems evident that whatever money he may raise (regardless of the sacrifices to which he submits in obtaining it) will be quickly thrown to the winds, and 'the dose will have to be repeated as before' until his resources are exhausted.

September 25, 1784. *Bookseller and Author.*—A characteristic drawing, in Rowlandson's best recognised style, bearing the name of Henry Wigstead as inventor, published by J. R. Smith. The persons of the publisher and author

present the marked and conventional extreme contrasts which the two spheres of
life were supposed to suggest—the one gross and prosperous, the other meagre
and miserable.   The scene of the interview may be assumed to be the back-shop
of the bookseller ; it is fitted around with shelves lined with books.   The trader
is stout and solid ; his spectacles are thrust up on his forehead, his pen is behind
his ear, and his hands are held beneath his coat-tails, in a self-assertive attitude,
implying well-to-do pomposity.

Wigstead, whose name is associated with authorship (although his professional position as a magistrate exempted him from the sufferings of a struggling

MONEY-LENDERS.

literary hack), has painted the professional gentleman in no flattering colours ;
the man of letters is wretchedly lean in person, and abjectly subservient in
manner to the trafficker who is buying his ideas ; his hat is held respectfully under
his arm, and his manuscript, which he is endeavouring to recommend to his
patron, is in his hand.   One of the bookseller's clients, a respectable Church
dignitary, who is looking through the library, with great owl-like horn spectacles
on his reverend nose, is present at the interview, and is regarding the poor
literary hack with an air of inflated superiority.

1784. *London, Made and Sold by Broderip and Wilkinson, 13 Haymarket.*—A plate for a trade advertisement, introducing the figures Apollo, Daphne, &c., drawn and etched with considerable grace and spirit. Among Rowlandson's renderings of the works of other men we may mention a sketch after T. Mortimer, etched by T. R., 1784. This study portrays the back view of an Italian or Spanish peasant woman, playing the flute.

1784. *The Historian Animating the Mind of a Young Painter.*—This subject represents the painting-room of a young artist, furnished with a drawing-table, an easel, a couple of chairs, a settee, and a bust, while a few sketches of figure subjects are pinned on the walls. The painter, who is a well-favoured youth, is seated with his back to his easel, on which is a classic study in course of execution. His palette is on the ground, and he is holding a crayon in one hand, and a folio, which is serving as his drawing-board, in the other, ready to dash down his conceptions as soon as his imagination is sufficiently inspired by the effects of his friend's readings. The learned historian, whose hat and gloves are at his feet, wears a full-bottomed wig and large round rimmed spectacles. His appearance is somewhat clerical, and he is evidently filled with enthusiasm for the subject on which he is declaiming, book in hand. The limner's wife, in a morning dress, is seated by the fire, amusing her infant son, who is standing on her knee in a nude state, the infant being probably impressed into the service of the fine arts as the model for a cherubim. No publisher's name is given on this plate, which is delicately rendered.

1784. The print of a group of three figures ; in the centre is a pretty simple maiden, whose face wears an artless expression, such as Rowlandson excelled in delineating, seated in an armchair, and grasping the hand of a youth, who has opened a vein in his arm, while another maid, in a morning cap and dress, is lending her assistance. The name of R. Batty has been given in MS. as 'sculpsit.' Both the drawing of the figures and the style of the etching are strongly indicative of Rowlandson's handiwork.

1784. *Rest from Labour on Sunny Days.* Designed and etched by T. Rowlandson.—A peasant is sitting in an easy attitude perched upon the ruins of a temple, playing the flute ; a pretty peasant maid is leaning beside him, with her dog at her feet. Etching and aquatinta.

1784. *Billingsgate.*—All the humours of this famous academy of slang are displayed. The fish-selling fags have their baskets planted in rows in front of the landing-place. The hampers of the porters and the masts of ships are seen beyond. The Billingsgate hawkers are offering their fish vociferously for sale, getting drunk, and generally behaving in the disorderly style attributed to them. A gouty customer, evidently an epicure, who has come to select a turbot for his table, is seized unceremoniously by his wig and coat-tails and tripped up in the exertions of a fishfag aided by her urchin to arrest the passer, and call attention to certain goods she is holding out for inspection.

1784.   *Miller's Waggon.*

1784.   *A Timber Waggon.*   Published by E. Jackson, 14 Marylebone Street, Golden Square.

1784.   *Country Cart Horses.*   ,,

1784.   *Dray Horses.   Draymen and Maltsters.*   ,,

1784.   *Higglers' Carts.*   ,,

1784.   *A Post-chaise.*   ,,

1784.   *A Cabriolet.*   ,,

Rowlandson's Imitations of Modern Drawings.   Folio.   1784–88.

F. Wheatley	A Coast Scene, fishermen, fisherwomen, &c.
,,	A Companion ,,
Gainsborough	A Sketch ; trees, cottages, &c.
,,	Cattle, river side.
F. Wheatley	A Fair.
Bartolozzi	A Pair of Cupids.
Barret and Gilpin	Mares and Foals.
,,	Cattle.
Gainsborough	Landscape sketch.
Mortimer	A Storm at Sea.
Gainsborough	Cows.
Zucchi	Harmony. Two nymphs singing, another playing a lyre.
Mortimer	The Philosopher.
Barret	Ruins, and a Park.
Mortimer	A Study.
Barret	Ruins, &c.
Gainsborough	A Cottage, &c.
,,	An Open Landscape.
Mortimer	Scene in ' The Tempest,' from Shakespeare. Republished 1801. J. P. Thompson, Soho.
G. Barret	Lake Scene.
Saurey Gilpin, R.A.	Horses.
G. Holmes	The Sage and his Pupil.
Michael Angelo	Leda and the Swan.
G. B. Cipriani	Sleeping Venus and Love.

1785.

January 7, 1785. The Fall of Achilles.—It was evident from the first that the chances of the members of the late Coalition Ministry returning to power were weakened in the new Parliament, and it soon became obvious that, even as an Opposition, their party was without either weight or influence. Fox in looking round the recently elected House found himself surrounded by country gentlemen, Pitt's following, whose faces were unfamiliar to him. Pitt was firmly settled, the unquestioned master of the situation. It is the youthful Premier who has come forth, in the character of Paris it is presumed, with a bow and a quiver of arrows, the better to shoot Whiggism on the wing; he has just sent a bolt straight into the flying Opposition; the arrow has lodged in the heel of the mighty Fox, who is represented double the size of his triumphant adversary.

> Thus do I strive with heart and hand
> To drive sedition from the land!

The Whig chief is disabled, in spite of his armour, and he is lying at the mercy of the enemy.

> There is nought but a place or a pension will ease
> The strain that I've got in my tendon Achilles.

The turns of North and Burke seem likely to follow; the prostrate form of Fox is tripping up his friend's retreat; North's sword and buckler seem of no service to him; he is crying in perplexity—

> This curs'd eternal Coalition
> Has brought us to a rare condition.

Burke is trying to make good his escape.

> Before thy arrows, Pitt, I fly;
> I d—n that word *prolixity*.

January 24, 1785. Mock-Turtle. Published by S. W. Fores.

March 2, 1785. The Golden Apple, or the Modern Paris. Published by J. Phillips, Piccadilly.—The Prince of Wales is represented in the enviable position of Paris, deciding between the respective attractions of the three Duchesses, Rutland, Devonshire, and Gordon, the rival luminaries whose brilliancy dazzled society, and whose beauties graced the Court of the Prince of Wales. A gallant songster of the day has perpetuated the charms of this dazzling trio in the following lines, appropriate to Rowlandson's agreeably-expressed cartoon :—

Come, Paris, leave your hills and dells ;
  You'll scorn your dowdy goddesses,
If once you see our English belles,
  For all their gowns and bodices.

Here's Juno Devon, all sublime ;
  Minerva Gordon's wit and eyes ;
Sweet Rutland, Venus in her prime :
  You'll die before you give the prize.

March, 1785. *The Admiring Jew.* (Etched 1784.) Published by T. Smith, 6 Wardour Street, Soho.—An old Jew, who is evidently a man of substance, but awkward, ugly, and ill-bred, is twiddling his fingers and thumbs and pouring

THE DEFEAT OF THE HIGH AND MIGHTY BALISSIMO CORBETTINO AND HIS FAMED CECILIAN FORCES, ON THE PLAINS OF ST. MARTIN, ON THURSDAY, THE 3RD DAY OF FEBRUARY, 1785, BY THE CHAMPION OF THE PEOPLE AND HIS CHOSEN BAND,

After a smart skirmish, which lasted a considerable time, in which many men were lost on both sides. But their great ally, at length losing ground, desertions took place, and notwithstanding their vast superiority in numbers and weight of metal at the first onset, this increased apace, altho' often rallied by the ablest man in command, till at length the forces gave way in all quarters and they were totally overthrown. This print is dedicated to the Electors of the City and Liberty of Westminster, who have so nobly stood forth and supported their champion upon this trying occasion, by

AN INDEPENDENT ELECTOR.

soft persuasions into the ear of a handsome and well-dressed lady, who is apparently a person of fashion.

March 7, 1785. *Defeat of the high and mighty Balissimo Corbettino and his famed Cecilian Forces*, on the plains of St. Martin, on Thursday, the 3rd day of February, 1785, by the Champion of the People and his Chosen Band.—Fox, at the head of his party, whose arms are legal weapons, such as *Law, Eloquence, Perseverance,* and *Truth*, is routing and putting to flight the combined forces of his opponents, led by Sir Cecil Wray and the High Bailiff, Corbett.   At the Westminster Election it will be remembered, Fox had gained the victory over his antagonists ; and the Scrutiny, moved for by Sir Cecil Wray, being concluded, the proper return was directed to be made ; and, as we have mentioned, the successful candidate brought an action and recovered heavy damages against the High Bailiff (who had made himself the tool of the Ministerialists).   Fox is protected by his buckler, inscribed ' Majority 38 ;' he is sweeping away the ' Cecilian forces' with the sword of ' Justice ; ' a laurel crown is placed on his brow by a celestial messenger, who is also charged with the decision of the Court—' It is ordered that Thomas Corbett, Esq., do immediately return.'   Fox is declaring, ' The wrath of my indignation is kindled, and I will pursue them with a mighty hand and outstretched arm until justice is done to those who have so nobly supported me.'   Sir Cecil Wray's shield of *Ingratitude* is no defence, and his weapon has snapped short ; he is crying in despair, ' My knees wax feeble, and I sink beneath the weight of my own apostacy !'   The High Bailiff is thrown down ; he confesses, ' My conscience is now at peace ; ' an ally is crying, ' Help, help ! our chief is fallen.   O conscience, support me !'   Corbett's lawyers have turned their backs on the cause of the client : ' Nor law, nor conscience, nor the aid of potent Ministers, can e'er support the contest 'gainst such a chief !'   ' Our support is gone and we are fallen into a Pitt ; yea, even into a deep Pitt ! '

March 27, 1785.   *The surprising Irish Giant of St. James's Street.*   ' *The surprising Irish Colossus, King of the Giants, measuring eight feet ten inches ; noble Order of St. Patrick, &c.*'—The figure of the famous Irish Giant is drawn with skill and originality by Rowlandson.   The person of this colossus, although gigantic, is graceful, and his proportions are such that the spectators who surround him are apparently dwarfed to half the usual standard.   The giant's right hand is resting on the head of a military commander, the tallest man in the room, who, while standing bolt upright, does not reach much above the waistband of the Irish mammoth.   Another officer, while standing on tiptoe on a chair, is still a full third short of the height of the prodigy.   The ladies are struck with wonder at such gigantic limbs, and one of them is comparing her tiny foot with the large and well-proportioned member of the giant ; while some of the audience are investing themselves in his top-boots.   The skeleton of this remarkable person is preserved in the Hunterian Museum, College of Surgeons.   ' Mr. Lynn related to-day that the surgeons, in spite of the vigilance of the Irish Giant's friends, obtained the body for dissection.   They made several attempts to bury it in the Thames, or to convey it to Dover. But the body-hunters were too keen for all they aimed at ; and after keeping the corpse fourteen days they sold it to John Hunter for 100*l.* The heart was preserved, and was very large. . . . The stature of the skeleton measures eight feet two inches.'—' MS. Journal of Captain E. Thompson, R.N.' (*Cornhill Magazine*, May 1868.)

April 12, 1785. *The Wonderful Pig.* Published S. W. Fores, 3 Piccadilly. —The artist has given a grotesque representation of the learned hog, spelling his words before a delighted audience ; the individual characteristics of the spectators are capitally diversified ; their actions and groupings are, as usual, marked with vivacity. According to a placard over the mantel-piece of the hall in which this intellectual entertainment was offered we learn : ' The surprising pig, well versed in all languages, perfect arithmetician, mathematician, and composer of music.'

May 27, 1784. Verses published 1785. *The Waterfall, or an Error in Judgment.* Published by Wallis, Ludgate Hill.

> The coxcomb, student, and attorney vile,
> Jew bail and tipstaff, added to the pile ;
> All rush in terror, or from gain or sport,
> And headlong tumble down the steps of Court.

The incident on which this print was founded occurred, according to the magazines, &c., in 1785 ; and, as numerous illustrations appeared at the time, it seems that the artist has put the date of the year wrongly. *The Waterfall* represents the Court of King's Bench in an uproar. The members of the Bench and the Bar, counsellors, attorneys, and clients, suitors and witnesses, are taking to flight indiscriminately, trampling over one another in their precipitate retreat, tumbling down the stairs of Westminster Hall, while robes, wigs, and briefs are lost in the struggle.

Rowlandson's illustration of this scene of consternation is used as the heading for a song to the tune of ' *The Roast Beef of Old England.*'

According to the song the recitative relates :—

> 'Twas at the Hall of Rufus, Woodfall tells,
> Where brawling, sneering Discord ever dwells ;
> Where honest men despond, where tricking thrives,
> And Law against plain Reason ever strives,
> A sudden fright seiz'd all the black-rob'd race,
> And inward horror mark'd each hideous face.
>
> A maiden appear'd on the roof of the Hall,
> And, washing a window, her water let fall,
> Which frighten'd the mighty, the short, and the tall.

Oh, the clean maid of Westminster!
And, oh, the clean Westminster maid!

Her trickling of water made such a sad noise,
It threw the Court into a horrid surprise ;
All feeling alike—alike they all rise.
    Oh, the stout hearts of the lawyers!
    And, oh, the lawyers' stout hearts!

They thought that the roof was all coming down ;
And knowing how much they deserv'd Heaven's frown,
All hasten'd, with loss of wig, band, and gown,
    Out of the Court of Westminster,
    And out of Westminster Court.

The Serjeants were wounded in limbs, nose, and eye ;
Like leaves of the Sibyls their briefs scattered lie-
A sight very pleasant to all standers-by.
    Oh, the torn robes of the Benchers!
    And, oh, the Benchers' torn robes!

For Ruspini's Styptic some half-dozen run ;
But the crowd stayed to laugh and enjoy the high fun ;
All hop'd the long thread of the Law was now spun.
    Oh, what a joy to Old England!
    And, oh, to Old England what joy !

But Heaven, to punish this half-ruin'd nation,
Permitted again each to take his old station,
The people to gall with the deepest vexation.
    Oh, what a grief to Old England !
    And, oh, to Old England what grief !

1785. *Comfort in the Gout.* (See July 1, 1802.) Republished 1802.

June 28, 1785. Vauxhall Gardens. Engraved by R. Pollard, aquatinted by F. Jukes. Published by John Raphael Smith.—It will be remembered by the reader that, in the earlier part of this sketch of *Rowlandson's Life, Works, and Times,* special reference is made by the artist's friend and the frequent companion of his adventures, Henry Angelo, to their expeditions to Vauxhall Gardens to study character. The varied humours discovered at this popular resort employed Rowlandson's pencil frequently, as we are told in the *Memoirs.* It seems, on the authority of those who were most intimate with the caricaturist, and who were also thoroughly well acquainted with the leading examples of his skill, that *Vauxhall Gardens* may be accepted as his *chef d'œuvre* in the general estimation. We can compare it to his drawing of the *Tuileries Gardens,* which is even fuller of diversified groups.

In the famous picture of *Vauxhall* we have the Rotunda, a marvellous construction, built from the designs of an inventive carpenter, a modest genius, who obtained a certain celebrity for his ingenuity.[1] 'The gilded scallop-shell,' described by Thackeray in the Vauxhall episode which is introduced in the opening of *Vanity Fair*, was, as it appeared within the writer's recollection, a melancholy, tawdry substitute for the vanished splendours as noted in Rowlandson's drawing. A portly lady, standing in front of the orchestra, is warbling ballads to the highly genteel company, the patrons of the entertainment; of the performers we are able to offer but scanty particulars.

COMFORT IN THE GOUT.

[1] 'The present Orchestra (1809) was first exhibited to the public on the 2nd June, 1735. It was built by an ingenious mechanic, named Maidman, a common carpenter employed in the gardens, from a design of his own. The composition with which it is ornamented was also his own discovery. This elegant orchestra is calculated to contain fifty performers, with an organ, &c. It is illuminated by about four thousand lamps, and presents an object of unparalleled brilliance. The same ingenious artisan erected the rotunda, which is seventy feet in diameter, and represents a magnificent pavilion. Within it is placed another orchestra, where the musical part of the entertainment is performed in unfavourable weather. Adjoining the saloon, with its *scagliola* columns, and its paintings by Hayman, is a supper room, one hundred feet long and forty feet wide, with a double row of columns. On the walls are represented paintings of rural scenery, which answer to the intercolumniations. At the end of the room was the statue of Handel, in white marble, and in the character of Orpheus singing to his

The figure of the fair vocalist is evidently intended for that of Mrs. Weichsel, a Vauxhall favourite, already mentioned as the mother of the great Mrs. Billington, the pride of English operatic celebrities. It was at Mrs. Weichsel's benefit, which Rowlandson attended at 'the little theatre in the Haymarket,' that our artist produced a sketch of this musical family. To return to Vauxhall. Angelo and other informants supply us with a hint or two of the company. Daniel Arrowsmith was engaged as one of the principal singers, 'where Mrs. Kennedy and that capital bass, Sedgwick, entertained the public for several seasons.' Joe Vernon, of Drury Lane Theatre, is mentioned among the performers. Barthelemon was leader of the band; Fisher played the hautboy; and Mr. Hook was conductor and composer.

To describe the visitors: the most conspicuous figures, which occupy the centre of the picture, and are exciting the admiring regards of the frequenters of Vauxhall scattered around them, are understood to be intended for the fascinating Duchess of Devonshire and her sister, Lady Duncannon. Among the 'freaks of folly' recorded by our invaluable authority Angelo he mentions having frequently 'seen many of the nobility, particularly the Duchess of Devonshire, &c. (the '&c.' expressing a whole crowd of fashionable notorieties), with a large party, supping in the rooms facing the orchestra, French horns playing to them all the time.'

Captain Topham, the macaroni-scribbler of fashionable intelligence and genteel scandalmonger to *The World*, a newspaper of which he was conjointly proprietor, editor, and principal contributor, is standing upright as a post, dressed in a smart uniform, and quizzing the fair through his glass. A stout old Commander, stranded on shore, with only one eye and one leg left from his naval glories, is planted, lost in admiration, on the Duchess's right. This gallant veteran is understood to represent Admiral Paisley, the reputed original, according to the caricaturist, who has drawn his portrait more than once, of '*The Tough Old Commodore*'—

> Why, the bullets and the gout
> Have so knocked his hull about,
> That he'll never like the sea any more!

A clerical person over the shoulder of Lady Duncannon is a free render-

---

lyre; but it is now removed behind the orchestra in the garden. This fine piece of sculpture first introduced the abilities of Roubiliac to the notice of the public. It was begun and completed in the place of which it was the ornament, while the noble subject and the superior artist were enjoying the friendly and protecting hospitality of Mr. Jonathan Tyers, who purchased the place in 1730, and opened it with an attractive entertainment which he called a *Ridotto al Fresco*.

'The grove, principal entrance, and other parts of the gardens are furnished with a number of small pavilions, ornamented with paintings, chiefly by Hogarth and Hayman: each containing a table and seats, to which the company retire to partake of refreshments.'—*Microcosm of London.*

ing, it is hinted, of Bate Dudley, who was the hero of a somewhat notorious Vauxhall adventure. By the side of the reverend sable-clad editor of the *Morning Post* stands a handsome figure, dressed in full Highland costume, with a veritable claymore under his arm, of which the bearer was reported to well know the use ; this gentleman's person is reported to be introduced as a compliment to another editor, James Perry, of the *Morning Chronicle*, who was, Angelo relates, very expert with the Highland broadsword, its exercise being 'his favourite diversion ; ' he might be frequently met at masquerades and places of entertainment, dressed in the costume of a Highlander, with a party of Scotch lassies, dancing Scotch reels. For variety of steps, Highland flings, &c., he was particularly noted ; crowds collected round him.'

Another conspicuous group introduces the Prince of Wales, afterwards George the Fourth, then a sweet youth, whose persuasions were supposed to be irresistible, and ' whose smile was victory ; ' he is represented whispering soft flatteries in the ear of a not unwilling fair, whose right hand is held captive under the arm of a gentleman, presumably her better half. This tender situation is reported to indicate a well-known episode in the career of the Heir Apparent, which, although somewhat threadbare, still retains an air of romance. ' Prince Florizel,' wearing his brilliant star on his breast, is addressing himself covertly to the most conspicuous figure of the party, the captivating Mrs. Robinson by general acceptation, the graceful *Perdita*, in connection with whom, as the artist has drawn him, the Prince is said to have

> Gazed on the fair
> Who caused his care,
> And sigh'd and look'd, and sigh'd again.

The lady is coyly trifling with a trinket suspended by a chain round her shapely throat, possibly the identical locket affectingly alluded to by the ' British Sappho' (as not impartial admirers subsequently dubbed the fair poetess) in her Memoirs; this *gage d'amour*, which is almost historical in the chronicle of small affections, containing Prince George's portrait, then a handsome, fine-complexioned youth, with a profusion of fair hair, as painted in miniature by Meyer, was presented in an early stage of the flirtation to the lady, through Lord Malden, the *Leporello* of the transaction. Within the case of this tribute of tenderness was a heart, appropriately cut in paper, on one side of which was inscribed, ' *Je ne change qu'en mourant* ; ' and on the other, ' *Unalterable to my Perdita through life* ; ' a lover's protestation which was not remarkably verified by the subsequent inconstancy of the impressible *Florizel*.

Within a supper-box—one of those grotesque-looking cabinets which many who have visited the shades of Vauxhall may still bear in vivid remembrance—is assembled another convivial party, the members of which have been described—we are inclined to suspect without any sufficiently valid foundation—as the representatives of an illustrious and very familiar literary coterie. A stout personage, in the centre, of massive proportions, has been adopted as a free rendering of the person of the famous Doctor Johnson, who is pictured as characteristically intent on his supper, and indifferent alike to his company and the sprightly society which surrounds his box; seated in a corner, on the great lexicographer's left, anecdotic Boswell is shown, pausing, open-mouthed, to catch the good things that may fall from his eminent leader; Mrs. Thrale, on Johnson's right, is saying something very pertinent to Oliver Goldsmith, who is endeavouring to carve the contents of his plate. His stolid features do not express anything approaching to rapturous appreciation of the accomplished blue-stocking's extraordinary flow of bewitching conversation.

Before we leave the attractive vicinity of *Vauxhall Gardens*, as its picturesque humours were noted by an able hand a century ago, we must offer a few traits of the delightful old haunt and the wicked ways of its frequenters. Our inexhaustible informant Angelo is considerate enough to enlighten our more repressive generation on the practices of the period.

The dashers of the day, instead of returning home in the morning from Vauxhall, used to repair to the Star and Garter, at Richmond; and, on some occasions, the madcap excursions were pushed farther. Angelo mentions a party of which he had formed a member, when, while crossing Westminster Bridge, the sight of a boat suggested a fresh act of extravagant frolic, no less than being rowed to the Tower, taking places, and straightway setting off in the famous hoy for the sea-trip to Margate, which in those times was quite a journey.

We have already introduced a certain witty and pugilistic divine; let us avail ourselves of Angelo's remembrances of an incident in his career, the scene of which belongs to the print we have been endeavouring to elucidate for our readers. Parson Bate—better known by this *soubriquet* than by his later title as Sir Bate Dudley—who was at the time editor of the *Morning Post*, obtained the nickname of the *Fighting Parson*, from a memorable affray in Vauxhall Gardens.

The particulars of the *fracas* are thus related in the *Reminiscences:*—'Mr. Parson Bate, as magnificent a piece of humanity, perhaps, as ever walked arm-in-arm with a fashionable beauty in the illuminated groves of Vauxhall, was promenading and chatting, with the celebrated Mrs. Hartley,[1] her Woodstock

---

[1] 'Mrs. Hartley was an actress of some popularity; more celebrated, however, for her beauty. She was one of those ladies whose career on the stage was without reproach. She was painted by several of the first artists, and among others by Sir Joshua Reynolds, in one of her best characters. No female, perhaps, that ever appeared on the stage looked more lovely than she in *Fair Rosamond*. Mr., afterwards Sir Bate Dudley, married the sister of this lady.'

glove gently rubbing against his sable sleeve; when Mr. Fitzgerald (who was subsequently hanged in Ireland for certain malpractices), in company with Lord Littleton and Captain O'Bourne, most ungallantly gave offence to the lady and her protector by severally turning short round upon her and, with the most marked rudeness, staring in her face. This offensive behaviour was resented by Mr. Bate, and, if my memory does not deceive me, he chastised the offenders on the spot.'

Mr. Bate's paper, *The Morning Post*, obtained much celebrity by the exposure of the three gentlemen for their rude attack upon a lady. The *rencontre* begot a paper war, which was, for some weeks, maintained with great rancour on both sides; but the superior wit and powerful satire of Parson Bate were so manifest that his opponents were beaten out of the literary arena.

'Subsequent proceedings led to a meeting of the parties at a tavern, where, it seems, some explanation was entered into and an apology was offered. This, as appeared later on, was a discreditable stratagem on the part of the aggressors to revenge themselves on this redoubtable priest, by procuring for him, as they anticipated, a sound drubbing; they had, however, once more mistaken their man.

'These three confederates met according to appointment, and Mr. Bate brought his friends too. A strapping spark was then introduced to the party as Captain ——, who had been prompted to insult the pugnacious reverend, with the hope of provoking him to a personal attack, as at Vauxhall. This mock captain was a well-known prize-fighter. The parson, not at all daunted by the insolent threats of the ruffian, fell upon him, and with his own weapons, so completely thrashed him that he was taken away almost senseless in a hackney-coach.'

A farewell incident of Vauxhall, and we will leave for good the precincts memorable in the history of the past. This time we are carried to the *rendezvous* with Angelo and his friends in company with the most incorrigible blades of the town.

'Lord Barrymore's fondness for eccentricities ever engaged his mind. Whether in London or Wargrave 'twas all the same—always in high spirits, thinking of what fun he should have during the day. Seated, after dinner, at eleven o'clock, on one of the hottest evenings in July, he proposed that the whole party should go to Vauxhall.

'The carriage being ordered, it was directly filled inside; and the others outside, with more wine than wit, made no little noise through the streets.

'We had not been long at Vauxhall when Lord Barrymore called out to a young clergyman, some little distance from us, who, when he approached and was asked, "Have you had any supper?" to our surprise answered, "Vy, as how, my lord, I have not as yet had none." A waiter passing by at the time, Lord Barrymore said, "You know me; let that gentleman have whatever he calls for;" when he told the parson to fall to, and call for as much arrack punch as he pleased. "Thank ye, my lord," said he, "for I begins to be hungry, and I don't care how soon I pecks a bit."

'Lord Barrymore had that morning, unknown to us, contrived to dress Tom Hooper, the tin-man (one of the first pugilists of that time), as a clergyman, to be in waiting at Vauxhall, in case we should get into any dispute. This fistic knight now filled the place of a lackey, and was constantly behind the carriage, a sworn votary of black eyes and disfigured faces. His black clothes, formal hat, hair powdered and curled round, so far disguised him that he was unknown to us all at first, though Hooper's queer dialect must have soon discovered him to the waiters. This was a *ruse de guerre* of Lord Barrymore's. About three o'clock, whilst at supper, Lord Falkland, Henry Barry, Sir Francis Molineux, &c., were of our party; there was at this time a continual noise and rioting, and the arrack punch was beginning to operate.

'On a sudden all were seen running towards the orchestra, the whole garden seemed to be in confusion, and our party, all impatience, sallied out, those at the further end of the box walking over the table, kicking down the dishes. It seems that the effects of the punch had not only got into Hooper's head but had excited an influence over his fists, for he was for fighting with everybody. A large ring was made, and, advancing in a boxing attitude, he offered to fight anyone; but all retired before him. Felix M'Carthy, a tall, handsome Irishman, well known by everybody at that time, soon forced his way through the crowd and collared him, at the same time saying, "You rascal, you are Hooper, the boxer; if you do not leave the garden this instant I'll kick you out." The affrighted crowd, who before retreated as he approached them, now came forward, when Hooper, finding himself surrounded, and hearing a general cry of "Kick him out!" made his retreat as fast as possible, thus avoiding the fury of those who would not have spared him out of the gardens, if he had been caught. We found him at five in the morning behind Lord Barrymore's carriage, with the coachman's great-coat on, congratulating himself upon having avoided the vengeance of those to whom, a short time previously, he had been an object of fear.'

July 24, 1785.   *The Slang Society.*

August 11, 1785.   *Introduction.*—There is hardly sufficient authority to warrant the editor in directly ascribing this print to Rowlandson; the work is evidently early, and very French in the characteristics of costumes, surroundings, and subject. There are points in the etched outline and in the general spirit and method of execution, which lead to the impression that

Rowlandson is at least answerable for the etching and mezzotinting of the design. From the costumes worn by the figures the date of the subject may be assumed to be some time before the French Revolution. An overdressed old abbess, her

AÉROSTATION OUT AT ELBOWS, OR THE ITINERANT AÉRONAUT.

head and shoulders enveloped in a cardinal, is introducing a French peer, who is toothless and decrepit, to a tall and fashionably-attired beauty, who is rising to receive the visitor with an air of dignified modesty.

September 5, 1785.   Aërostation out at Elbows, or the Itinerant Aëronaut.

Vincent Lunardi.

Behold a hero, comely, tall, and fair!
His only food is philogistic air!
Now on the wings of mighty winds he rides!
Now torn through hedges! dash'd in ocean tides!
Now drooping roams about from town to town,
Collecting pence to inflate his poor Balloon.
Pity the wight and something to him give,
To purchase gas to keep his frame alive!

TOO MANY FOR A JEW.

1785.   *Going, a-going.*—A handsome young huntsman has encountered, in the course of his sport, a pretty country maiden, neatly apparelled, and beaming with all the freshness of rustic simplicity and artlessness.   Her budding charms are tempting the youth to court the maiden, to her own manifest embarrassment: meanwhile the gay Lothario's huntsman is shown in the distance 'going' off with the horses: the young squire's hunting, as far as the chase of the fox is concerned, being evidently finished for the day.

1785.   *Gone!*

September 30, 1785.   Too Many for a Jew.   Published by S. Alken, Soho.

October 1, 1785.   *An Essay on the Sublime and Beautiful.*   Published by T. Cornell, Bruton Street.—A ragged enthusiast, who, as we gather from the shoe half-thrust into his coat-pocket, combines the cure of human souls with the cobbling of leather soles, is holding forth to a devout congregation.

AN ESSAY ON THE SUBLIME AND BEAUTIFUL.

The companion print to this caricature is called *The Maiden Speech*, and represents a Member, on the floor of the House, favouring the representatives of the people therein assembled with their first experience of his oratorical powers within the Parliamentary walls.

October 5, 1785.   *Captain Epilogue* (Major Topham, Editor of 'The World') *to the Wells* (Mrs. Wells).   (See March 7, 1786.)

Col. Topham endeavouring with his Squirt to Extinguish the Genius of Holman.   (See December 1784.)

To what, O Muse! can I compare
In heaven, water, earth, or air!
    The furious Epilogue.
His dress to ape, if ape they can,
Of every fop is now the plan,
    And he's alone the vogue.

See to the side-box now he flies,
The optic to his eye applies
    To aid his *piercing* sight ;
Whate'er he cannot comprehend
His *fiat* to the Shades shall send,
    And damn to endless night.

COL. TOPHAM ENDEAVOURING WITH HIS SQUIRT TO EXTINGUISH THE GENIUS OF HOLMAN.

Should Holman *Garrick's* art display,
'Tis twaddle, boreish, damn'd *outré*,
    Quite vulgar, unrefin'd ;
His Wells and Henderson alone
Possess'd of merit will he own ;
    To others' worth is blind.

The macaroni Col. Topham, held in leading strings by Henderson and Mrs. Wells, is vainly trying, armed with a critical squirt, to suppress the rising celebrity of Holman, the actor, and writer for the stage.   Holman, it will be remembered (see life of Rowlandson), was one of the caricaturist's schoolfellows.

October 5, 1785. *Captain Epilogue.* Republished March 7, 1786, by E. Jackson, 14 Marylebone Street, Golden Square.—The figure of Captain Topham, (afterwards Colonel) of the *World* newspaper, of which he was proprietor, editor, critic, and scandalmonger—the fashionable intelligencer, *arbiter elegantiarum*, and man of fashion and gallantry. We find the macaroni soldier and journalist a prominent personage in the satirical effusions of his time; we recognise him among Gillray's caricatures as the *Thunderer* (August 20, 1782), and later as the *Windmill*, standing forth advocating the interests of Mrs. Robinson, the *Perdita* who, deserted by the Prince of Wales, found, it was hinted, refuge in the championship of *Captain Epilogue.* In another cartoon Major Topham is bringing his lengthy accounts to Pitt's pay-table, 'for puffs and squibs,' the literary services which he had placed at the Ministerial disposal, and directed against the Whig candidate, Lord John Townshend, during the Westminster Election (August 14, 1788), which occurred when Lord Hood was appointed to the Treasury Board. We find the gallant quill attacking merit where it crossed his partialities, and the present caricature seems designed to expose the Captain's *tendresse* for the actress of his choice. Epilogue is dressed, as he is always represented, in the height of the latest French fashion, his coat, his stockings, his pumps, his frill and ruffles, and his wig and queue being the very latest importations from Paris; a finger-post is pointing to the *Wells*, and the somewhat suggestive and highly modish figure of the lady is drawn below it.

1785. *A Cully Pillaged.* (Same date as *Comfort in Gout.*)—A stalwart-looking bully has suddenly burst into an apartment; he has seized and is securely holding an alarmed individual, whose hat is thrown off and his wig is knocked awry; his pigtail is rigid with terror; he is standing on tiptoe, his limbs paralysed with fear, while a very picturesque-looking Cyprian, with hair and dress in somewhat dishevelled condition, is deliberately exploring the pockets of the victim.

1785. *Copper-plate Printers at Work.*—This sketch, which is vastly interesting, is probably drawn from the room in which the caricaturist's etchings were pulled, an apartment evidently near the sky. A couple of stalwart printers are hard at work rubbing ink into the copper-plates. A sturdy workman is turning the press, while a little oddity of a printer is drawing an impression from the copper lately under pressure. A connoisseur, in spectacles, of the old-fashioned type, is holding up a print at arm's length with a deeply critical expression on his sharp features. Numerous prints are hung up to dry on lines stretched across the chamber.

About 1785. *A Bed-warmer.*—Another print, which was published about this date, bears the name of H. Wigstead as *delt. et fecit*; but, by a strange anomaly, although a few strokes of the outline here and there belong to

Wigstead's hand, which, from its untutored, straggling style, is easy of recognition, the figures and filling in are unmistakably by Rowlandson, who has paid his friend the compliment of ascribing the entire credit of the composition to his name. The subject represents a bedchamber; clothes, &c., are scattered about the room; a venerable libertine, whose bed has evidently been recently warmed, is endeavouring to retain by her skirt a remarkably handsome and sprightly-looking chambermaid, whose figure is gracefully expressed in Rowlandson's most felicitous manner, both as regards ease and action. The offended nymph is making off with the chamber candle and the warming-pan, the latter a formidable weapon for the defence of assaulted virtue.

1785. *Temptation.*—A companion plate was executed under the same auspices, but the name of H. Wigstead in this instance appears as designer only. It represents a scene of temptation. A decrepit and, as far as years go, venerable libertine is offering certain proposals to a pretty and finely-shaped maiden, who is weighing a purse with an air of indecision, while the vicious dotard is pressing her disengaged hand and leaning on her shoulder. The chamber is evidently the workroom of a cobbler; his bench and a pile of shoes in the foreground have been thrown over by the gambols of a dog and cat. In this case it is easy to see that if the maiden does not retire from the struggle with unstained hands, the elderly reprobate, whose crutch is under his arm, will not come off unscathed, for behind the curtains of the bed, in the shadow of the apartment, which seems to serve as workroom, kitchen, parlour, and bedroom in one, appears the half-concealed and brawny person of the cobbler himself, who is evidently enjoying the prospect of the vengeance which he is about to let fall on the head of the old sinner.

1785. *Grog on Board.* (See Jan. 1794.) Published by S. W. Fores, 3 Piccadilly.

1786. *Tea on Shore.* (See June 1794.) Published by S. W. Fores, 3 Piccadilly.

November 24, 1785. By Authority Persons and Property Protected. Published by S. W. Fores.—His Majesty's (G.R.) Royal Mail Coach is in a quandary; one horse is down, and a second is rearing; the hind wheel is off; a fair traveller is sent sprawling on the ground in an attitude which is neither easy nor becoming. An unfortunate passenger has lost his wig, and in seeking to recover it has become jammed in the coach-window. The coachman has lost his balance, and the shock is capsizing his seat; the concussion has discharged the huge blunderbuss borne by the guard through the letter-bags; the mails, and other contents are scattered to the winds by the explosion; and, to cap the misfortune, the lurch has accidentally loosened the trigger of a huge horse-pistol carried in the guard's

INTRUSION ON STUDY, OR THE PAINTER DISTURBED.

belt for extra security, and the contents are peppering an unfortunate lady who has fallen on the highway.

November 28, 1785. *Doctors Differ.* Published by S. W. Fores, 3 Piccadilly.

November 30, 1785. *The Sad Discovery, or the Graceless Apprentice.* Published by J. R. Smith, 83 Oxford Street.

November 30, 1785. *Intrusion on Study, or the Painter Disturbed.* Published by S. W. Fores.—The studio of an artist, who is somewhat of a macaroni ; the painter is hard at his work ; on his easel is a classic subject ; the principal figure is drawn from a pretty girl, his model, who is 'sitting' before him ; a squire and a young foxhunter are dashing in, alike disregardful of the remonstrances of the artist and the confusion into which their unceremonious entry has thrown his blushing model, whose nude figure he is endeavouring to block out with his palette. (Republished July 1, 1802.)

November 31, 1785. *Jockeyship.* Published by J. R. Smith, 83 Oxford Street.—A view of that portion of the racing-ground where the jockeys are about to mount. Various interested groups are represented as surrounding the riders, and secret counsel, at the last moment, is given to jockeys by owners of horses—possibly parting instructions to ride either a winning or a losing race, as their private arrangements may require. That the proceedings of the Turf were not perfectly pure and above the comment of suspicion in the infancy of horse-racing is Indicated by the caricaturist in the last action of 'jockeyship ;' the riders, while shaking hands finally with their owners and backers, are shown taking care to keep their left hands open behind their backs for bribes from the other side ; this signal is meeting a golden response. The crowded stand and the racecourse are sketched in the background.

December 1785. *An Italian Family.* Rowlandson, delt. ; Alken, fecit. (See 1792.) Published December 1785 by S. Alken, Dufour's Place, Broad Street, Soho. Sold by W. Hinton, Sweetings Alley, Cornhill.

A French Family. Sold by W. Hinton, Sweetings Alley, Cornhill. (Republished 1792.)

December 15, 1785. *Courtship in High Life. Courtship in Low Life.*—A pair of prints designed and executed by Rowlandson in imitation of drawings, and belonging to the same period as the more finished and special works which the artist produced published by J. R. Smith. In the former subject *High Life Courtship* is represented in the figure of an elegant young noble—probably meant for the Prince of Wales—kneeling at the feet of a graceful and charming young lady of extreme fashion ; the portrait exhibits certain indications of being intended for that of Mrs. Fitzherbert. There is a great deal of animation and good taste in the composition. The companion print of *Low Life Courtship* introduces a

British sailor, (who has lost an eye and gained a wooden leg in the service of his country), pouring out a bumper of spirits and regarding with a longing eye a careless and semi-intoxicated-looking damsel, who, in spite of evident symptoms of dissipation, is represented as buxom, fresh-looking, and well-favoured.

December 15, 1785.   *City Courtship.*

December 15, 1785. *Rustic Courtship.*   Published by J. R. Smith, 83 Oxford Street.   H. Wigstead, del.—Rowlandson has given his unmistakable characteristics to this plate, which is executed in outline etching, and filled in in aquatint, in admirable facsimile of the artist's drawings, washed in Indian ink, and tastefully coloured.   A fair cottage beauty is spinning flax; her wheel is placed outside the cottage-door; she is being stared at in vacuous admiration by a rustic Colin Clout, who is grinning from ear to ear and scratching his forehead in perplexity. Hop-poles are seen in the distance, and the landscape is one of those pretty country scenes such as may often be seen in England.

December 1785, *Filial Affection, or a Trip to Gretna Green.*   (Companion to *The Return from Gretna Green, or Reconciliation.*)—This plate, which is executed in mezzotint, is usually worked up in imitation of a water-colour drawing —its resemblance to the original sketch, if judiciously tinted after Rowlandson's drawing, is sufficiently close to prove deceptive.   A post-carriage is tearing along down hill, on the road to Gretna Green, drawn by four prancing horses, ridden by a pair of jockeys, and pursued by a posse of mounted horsemen.   The foremost rider, a squire, booted and spurred, is coming close to the elopers and flourishing his whip revengefully at the occupants of the chaise; his horse is turned aside by the threatening attitude of the fugitives.   The lady, her feathers flying in the wind, is leaning out of one window, pointing a formidable pistol at her parent's head; while the dandified young swain who is the abductor in this case is pointing a second pistol through the other window.   The rest of the chase are lost in the clouds of dust which the wheels of the post-chaise are throwing in the rear.   One venerable gentleman's hat and wig are being left far behind, like those of our old friend John Gilpin.

December 17, 1785. *The Reconciliation, or the Return from Scotland.*   Published by W. Hinton, 5 Sweetings Alley, Royal Exchange.—The pair of fugitives we saw in the previous subject are now, like a brace of repentant turtle-doves, returning to the family nest which they had rashly forsaken.   The gallant husband is all submission and civility, pointing to the tears of his bride as their intercessors to the hearts of the parents.   The father is indicating that a place at his fireside is still the right of his child; the old footman is joyfully placing a chair for his young mistress; and the servants, introduced in the doorway of the apartment, are in ecstasies to see the runaway couple return and the domestic breach happily repaired.

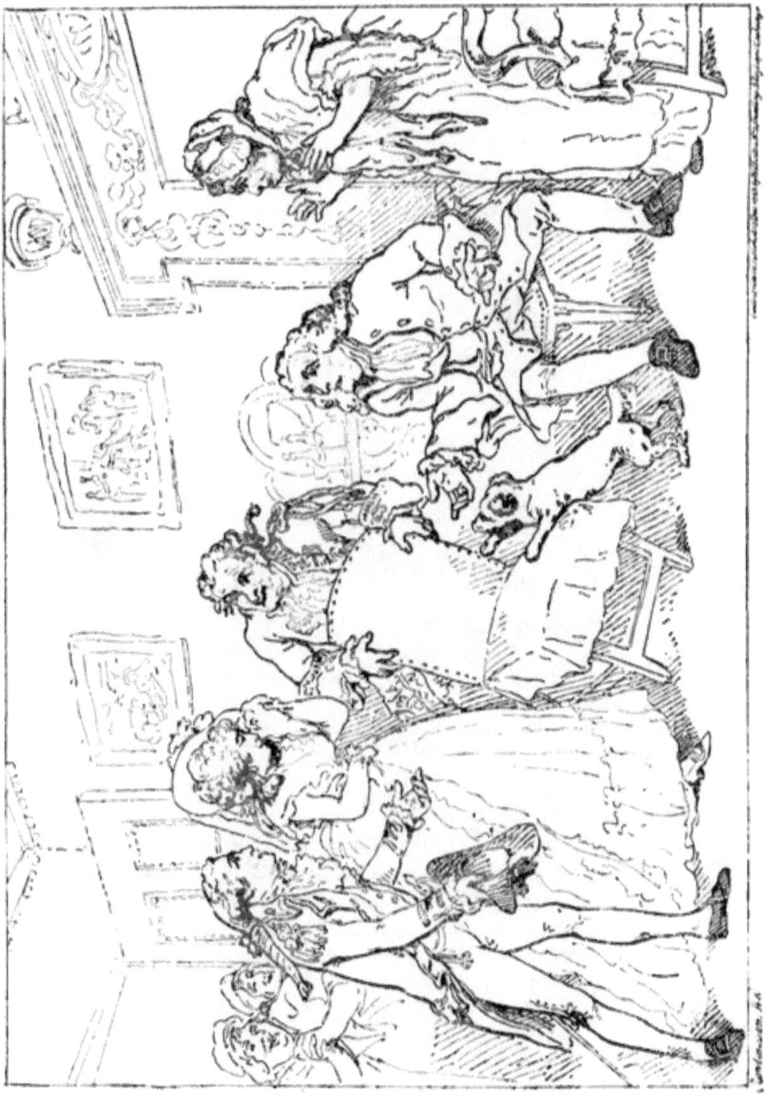

THE RECONCILIATION, OR THE RETURN FROM SCOTLAND.

December 21, 1785. *Botheration* (Bar). Published by W. Hunter. (Engraved by Alken.) Dedicated to the Gentlemen of the Bar.

December 21, 1785. *The Loss of Eden and Eden Lost.* N.B ' Every man has his price.'—*Sir Robert Walpole's politics.* Published by W. Hinton, 5 Sweetings Alley, Royal Exchange.—This caricature gives the portraits of two would-be benefactors of their country, who, the satirist is inclined to hint, were not acting from purely disinterested motives. General Arnold, dressed in his uniform,

HARMONY.

and with his sword drawn, while offering up an invocation to *Liberty*, is one of the figures ; Eden (Lord Auckland) is the other ; the patriotic statesman has also apostrophised *Liberty*, and successfully in his instance, with his pen ; his pocket is well supplied with those good things which have fallen to his share—' 6,000*l.* per annum,' ' *Commissioner to America*,' ' *Commercial Negociator to France*.'

> Two patriots in the self-same age were born,
> And both alike have gain'd the public scorn :
> This to America did much pretend,
> The other was to Ireland a friend.
>
> Yet sword or oratory would not do,
> As each had different plans in view.
> America lost ! Arnold, and, alas !
> To lose our Eden now is come to pass.

1785. *Sympathy, or a Family on a Journey laying the Dust.* Designed and etched by T. Rowlandson. Published by W. Humphrey.—The halt of a coach on the road. The occupants have descended, and the coachman and footman, horses, &c., are occupied as described by the title.

1785. *John Gilpin's Return to London.* Aquatinta by F. Jukes.

> Away went Gilpin, and away
>   Went Postboy at his heels,
> The Postboy's horse right glad to miss
>   The lumbering of the wheels.

TASTES DIFFER.

> Six gentlemen upon the road,
>   Thus seeing Gilpin fly,
> With Postboy scamp'ring in the rear,
>   They rais'd the hue and cry :
>
> 'Stop thief! stop thief! a highwayman !'
>   Not one of them was mute ;
> So they, and all that pass'd that way,
>   Soon join'd in the pursuit.

1785. *Harmony—Discord.* A pair of contrasts.—*Harmony* is a remarkably graceful example of the artist's skill in indicating pleasing forms and easy, flowing outlines. The warrior, we presume, is relaxing the stern front of Mars by the practice of the softer arts, and is seated at the side of a fair companion, who is holding her hero's music-book on her lap.

1785. *Effects of Harmony.* (Companion to the above.)

1785. *Tastes Differ.*—An antiquated individual, evidently a connoisseur of old prints, dressed in his morning cap and dressing-gown, is buried in the study of a large folio spread before him ; all his admiration is absorbed in his hobbies, to the neglect of a young and pretty woman by his side, who is consoling herself,

in dreams, for the neglect with which as the plate seems to hint, the superannuated spouse is treating the charms of her company and person.

1785. *Nap in the Country. Nap in Town.* Published by S. Alken, Dufour's Place, Soho.—A *Nap in the Country* represents the mid-day rest of a rustic pair, who, while their sheep are calmly grazing and their dog is keeping faithful watch, are, beneath the shadows of spreading trees, indulging in ' forty winks ' in the open country, after their early morning toils.

A *Nap in Town,* which may also be taken as an afternoon siesta, though equally luxurious, is not enjoyed under such healthy conditions as the preceding :

NAP IN TOWN.

SEA AMUSEMENT, OR COMMANDER-IN-CHIEF OF CUP AND BALL ON A CRUISE.

the town pair are taking their repose with as much lazy ease as the circumstances
will permit.

1785. *Sea Amusement, or Commanders-in-Chief of Cup and Ball on a Cruise.*
—It appears from this print, which in the coloured editions is judiciously tinted

to make it resemble a drawing, that the inactivity of our commanders at sea was
attracting popular censure.   In the plate we find the admiral and his commodore,

OPERA BOXES.

instead of sweeping the foes of Britain from the ocean, as was the desire of the
entire nation, seated in the state-cabin, with a pile of gold-pieces on the ground,

devoting their energies to gambling with a child's toy. Scattered around and trodden upon unheeded are plans of fortifications to be bombarded, the charts of oceans to be navigated, and rough draughts for the arrangement of the ships at the beginning of a sea-fight, such as we find Nelson drew up for the guidance of his captains before going into action on the eve of his glorious victories. An old salt, who is pouring out tea for these degenerate warriors, is regarding their puerile dispositions with an air of disgust and distress.

December 26, 1785. *French Travelling, or the First Stage from Calais.*
December 26, 1785. *English Travelling, or the First Stage from Dover.*
1785. (?) *Opera Boxes.*

1786.

January 1, 1786. *The Supplemental Magazine.* Published January 1, 1786, by S. W. Fores, 3 Piccadilly.

January 1, 1786. *Private Amusement.* (See October 28, 1781), *E. O. or the Fashionable Vowels.*

January 5. 1786. *Box-Lobby Loungers.* Designed by H. Wigstead; etched by Rowlandson; published January 5, 1786, by J. R. Smith, 83 Oxford Street.—The diversities of character introduced into this drawing, which is one of Rowlandson's larger productions, entitle it to a prominent place in a collection of the artist's works. Glimpses of the theatre are seen through the open doors. In the coloured editions of this plate, which is scarce and valuable, the most conspicuous figure is that of a military hero, the adventurous Colonel George Hanger (afterwards Lord Coleraine), companion and instigator of the Prince of Wales's early frolics; well known to the satirists, and in short one of the notorieties of his generation. This inveterate 'man about town' is shown with his invariable companion, christened by the eccentric Colonel, who rejoiced in a vocabulary of his own, his '*Supple-Jack*,' a thick stick carried under his arm; the gallant lounger, who has left the world a volume of eccentric *Memoirs*, with his *Advice to Lovely Ciprians* by way of Appendix, is lost in admiration of two highly attractive nymphs, possible members of the 'Sisterhood;' while Georgey Hanger's truant eyes are engaged in the contemplation of the personal charms of these butterflies of fashion, the hand of a pickpocket is equally ready to carry off the Colonel's seals from his fob, as a souvenir of the *rencontre*. On the right of the ubiquitous hero another pair of lovely damsels, displaying the follies of the mode in their attire, are attracting the somewhat marked attentions of a circle of elderly admirers. A dwarfed and deformed beau, elaborately dressed in the French fashion, probably designed for the figure of Sir Lumley Skeffington, who was the authority, among the *bucks* and '*fashionables*' of his day, on theatrical matters, is getting into trouble by the awkwardness into which his near sight and his gallantry are combining to betray him; the train of an antiquated belle is coming to grief through the clumsiness of *The Skeffington*. The lady, whose native charms, in their decay, are considerably heightened by art, has evidently availed

LONDON LOUNGERS.

herself of her fortune to secure a handsome dandified young cavalier ; two sturdy old retired sea-captains are contemplating the ' *Skittish Skeffy*,' and his monkey-like escapades with expressions of profound contempt. A superannuated man of quality, a venerable *beau* of scarecrow aspect, is foppishly cultivating the good graces of a dashing 'girl of the period ;' while two extraordinary Don Juans, who, judging from their exteriors, would not be suspected of engaging themselves in amorous intrigues, are enlisting the friendly offices of a comfortable old body, who unites the twin occupations of selling oranges and play-bills, with the manipulation of delicate negociations, a recognised and experienced ambassadress, in fact, to the court of Cytherea, duly credentialised, and, as far as appearances can be relied on, a thoroughly discreet and capable person in her profession. A play-bill, adhering to the green-baize-covered walls of the Lobby, is intended to apply to the situation of the frivolous habitués who are haunting the crowded lounge— ' *The Way of the World*,' and ' *Who's the Dupe ?* ' Beyond the main groups we have particularised, there are numerous individuals scattered about, probably well-known characters in their generation, whose persons and portraits were doubtless familiarly recognised at the date Rowlandson favoured his contemporaries with this suggestive view of their private amusements in the *Box Lobbies*.

January 13, 1786. *Love and Learning, or the Oxford Scholar.* Drawn by Rowlandson Engraved and published by B. Smith, 10 Pleasant Row, Battle Bridge.—A print engraved in somewhat peculiar style as an attempted *facsimile* after the original drawing. The subject is an undergraduate, who is leading a tall and graceful female tastefully dressed in white, through a wood ; the cavalier is pointing out the beauties of the scene ; the face of a forsaken lady, wearing a malignant expression, appears from the concealment afforded by the forest shade.

> Beauty invites, and love and learning plead ;
> The Oxford scholar surely must succeed.
> Yet oh ! ye blooming, soft inclining fair,
> Of his too fatal eloquence beware ;
> For see, a slighted fair one is behind,
> With jealous eye and most distracted mind !

February 10, 1786. *Sketch of politics in Europe January* 24, 1786. *Birthday of the King of Prussia. Toasts upon the occasion.* ' *King of Prussia*,' ' *King of Great Britain*,' ' *The Berlin Union*,' ' *Confusion to the Bavarian Project*,' ' *The Wooden Walls of Old England*,' ' *The Illustrious House of Brunswick and Wolfenbuttel*,' ' *Destruction to the French Interest in Holland, and prosperity to the House of Orange*,' ' *May the British Lion and the Prussian Eagle remain united for times everlasting*,' ' *May the United strength of the British Lion and the Prussian Eagle preserve the Ancient Constitution of the German Empire, and the Protestant interest,'* ' *May Universal Monarchy, the bane of Human Nature, for ever remain a baseless vision!'* This general view of the political prospects of Europe is pictorially set forth in the fashion of an escutcheon, representing the two Protestant monarchs under a pavilion, and seated side by side on one throne —a Prussian grenadier behind the Great Frederick, and a British sailor behind George the Third. Frederick is holding the double-headed eagle of Austria in golden fetters, with his feet on the motto *Universal Monarchy*. The names of the various German States, Hanover, Brunswick, Hesse, Saxony, Deuxpont, and Mayence, are on two shields at the sides of the pavilion. The reigning Duke of Brunswick, and Prince Ferdinand of Brunswick, are standing on either side of the monarchs in the centre, as supporters, with their hands on their swords ; both are declaring to ' the twin Protestant heroes,' ' When you agree, I am ready.' The neighbouring States are variously symbolised. The Prince of Orange is praying for protection ; Holland is figured as a milch cow, of which France is monopolising the produce ; and above, a monkey, with the Crown and Insignia of France, has perched on the globe, and is pointing his claw to Holland. Busts of the reigning monarchs are ranged around. Denmark ' lays by ' for the present ; Sweden is ' in the pay of France ;' Portugal is crying, ' Oh ! buy my wine ;' Spain wants ' the Rock ;' Sardinia is declaring, ' You shall not settle without me !' The Polish Bear, who is announcing that he ' is not muzzled,' is standing between Russia and the Sultan of Turkey ; the latter is hurling defiances at Catherine, ' By the great prophet thou art but a woman !' Russia, as a crowned beast of prey, is ' tortured by ambition, and backed by Brother Joseph.'

March 6, 1786. *La Négligé.* Designed by ' *Simplex Mundities.'* Published by S. W. Fores.

March 7, 1786. *Captain Epilogue*, published by E. Jackson, 14 Marylebone Street.—The macaroni editor's portrait, as described in the previous print (October 25, 1785), with the addition of a notice-board, introduced above the post which points *To the Wells,—A Prospectus for the* ' *World and Fashionable Advertiser.'*

March 7, 1786. *An Ordnance Dream, or Planning of Fortifications*, published by S. W. Fores, 3 Piccadilly.—The Duke of Richmond—who, perhaps in some degree on account of his partial French extraction, and his left-handed Stuart descent, did not enjoy unmixed popularity, was constantly brought into ridicule, with which the satirists met his abortive fortification schemes, and a certain gun, of his own construction, reputed of leather, which it is said he was anxious to introduce.

The caricaturist has represented the distinguished Master-General of Ordnance, an insipid edition of *Uncle Toby*, as the Duke was frequently nick-named. The Duke is in his study, fast asleep in his arm-chair, surrounded by his novel experiments. His foot is resting on the 'Trial of Colonel Debbeig.' A case of fresh ammunition, in the form of tobacco pipes, is lying by his side, and a number of rolled up plans of the projected fortifications are thrown about the place. On the walls are a pair of views on the subject of the proposed fortifications; one picture represents the bare ground, with labourers and wheel-barrows, and the skeletons of a projected fleet; the second view gives the fortifications under the state of their imaginary completion, furnished with guns and ammunition, and duly manned, with a bulwark of our wooden walls beyond. The solid and

AN ORDNANCE DREAM, OR PLANNING OF FORTIFICATIONS.

assuring conditions of the preparations on paper are badly sustained in practice. A pile of card-houses, disposed round the study-table, do duty for fortresses; broken pipe-bowls and stems take the place of stoneworks and guns. An empty decanter accounts for the Duke's faith in this imaginary system of protection. A cat is clawing at the table-cloth, and threatening the total destruction of the projected defences at one swoop; she is mounted on the muzzle of a sample gun of the problematical leathern ordnance, of which, rumour asserted, the Duke of Richmond had ordered a snuff-box maker to supply him patterns. In the struggles in Parliament, where the Duke's plans were the subject of vexed discussion, more stress was laid on his political apostasy than upon the inefficiency of his propositions, patriotism in the senate being subordinated at all times to the workings of party, and the intrigues for political power.

LUXURY.

MISERY.

March 7, 1786. *Luxury—Misery.* Published by E. Jackson, 14 Marylebone Street, Golden Square.—The luxury of a breakfast in bed on downy pillows, surrounded by all the allurements of ease and other superfluities, is contrasted with the *Misery* of perishing of starvation and thirst on the wide ocean, with nothing but a mast between the frozen unfortunates and a watery grave, and no object of relief on the bare horizon to suggest a ray of hope to the solitary sufferers.

March 8, 1786. *The Morning Dram.* Published by J. Phillips, 164 Piccadilly.—The toilette of a lady whose tastes are, to say the least of them, slightly inclined to the social glass ; while her French hair-dresser is attending to her luxuriant locks, the fair, free and easy divinity is not too ethereal to decline recruiting her spirits with a cordial.

THE MORNING DRAM.

March 1786. *The Polish dwarf* (Count Boruwloski) *performing before the Grand Seigneur.* Published by E. Jackson, 14, Marylebone Street.

The famous Count Boruwloski visited nearly all the courts of Europe, where he was made the most of on account of his remarkable diminutiveness, as at the age of twenty his height was but two feet four inches. This Polish miniature man differed from dwarfs in general, as his figure was well-proportioned, and he further possessed perfect breeding, was intellectual, good-natured, and accomplished, and, among other gifts, enjoyed a talent for music, which he had cultivated. His memoirs, written by himself, first appeared in 1788 ; he lived to the advanced age of ninety-eight, he was born at Chaliez, in Russian Poland, November 1739; he died at Banks' Cottage, near Durham (the gift, it is said, of some of the prebendaries of Durham Cathedral), September 13, 1837.

The artist, who had an opportunity of studying this duodecimo edition of humanity from the life, has represented Count Boruwloski in the act of favouring that mysterious potentate, the Grand Seigneur, with a tune on the violin, within the sacred and unapproachable precincts (as far as mankind is concerned) of the harem.   The contrast presented between this perfect miniature and the

THE POLISH DWARF (COUNT BORUWLOSKI) PERFORMING BEFORE THE GRAND SEIGNEUR.

full-blown and highly developed beauties of the seraglio, the overfed Grand Turk, and his gigantic guards, is ludicrously marked.

April 1, 1786.   *The Dying Patient, or the Doctor's Last Fee.*   Published by H. Brookes, Coventry Street.

1786.   *Brewer's Drays.*   Published by E. Jackson, 14, Marylebone Street, Golden Square.—An unusually careful sketch—for Rowlandson—of the interior of the premises of a certain great brewer, most probably those of the renowned Mr. Whitbread, in Chiswell Street, visited in state by their gracious Majesties about this period, when the Royal condescension was made the subject of the famous ode by Peter Pindar—

Full of the art of brewing beer,
    The monarch heard of Whitbread's fame ;
Quoth he unto the queen : ' My dear, my dear,
    Whitbread hath got a marvellous great name.
Charly, we must, must, must see Whitbread brew
Rich as us, Charly, richer than a Jew.
Shame ! shame ! we have not yet his brewhouse seen ! '
Thus sweetly said the king unto the queen.

Now did the king for other beers inquire,
For Calvert's, Jordan's, Thrale's entire ;

BREWER'S DRAYS.

And after talking of these different beers,
Asked Whitbread if his porter equalled theirs—
A kind of question to the Man of Cask
That even Solomon himself would ask.

1786.   *Contrasts: Youth and Age.*—An exceedingly witch-like looking elderly female is endeavouring to entertain a young beauty with some piece of news from a paper, to which the maiden, it appears, is most indolently indifferent.

1786 (?).   *Sailors Carousing.*—A bacchanalian scene, picturing the diversions of salts on shore in the days when tars indulged in such jocularities as frying

gold watches, and eating one-pound Bank Notes on bread and butter. The
'Pollies from Portsmouth' have evidently exceeded the bonds of strict moderation in their applications to the punch-bowl. A Dutch skipper is calmly smoking

CONTRASTS—YOUTH AND AGE.

and drinking himself into philosophic stupidity, regardless of the uproar proceeding around him, of singing, shouting, and fiddling, in drunken discordance.

1786 (?). *The Return from Sport.*—A bold and well-executed etching, to

SAILORS CAROUSING.

which a further interest is added by Rowlandson's easy and flowing touch, of a
rustic subject in Morland's manner. The results of the morning's sport are
chiefly remarkable for their ludicrous insignificance.

May, 1786. *A Theatrical Chymist.*—We have already seen the genius of Holman, who was, as we have noticed, at school with the Caricaturist, rising like the sun as represented by Rowlandson's pencil and graver: we now find the satirist giving his alliance to the other side, although the former print, *Topham endeavouring with his squirt to extinguish the rising genius of Holman*, was being reissued. Probably the success on one side induced the artist—who, we presume, sought only to exercise his art, and was not inconvenienced by party prejudices—

THE RETURN FROM SPORT.

to try and make as fair a counter-hit as we so often find him doing. The figure of Holman, a mean and by no means imposing-looking personage, is issuing from a still, together with a discharge of 'puffs,' &c. The *Theatrical Chymist* is a clerical-looking worthy, our old friend Parson Bate, who is employing a decayed military buck, in tattered regimentals, seated on a pile of paper, to fan the furnace *Academy* with the *Morning Post* bellows; the materials, from which the actor Holman is being distilled, are *Ignorance, Impertinence, Coxcomity, Misconception, Raving, Ranting, Grinning, Snarling, Tortured Attitudes, Envy, Detraction.*

1786. *A Box-Lobby Hero.* *The Branded Bully, or the Ass stripp'd of the Lion's Skin.*—The incident which forms the subject of this plate is now forgotten, but it appears some over-grown and swaggering personage had constituted himself the tyrant of the box lobbies. The old fable of the Ass in the Lion's skin is verified. Although a head and a half taller than any of those present, the *Branded Bully* is allowing a mere dwarf to pull his enormous pigtail, and kick him. The ladies are jeering at the discomfitted swaggerer, who, it seems, is in such abject fear that he is suffering all sorts of indignities without attempting to resent them.

May 6, 1786. More of Werter. The Separation. Charlotte preserved from destruction by Albert and Hymen, whilst Werter in the excess of frenzy puts an end to his existence. Designed by Collings, etched by Rowlandson, published by E. Jackson, Marylebone Street.—The last scene of Werter's tragedy is represented as taking place on the brink of a precipice. The adolescent divinity Hymen. in whose path flowers are strewn, is conducting Charlotte away from the fate which is hanging over her lover; Hymen's torch is interposed between them, and his hand is on the matrimonial chain by which

Charlotte is bound to her faithful husband, about whose head is a vision of antlers. Charlotte is hurried off in despair. As to the hero of the story, he is writhing about in a passionate paroxysm, a serpent is stinging him, a death's head looms above his own, the suicide is grasping a pistol in each hand, and a devil with a scourge of snakes and a vial of poison, is pouring the fatal potion over his head like Macassar oil, of which his locks, like a Turk's head broom, standing bolt on end with excitement, do not appear to have any need.

July 20, 1786. *Covent Garden Theatre.* Published by H. Brookes, Coventry Street.—An interior of the old theatre filled on all sides with a diversified and appreciative audience. The etching is made with a bold free point, and from its ease and simplicity bears the closest resemblance possible to the artist's original outlines, drawn with his famous reed pen, in the facile exercise of which Rowlandson attained peculiar excellence.

September 1, 1786. *Outré Compliments.*

October 1, 1786. *The Jovial Crew.* Published by S. W. Fores, 3, Piccadilly. —This print, which is somewhat suggestive of Rowlandson's manner, has evidently lost much in the engraving, which is due to another hand. The group consists of a brace of jolly mariners—probably intended for captain and mate— whose characteristics are somewhat of the Dutch skipper type, in company with a black sailor, who is holding a punch-bowl, and is seated on a coil of rope on the deck of the vessel.

1786. *A Visit to the Uncle.* Published by E. Jackson, Marylebone Street. (See 1794.)

A Visit to the Aunt. Published by E. Jackson, Marylebone Street. (See 1794.)

1786. *The Wood Eater (Fox).* (See December 20, 1788.)

Illustrations to poems by Peter Pindar, 1786–92. Printed for G. Kearsley at the Johnson's Head, 46, Fleet Street.

Peter's Prophecy, or the President and Poet;

OR AN IMPORTANT EPISTLE TO SIR JOSEPH BANKS ON THE APPROACHING ELECTION OF A PRESIDENT OF THE ROYAL SOCIETY.

BY PETER PINDAR.

The Banquet Scene: a Repast of the Acclimitative Order.

SIR J. BANKS (*loquitur*).

Zounds! ha'nt I swallow'd raw flesh like a hound?
On vilest reptiles rung the changes round?
Eat every filthy insect you can mention;
Tarts made of grasshoppers, my own invention?
Frogs, tadpoles by the spoonful, long-tail'd imps,
And munch'd cockchaffers just like prawns or shrimps?

Hell seize the pack! unconscionable dogs!
Snakes, spiders, beetles, chaffers, tadpoles, frogs,
All swallow'd to display what man can do—
And must the villains still have something new?
Tell, then, each pretty President creator—
Confound him—that I'll eat an alligator.

Picturesque Beauties of Boswell.

'Part the First, containing ten prints, designed and etched by two capital artists' (Collings and Rowlandson). 'Published in May, 1786, by E. Jackson, 14 Marylebone Street, Golden Square.

'To any serious criticism or ludicrous banter to which my journal may be liable, I shall never object, but receive both the one and the other with perfect good humour.'—*Vide* Boswell's Letter in the *Public Advertiser* of March 10, 1786.

1. *Frontispiece.*—Representing General Paoli, Dr. Johnson, and the Journalist practising his celebrated imitations.

Ursa Major and the General are drawing the elated advocate in a go-cart, which bears his initial, with a fool's cap worn over an advocate's wig. The Journalist has bells to his Scotch bonnet, a pen behind his ear, a portrait of Bruce, his reputed ancestor, round his neck, a rattle is in his hand, while his publications, *Journal to the Hebrides*, and *Corsica*, are by his side; he is indulging his famous imitation of a '*Moo, oah*' cow (see plate 10, vol. ii). 'All hail, Dalblair! Hail to thee, Laird of Auckinleck.'—*Vide Journal*, p. 38.

2. *The Journalist, with a view of Auckinleck or the Land of Stones.*

Bozzy is shown strutting with his short legs very wide apart, posed for the heroic, with a plaid blowing over his shoulder, a feather in his bonnet, an ink-bottle at his button-hole, and an advocate's wig and bands: a bulky manuscript, 'Materials for the Life of Samuel Johnson, LL.D.,' is serving as his buckler, and the *Journal* is flourished as a claymore. *Ogden on Prayer* is in his pocket.

'I am, I flatter myself, completely a "Citizen of the World." In my travels through Holland, Germany, Switzerland, Italy, Corsica, France, I have never felt myself from home; and I sincerely love every kindred, and tongue, and people, and nation'—(p. 11).

'My great-grandfather, the husband of Countess Veronica, was Alexander, Earl of Kincardine. From him the blood of Bruce flows in my veins; of such ancestry who would not be proud, and glad to seize a fair opportunity to let it be known?'—*Vide Journal*, p. 16.

3. *The Embrace at Boyd's Inn.*

'On Saturday, August 14, 1773, late in the evening I received a note from Dr. Johnson that he was arrived at Boyd's Inn at the head of the Cannongate; I went to him directly.   He embraced me cordially, and I exulted in the thought that I now actually had him in Caledonia.'—*Vide Journal*, p. 12.

4. *Walking up the High Street, Edinburgh.*

'Dr. Johnson and I walked arm in arm up the High Street to my house in James's Court.   It was a dusky night, I could not prevent his being assailed by the evening effluvia of Edinburgh.

'As we marched along he grumbled in my ear, "I smell you in the dark." '— *Vide Journal*, p. 13.

5. *Tea at the Journalist's House in James's Court.*

'My wife had tea ready for him, which it is well known he delighted to drink at all hours, particularly when sitting up late.   He showed much complacency that the mistress of the house was so attentive to his singular habit, and as no man could be more polite when he chose to be so, his address to her was most courteous and engaging, and his conversation soon charmed her into a forgetfulness of his external appearance.'—*Vide Journal*, p. 14.

6. *Chatting 'till two o'clock in the Morning.*

'We talked of murder, and of the ancient trial by duel.   We sat till near two in the morning, having chatted a good while after my wife left us.   She had insisted that, to show all respect to the sage, she would give up our own bedroom to him, and take a worse.   This I cannot but gratefully mention as one of a thousand obligations which I owe her since that great obligation of her being pleased to accept of me as her husband.'—*Vide Journal*, p. 15.

7. *Veronica, a Breakfast Conversation.*

'Dr. Johnson was pleased with my daughter Veronica, then a child about four months old.   She had the appearance of listening to him.   His motions seemed to her to be intended for her amusement, and when he stopped she fluttered, and made a little infantine noise, and a kind of signal for him to begin again.   She would be held close to him, which was a proof, from simple nature, that his figure was not horrid.   Her fondness for him endeared her still more to me, and I declared she should have five hundred pounds of additional fortune.'— *Vide Journal*, p. 17.

8. *Wit and Wisdom making preparations for dinner.*

'We gave him as good a dinner as we could.   Our Scotch wild-fowl or grouse were then abundant, and quite in season; and so far as wisdom and wit can be aided by administering agreeable sensations to the palate, my wife took care that our great guest should not be deficient.'—*Vide Journal*, p. 123.

9. *Setting out from Edinburgh on the Tour.*

'Wednesday, August 18.   On this day we set out from Edinburgh, attended only by my man, Joseph Ritter, a Bohemian, a fine stately fellow, above six feet high, who had been over a great part of Europe, and spoke many languages.

He was the best servant I ever saw. Let not my readers disdain his introduction, for Doctor Johnson gave him this character : " Sir, he is a civil man, and a wise man." My wife did not seem quite easy when we left her, but away we went.'—*Vide Journal,* p. 47.

10. *Scottifying the Palate at Leith.*

'I bought some speldings, fish salted and dried in a particular manner, being dipped in the sea and dried in the sun, and eaten by the Scots by way of relish. He had never seen them, though they are sold in London. I insisted on

SCOTTIFYING THE PALATE AT LEITH.

Scottifying his palate, but he was very reluctant. With difficulty I prevailed with him. He did not like it.'—*Vide Journal,* p. 50.

> I see thee stuffing, with a hand uncouth,
> An old dry'd whiting in thy Johnson's mouth ;
> And, lo ! I see, with all his might and main,
> Thy Johnson spit the whiting out again.—PETER PINDAR.

Second Volume. Same title as the first part.

1. *Frontispiece.   Revising for the Second Edition, under the inspection of a learned friend.*

'Having found, on a revision of this work, that a few observations had escaped me, the publication of which might be considered as passing the bounds of strict decorum, I immediately ordered that they should be omitted in the present edition.'

> Let Lord M'Donald threat thy breech to kick,[1]
> And o'er thy shrinking shoulders shake his stick ;
> Treat with contempt the menace of this Lord—
> 'Tis Hist'ry's province, Bozzy, to record.

Vide *Poetical Epistle to Jas. Boswell, Esq.*, by PETER PINDAR, Esq.

2. *The Procession to St. Leonard's College.   St. Andrews.*

'After supper we made a procession to Saint Leonard's College, the landlord walking before us with a candle, and the waiter with a lantern.'— *Vide Journal*, p. 54.

3. *The Vision at Lord Errol's.   Slain's Castle.*

'I had an elegant room, but there was a fire in it that blazed ; and the sea, to which my windows looked, roared ; and the pillows were made of some seafowls' feathers, which had to me a disagreeable smell, so that by all these causes I was kept awake a good time. I saw in imagination Lord Errol's father, Lord Kilmarnock (who was beheaded on Tower Hill in 1740), and I was somewhat dreary, but the thought did not last long, and I fell asleep.'—*Vide Journal*, p. 110.

4. *Lodging at Mr. M'Queen's, in Glenorison : the celebrated Spider Scene.*

'There were two beds in the room, and a woman's gown was hung on a rope to make a curtain of separation between them. . . . Doctor Johnson fell asleep immediately ; I was not so fortunate for a long time. I fancied myself bit by innumerable vermin under the clothes, and that a spider was travelling from the wainscot towards my mouth. At last I fell into insensibility.'—*Vide Journal*, p. 153.

5. *Reconciliation at Glenelg, after the Journalist had ridden away from Ursa Major.*

'I resumed the subject of my leaving him on the road, and endeavoured to defend it better. He was still violent upon that head. I had slept ill ; Dr. Johnson's anger had affected me much. I considered that, without any bad intention, I might suddenly forfeit his friendship, and was impatient to see him this morning. I told him how uneasy he had made me by what he had said.

---

[1] A letter of severe remonstrance was sent to Mr. B., who, in consequence, omitted, in the second edition of his Journal, what is so generally pleasing to the public, viz., the scandalous passages relative to this nobleman.

He owned he had spoken to me in passion, and that he would not have done what he had threatened, and added, " Let's think no more on't."—Boswell : " Well, then, sir, I shall be easy.   Remember, I am to have fair warning in case of any quarrel.   You are never to spring a mine upon me.   It was absurd in me to believe you."   Johnson : "You deserved about as much as to believe me from night to morning." '—*Vide Journal*, p. 164.

6. *Highland Dance on the top of Dun-Can.*

'Old Mr. Malcolm McCleod, who had obligingly promised to accompany me, was at my bedside between five and six.   I sprang up immediately, and he and I, attended by the two other gentlemen, traversed the country during the whole of this day.   Though we had passed over not less than four-and-twenty miles of very rugged ground, and had a Highland dance on the top of Dun-Can, the highest mountain in the island, we returned in the evening not at all fatigued, and piqued ourselves at not being outdone at the nightly ball by our less active friends who had remained at home.'—*Vide Journal*, p. 192.

7. *The Recovery, after a severe drunken frolic at Corrichatachin.*

'I awaked at noon, with a severe headache ; I was much vexed I should have been guilty of such a riot, and afraid of a reproof from Dr. Johnson. About one he came into my room and accosted me, "What, drunk yet!". When I rose I went into Dr. Johnson's room, and taking up Mrs. McKinnon's Prayer-book, I opened it at the twentieth Sunday after Trinity, in the Epistle for which I read : "And be not drunken with wine, wherein there is excess." Some would have taken this as a divine interposition.'—*Vide Journal* p. 318.

> At Corrichatachin's, the Lord knows how,
> I see thee, Bozzy, drunk as David's sow,
> And begging, with rais'd eyes and lengthen'd chin,
> Heav'n not to damn thee for the deadly sin.
>
> PETER PINDAR'S *Epistle.*

8. *Sailing among the Hebrides,—the Journalist holding a rope's-end.*

'As I saw them all busy doing something, I asked Col with much earnestness what I could do.   He with a happy readiness put into my hand a rope which was fixed to the top of one of the masts, and told me to hold it till he bid me pull.   If I had considered the matter I might have seen that this could not be of the least service, but his object was to keep me out of the way of those who were busy working the vessel, and at the same time to divert my fear by employing me and making me think that I was of use.   Thus did I stand firm to my post, while the wind and the rain beat upon me, always expecting a call to pull my rope.'—*Vide Journal*, p. 349.

9. *The Contest at Aucklinleck, in which Ursa Major made a severe retort on the Journalist's father.*

'The contest began whilst my father was showing him his collection of medals; and Oliver Cromwell's coin unfortunately introduced Charles the First and Toryism; in the course of their altercation Whiggism and Presbyterianism, Toryism and Episcopacy, were terribly buffeted.

'They became exceedingly warm and violent, and I was very much distressed at being present at such an altercation between two men, both of whom I reverenced; yet I durst not interfere. It would certainly be very unbecoming in me to exhibit my honoured father and my respected friend as intellectual gladiators for the entertainment of the public; and therefore I suppress what would, I daresay, make an interesting scene in this dramatic sketch—this account of the transit of Johnson over the Caledonian hemisphere.' —*Vide Journal*, p. 482.

10. *Imitations at Drury Lane Theatre by the Journalist.*

'At Mr. Tyler's I happened to tell that one evening, a great many years ago, when Dr. Hugh Blair and I were sitting together in the pit of Drury Lane playhouse, in a wild freak of youthful extravagance I entertained the house *prodigiously* by imitating the lowing of a cow. I was so successful in this boyish frolic that the universal cry of the galleries was, "*Encore* the cow! *Encore* the cow!" In the pride of my heart I attempted imitations of some other animals, but with very inferior effect. My reverend friend, anxious for my fame, with an air of the utmost gravity and earnestness addressed me thus: "My dear sir, I would *confine* myself to the *cow*!"

'A little while after I had told this story I differed from Dr. Johnson, I suppose too confidently, upon some point which I now forget. He did not spare me. "Nay, sir (said he), if you cannot talk better as a man, I'd have you bellow like a cow."'

THE authorship of the following pair of prints is doubtful; they present many indications of Rowlandson's manner, and they were issued by his publisher, S. W. Fores, 3 Piccadilly; they are sometimes ascribed to Gillray :—

January 1, 1787. A pair of single figures, respectively described as *London Refinement* and *Country Simplicity*. As the titles sufficiently indicate, the former sets forth a town 'macaroni' dressed in the height of the mode, and the latter represents a pretty youth, of rustic fashion, long-haired, and clad in picturesque and homely country garb.

January 11, 1787. *Uncle George and Black Dick at their New Game of Naval Shuttlecock.*—From this caricature it seems that the conduct of the Admiralty in 1787 gave reasonable grounds for dissatisfaction. The state of things is pictorially set forth by Rowlandson. In the centre of the picture stand the compound heads of the Admiralty, a single figure with two fronts—those of the King and Lord Howe, who was popularly designated 'The Prince of Duskey Bay.'

A bevy of admirals are applying to the King for recognition of their services to their country; they are all partially disabled by the loss of limbs. A petitioner is offering a statement of their situation to the King, who is made to declare, ' I never interfere with your First Lord; no, never ;' while the second head of this Janus, Howe, in replying to a petition from sundry aggrieved captains, is dismissing the applicants with " Go, go! I can do nothing ; it is his Majesty's pleasure that——' The abused admirals are expressing their wrongs : ' I see I shall lose my rank after all my long services !' ' I am set aside, although I've lost a son and one eye !' ' Humbug'd, by Jove, by ye old Jesuit !' ' Had I my arm again, to find a better country !' ' Brothers, our Lords and Commons will not suffer this game !'

The captains have evidently a bad opinion of their First Lord, *Vultus est Index Animi*: ' Our navy has now two heads and no helm ; rare work !' ' Rascal!' ' The King's pleasure! That's a falsity added to a mean *finesse !*' ' He's fond of manœuvres if ever so bad; you know him !'

THE LOUSIAD.

For Peter nat'ral 'tis to speak
In rhyme, as 'tis for pigs to squeak.

PETER PINDAR TO THE READER.

Gentle Reader,—It is necessary to inform thee that his Majesty actually discovered, some time ago, as he sat at table, a *louse* on his plate. The emotion occasioned by the unexpected appearance of such a guest can be better imagined than described.

An edict was, in consequence, passed for shaving the cooks, scullions, &c., and the unfortunate louse condemned to die.

Such is the foundation of the Lousiad: with what degree of merit the poem is executed, the *uncritical* as well as the critical reader will decide.

The ingenious author, who ought to be allowed to know somewhat of the matter, hath been heard privately to declare, that in his opinion the *Batrachomymachia* of Homer, the *Sechia Rapita* of Tassoni, the *Lutrin* of Boileau, the *Dispensary* of Garth, and the *Rape of the Lock* of Pope, are not to be compared to it,—and to exclaim at the same time, with the modest assurance of an author —

Cedite, scriptores Romani; cedite, Graii—
Nil ortum in terris, Lousiadâ, melius.

Which, for the sake of the mere English reader, is thus beautifully translated :—

Roman and Grecian authors, great and small,
The author of the Lousiad beats you all.

What dire emotions shook the monarch's soul!
Just like two billiard-balls his eyes 'gan roll.
'How, how—what, what? . . . what's that, what's that?' he cries
With rapid accent and with staring eyes.
'Look there! look there!—what's got into my house?
A louse, God bless us!   Louse, louse, louse, louse, louse.'
The Queen look'd down, and then exclaimed, 'Good la!'
And with a smile the dappled *stranger* saw.
Each Princess strain'd her lovely neck to see,
And, with another smile, exclaimed, 'Good me!'
'Good la! good me!'   'Is that all you can say?'
(Our gracious monarch cry'd, with huge dismay).
'What! what a silly, vacant smile takes place
Upon your Majesty's and children's face,
Whilst that vile louse (soon, soon to be unjointed!)
Affronts the presence of the *Lord's anointed!*'
Dash'd, as if tax'd with hell's most deadly sins,
The Queen and Princesses drew in their chins,
Look'd prim, and gave each exclamation o'er,
And, prudent damsels, 'word spake never more.'
Sweet maids! the beauteous boast of Britain's isle,
Speak—were those peerless lips forbid to smile?

Lips! that the soul of simple *Nature* moves—
Form'd by the beauteous hands of all the *Loves :*
Lips of delight! unstained by satire's gall!
Lips! that I never kiss'd—and never shall.
Now to each trembling page, a poor mute mouse,
The *pious* monarch cry'd, 'Is this *your louse?*'
'Ah! Sire,' replied each page, with pig-like whine,
'An't please, your Majesty, it is not *mine.*'
'*Not thine?*' the hasty monarch cry'd again—
'What, what?   Who's, who's, then?   Who the devil's, then?'

'IS THIS YOUR LOUSE?'

Now at this sad event the sovereign, sore
Unhappy, could not take a mouthful more ;
His wiser Queen, her gracious stomach studying,
Stuck most devoutly to the beef and pudding ;
For Germans are a very hearty sort,
Whether begot in hog-styes or a court,
Who bear (which shows their hearts are not of stone)
The ills of others better than their own.
    Grim terror seiz'd the souls of all the pages,
Of different sizes and of different ages ;
Frighten'd about their pensions or their bones,
They on each other gap'd, like Jacob's sons.

Now to a page, but which we can't determine,
The growling monarch gave the plate and vermin :
' Watch well that blackguard animal,' he cries,
' That, soon or late, to glut my vengeance, dies !
Watch, like a cat, that vile marauding *louse*,
Or George shall play the devil in the house.
Some *spirit* whispers, that to cooks I owe
The precious *visitor* that crawls below.
Yes, yes ! the whisp'ring *spirit* tells me true,
And soon shall vengeance all their locks pursue.
Cooks, scourers, scullions, too, with tails of pig,
Shall lose their coxcomb curls, and wear a wig.'
Thus roar'd the King—not Hercules so *big*;
And all the palace echo'd, ' Wear a wig ! '
Fear, like an ague, struck the pale-nos'd cooks,
And dash'd the beef and mutton from their looks,
Whilst from each cheek the rose withdrew its red,
And pity blubbered o'er each menac'd head.

But, lo ! the great *cook-major* comes ! his eyes
Fierce as the redd'ning flame that *roasts* and *fries* ;
His cheeks like *bladders* with high passion glowing,
Or like a fat *Dutch trumpeter's* when *blowing*.
A neat white apron his huge corpse embrac'd,
Tied by two comely strings about his waist ;
An apron that he purchas'd with his riches,
To guard from hostile grease his velvet breeches.

' Ye sons of dripping, on your *major* look !
(In sounds of deep-ton'd thunder cry'd the cook),
I swear this head disdains to lose its locks ;
And those that do not, tell them they are *blocks*.
Whose head, my cooks, such vile disgrace endures ?
Will it be yours, or yours, or yours, or yours ?
Then may the charming perquisite of grease
The mammon of your pocket ne'er increase ;
Grease ! that so frequently hath brought you coin,
From veal, pork, mutton, and the great *sirloin*.
O brothers of the spit ! be firm as rocks—
Lo ! to no King on earth I yield these locks.
Few are my hairs behind, by age endear'd !
But, few or many, they shall *not* be shear'd.

  .   .   .   .   .

Sooner shall ham from fowl and turkey part,
And stuffing leave a calf's or bullock's heart :
Sooner shall toasted cheese take leave of mustard,
And from the codlin tart be torn the custard.
Sooner these hands the glorious haunch shall spoil,
And all our melted butter turn to oil :

Sooner our pious *King*, with pious face,
Sit down to dinner without saying grace ;
And every night salvation-pray'rs put forth
For Portland, Fox, Burke, Sheridan, and North.
Sooner shall fashion order frogs and snails,
And dishclouts stick eternal to our tails !
Let George view *ministers* with surly *looks*—
Abuse 'em, kick 'em—but revere his cooks !'
' What ! lose our locks !' reply'd the roasting crew,
' To barbers yield 'em ?—Damme if we do !
Be shav'd like foreign dogs, one daily meets,
Naked and blue, and shiv'ring in the streets ?
And from the palace be asham'd to range,
For fear the world should think we had the mange ? '
' Rouse, *Opposition !*' roar'd a tipsy cook,
With arms akimbo and bubonic look.
' Be shav'd !' a scullion loud began to bellow—
Loud as a parish bull, or poor Othello.
' Be shav'd like pigs !' rejoin'd the scullion's mate,
His dishclout shaking, and his pot-crown'd pate—
' What barber dares it, let him watch his nose
And, curse me !—dread the rage of these ten foes.'
' Be shav'd !' an understrapper turnbroche cry'd,
In all the foaming energy of pride—
' Zounds ! let us take His Majesty in hand !
The king shall find he lives at our command.
Yes—let him know, with all his wond'rous state,
His teeth and stomach on *our* wills shall wait.
We rule the platters, *we* command the spit,
And George shall have his mess when *we* think fit ;
Stay till *ourselves* shall condescend to eat,
And then, if *we* think proper, have his meat.'
' Heav'ns !' cry'd a *yeoman*, with much learning grac'd,
In books as well as meat a man of taste—
' However *modern Kings* may cooks despise,
Warriors and *Kings* were cooks, or hist'ry lies.
Patroclus broil'd beef-steaks to quell his hunger ;
The mighty Agamemnon potted conger !
And Charles of Sweden, 'midst his guns and drums,
Spread his own bread and butter with his thumbs.
Be shav'd !—No !   Sooner pill'ries, jails, the stocks
Shall pinch this corpse, than barbers snatch my locks.'

.   .   .   .   .   .

Around the table, all with sulky looks,
Like culprits doom'd to Tyburn, sat the cooks.
At length, with phiz that show'd the man of woes,
The sorrowing king of spits and stew-pans rose ;

With outstretch'd hands and energetic grace,
He fearless thus harangues the roasting race :
' Cooks, scullions—hear me, every mother's son—
Know that I relish not this royal fun.
What's life,' the major said, ' my brethren, pray,
If force must snatch our first delights away ?
Relentless, shall the royal mandate drag
The hairs that long have grac'd this silken bag ?—
Hairs to a barber scarcely worth a fig—
Too few to make a foretop for a wig !

'COOKS, SCULLIONS—HEAR ME, EVERY MOTHER'S SON.'

Hairs, look, my lads, so wonderfully thin
Old Schwellenberg has more upon her chin !'

'—What ! what ! not shave 'em, shave 'em, shave 'em, shave 'em ?
Not all the world, not all the world shall save 'em.
I'll shear 'em, shear 'em, as I shear my sheep !'
Thus spoke the mighty monarch in his sleep :
Which proves that kings in sleep a speech may make,
Equal to what they utter broad awake.

Now did the *major* hum a tune so sad !
Chromatic—in the robes of sorrow clad ;

But, lo! the ballad could not fear control,
Nor exorcise the barbers from his soul.
And now his lifted eyes the ceiling sought ;
And now he whistled—not for want of thought.

   .   .   .   .   .

Scarce had he utter'd when a noise was heard ;
And now, behold, a motley band appear'd !
With Babel sounds at once the kitchen rings,
Of groom, page, barber, and the best of Kings !

'AND NOW HIS LIFTED EYES THE CEILING SOUGHT,
AND NOW HE WHISTLED—NOT FOR WANT OF THOUGHT.'

And lo ! the best of Queens must see the fun ;
And lo ! the Princesses so beauteous run ;
And Madam Schwellenberg came hobbling, too—
Poor lady, losing in the race a shoe !
But, in revenge-pursuit, the loss how slight !
The world would lose a *leg* to please a spite.
And now for peace did Seeker bawl aloud ;
And lo, *peace* came at once among the crowd.

In courts of justice thus, to hush the hum,
' Silence !' the crier calls, and all is mum.
' Cooks, scullions, all, of high and low degree,
Attend and learn our monarch's will from *me*.
Our sovereign lord, the King, whose word is fate,
Wills in his wisdom to see shav'd each pate :
Then, gentlemen, pray take your chairs at once ;
And let each barber fall upon his sconce.'
Thus thunder'd Seeker, with a Mars-like face,
And struck dire terror through the roasting race.
Thus roar'd Achilles, 'mid the martial fray,
When ev'ry frighted Trojan ran away.
Calm was the crowd when thus the King of isles,
Firm for the shave, but yet with kingly smiles :
' You must be shav'd—you shall—you must, indeed.
No, no—I shan't let slip a single head.
A very filthy, nasty, dirty trick :
The thought on't turns my stomach—makes me sick.
Louse, louse—a nasty thing—a louse I hate :
No, no—I'll have no more upon my plate.
One is sufficient—yes, yes—quite a store :
I'll have no more—no more—I'll have no more.'
Thus spake the King, like ev'ry King who gives
To trifles lustre that for ever lives.
Thus stinking vapours from the oozy pool,
Of cats and kittens, dogs and puppies full,
Bright *sol* sublimes, and gives them golden wings,
The cloud on which *some* say the cherub sings.

PETER'S PENSION.

A SOLEMN EPISTLE TO A SUBLIME PERSONAGE.

Non possum tecum vivere, nec sine te.

Nebuchadnezzar, sir, the *King*,
As sacred hist'ries sweetly sing,
Was on all fours turn'd out to grass,
Just like a horse, or mule, or ass.
    Heav'ns ! what a fall from kingly glory !
I hope it will not so turn out
That we shall have (to make a pout)
    A second part of the old story !

This pension was well meant, O glorious King !
And for the bard a very pretty thing ;
But let me, sir, refuse it, I implore !
I ought not to be rich whilst you are poor.

No, sir, I cannot be your humble hack ;
I fear your *Majesty* would break my back.

A great deal, my dear liege, depends
On having clever bards for friends.
What had Achilles been without his Homer ?
A tailor, woollen-draper, or a comber !
In poetry's rich grass how virtues thrive !
Some when put in, so lean, seem scarce alive,
And yet so speedily a bulk obtain,
That e'en their *owners* know them not again.

PETER'S PENSION.

Could *you*, indeed, have gain'd my muse of *fire*,
Great would your luck have been, indeed, great *sire !*
　　Then had I prais'd your nobleness of spirit !
Then had I boasted that myself,
Hight Peter, was the first blest, tuneful elf
　　You ever gave a farthing to for merit.

Though money be a pretty handy tool ;
Of mammon, lo ! I scorn to be the fool !
If fortune calls she's welcome to my cot,
Whether she leaves a guinea or a groat ;
Whether she brings me from the butcher's shop
The whole sheep or a single chop.

For lo! like Andrew Marvel I can dine,
And deem a mutton bone extremely fine.
Then, sir, how difficult the task you see,
To bribe a moderate *gentleman* like *me*.
I will not swear, *point blank*, I shall not alter—
A *saint* (my namesake) e'en was known to falter.

And who is there that may not change his mind?
Where can you folks of that description find
Who will not sell their souls for cash?
That most angelic, diabolic trash!
E'en grave divines submit to glitt'ring gold!
The best of consciences are bought and sold:
Yet should I imitate the fickle wind,
Or Mister Patriot Eden—change my mind;
And for the bard your Majesty should send,
And say, 'Well, well, well, well, my tuneful friend,
I long, I long to give you something, Peter—
You make fine verses—nothing can be sweeter—
What will you have? what, what? speak out, speak out:
Yes, yes, you something want, no doubt, no doubt.'

Then would the poet thankfully reply,
With falt'ring voice, low bow, and marv'ling eye
    All meekness! such a simple, dove-like thing!
'Blest be the bard who verses can indite,
To yield a *second Solomon* delight!
    Thrice blest, who findeth favour with the King!

'Since 'tis the royal will to give the bard
In whom the King delighteth some reward,
Some mark of royal bounty to requite him,
O King! do anything but *knight him*.'

ODES FOR THE NEW YEAR.

Know, reader, that the laureate's post sublime
Is destin'd to record, in handsome rhyme,
    The deeds of British monarchs twice a year:
If *great*, how happy is the tuneful tongue!
If *pitiful*, as Shakespeare says, the song
    Must 'suckle fools and chronicle small beer.'

But bards must take the *up hill* with the *down*;
    Kings cannot always oracles be hatching:

Maggots are oft the tenants of a crown—
    Therefore, like those in cheese, not worth the catching.

O gentle reader ! if, by God's good grace,
    Or (what's more sought) good interest at court,
Thou get'st of lyric trumpeter the place,
    And hundreds are, like gudgeons, gaping for't ;
Hear ! (at a palace if thou mean'st to thrive)
And, of a steady coachman, learn to drive.

ODES FOR THE NEW YEAR.

Whene'er employ'd to celebrate a King,
Let fancy lend thy muse her loftiest wing—
    Stun with thy minstrelsy th' affrighted sphere ;
Bid thy voice thunder like a hundred batteries ;
For common sounds, conveying common flatteries.
    Are zephyrs whisp'ring to the royal ear.

Know, glutton-like, on praise each monarch crams ;
    Hot spices suit alone their pamper'd nature :
Alas ! the stomach, parch'd by burning drams,
    With mad-dog terror starts at simple water.

Fierce is each royal *mania* for applause ;
And, as a horse-pond wide, are monarch's maws—
　　Form'd, therefore, on a pretty ample scale :
To sound the *decent* panegyric note,
To *pour* the *modest* flatt'ries down their throat,
　　Were off'ring shrimps for dinner to a whale.

And mind ! whene'er thou strik'st the lyre to kings,
To touch to Abigails of court the strings ;
　　Give the Queen's toad-eater a handsome sop,

THE TRIUMPH OF SENTIMENT.

And swear she always has more grace
Than e'en to sell the *meanest* place—
　　Swear, too, the woman keeps no title-shop.

Thus, reader, ends the prologue to my odes !
　　The true-bred courtiers wonder whilst I preach—
And with grave vizards and stretch'd eyes to gods,
　　Pronounce my sermon a most impious speech :
With all my spirit—let them damn my lays—
A courtier's curses are exalted praise.

January, 1787.   *The Triumph of Sentiment.*
January, 1787.   *The Triumph of Hypocrisy.*

1787.   *Transplanting of Teeth.*   Published by J. Harris, 37 Dean Street, Soho.—Among the schemes of charlatans, which were popularly successful in the days of *The Temples of Health, Mud Baths,* and other devices by which pretenders flourished on the gains extorted from fashionable credulity at the end of the last century, was a new theory of dentistry, according to the practice of which a sound tooth was to be torn from the jaws of a healthy individual, and,

THE TRIUMPH OF HYPOCRISY.

while still warm, was to be inserted in the gums of some patient whose decayed molar had been extracted simultaneously, and the rest of the operation was left to nature.   According to the caricaturist, who has produced a large, spirited, and well-executed plate on this novel operation, we are informed by advertisement that this truly extraordinary performance is taking place in the surgery of '*Baron Ron, Dentist to her High Mightyness the Empress of Russia.*' The professor has appended to this important announcement the further statement, '*Most money given for Live Teeth.*'

The dual operations of depriving the poor of their sound teeth for a small pecuniary consideration, that their lost molars may regarnish the gums of patients who are prepared to pay for the accommodation, and the substitution of whole teeth for decayed ones, are proceeding at once. The artist has sketched two wretched young creatures, in rags, who are stealing out of Baron Ron's surgery, weeping and bewailing the loss of their teeth, and regarding a coin held in the palm of their hands, with mourning and reproachful looks. An old dandy, a military buck, is examining the adjustment of his new teeth, which do not appear to fit as accurately as could be desired. An assistant dental professor is planting a live tooth in the gums of a lady of quality, who is kicking violently, in disapproval of the sensation. An elderly dowager is seated

SHOEING : THE VILLAGE FORGE.

in suspense in a chair beside a young sweep, whose odoriferous vicinity she is counteracting by applications to a scent-bottle held to her susceptible nose, while the Baron—a modishly costumed foreigner—is tearing out a beautiful healthy white tooth from the jaws of the sooty patient, to be straightway transplanted into the gums of the customer of quality.

May 9, 1787. *The Brain-Sucker, or The Miseries of Authorship.*

In 1787 Rowlandson issued a series of rustic sketches, including such subjects as horses, dogs, coaches, carts, haymakers, cottages, farrier's forges, and roadside inns ; similar views to those selected by Morland, but treated in Rowlandson's own original style.

Among these rural studies we may particularise :—

A BREWER'S DRAY.

A POSTING INN.

Shoeing: the Village Forge. Published by Laurie and Whittle, 53 Fleet
Street.

A Brewer's Dray.

A Posting Inn. Republished July 1, 1803.

A Rural Halt. Published by J. Harris, Dean Street, Soho.

A RURAL HALT.

HAYMAKERS.

A SAILOR'S FAMILY.

A COLLEGE SCENE, OR A FRUITLESS ATTEMPT ON THE PURSE OF OLD SQUARE-TOES.

Haymakers.   Published by J. Harris, Dean Street, Soho.

1787.   *A Post Chaise.*

1787.   *A Sailor's Family.*—One of those charming pieces to which so much of Rowlandson's reputation is justly due.   Unaffected simplicity, an easy effortless style of drawing, natural grouping, and the most perfect felicity in rendering graceful attitudes and depicting faces, unequalled for a certain innocent beauty and expressiveness.

August 1, 1787.   *A College Scene, or a Fruitless Attempt on the Purse of old Square-toes.*   Engraved by E. Williams; published by J. R. Smith, King

TRAGEDY SPECTATORS.

Street, Covent Garden.—*Old Square-toes* has called to see his scapegrace— on the subject of supplies, it is needless to particularise.   Young *Hopeful,* who is obviously destined for the Bar—where, we may feel convinced in advance he is bound to shine—has assumed his most specious deportment, and has donned his cap and gown, with the other semblances of decorum.   The title, *Fruitless Attempt,* seems somewhat of a misnomer, for the special pleading of young *Hopeful* is evidently producing a favourable impression.   Old *Square-toes* has banged himself down into a chair, and planted his stick on the ground with an air of determination, in a very square attitude, to demonstrate that his resolution is not to be shaken, and that young *Hopeful* is losing his pains ; but,

COMEDY SPECTATORS.

LOVE IN THE EAST.

as in the old comedies, the paternal heart is yearning towards his progeny,
while his most relentless denunciations are thundered forth; the lines of his
stern face are relaxing, an amused smile is twitching at the corners of his
mouth, and we are convinced that the next remark will embody the sentiments immortalised by the Georgian dramatists: 'You dog, this time your
father forgives you; boys will be boys; I was a gay young spark myself once;
I'll pay your debts this time, but never again, &c. &c.'

THE ART OF SCALING.

October 18, 1787. *Tragedy Spectators. Comedy Spectators.* Published by
T. Rowlandson, 50 Poland Street.—The contrast of the respective attractions
between the two classes of entertainment is pictured with the artist's characteristic force and spirit. The humour of these two designs is suggestive of
Hogarth's genius. While the woes of 'Romeo and Juliet' are influencing the
spectators to the most profound melancholy, and reducing the audience to tears
and hysteria, the attendants on *Comedy* are enjoying the humours of the performance with the most frank and unrestrained merriment.

1787.   *Love in the East.*—Oriental luxuriousness seems to have had a charm for Rowlandson's pencil. It is true that the customs of the East were not represented, at the caricaturist's day, with the strictest adherence to facts; their salient points have since been made more familiar by the graphic pictures of our travelled artists, for whom the East has always had a peculiar fascination.

Rowlandson's fancy has supplied those details which he could not furnish from actual experience, and as far as the general theories of oriental splendour

MODISH.

are concerned, the imaginative delineations of our artist will be found far more realistic and in accordance with our preconceived impressions than the actuality.

November 5, 1787.   Reformation, or the Wonderful Effects of a Proclamation.— The Chapel Royal is apparently the scene of this subject. King George, Queen Charlotte, with a Lord and Lady-in-waiting, are in the Royal pew; near them are the law Lords; the Prince of Wales and Mrs. Fitzherbert, with Col. George Hanger, are in the centre; Burke is between them, with Lord North, who is of course represented as sleeping soundly, in spite of the efforts made by a pretty maiden to awaken him.   Pitt is acting as clerk.   The sermon is evidently one of no common significance.   Fox is standing in a sheet, with a placard, '*For playing cards on the Lord's Day !*'   A stout lady, armed with a whip, is driving a pack of dogs out of the chapel.

1787(?).   *The Art of Scaling.*

1787(?).   *Modish.*   Published by S. W. Fores, Piccadilly.

PRUDENT.

1787(?).   *Prudent.*   Published by S. W. Fores, Piccadilly.

1787.   *Landscape and other Etchings, by T. Rowlandson.*

1787.   *Embarking from Brighthelmstone to Dieppe.*—The spectators are scattered about the shore, with various fishing smacks ; the passengers are being pushed off in rowing boats to the sailing lugger, which is to take them and their luggage across the Channel.   There is a fresh breeze blowing ; the whole view is animated, and complete as a picture.

1787.   *A Sea-coast Scene.   Cottages by the Sea-shore : a Storm coming on.*

1787.   *Deer-Hunting: a Landscape Scene.*—A noble park is capitally etched; the subject is diversified by the introduction of a stag hunt. The hunters are riding up as the stag, followed by the pack of hounds, is taking the water.

December 18, 1787.   *A Travelling Knife-grinder at a Cottage Door.* Published by T. Rowlandson, Poland Street.—A pretty rustic scene, etched with spirit and well finished.

The Three Horse-shoes—A roadside inn.

1787.   *View on the French Coast.*—Partially dismantled ships of war, canted for caulking.

1787.   *Fox-Hunting: a Landscape Scene.*—The artist has taken great pains with the trees and rich foliage which grace this view. The pack have come up with the fox, and the huntsmen are in ' at the death.'

October 15, 1787.   *Stage Coach setting out from a Posting House.*

1787. *Cribbage Players.*—A lady and gentleman are opponents ; a second lady and gentleman are watching the respective hands. Etched in a brilliant outline, probably intended to be coloured in facsimile of an original drawing.

December 15, 1787.   *Postboys and Post-horses at the White Hart Inn.*— Published by J. Harris.

1787. *Boy bringing round a Citizen's Curricle.*

1787. *Civility.*

1788.

1788.   *The Morning of the Meet.*—One of a series of large hunting pictures, somewhat in the style of Morland, more especially as respects subject, but treated with Rowlandson's individuality as regards boldness, spirited action, and ease.

There are five successive subjects which may be considered to form part of this series, respectively entitled *The Meet, The Start, The Run, In at the Death,* and *The Dinner.*

February 20, 1788.   *The Humours of St. Giles's.*   Published by T. Harmar (Engraver), 161 Piccadilly. The honours of this plate are, we understand, divided between Rowlandson and Ramberg.   The *Humours of St. Giles's* are of a diversified nature, as might be supposed.   Both artist and engraver seem to have seized the passing incidents with true Hogarth-like aptitude, and collected them in one group.   There is nothing but the evidence of Rowlandson's peculiarities to warrant us in including this print among his works.   It is very scarce, and we have not met with his name on any copy of the plate, which is engraved by T. Harmar, the publisher, after a method bearing some resemblance, as far as mechanical execution is concerned, to the early style of James Gillray.   We believe the etching is due to Ramberg, but the female figures, and the person of the hairdresser, are unmistakably characteristic of our artist's manner, both as concerns expressions and attitudes, and particularly as regards the drawing of the extremities.

A 'gin slum' is the centre of attraction ; at the sign of the ' Fox and Grapes ' the landlord is serving a buxom and somewhat dishevelled Irish beauty with a glass of ' blue ruin.'   A drunken-looking butcher is standing treat; another fair member of the hundreds of Drury is entirely overcome, and is a ' deadly lively ' illustration of the usual advertisements traditionally found outside the spirit cellars of Hogarth's period : ' dead drunk for a penny, clean straw for nothing.' A dandified French barber, returning from the mansions of his clients in St. James's, with his powdering-bag and paraphernalia under his arm, is stooping, from a motive of gallantry, over the semi-conscious nymph, while an urchin is possessing himself of the tonsor's handkerchief.   A baker, taking home ready-

THE MEET.

THE HUMOURS OF
ST. GILES'S.

cooked joints to the respective owners, is pausing awhile to enjoy the farces transacting around him, while the lamplighter, perched on a ladder above to attend his lamps, is pouring some of his oil over the baked meats by way of sauce.   In the distance is shown an altercation between a milk-maid and a fish-fag, and a bout of fisticuffs is proceeding farther on.

March 6, 1788.   *The Q. A. loaded with the Spoils of India and Britain.*— The Q. A. is a zebra; Pitt is seated, with well-stuffed panniers, in front of this novel steed, loaded with costly spoils, *Rights and Wrongs*; round the Zebra's neck is a bag of *Bulse*, containing some of Warren Hasting's famous ill-gotten diamonds.   Pitt is sharply whipping his beast, and declaring ' I have thrown off the mask, I can blind the people no longer, and must now carry everything by my bought majority.'   The Q. A. is also trumpeting forth, ' What are children's rights to ambition ? I will rule in spite of them, if I can conceal things at Q.'   A law lord, said to be intended for Lord Thurlow, who has hold of the animal's head, is filled with certain gloomy apprehensions : ' So many Scotchmen have left their heads behind in this d—d town for treason, I begin to tremble as much as the thief in the rear for my own.'   The thief in the rear is the Duke of Rich-mond, who, with one of his famous defence guns between his legs, is assisting Pitt's advance with a goad, and crying ' Skulking in the rear, out of sight, suits best my character.'   A finger-post is pointing to *Tower Hill*, by *B—m (Buck-ingham) House.*

March 29, 1788.   *Ague and Fever.*   (Companion print to *The Hypochondriac*, November 5, 1792.)   Designed by James Dunthorne.   Etched by T. Rowland-son.   Published by Thomas Rowlandson, 50 Poland Street.

> And feel by turns the bitter change of fierce extremes—
> Extremes by change more fierce.—MILTON.

James Dunthorne seems to have had a taste for inventing symbolical renderings of human infirmities ; in the present case the two conditions of *Ague and Fever* are at least ingeniously portrayed.   The cold snake-like folds of *Ague* are twining round the shivering victim, seated as he is in the full heat of a blazing fire ; while the quivering heats of *Fever* personified are in attendance, between the patient and his physician, waiting to add his persecutions to the infirmities which the sick man is already enduring.

July 9, 1788.   *Going to ride St. George ; a Pantomime Scene lately performed at Kensington before their Majesties.*   Published by William Holland, 50 Oxford Street.—This print, with a crowd of others on the same incident, had its rise in an accident : the Prince of Wales, being out driving in a curricle with Mrs. Fitz-herbert, by some misadventure was thrown from his vehicle, and his companion shared his fall.   In Rowlandson's print the Prince has fallen on his back, and

AGUE AND FEVER.

the lady is taking a Phaeton-like flight on to his body. The positions are reversed in the caricatures Gillray and other satirists produced on the subject. George the Third and his Queen, with an escort of Guards, are riding past at the very moment, and they seem greatly interested in the spectacle of their son's downfall.

July 22, 1788. *Old Cantwell Canvassing for Lord Janus.*—The Westminster Election again created further excitement in 1788, as the old field on which the Whigs had gained their triumph against Court interest. The appointment of Lord Hood, in the beginning of July, to a seat at the Admiralty Board rendered a new election necessary. Hood, as the supporter of Pitt, enjoyed the advantage of the Ministerial assistance ; the Opposition, however, contested the seat so efficiently in favour of Lord John Townshend, in the Whig interest, that, in spite of the manœuvres of the Ministry, the Liberal member was returned.

In Rowlandson's print a Methodistical congregation is being harangued by the pastor on the respective qualities of the candidates. Lord Hood, whose countenance is wearing a look of sanctified horror, is accommodated with a seat behind his advocate ; and a sailor, with a bludgeon and the union-jack unfurled, is also in the pulpit. *Old Cantwell* has a work in his hand setting forth representations of *Devil Townshend* and *Saint Hood.* The eloquence of the preacher is directed against the failings of his opponents : ' Lord Hood is a saint, my dear brethren, as immaculate as a newborn babe ; but as for Lord Townshend, he'll be d——d to all eternity. I shudder when I tell you he loves a pretty girl ; the Opposition to a man are all fond of pretty girls ! They go about like lions in pursuit of your wives and daughters. Lord Hood's pious Committee will swear to it,' &c.

July 27, 1788. *Effects of the Ninth Day's Express from Covent Garden, just arrived at Cheltenham.*—The King had retired to Cheltenham, where, according to the artist, he was taking the waters with his family ; a postilion has arrived express from London with the latest intelligence concerning the election for Westminster. The ' result of the ninth day's poll—majority for Lord John Townshend, 218,' is too much for his Majesty, who is quite overcome ; he has dropped the tumbler from which he was taking the waters, and has fallen into the arms of a page ; a peasant, who has been drawing the water for his sovereign, is, in consternation, deluging the royal shoe with a few quarts of the same fluid ; Queen Charlotte is horrified, and the pretty Princesses are clasping their hands in consternation. In Court circles it was represented that the Whigs were capable of any atrocity, however deep.

August 1, 1788. *The School for Scandal.* Published by V. M. Picot, 6 Greek Street, Soho. T. Rowlandson, invt. ; V. M. Picot, direxit.—One of the long strips containing subjects arranged in series, which were popular at this period, belonging to the same order as *The Bath Minuet* and *The Progress of a Lie*, by H. Bunbury; *A Country Dance* and *A Cotillon*, by W. H. Kingsbury; *The Installation Supper, as given at the Pantheon, by the Knights of the Bath* (on May 26, 1788), by James Gillray; *The Prince's Bow*, by F. G. Byron; *English Slavery, or a Picture of the Times*, 1788; *Chesterfield Travestied*, by Collings, &c., &c.

The School for Scandal consists of seventeen females, of ages varying from a tender maid to an antiquated grandmother; the respective characteristics of the different individuals are hit off with Rowlandson's usual spirit and success; the pretty maidens being extremely flattered, and the traits of less favoured dowagers coming in for grotesque exaggerations. The fair members of this coterie are supposed to be making their several comments, as exclamations, upon a recent elopement, a proceeding not unusual at the time *The School for Scandal* was given to the public: 'Off! positively off!' 'I'm thunderstruck!' 'Poor creature, I pity her!' 'And with a low-bred fellow!' 'Did you expect anything else?' 'A footman too!' 'Even so!' 'Mind, it's a secret!' 'Not a syllable!' 'Poor as we are, my daughter would not have done so!' 'I! God forbid!' 'Oh! 'tis fashionable life!' 'She vow'd she'd go!' 'So fine a girl! with so good a fortune!' 'I say nothing!' 'An ill-made scoundrel too!' 'He's good enough for her!'

November 25, 1788. *Filial Piety.* Published by S. W. Fores, 3 Piccadilly. —The King's illness gave serious grounds for apprehension; as his chances of recovery became more precarious the Tories thought fit to insinuate that the Prince and his adherents were awaiting the royal dissolution with ill-concealed satisfaction. In *Filial Piety* we find the King almost at his last gasp; he is stretched on the bed, from which, it was generally concluded, he would never be able to get up; his hand is raised to his head in token of suffering, and he is turning away his face from a spectacle well calculated to disturb the last moments of a pious and suffering parent. The Prince and his friends have just risen from a drunken bout; their spirits have evidently been well sustained; the Heir Apparent is reeling in, with 'Damme, come along; I'll see if the old fellow's —— or not?' Georgey Hanger has come dancing in to support his comrade; under his arm is his *Knock-me-down Supple-Jack*, and he has a bottle held in readiness for emergencies. Sheridan, who became prominent at this period as the Prince's confidential adviser, is capering and huzzaing. A table is knocked over, and the Sacrament is thrown on the ground; a bishop on his knees, who is offering a prayer for the *Restoration of Health*, is horrified at the scandalous improprieties committed by these boisterous intruders. On the wall is a representation of the *Prodigal Son*, as appropriate to the occasion.

December 26, 1788.   *The Prospect before us.*—Although the satirists took some pains to point out the aspirations of the Whigs, they did not conceal their sympathies for the position of the Prince, and the necessity of providing for the security of his interests in the future, as threatened by the Regency restrictions. *The Prospect before us*, at the end of 1788, seemed likely to be shortly realised, until the unexpected recovery of the King put an end to the hopes and intrigues of both parties.   The prospect which threatened the hopes of the Prince and his Whig adherents was the practical investment of the sovereign power in the hands of the Queen and Pitt, to the setting aside of the Prince's influence save in name.   The crown is divided ; one-half is wavering over the head of Pitt, and the other is suspended over the head of the Queen, who is trampling on the coronet and triple plume of the Heir Apparent, 'my son's right.'   Queen Charlotte is held by the Minister in leading-strings.   Pitt, who had suffered his zeal to outrun his discretion, is understood to have made a statement, in the heat of debate, which his opponents characterised as downright treason ; the question-able expression,[1] with some additional colouring, is set down in a written speech which he is displaying in his hand : '*I think myself as much entitled to be Regent as the Prince of Wales.*'   Pitt, under the shelter of the Queen, is declaring : ' Behind this petticoat battery, with the assistance of *Uncle Toby* (Duke of Richmond), I shall beat down the legal fortifications of this isle and secure the Treasury at the next general election !'   Queen Charlotte is holding a draft of special *Taxes, 1789, by Billy's desire.   Petticoats, Blue and Buff Cloth ; Devon-shire-Brown Silk, Portland Stone, Fox Muffs.*   The bulky form of Madame Schwellenberg, Mistress of the Robes—the German favourite of the Queen and the popular detestation of the rest of the community—is swaggering along to the House of Lords, with the Mace and Purse ; she has supplanted Thurlow as Lord Chancellor, and is already dictating the policy her mistress is to follow : ' Take care to secure the jewels ; I have hitherto been confined to the wardrobe, but now mean to preside at the Council, and, with Billy's assistance, the name of Schwel-lenberg shall be trumpeted to the remotest corner of Rag Fair.'   The Queen is proclaiming herself a passive agent : ' I know nothing of the matter.   I follow Billy's advice !'

The Treasury gates are securely closed ; the spectators are declaring that the Premier, Pitt, ' never meddled with a petticoat before ; ' and Warren Hastings is observing with delight that his apprehensions concerning the action of his enemies are at an end, and that the influence he had made with the Queen, in

---

[1] The words taken exception to were : ' I say the Prince of Wales has no more right to assume the government without the consent of the Parliament, who represent the people, than any other person,' &c.

the form of gifts of jewels, is now likely to become of service : 'My diamonds will now befriend me. Huzza !'

December 1788. *The English Address.*—To this further satire upon the *Regency Restrictions* Rowlandson has attached the name of H. Wigstead. Pitt is standing on a platform receiving the congratulations of a drove of donkeys. The Prince of Wales, wearing his coronet, plume, and broad riband, is held in fetters, a powerless victim in the hands of 'the Pitt party.' The Duke of Richmond has secured one end of the chain ; on the reputation of his abortive fortification propositions he declares, while alluding to the lean figure of his leader, 'Billy's virtue is bomb-proof, gentlemen ; he is well fortified in his own good works.' Both the personal peculiarities of the Prime Minister and his attitude are well hit off ; he is giving his followers this assurance : 'Gentlemen, I have chained up your Prince ; your enemies may insult him as they please ; he cannot resent it. I expect to receive all your thanks for this service I have done your Constitution. Should a war break out you have now nobody to defend you— look upon me, gentlemen, as your saviour ; I will only tax you a little more, and quarter a few more of my needy relations on you, and will then retire to my new office of Treasurer and Secretary, at Buckingham House.' For these patriotic services the members of the asinine assembly are duly acknowledging their gratitude.

December 26, 1788. *The Political Hydra.*—Fox, in this case, enjoys the distinction of having his career pictorially illustrated in six phases : *Out of place, and in character* ; black-bearded and swarthy, his rugged locks unkempt. *In place ; out of character* ; his beard shaven, his locks powdered. *As he might have been* ; crowned with the cap of Liberty. *As he would have been* ; wearing a coronet. *As he should have been* ; his head severed by the executioner's axe, the punishment awarded traitors. *As he will be* ; enjoying the supreme power under the Prince of Wales's diadem. This last prophecy was premature, as was soon seen.

December 29, 1788. *A Touch on the Times.*—Rowlandson has taken his own print of the *Times*, 1784, and has produced a parody upon the same theme. In this case the Prince is again represented as being led to the steps of the throne ; one foot is placed on a solid base, the *Voice of the People* ; the second step, however, *Public Safety*, is sadly injured ; *Virtue*, as indicated on the throne, is a money-bag ; the coming ruler is making patriotic professions : 'I would do the best to please my people.'

Fox is leaning on the throne ; his figure is intended to personify that of *Justice* ; a brace of dice-boxes form the new scales of Justice, a bludgeon, topped with an eye, is *the Sword of Justice.* Fox is declaring : 'I have the voice of the people in my eye.' Sheridan is playing the part of *Liberty out at elbows* ; while leading the Prince to the throne he is picking his pockets. *Britannia* is showing a cloven foot ; Pitt, provided with a huge extinguisher, is stumbling over the *British Lion* ; he is boasting, in reference to the incendiary torches of *Envy, Rebellion, &c.*, which sundry Furies are flourishing around, ' I could soon extinguish these puppet-show vapours, if properly supported.' The City Corporation has sent its deputies, as in the former print ; their complaint is, 'We have not been taxed this twelvemonth !' *Commerce* in this instance is depicted as a dissolute harridan, deep sunk in gin.

December 30, 1788. *Sir Jeffery Dunstan Presenting an Address from the Corporation of Garratt.*—Pitt is crowned ; his throne is not, however, exactly a seat of dignity ; his secretary, Dr. Prettyman, Bishop of Lincoln, is holding an *Address from Manchester.*

Sir Jeffery Dunstan, a poor deformed, half-witted, and 'eccentric character' of the time, has shouldered the civic mace, and is presenting an address from the very ancient and respectable Corporation of Garratt, beginning : ' High and mighty Sir.' Pitt is replying : ' Thanks, thanks, my respectable friend ; this is the most delicious cordial I have tasted yet.' Brook Watson, Alderman Wilkes, and others are supporting the address. A tomfool, who, as trainbearer, has hold of Sir Jeffery's cloak, is enquiring, ' Did you ever see such grace and dignity in your life, Mr. Alderman ?' To which Wilkes is responding, ' Grace— he shall be made Master of the Ceremonies at St. James's !'

December 30, 1788. *The Word-Eater.* Published by S. W. Fores, 3 Piccadilly.

ADVERTISEMENT EXTRAORDINARY.—This is to inform the public that this extraordinary phenomenon is just arrived from the Continent, and exhibits every day during the sittings of the House of Commons before a select company. To give a complete detail of his wonderful talents would far exceed the bounds of an advertisement, as indeed they surpass the powers of description. He eats single words and evacuates them so as to have a contrary meaning. For example, the word Treason he can make Reason, and of Reason he can make Treason ; he can also eat whole sentences, and will again produce them either with a double, different, or contrary meaning, and is equally capable of performing the same operation on the largest volumes and libraries. He purposes, in the course of a few months, to exhibit in public for the benefit and amusement of the Electors of Westminster, when he will convince his friends of his great abilities in this new art, and will provide himself with weighty arguments for his enemies.'

The hero of this specious advertisement is Fox ; he is standing near the Speaker's table, in the House of Commons, where the members are struck with amazement at his dexterity in this novel accomplishment. In one hand the Whig performer is holding out his speech on the *Rights of the Prince*, and the *Explanation of that Speech* in the other. ' All these,' he declares, ' I will devour

---

¹ It must be remembered that in 1788 the public were flocking to the performances of a famous stone eater.

next.' Two important and bulky works are at his feet, waiting their turn to be devoured—*Jus Divinum of Kings* and *Principles of Toryism.* On the table, placed before the 'Word-Eater,' is a provision of considerable substance which will test his further powers of digestion—*Statutes at Large, Magna Charta, Principles of the Constitution,* and *Rights of the People.*

December 31, 1788. *Blue and Buff Loyalty.*—The sympathy openly manifested by the Whig faction for the Prince's prospects of succeeding to power is

HOUSEBREAKERS.

satirised at the expense of *Blue and Buff* susceptibilities. *Saturday.*—The Royal Physician is drawn looking very downcast, with his gold-headed cane to his lips. 'Doctor: How is your patient to-day?'—'Rather worse, sir.' *Blue and Buff Loyalty* is made to exult somewhat indecorously: 'Ha, ha! rare news!' *Sunday.*—'Doctor: How is your patient to-day?' The physician's face expresses restored confidence: 'Better, thank God!' An expression the reverse of loyal or pious is put into the mouths of the disappointed faction.

1788. *Housebreakers.* Drawn and etched by T. Rowlandson; aquatinted

by T. Malton. Republished by S. W. Fores, 3 Piccadilly, August 1, 1791.—
This plate represents the domestic felicity of well-to-do citizens being rudely
broken in upon by robbers and threatening assassins.

LOVE AND DUST.

A very critical situation for all the actors concerned. What the next moment
may produce it is impossible to conjecture, so much depends upon the first shot ;

it is truly a moment of suspense.   Whether the horse-pistols of the burglars will miss fire, and the formidable blunderbuss held by the respectable householder will lodge its contents—which would be, seemingly, enough to mow down a regiment—in the dastardly bodies of the midnight marauders, must remain a problem, the solution of which is lost beyond recovery.

1788.   *Love and Dust.*—Cinder-sifters pursuing their grimy avocation somewhere in the outskirts, in the neighbourhoods where the great pyramidal heaps of dust and cinders were to be found in the last century.   That romance should soften

LUXURY AND DESIRE.

the front of labour, and that *Black Sal* and *Dusty Bob* should lighten the sifting of cinders with a mixture of conviviality and flirtation, is but another proof that human nature is everywhere constituted on the same susceptible principles— a fact open to demonstration.   The present print, which, in its way, is about as terrible in its vagabond fidelity and grim humour as anything which Rowlandson has left us, has been included in the present series, with a due sense of editorial responsibility, as affording a fair instance of our caricaturist's talent in Hogarth's realistic walk.

To draw this and similar groups from the life, Rowlandson had only to take

a stroll from Soho to the corner where the Gray's Inn Road now stands.   On
the ground which Argyle Street, Liverpool Street, and Manchester Street at
present occupy, in the caricaturist's day was spread 'that sublime, sifted
wonder of cockneys, the cloud-kissing dust-heap, which sold for twenty thousand
pounds.'

The sum quoted is apocryphal; but it is known that, by some chance, Russia
heard of these famous accumulations of dust and cinders—said to have been
existing on the same spot since the Great Fire of London—and, as the fallen

LUST AND AVARICE.

city of Moscow required rebuilding after Napoleon's famous Russian campaign,
the government of the Czar purchased the vast piles and shipped them to
Moscow.

This estate—the site of the ground on which the dust-heap stood—was
purchased by the 'Pandemonium Company' in 1826, for fifteen thousand pounds.
The Liverpool Street Theatre was erected, and the surrounding grounds subsequently let on building leases. Beyond the Gray's Inn Road heap—when the
Caledonian Road was a rural thoroughfare—was the Battle-Bridge Estate of

some twenty acres, described in the 'New Monthly Magazine' (1833) as 'the grand centre of dustmen, scavengers, horse and dog dealers, knackermen, brick-makers, and other low but necessary professionalists.' As Mr. T. C. Noble—the descendant of the original lucky speculator who secured the dustheap, and sixteen dilapidated tenements, as he relates, for about 500*l.*—communicated to Pink's *History of Clerkenwell*, 'the site of the mountain of cinders is now covered by the houses of Derby Street; the names of the thoroughfares erected on this estate were derived from the popular ministers of that day.'

November 28, 1788. *Luxury and Desire.* Published by W. Rowlandson,

STAGE COACH AND BASKET.

49 Broad Street, Bloomsbury.—A battered old hulk—a regular ancient com-modore—is forcing a well-filled purse on the acceptance of a graceful and well-favoured maiden.

November 29, 1788. *Lust and Avarice.* Published by W. Rowlandson, 49 Broad Street, Bloomsbury.—A pretty simple-looking girl, dressed in a countrified garb, is exacting contributions from a miserly curmudgeon, who it seems is extremely reluctant to part with his money.

December 3, 1788. *Stage Coach with Basket: the Dolphin Inn.*—Published by William Rowlandson, 49 Broad Street, Bloomsbury.—A scene of bustle and

activity, consequent upon the departure of a stage coach from a posting-house in
a flourishing country town.   From the business going on in the background it is

AN EPICURE.

evidently market-day.   The coach is taking up its complement of passengers at
the *Dolphin Inn* ; the landlord of the house is civilly doing the honours of his

establishment, and conducting a party of new arrivals to the comforts of his hostelry.

1788.   *An Epicure.*—Another Hogarth-like study, but touched with all the knowledge and spirit peculiarly the attributes of Rowlandson.   An over-fed gourmand, whose hopes of happiness are evidently centred on perishable things, is exulting, with pantomimic rapture, over a delicacy in the way of fish.   (See 1801, republished.)

1788.   *A Comfortable Nap in a Post-chaise.*—A well-fed easy-going pair, reposing in a jogging post-chaise, are soothed into slumber by the motion, and are being rattled along oblivious of their surroundings.

1788.   *A Fencing Match.*—Rowlandson was an amateur, as we have noticed,

A COMFORTABLE NAP IN A POST-CHAISE.

of all manly exercises.   In his day riding, boxing,[1] and especially fencing, were considered indispensable accomplishments for the man of 'ton.'   We have had occasion to allude to our artist's intimacy with Angelo, the fashionable professor of sword exercises, who notices the caricaturist's works with appreciation, and mentions him with the highest personal esteem, in various passages of his memoirs and anecdotes.   Rowley executed numerous sketches for his friend Angelo; and he further engraved a series of plates for him, besides a large and interesting view of his fencing-rooms.

[1] The caricaturist is said to be the hero of the sparring roysterer in his unflattering delineation of *A Brace of Blackguards,* introducing George Moreland the painter and himself under a situation little complimentary to the softening influences of the fine arts.   The plate is given in this work under the date *May* 30, 1812, when it was re-issued by the artist, but the original etching properly belongs to a much earlier period, and was probably executed about a quarter of a century anterior.

A FENCING MATCH.

THE PEA-CART.

The present subject, which is particularly excellent as regards grouping and execution, probably represents an encounter at Angelo's rooms, either in the West or in the City, in both of which parts of town he held establishments. The principal figures, and the personages grouped around the fencers, were no doubt meant to designate portraits ; but as no evidence has been preserved to this date that would assist in more than a partial identification of one or two professional celebrities, it is nearly impossible to recognise the major part of the individuals present.

1788. *A Print Sale. A Night Auction.*—The rooms of an old auctioneer, where night sales of pictures, drawings, and prints, were held. The auctioneer is seated under a candelabra, at his desk, which is placed upon a circle of boards running round the apartment, and forming a trestle for the display of engravings. The customers, connoisseurs, collectors, artists, &c., are seated on the outside of the circle, and on either side of the seller. The sale-clerk, and the men who are showing the lots, are in the space within the centre.

Contemporary references further describe these 'night auctions,' where the caricaturist's drawings frequently figured, and which Rowlandson occasionally attended, in company with his friends Mitchell the banker, Parsons and Bannister the comedians, *Antiquity* Smith, *Iron-wig* Heywood, Caleb Whiteford, and other *dilettanti.* See page 70.

1788(?). *The Pea-cart.*

1789.

Several of the prints included under our description of the political caricatures
for 1789 are confessedly of somewhat doubtful parentage. In one or two
cases, other artists, like Kingsbury, are entitled to the credit of having a share
in the prints we here include with Rowlandson's works.

After carefully examining and comparing the questionable plates with those
whose authenticity is certain, we have selected only such examples as we feel
convinced are not altogether out of place in this volume, while we acknowledge
a doubt of their precise authenticity. It is the old story of the engraver with
more than one publisher disguising his handiwork, as Gillray and other caricaturists are well known to have done, to accommodate rival print-selling firms,
without appearing to depart from the loyalty due to their principal employer. In
the case of Gillray, it will be remembered, his allegiance was enlisted, and in a
more special manner than is usual in the relation between artist and publisher,
in the interests of the Humphreys. In the instance of Rowlandson, although he
did not supply any one firm with his works, to the exclusion of other publishers, at
the period we are describing—and before either Mr. Ackermann, of the Strand,
took our artist under his protecting care, or Mr. Tegg, of Cheapside, began to
pour his cheaper caricatures into the market—it will be recognised that Rowlandson's best prints were issued by Mr. S. W. Fores, of Piccadilly. He occasionally,
when a popular subject gave unusual impulse to the demand for satirical plates,
supplied Mr. W. Holland of Oxford Street with his etchings, slightly varying
his style as far as the manipulative portion of the engraving was concerned,
but retaining all the more special features of his identity. Indeed it is doubtful
if he sought to disguise his handiwork in the sense adopted by Gillray, who did
not hesitate, it has been said, to produce inferior piracies, executed by his own
hand, with intentional clumsiness and apparently defective skill, after his own
masterpieces, to accommodate caricature-sellers who wished to secure his works
otherwise than through the legitimate channel of his own publishers, who are
known to have been both respectable and liberal in their dealings with this
wayward and unscrupulous genius.

January 1, 1789. *The Vice Q——'s Delivery at the Old Soldier's Hospital in Dublin.*—Published in Dublin; republished by W. Holland, 50 Oxford Street.—This print alludes to a certain interesting event. The Lord Lieutenant's lady has apparently been confined in a ward of the Soldier's Hospital, Dublin. One old veteran, who is nursing the bold young stranger, is declaring: 'Deel, my saul, but he'll be a brave soldier.' The distinguished parent is responding: 'Thanks, thanks, my brave sergeant, you shall be knighted this day.' Soldier's porridge is supplied, as a substitute for caudle. An invalided warrior is inclined to quarrel with this proceeding: 'Downright robbery, by St. Patrick! We'll soon be famished if our broth is to be stole from us in this manner.'

January 8, 1789. The modern Egbert, or the King of Kings.—The Prince of Wales is pictured in the position of Egbert when towed by kings on the river. The vexed question of the '*Regency Restrictions*' is still the difficulty of the situation. His Royal Highness is held captive; his hands and feet are bound in golden chains. The arms of the *Stork and Anchor*, as hung out upon Pitt's barge, are placed above the *Royal Standard of England.* The modern Egbert, while passing St. Stephen's, is declaring, in reference to his fettered condition, 'I feel not for myself but for my country.' Pitt, wearing the dress in which he is usually represented—the Windsor uniform—and with an imperial diadem placed upon his head, is acting as steersman to his barge, which carries a huge flag inscribed with his arms, and the words '*Devil take right, P. W.'* The young statesman is encouraging his crew to 'pull together, boys!' The four oarsmen are all crowned as kings. Thurlow the Thunderer, with his diadem perched above his chancellor's wig, is acting as stroke, and pulling away vengefully: 'Damme, I've got precedence of the young lion!' The Marquis of Buckingham is asserting, 'I'll answer for the Shillalagh without authority!' Dundas is rowing with a long golden spoon; he is declaring, 'The prince shall remember old *Nemo Impune*;' and the Duke of Richmond, with one of his famous guns as an oar, is promising 'We'll show him Gallic faith!'

1789. *The Pittfall.*—The chance of catching the Crown—in the print a kind of *ignis fatuus*, has lured Pitt and the parliamentary allies (who supported his measures for 'restricting the powers of the Regent') to the brink of destruction. The Pittfall is nothing less than the infernal regions, pictorially set forth as smoke, and a great deal of flame, with fantastic devils, furies and pitchforks, all seething together. Pitt is making a flying leap to seize the Crown, which is fluttering above his reach: 'I'll have thee or perish in the attempt, for my ambition knows no bounds!' The leading demon is prepared with a barbed prong, to receive the Minister on his descent below, while offering Pitt the comforting assurance: 'You will be elected Regent in our dominions *nem. con.*' The Duke of Richmond has overstepped the margin, and is plunging headlong into the clutches of his tormentors. 'Spare me this time,' he cries; adding, with a liberality little likely to be appreciated in the quarter to which it is addressed, 'and you shall have coal in future without duty.' A friend is assuring the Duke, in allusion to his left-handed descent from Charles the Second, 'All your great grandfather's w——s are waiting dinner for you!'

Thurlow is hurling at the flitting diadem with the Chancellor's mace. He is proclaiming his resolution with a strong asseveration, 'I'll have a knock at it!' The Duke of Grafton also descended, it will be remembered, from the 'Merry Monarch,' is declaring, 'Junius has lamed me, or I'd have a knock at it too!'

January 30, 1789. *The Propagation of a Truth.* H. W. invt. Published by Holland, Oxford Street.—Bunbury's long serial slip, '*The Propagation of a Lie,*' enjoyed a wide reputation. In the present print Rowlandson, under the suggestion of his friend Wigstead, has turned the social satire to political purposes. The Tory chances seemed utterly forlorn at the time of the King's illness; indeed, the loss of their offices was only a question of days, until an unexpected change in the royal health cleared off their apprehensions. At the beginning of the year 1789, however, no one doubted that a week or two would see Fox and the Whigs back in power. In the *Propagation of a Truth* the members of the threatened Ministry are represented as imparting their personal apprehensions to one another confidentially. R——e (*Rose*), one of the Treasury Secretaries, is rushing in with this gloomy intelligence: 'The people refuse to address.' The profane Thurlow is invoking objurgations upon the optics of the public. Pitt is collapsing: 'Then I am done up!' Lord Sidney is declaring: 'It is all dickey with me!' Dundas is stamping with vexation: 'I'll gang to my own country, and sell butter and brimstone!' The Duke of Richmond is admitting his fears: 'I begin to smell powder;' and the Duke of Grafton is corroborating his colleague's theory. Lord Chatham, at the Admiralty, is asserting: 'I thought myself snug.' Lord Camden confesses, from his experience, 'I should have known better.' Brook Watson, with his wooden leg, is saying: 'I cannot Brook this, I'll hop off!' Grenville, who occupied the Speaker's chair (January 5 to May), does not relish losing his new wig. Old Alderman Wilkes, who had ratted extensively in his time, and who was, at the date of the present caricature, slyly paying his court to both sides simultaneously, is congratulating himself upon the famous squint immortalised by Hogarth: 'I can look either way!' Lord Carmarthen is uncomfortable: 'I've been in anguish all night!'

Both factions of Tories and Whigs alike were satirised alternately. If one print was severe on the Ministry and their adherents, it was certain to be followed in turn by no less cutting strictures upon their antagonists of the Opposition.

January 21, 1789. *Loose Principles.* Published by S. W. Fores, 3 Piccadilly.—Fox is represented in his study; the busts of Wat Tyler and Jack Cade are its ornaments. His book shelves offer '*The Laws of Pharaoh*,' '*Political Prints*,' '*Life of Oliver Cromwell*,' '*Cataline*,' '*Memoirs of Sam House*,' and kindred literature. Fox is plunged in distress; Burke is engaged in a certain quest; 'not searching for precedents, but consequences.' Sheridan—whose foot is standing on a volume of Congreve's plays, marked '*School for Scandal*,' indicating that this comedy was somewhat of a plagiarism from the works of his predecessor —has charge of the Regent's clyster-pipe, his confidential appointment being that of 'Principal Promoter of Loose Principles.'

January 28, 1789. *Suitable Restrictions.* Published by S. W. Fores, 3 Piccadilly.—The Heir Apparent, according to this print, is treated as an infant. A long pinafore, and a child's cap, are employed to carry out the theory of his puerility. Pitt, in court dress, is making sure of his ward, for he is holding him in leading-strings. Pitt's *restrictions* effectually prevent the Prince from stooping to take up the Crown, which is the subject of a new game of ring-tor. The leading Whigs, shown kneeling down at a little distance, are taking part in the sport. Fox is making a shot at the ring, in the centre of which stands the Crown of England: 'My game for a crown!' Sheridan's chief anxiety is for his own interests: 'Knuckle down, and don't funk, Charley.' Burke, who is eager to take his chance, is exclaiming: 'My turn next, Sherry!'

January 30, 1789. *Neddy's Black Box, containing what he does not value three skips of a louse.* Published by S. W. Fores.—The Prince appears on his throne, a full-fledged Regent by anticipation, with all his plumes and paraphernalia. The ex-patriot Burke is kneeling in an attitude of courtier-like servility, and presenting the head of Charles the First, preserved in the *Treasury Box*: 'My Liege, I told them in the House no day so proper to settle the Regency as Charles's martyrdom.' Sheridan, who wears the blue and buff uniform like his colleague, is supporting the orator: 'I, too, am for despatch; such days best suit our purpose.' From Sherry's pocket is peeping the pamphlet, '*Horne Tooke's Letter on the Prince's Marriage*,' which operated somewhat like a spark in a powder magazine at this date. A quotation from Edmund Burke's speech, referring to the day most suitable for the discussion of the Regency Bill, is added at the foot of the plate: 'Why not debate it on Friday? I say it is the only day in the year on which it ought to be debated (Charles's martyrdom), and carried up in the *Black Box*.'

1789. *State Butchers.*—In this view of the Prince's situation, the Heir Apparent is pictured as the victim of the combinations which Pitt contrived to hinder the Prince's accession to power by vexatious restrictions. The principal figure is that of the future Regent, laid out at length on the anatomy table, ready to be operated upon by the dissecting knives which his antagonists are eagerly setting to work. Pitt occupies the chair as president of this college of Surgeons; in his left hand is a paper, '*Thanks from the City of London with 50,000l.*' He is holding a wand in his right hand, with which he is pointing to the heart of his subject, beneath the Prince's Star of Brunswick; he is thus directing his head anatomist, Dundas :—'The good qualities of his heart will certainly ruin our plan; therefore cut that out first.' Lord Thurlow, in his Chancellor's robes, is, like Hamlet, musing over the head of the fallen prince. Lord Sydney has his knife held ready for a desperate gash. The two Stuart peers are assisting as amateur butchers. The Duke of Grafton has a dissecting knife in either hand; at his feet is a formidable basket of saws and cutting in-

A NEW SPEAKER.

struments; his preparations are on an extensive scale, while the Duke of Richmond is prepared to resort to even clumsier methods, since *Uncle Toby* is wielding a heavy executioner's axe in readiness to cut in at any signal.

February 6, 1789. *A New Speaker.* Published by H. Holland, Oxford Street. —Addington, the Speaker, is at his table. Pitt, standing behind him, has thrust a speaking trumpet into his mouth, through which the orator, to the amazement of the other members, is holding forth : 'Eyes has he and sees not, neither is there any breath in his mouth, but through the hollow of his head shall the sound of my own voice be exalted, and through the stuttering of his tongue my intentions be more fully explained. Keep together, my good friends, till I go out, and you will then probably follow me, but I will work changes for you. See how this rank Tory becomes a good Whig!' The mace is lying on the table beside the '*City Address, 50,000l.*; *Aldermen Hoppikicky, Squintum, Peter Grievous, &c.*,' and a proposed *List of Taxes*, which includes such items as *Fox-tails, Play (i.e* gambling) *Houses* &c., fanciful personal enactments levelled against Pitt's great rival.

February 7, 1789. *Britannia's Support, or the Conspirators Defeated.* Published by H. Holland, Oxford Street.—The Prince, who is looking somewhat ill at ease under the circumstances, has been attacked by Pitt and his allies, the Stuart dukes. Pitt is aiming an awkward blow at the tutelary divinity and her protégé with a terrible-looking axe. The Duke of Richmond is firing a musket; and the Duke of Grafton, as a midnight assassin, is operating with a dagger and a dark lantern. Britannia has taken the Heir Apparent to her arms, and is shielding the menaced Prince with her person.

February 7, 1789. *The Hospital for Lunatics.*—A companion to the preceding. The results of the Tory excitement have landed certain sufferers in the Lunatic Asylum. The mad doctor is going his rounds, he is declaring; 'I see no signs of convalescence!' His assistant, following with a few strait-waistcoats for the refractory patients, is supporting the opinion of his chief : 'They must all be in a state of coercion!' Pitt is the first sufferer; he is wearing a coronet of straws, and is waving a sceptre of twigs ; over his head is the notice : *Went mad, supposing himself next heir to a Crown.*' In the adjoining cell is the Duke of Richmond, who is buried in the contemplation of toy cannons—'*Went mad in the study of fortifications.*' Next to him is another victim, '*Driven mad by a political itching.*'

February 7, 1789. *Britannia's Support.*

February 15, 1789. *Going in State to the House of Peers, or a Piece of English Magnificence ; dedicated to Mr. Pitt and his 267 Liberal friends.* Published by William Holland, 50 Oxford Street.—This print, with one or two others of similar character, have been attributed to Kingsbury. A careful comparison of these doubtful plates, with the more recognised etchings of both Rowlandson and Kingsbury, has led the writer to the conclusion that several at least of the caricatures published by Holland at this time, owe their existence, at least in part, to the skill of the former, although he has in some degree modified his usual handling.

The Heir Apparent is proceeding in burlesque state to the chamber of Peers. A ragged mob is in attendance. The arms on his carriage are turned upside down, coachman and footmen are of the shabbiest, and the slovenly coach is drawn by eight miserable animals, who can barely crawl, while one of the broken-kneed leaders has actually come to grief. The Tories have taken their places at certain windows to view the procession.   The Duke of Orleans (who was on a visit to this country), or the French Ambassador, is amazed at such a dowdy spectacle ; next to his window is Lord Amherst.   The Stuart-Dukes of Richmond and Grafton, sharing a window, are agreeing that the Prince's turn-out is ' Well enough for any of the Brunswick race ;' they have put up at the sign of the ' *Lion in the Toils.*'   The Marquis of Carmarthen is saying, ' Very pretty indeed ;' he is at the sign of ' *The Restrictions*' (a picture of the Prince in the pillory is on the signboard) ; his neighbour Pitt is declaring the show to be ' a very magnificent spectacle, upon my honour.'   Lords Hood and Chatham, at the sign of ' *The Chatham and Hood,*' a frigate labouring in a storm being the signboard, are on the look-out : ' The great naval review was nothing to it.'   Lord Chatham is assuring his companion that the show is ' infinitely superior to my father's funeral.'   Lord Thurlow is asseverating with an oath, ' It eclipses all that has been ever seen in Rome !'

March 6, 1789.   A Sweating for Opposition, by Dr. Willis Dominisweaty and Co.   Published by S. W. Fores.—The health of the King, according to the reports of his physicians, began to improve from this date.   It was hinted rather broadly that this intelligence was not so agreeable to the Opposition as they might desire.   The print sets forth the new treatment by which the growing consequence of the Whigs was to be reduced.   The several patients are placed in small furnaces, with a blazing fire below each ; the doctors are attending to the stoking with a will.   Burke is becoming quite limp in the process : ' I have got no juice left.'   Fox is becoming furious ; he is gesticulating and shouting, ' I have sweated enough.'   Sheridan is venemous : ' This is scandalous ; the Baily's (Bailiffs) have sufficiently sweated me !'   The Prince, in an agony, is crying : ' I suppose they call this a Regency sweat.'   A lady next to him is declaring : ' I sweat with desire.'   Weltjé, the Prince's house steward and head cook—a man who enjoyed considerable reputation in spite of the satirists—is asserting : ' I never sweat so much at cooking in my life.'   Mrs. Fitzherbert, who is separated from her admirer, is highly indignant : ' I sweat with jealousy ; what disregard to the marriage right !'

March 10, 1789.   Edward the Black Prince receiving Homage.   Published by William Holland, 50 Oxford Street.—Thurlow, in his Chancellor's robes, is assuming the sovereign position ; he has the crown and sceptre ; Adam, wearing his counsellor's gown, has come to ' kiss hands.'   According to the print *the black-browed Thunderer* is blessed with the hairy paws of a bear, not omitting the claws.   On the wall, in the background, is a picture of *Blood stealing the Crown.*

March 7, 1789.   The Irish Ambassadors Extraordinary.   A gallantee Show.   Published by S. W. Fores.—The six members of the so-called Irish Embassy are galloping up to the colonnades of Carlton House, each mounted on a jibbing

Irish bull; the riders have their faces to the tails, by which they have taken hold in order to secure their seats. The Marquis of Lothian and the Duke of Leinster are urging the deputation forward. It is understood they have arrived somewhat late. The holder of the address is declaring: 'Aye, aye, the Marquis of Buckingham will remember me when I go back again.' The other deputies are making pertinent observations: 'The folks stare at us as they would at wild beastises!' 'What a nice errand is this; make him Regent whether or no!' 'I say, my friend, we shall be there the day before the fair!' 'Well! yes, I dare say well! why, he was so bad he could say nothing but " *What, what, what*," when we left Dublin!' 'What, no occasion for a Regent? then we will go back again and tell the lads we are all mad, and, by the powers, 'tis my opinion we are come over for nothing at all, at all!' The cook of the *Pall Mall Ordinary* is thrusting his stout body out of a window opposite Carlton House and declaring: 'Begar, I must go prepare more sourkraut for dese wild bullocks!'

March 15, 1789. *Irish Ambassadors Extraordinary ! ! ! In a few days will be published the Return of the Ambassadors.*—The memorable six are mounted on their prancing bulls, with a sack of potatoes behind each for a saddle, and as provisions for the journey; all are armed with bludgeons. The delegates are headed by a personage with a crozier and a mitre, a sort of episcopal leader, who is exhorting his followers to ' Make haste, my honies!' The Duke of Leinster is flourishing his shillalagh: 'No restrictions, by the Holy Cross of St. Patrick!' Others are crying: ' How our Majority will astonish the young King!' Some doubt crosses their minds as to his Majesty's possible restoration to health: ' My dear, I was told that he was recovering fast!' ' No! as mad as a hatter!'

Press Notices. March 2, 1789. *Address from the Parliament of Ireland to the Prince of Wales.* (*Morning Herald*).—' We have, however, the consolation of reflecting, that this severe calamity hath not been visited upon us until the virtues of your Royal Highness have been so matured as to enable your Royal Highness to discharge the duties of an important trust, for the performance whereof the eyes of all his Majesty's subjects of both kingdoms are directed to your Royal Highness.'

March 4, 1789. *Irish Embassy Uniform.* (*World*).—The great open pocket *on either side* is this : When the Duke of Leinster was coming, he wrote indefinitely to have a new coat. ' I would not be in his coat for something,' said Lord Robert Fitzgerald pleasantly, when he heard of the mischievous folly. But wishing to do the best he could for his brother, he ordered him the *Constitutional* uniform of *Blue* and *Orange.* This, of course, the Duke, when he came, would not wear; and new clothes being hastily wanted, Jennings and Headington, the tailors, were left at liberty, *and they made the* GREAT OPEN POCKET *on either side !*

March 19, 1789. *Ireland—by Express: The Six Amazing Bulls.* (*World.*) —' The proprietor of these unruly animals begs leave, through the channel of the *World*, to return his most grateful thanks for the great encouragement Mr. GRATTAN's *Bulls* met with in London, and most particularly from their Royal Highnesses the Prince of Wales and the Duke of York.

' He is sorry to say that upon the road these animals grew very unruly. The completely horned one was four times beaten, for taking what did not belong to him ; and the *little bull*, called 'my lord,' who had but a stump of a tail, had that cut off by a wicked boy for his diversion.

' The other four all tumbled into the water, as they landed at Dublin, and looked so ill, when they were driven into Mr. Grattan's stable, " that he wished to heaven he had never sent them over ! "

' The proprietor has likewise to add, that they were so well fed by the kindness of the gentlemen in London, that they do not again take kindly to Irish potatoes. He hopes, however, by beating them regularly every day, he shall drive sense into them.

' The collection for seeing these amazing animals upon the road was very handsome. Since their arrival here, the Lord-Lieutenant has had an offer of them for sale, and *very cheap* ; but he thought they had been so " hawked about," by being up at public show in London, he would have nothing to do with them. So the bulls are where they were—with the proprietor.'

March 9, 1789. *The Answer to the Irish Ambassadors.* (*Morning Chronicle*).

Your duty to the King is great,
    As all mankind must see ;
And, though you're come a day too late,
    You're welcome still to me.

You'll guess what want of speech conceals,
    As Irishmen should do ;
You'll guess my understanding feels,
    My heart remembers, too.

You take a different line, I see,
    From England and oppose her ;
But well I know you disagree
    To make the Union closer.

As to the rest of your Address,
    I know not what to do ;
I fear 'tis treason to say Yes,
    I'm loth to answer No.

    Should he relapse, indeed, I might
        Accept the Irish sway ;
    But that I cannot learn to-night,
        So come another day.

March 2, 1789. *The Prince's Answer to the Address of the Deputation from Ireland.* (*Morning Herald*).—' " If, in conveying my grateful sentiments on their conduct, in relation to the King, my father, and to the inseparable interests of the two kingdoms, I find it impossible adequately to express my feelings on what relates to *myself,* I trust you will not be the less disposed to believe that I have an understanding to comprehend the value of what they have done, a heart that must remember, and principles that will not suffer me to abuse their confidence.

'" But the fortunate change which has taken place in the circumstances which gave occasion to the Address agreed to by the Lords and Commons of Ireland induces me for a few days to delay giving a final answer ; trusting that the joyful event of his Majesty's resuming the personal exercise of his Royal authority may then render it only necessary for me to repeat those sentiments of gratitude and affection for the loyal and generous people of Ireland which I feel indelibly imprinted on my heart."

'The Prince of Wales has conducted himself in this delicate point with the circumspection and propriety that has marked the whole of his conduct in the late melancholy and critical circumstances.   He called to his aid the first legal ability in the kingdom ; and on the subject of the answer to the Irish Address had a conference of several hours with the Lord Chancellor and Lord Loughborough.'

March 16, 1789.   *The Ambassadors' Extraordinary Return, on Bulls without Horns.*   Published by S. W. Fores.—The same personages we saw caricatured on the previous plate are represented in the sequel returning to Dublin.   They have exchanged their famous Irish bulls for donkeys ; their potatoes have gone, but they are liberally provided with *Regency Cakes* in their place.   Their Pope, whose donkey's head is ornamented with the plume of three feathers as borne by the Prince of Wales, is received by an eager deputation on his arrival : 'What news, what news ? The tidings tell. Make haste and tell us all ; say why are they thus mounted ? Is the Regent come and all ?'   The leader is replying : 'I'll tell you all in no time. Why, you must know the King is better than the Regent—that is all!'   The Marquis of Lothian is declaring, 'Master Walgee (Weltjé) made us such Regent's and Regency cakes!'   The Duke of Leinster is crying, 'Aye, my lads, Dr. Willis has done the King over, and the Regent won't take it !'   Other members of the deputation are remarking, 'The English lads were so merry, by my shoul, they were always a-laughing at us !' 'Ambassadors Extraordinary, by St. Patrick, but I've forgot what we have done !' 'Done ? Why carried the address, and brought it back again, with all these cakes. A deal better than potatoes !'

April 4, 1789.   *The Rochester Address, or the Corporation going to Eat Roast Pork and Oysters with the Regent.*—The procession of the Corporation of Rochester is headed by the Mayor (Matthews), who is holding the *Address* at the end of a pole ; he proposes to send the Regent 'some chips.'   The rest of this train, professional men and traders of Rochester, are promising to favour the heir to the throne with their specialities.   Alderman Spice will 'assist him with long sixes.' Alderman Thompson will favour him with his *Preventative*; another, a brewer, will send him 'some *Chatham Butt*:' Prentice professes to 'give him thirteen to the dozen, and all sour;' another member of the Corporation, a barber by trade, is proposing to 'shave him.' Sparks, a lawyer, is declaring, 'I'll beg to speak to Sherry for his business, bailing, actions, demands, writs of error; that is, if he'll promise to see me paid!' Bristow is guaranteeing 'he shall never be tried by the Court of Conscience.' Robinson is asserting, 'These are your right sort; none of your quack;' and Alderman Nicholson, who is bringing up the rear, with a brick and trowel, is looking forward to the job 'of making him some fortifications!'

April 22, 1789. The Grand Procession to St. Paul's on St. George's Day, 1789: an exact view of the Lord Mayor carrying the City Sword, bareheaded, &c. Published by Holland, Oxford Street.—Upon the King's recovery the popular tide turned abruptly, and, before the end of April, the satirists were making capital out of the excessive gush of loyalty which greeted the King's restoration to health. The felicitations offered on this occasion were not, however, more extravagant than the congratulations which would have been offered the Regent had the case been altered. In the present print the procession is on its way to St. Paul's to return thanks; the Volunteers are keeping the line of route; the windows are filled with rejoicing spectators, smiling and bowing, with ribands, favours, and mottoes, inscribed with printed sentiments complimentary to the monarch. A man, wearing a leek in his hat, is at the head of the train, seated on a goat; the Aldermen, without hats or wigs, are finding some difficulty in keeping their seats. The Lord Mayor has a nervous time of it, while holding the Sword of State; two footmen are steadying him by the leg—his horse has been slightly startled—as he is passing a noisy band of musicians, stationed in a balcony. 'And all the people rejoiced and sung, Long live the King! May the King live for ever!' The King's well-appointed team of eight white horses is passing a show—the Royal Waxworks: 'Here you may see King Solomon in all his glory!' The state carriage contains the King, the Queen, and the coarse-featured Madame Schwellenberg; the Guards are bringing up the rear.

October 23, 1789. An Antiquarian. Published by W. Holland, 50 Oxford Street.

October 24, 1789. Sergeant Kite, Sergent Recruiteur. Published by S. W. Fores, 3 Piccadilly. (N.B. Fores' Museum now opened. Admission, one shilling.)—The Duke of Orleans is represented as Sergeant Kite, dressed in the uniform of a hussar—a tight tunic and breeches, given, in the coloured versions of the plate, as green, faced with crimson, and richly laced with gold; with a furred cocked hat and enormous cockade; inscribed on the scarf he is wearing are the words '*Vive la Liberté!*' destined shortly to become the keynote for all the reckless destruction, indiscriminate slaughter, and bloodthirsty atrocities of the great French Revolution. An enormous sabre is trailed by his side, and he is resting on a halbert with a head shaped like an axe. By his side is his drummer, whose figure the artist has treated with the broadest grotesque; the Frenchman's enormous earrings, together with a pigtail of inordinate length, are exciting the wonder of the spectators. The *Sergent Recruiteur* is beating up his recruits at Billingsgate amongst the fishfags. The *Poissardes* of France were making themselves a terrible reputation throughout Europe by the violence of their behaviour, and the satirist hinted in the present plate that the Duke of Orleans would be able to secure congenial revolutionary levies amongst the muscular vixens of the fish-market here. The viragoes of Billingsgate do not seem to favour the Duke's mission; they are giving the Frenchman what may be termed a warm reception: his advances are met with taunts, contumely, and apparently by challenges to ignominious personal combat.

January 1, 1789. *Grog on Board.* Published by S. W. Fores, 3 Piccadilly. Republished January 1794.—'Sweet Poll of Plymouth' has been smuggled on board during the absence, let us believe, of the chief officers, who have genteelly gone to take *Tea on Shore* in the port. A pretty 'mid-shipmite' and a black boy are deep in the perusal of a volume of fascinating voyages. The rest of the persons represented are, from the dog upwards, variously interested in their fair female visitor. One tar, in a fur cap, is singing verses, with his truant eye fixed on the nymph instead of on his music; another old salt, who is handing the punchbowl about, has evidently neglected his pipe, which he is vainly endeavouring to rekindle from the bowl of a comrade, who has eyes for nothing but the lady. 'Poll' is quite a Cleopatra for beauty, grace, and love of pleasure, if not for frailty and splendour; she is reposing with negligent ease in the stalwart arms of a good-looking sailor, for want of a more luxurious couch, and her foot is resting on the knee of another favoured swain, who seems proportionately proud of the honour. Her *débonnaire* ladyship is not only distinguished for the beauty of person and condescension of manners essential to make herself adored by poor Jack; she sports the wealth of jewellery supposed to be irresistibly gratifying in his sight—a pair of bracelets, earrings, imposing shoe-buckles, and, to cap all, a *pair* of watches, with massive chains and heavy trinkets galore, disposed on either side.

January 1789. *Tea on Shore.* Published by S. W. Fores, 3 Piccadilly. Republished January 1, 1794.—A companion to the last print, affording the supposititious contrast between high and and low life in port. The officers are leaving the vulgar jollifications of *Grog on Board* for delicate flirtations over the tea-table on shore. In those days, when opportunities for personal

distinction were more frequent, commanders were recognised and entertained
as heroes, and their visits on shore were not unfrequently a round of agreeable

festivals and social triumphs.   Rowlandson has shown how graciously the
fair are regarding the sons of Neptune, who are doing their best to create

favourable impressions in return.   The head of the house, who is not apparently of the slightest consequence on this occasion, is left to indifference and the

charge of the tea urn ; while the naval commanders are carrying all the admiration before them, on the venerable principle, lyrically rendered by John Dryden

(although the sentiment was no novelty in his day), that 'none but the brave
deserve the fair.'

February 1, 1789.   *Careless Attention.*   Published by J. Griggs, 216
Holborn.—A corpulent sufferer, disabled by gout, is thrown into a dreadful
quandary; he is seated by the fire, where the kettle is boiling over, deluging the
place, and threatening the invalid with the dangers of scalding.   The table, and
the little comforts spread thereon, are thrown down in the struggle to get out
of the dangerous vicinity; the gouty cripple is vainly shouting and storming for
assistance; his nurse, who is much too young, sprightly, and good-looking for
her situation, is seen at the door of the apartment, struggling in the embraces of

INTERRUPTION, OR INCONVENIENCE OF A LODGING-HOUSE.

a dashing young spark—probably the master's undutiful heir; the *coquetteries*
of the pair have engaged their full attention, to the neglect of the unfortunate
head of the house, of whose critical position they are delightfully unconscious.

April 1, 1789.   *Interruption, or Inconvenience of a Lodging-house.*   Published by S. W. Fores, 3 Piccadilly.   Republished April 1, 1824.—A stout
dowager and her maid are thrown into a state of consternation easy to appreciate by the sudden entrance on the occupations of the toilette of a roystering
young 'blood,' who, from the disorder of his dress and the recklessness of his
attitude, has evidently returned from the tavern, something the worse for his
evening's potations, and not strikingly clear in his head as to his ultimate
destination.

June 20, 1789. *A Sufferer for Decency.*—The interior of a barber's shop, conducted on popular principles, as the notice on the lantern has it : '*Shave with ease and expedition for one penny.*' It will be noticed that the lathering is accomplished on a wholesale scale; a boy is waiting on the customers with a small pail of soap, and is officiating with a lathering-brush of the size of a decent hearth-broom; the barber is waiting, with his razor poised in the air, ready to

A SUFFERER FOR DECENCY.

let it descend with a swoop on the face of the sufferer; expedition of execution rather than an artistic delicacy of handling being the order of the day at the class of establishment delineated by the caricaturist, who in the days of universal shaving must have known the cost of sacrificing to custom.

1789. *A Penny Barber.* Companion to *Sufferer for Decency* (June 1789). Published by W. Holland, 50 Oxford Street.—A stout old gentleman, enveloped

in a barber's cloth, has taken his seat in the shaving-chair; his wig is removed
and his chin plenteously lathered; the aproned barber is still employed with
his soap and basin.   One customer is performing an ablution; and the assistant,
whose hair is dressed in the wildest French style, is smoothing down a compact
full-bottomed old-fashioned wig.   One or two barber's blocks, a cracked
glass, and a bird in a cage form the chief embellishments, to which must be
added a lantern lighted by a single candle and inscribed with this information,
' *The oldest shaving shop in London.   Most money for second-hand wigs.*'

   About 1789.   *Domestic Shaving.*—A family group, delicately executed in

stipple in imitation of a chalk drawing.   The scene is pictured with considerable care and truthfulness to nature.   A stout gentleman, wigless and
with lather-spread chin, is rasping away at his ample throat before a hand-glass,
which a gracefully-drawn female, in a simple morning dress, is holding before the
' shaver.'   A pretty child is seated in an infant's chair by his side, watching,
with a pleased smile on her face, the gambols of a cat and kitten.

   August 4, 1789.   *A Fresh Breeze.*   Published by S. W. Fores.—A party
of distinguished guests are represented as trying a cruise on board the Southampton frigate.   An elevated personage, judging from his star and riband,
has secured his cocked hat with a handkerchief tied under his chin; he is suffering
the discomforts of sea-sickness.   The helmsman has some difficulty in steering,

surrounded as he is by a group of limp persons of fashion ; a fat dowager, who has propped herself against the back of the steersman, is trying to subdue her qualms by applying to cordials ; a more dignified lady is indulging in attitudes expressive of tragic despair. Three fair creatures have abandoned themselves to utter prostration on the opposite side. The sailors are exhibiting their disgust at the operation of washing down the decks and attending to the necessities of the sufferers ; fresh supplies of buckets, for the accommodation of the indisposed, are being handed up from below by a brace of 'Beef-eaters,' whose presence, so far from adding dignity to the company, is a source of inconvenience, since they

THE BETTING POST.

too are painfully sea-sick ; and their halberts, from the incapacity of the holders are threatening mischief to the helpless passengers around.

1789 (?). *The Start.*

1789 (?). *The Betting Post.*—The stout veteran on his cob, with a crutch in one hand, is intended for Colonel O'Kelly,[1] one of the most prosperous

[1] 'Colonel Dennis O'Kelly, the celebrated owner of *Eclipse* (this racehorse won everything he ran for), amassed an immense fortune by gambling and the turf, and purchased the estate of Canons, near Edgware, which was formerly possessed by the Duke of Chandos, and is still remembered as the site of the most magnificent mansion and establishment of modern times. The Colonel's training stables and paddocks, at another estate near Epsom, were supposed to be the best-appointed in England.'— *Hone's 'Table Book.'*

turfites of his day, and the owner of the most successful racehorse in the annals of racing.

1789 (?).   *The Course.*

1789 (?).   *The Mount.*—Colonel O'Kelly, the gouty veteran who figures throughout the Racing series, is again introduced ; this eminent patron of the turf is giving his parting injunctions to his jockey.[1]

1789.   *A Cart Race.*   Published by William Holland, Oxford Street, 1789. —This plate bears Rowlandson's signature, and is dated 1788.   The print is executed in bold outline, filled in with aquatint, and coloured in capital imitation of the original drawing.   The lowly cottages of some hamlet are partly distinguish-

THE COURSE.

able through the prodigious clouds of dust raised by the unruly eccentricities of a pleasure-party, represented as taking the air in three overladen and ramshackle carts, drawn by wretched horses barely one remove from the knacker's yard.

The amusement of the moment is an extemporised race.   One cart is leading triumphantly ; the horse is dashing along, urged on by the bludgeon of a coster-monger, who is conducting a party of beauties from St. Giles's, of the most florid and *dégagé* type.   Cart number two is considerably overmanned ; the horse is down ; the driver is alternately trying to whip his horse into animation or to lash

---

[1] A clever drawing, which has never, apparently, been engraved, *Colonel O'Kelly Enjoying a Private Trial previous to his Making a Match*, belonging to John West, Esq., is noticed in the Appendix.

his antagonists.   One free-and-easy lady is falling over the head of the cart, and
two more are being spilt over the tail. where they are sprawling in attitudes of
considerable freedom; a dog is indignantly barking at the fallen.   A third cart,
which is in the rear, is loaded so heavily that it seems there is difficulty in
persuading the horse to start at all.

   July 20, 1789.   *The High-mettled Racer.*

   1789.   *Don't he Deserve it?*   Designed and etched by T. Rowlandson; aquatinted by I. Roberts.   Published by William Holland, 50 Oxford Street.—An
elderly rake, evidently an old offender, taken in the fact. is receiving the well-
merited abuse of his modishly-apparelled better half; the fair companion of this

THE MOUNT.

compromising disclosure is covered with blushing confusion ; and various witnesses, summoned by the sounds of the wife's indignant eloquence, are expressing
their horror at the husband's obliquity.

   1789.   *She don't Deserve it.*   Designed and etched by T. Rowlandson ;
aquatinted by I. Roberts.   Published by William Holland, 50 Oxford Street.—
A pretty servant-maid, who has evidently been detected in some irregularity, is
literally ' kicked out,' *en deshabille,* by a tartar of a mistress.   The old master, who
is evidently the cause of the damsel's disgrace, and who has lost his wig in the
confusion of the disclosure, is ' starting like a guilty thing,' obviously anticipating
the connubial wrath which, in due course, will descend on his reprobate head.

September 1789. *Bay of Biscay.* Designed and published by T. Rowlandson, 1 James Street, Adelphi.—A ship is tossing on the stormy waters of the Bay of Biscay; a boatload of passengers, who have put off from the distant vessel, seems likely to be swamped by the waves, which are rolling mountains high. Fear and helplessness prevail on all sides; the sea is running too roughly for the oars to be of much avail; the captain and his crew have, it appears, abandoned their ship for the questionable chance of escaping in the long-boat; there are three ladies with them; one has apparently swooned, another is leaning over the side, with clasped hands, terrified at the imminence of the danger; and the third is in paroxysms which necessitate her forcible restraint. Rowlandson possessed the skill and perception to bring out every point in a desperate situation with thrilling effect, and his masterly power of depicting 'horrors,' &c., is in its way more striking, perhaps, even than his felicitous art of hitting off the salient humours of any of those ludicrous situations which his fanciful and inventive faculties suggested in exhaustless succession.

1789. *Chelsea Reach.* Designed and published by T. Rowlandson, 1 James Street, Adelphi.—A wondrous contrast to the horrors of the companion print, the *Bay of Biscay*; all is sunshine, jollification, and happiness. A gaily-decorated shallop, somewhat like a miniature edition of a state barge, is proceeding up the river with a pleasure-party, rowed by six gaily-clad watermen, wearing jockey caps, as was the custom of the time. A party of highly genteel ladies and gentlemen are exchanging courtesies, and pledging healths and toasts, under the shade of their parasols; an amateur musician is entertaining his friends with serenades on his flute, players on French horns are contributing to the diversion, a servant in livery is at the helm, and a large union-jack is flying. In the background is seen the tranquil river, with its distant bridges.

November 1789. *La Place des Victoires.*—If Rowlandson's visits to Paris had produced no other memorial than his inimitable picture *La Place des Victoires, Paris,* we should be satisfied with the result of his familiarity with Parisian life at the period immediately antecedent to the Revolutionary era.

The study, as a whole, is one of the most memorable we can ascribe to his skilful hand and his remarkable powers of profitable observation. The Circus, built by Mansard, one of the features of Paris under the Grand Monarque, remains in all its freshness to the present day; but it has shared the fate a similar monument would have suffered had it remained in the busy precincts of the East of London. Finding itself in the heart, as it were, of the trading centre of the city, near the Bourse, and hedged and elbowed around by the warehouses and industries of the busy commercial population, it has undergone an indignity which would vex the spirit of its founder and make the shade of the little monarch, in honour of whose victories it was erected and christened, exclaim against the degeneracy which the taste of his countrymen has undergone, and he would probably deplore the concession to utilitarianism which has transmogrified the well-known spot. *La Place des Victoires* in its present aspect is curiously disguised by hideous placards ; between each of the columns appear two or more humorous advertising boards, filling up the intermediate spaces, and inscribed with recommendations to purchasers to secure their wardrobe *au bon Diable*, and notices of a similar inviting character. Rowlandson has given a further indication of the Parisian centre—at the expense of topographical accuracy, it must be admitted—by introducing the towers of Notre Dame in a proximity somewhat closer than is legitimately warranted by the actual position of the mother church.

The monument, as seen in Rowlandson's veracious representation, is a splendid example of exaggerated glorification. The statue of a warrior—surely not intended to resemble the stout little monarch to whose glory it is dedicated—is trampling on an allegorical personage typifying the conquered enemies of France ; while the figure of Fame, holding her trumpet ready to sound the victor's praises, is crowning the hero with a wreath. Four chained slaves, cast in bronze, indicative of Louis' triumphs, are shown at the base ; these figures may now be seen in the Louvre. A courtier, or a disabled general, is pushed along in a ramshackle carriage, a sort of wheeled sedan, drawn by an old soldier, with two footmen to follow ; the Frenchman is regarding the stupendous monument raised to the glories of the Grand Nation with rapturous devotion. An *abbé*, with his hands in an enormous muff, is passing, with his nose in the air ; a *coquette à la mode* is leaning on his arm and raising her hood to shoot forth glances of fascination ; a handsome young officer, wearing a monstrous *queue*, is launching an admiring look towards the fair beguiler ; but her attention is engaged elsewhere, and the Parthian shot falls harmless. A shoeblack in the foreground is teaching a poodle to dance ; the comical animal's head is decorated with an old peruke. A pair of extensive beaux of the period are seen saluting each other with elaborate bows which would have filled the late Mr. Simpson, M.C., with despair. In the right-hand corner is shown a monk (Sterne's original *Brother Lorenzo*), shrinking away from recollections of the past. A downright English John Bull, in huge riding-boots, and a pretty English girl, his companion, in a habit, lacking the surrounding enthusiasm, are looking at the monument with the indifference of travellers who are in duty bound to take note of all the sights, but who, beyond the principle involved, find small gratification in the ordeal ; an English mastiff, the property of the strangers, is curiously regarding another exotic, an Italian greyhound. In the distance is shown a female porter and her donkey, followed by a procession of friars ; a French nobleman and his lady are driving by in gallant state, with a *Suisse* and a whole string of genteel footmen clinging like flies behind their chariot.

As the founder took some pains to inform the world (that is to say, Paris, which, to Frenchmen under the reign of the Grand Monarque, meant the universe), this wonderful structure, *à la gloire de Louis le Grand*, was erected by the Duc de la Feuillade, one of the idols of his age, and first satellite to the *Sun of Versailles*; Peer and Marshal of France, Governor of the Dauphin, Colonel of the Guards, &c.—in every way a most distinguished person. The statue was erected in front of this eminent courtier's Paris mansion, the *Hôtel de la Feuillade*. The principle of its erection was ingenious, ostensibly commemorating the glories of his master, the 'father of his people, and the conductor of invincible armies;' the celebrity of the patriotic founder of this monument is barely of secondary prominence, since his name and various high offices, emblazoned on the same pile, were bequeathed at the same time to the everlasting regard of posterity. The perpetual durability of fame in this case was doomed to last one century, and no more: the calculations of the Marshal did not include the coming French Revolution. In the January of 1793, the 'grand nation' became intoxicated with a saturnalia of blood, in which they avenged imposts, burdens, and slavery—evils which they had suffered in the past—by sacrificing the descendant of *le Grand Monarque*, a passive victim, on the scaffold to the vicious legacies of his predecessors. The fury which had made a martyr of the king, whose chief enjoyment had been the alleviation of the condition of his subjects, taking a retrospective turn, vented its destructive rage on every relic which recalled the servitude of generations—after the slaughter of the living, the national vengeance was wreaked on inanimate objects, and very naturally the ill-advised monument of the Place des Victoires came in for an early share of attention; and the memorial bequeathed to the everlasting admiration of posterity was scattered to the winds in a manner which effectually defeated the intentions of the testator; the only wonder being how the bronze figures escaped the fate of the furnace, and were spared being converted into artillery.

Under the circumstances, of the complete disappearance of this triumph of servile adulation, it is interesting to recall, in a remote degree, the incidents which attended its foundation. In the letters of Madame de Sévigné we trace a picture indicative of the events; first we are introduced to the zeal displayed by the Duc de la Feuillade, that inveterate and unequalled courtier, and his passion for raising monuments to the glorification of his master and himself. We follow the Marshal's first intentions, and are told how they were modified; we notice the erection of the pedestrian statue, with its glaring anomalies, sent to adorn the gardens of Versailles; and then we are instructed how the sculptor, Van den Bogaert—who, in compliment to his patrons, had changed his name to *de Desjardins*—was entrusted with the execution of the extraordinary conception which was to shed a lustre on the *Place des Victoires* to perpetuity.

*Lettre DCC. de Madame de Sévigné au Comte de Bussy, à Paris, ce 20 Juillet,
1679.*—'. . . . Il vous dira les nouvelles et les préparatifs du mariage du Roi
d'Espagne, et du choix du Prince et de la Princesse d'Harcourt pour la conduite
de la reine d'Espagne à son époux, et la belle charge que le roi a donnée à M.
de Marsillac, sans préjudice de la première ; et du démêlé du Cardinal de Bouillon
avec M. de Montausier, et comme M. de La Feuillade, courtisan passant tous
les courtisans passés, a fait venir un bloc de marbre qui tenoit toute la rue Saint
Honoré : et comme les soldats qui le conduisoient ne vouloient point faire place
au carosse de M. le Prince qui étoit dedans, il y eut un combat entre les soldats
et les valets de pied : le peuple s'en mêla, le marbre se rangea, et le prince passa.
Ce prélat vous pourra conter encore que ce marbre est chez M. de La Feuillade,
qui fait ressusciter Phidias ou Praxitèle pour tailler la figure du roi à cheval dans
ce marbre, et comme cette statue lui coûtera plus de trente mille écus.'[1]

In a footnote, by the editor, we are further enlightened on the use to which
this marble was finally applied, by order of the Duke de la Feuillade :—

'La Feuillade changea d'avis et fit sortir du bloc de marbre en question une
statue pédestre qui prêtoit à la critique, par le mélange bizarre du costume romain
recouvert du manteau royal françois. Cette statue du ciseau de Desjardins
(autrement Van den Bogaert) a été placée à l'Orangerie de Versailles.'

The next piece of information, also given in the editor's footnote, is more to
the point :—

'C'est le même artiste qui, six ans plus tard, a exécuté le monument de
la Place des Victoires, aussi magnifique qu'impolitique, et renversé en 1793 au
milieu des fureurs de l'anarchie. Il ne reste de ce monument que les quatre
figures, en bronze, d'esclaves enchaînés qui désignoient les nations dont la France
a triomphé dans le XVII* siècle. Ces figures sont dans la Collection de France.
—G. D. S. G.'

A fair-sized view of the Circus, Place des Victoires, and of the monument,
taken from the Hotel de la Feuillade, which would seen to have occupied
a frontage facing the semicircle, was published about 1686, engraved by N.
Guerard. The title runs thus :—

'Veue de la Place des Victoires où M. le Mareschal Duc de la Feuillade a
dressé un monument public à la gloire de Louis le Grand, de la statue de ce
Monarque couronné par la Victoire, accompagnée de Trophées, de Médailles, de
bas-reliefs, et d'inscriptions, sur les actions glorieuses de sa vie et de son règne.
Le 28 Mars, 1686.'

Numerous highflown praises of the King were engraved on the base of this
vainglorious monument, as well as a list of the various engagements fought in
the reign of Louis the Magnificent.

[1] Sévigné, vol. vi. pp. 98–157.

The principal inscription will give a fair impression of the nature of these panegyrics :—[1]

'*A Louis le Grand, le père et le conducteur des armées toujours heureux.*—Apres avoir vaincu ses Ennemis, Protegé ses alliez. Adjousté de tres puissants peuples à son Empire, Assuré les Frontières par des places imprenables, joint l'Ocean à la Méditerranée. Chassé les pirates de toutes les mers, Reformé les Loix, Destruit l'hérésie, porté par le bruit de son nom les nations les plus Barbares à le venir révérer des extremitez de la terre. Et reglé parfaitement

A DULL HUSBAND.

toutes choses au dedans et au dehors par la grandeur de son courage et de son génie.

'Francois Vicomte Daubusson, Duc de la Feuillade, Pair et Mareschal de France, Gouverneur du Dauphine, et Colonel des Gardes Françoises,

'Pour perpetuelle memoire

'A la postérité.'

---

[1] Place des Victoires. A circular open space, surrounded by houses, forming together one design, built by Mansard, 1686. Portions of the original statue of Louis XIV., raised by the Duc de la

November 29, 1789. *Mercury and his Advocates Defeated, or Vegetable In-trenchment.*—This print introduces a collision between two systems of medical treatment. The scene is Swainson's depôt for *Velno's Vegetable Syrup*, Frith Street, Soho. *List of Cures, in* 1788, 5,000 ; *in* 1789, 10,000. Swainson has entrenched himself in the centre of a barricade, formed of his specifics, a bottle of which he is exhibiting, with an air of triumph, to the posse of old practitioners, who, armed with dissecting-knives, mortars, mercury, prescriptions, and mineral pills, are preparing for a furious onslaught upon the innovator, whose introduction of *Velno's Syrup* has deprived them of the support of their profitable clients.

1789. *A Dull Husband.*—An interior scene, introducing us to a drawing-room of more refined character than Rowlandson generally selects for representation. The owners evidently occupy a wealthy position in life. The lady has musical tastes, it appears ; in the background is a harpsicord, the fair performer is playing the harp, and a guitar is lying at her feet. The husband has no soul for sweet sounds, or the soothing harmonies which his elegant companion has produced have lulled him into forgetfulness ; however it may happen, the gentleman is very evidently, and unpoetically, fast asleep.

Feuillade, in the middle, which was destroyed during the Revolution, are now in the Louvre : it was replaced by a statue of General Desaix, which, in its turn, was removed for the present one of Louis XIV. in the costume of a Roman emperor, by Bosio.

1790.

January 1, 1790.   *Tythe Pig.*   Published by S. W. Fores, 3 Piccadilly.—
Rowlandson has taken a vexatious institution, as enforced in his day, and turned

TYTHE PIG.

it to satiric account.   A vicar, who we presume is suffering for the sin of
gluttony—a failing to which at one time, if tradition is in any degree reliable, the
sons of most churches were more than slightly prone—since he is invalided by
an attack of gout, is seated in the official reception-room of his residence, within
view of his cure, in state, as becomes a dignitary of the Establishment, to receive
the tithes of his parish. His clerk is planted by his side, auditing *An Estimate of
the Tythes of this Parish.* This functionary is examining, with somewhat minute
scrupulousness, a fat pig which is borne in for approval by a comely maiden.

The contributor of the said pig, a country clown, who is evidently but half resigned to part with his belongings, is standing in the doorway scratching his shock head, wearing a face which expresses anything but approval of the surrender of his porker.

No date: about 1790. *A Roadside Inn.*—Two travellers are stopping to take refreshment at a pretty rustic hostel. A wain, drawn by a yoke of horses, is shown passing up the road.

January 1, 1790. *A Butcher.* Published by T. Rowlandson, 50 Poland Street.—In point of refinement this print has nothing to recommend it; a more barbarous rendering of a subject, which has in itself little of the picturesque,

A ROADSIDE INN.

cannot be well imagined. The subject is, however, treated with so much force and originality, that we considered it worthy to be inserted in our selection, as a representative example of Rowlandson's abilities in the savage walk—a branch to which he brought especial qualifications. And as it is the object of this work to give our readers a fair estimate of the abilities of an artist whose pictures reflect, in a great measure, the dispositions and tastes of his times, we have introduced more than one subject which may, on its individual merits or defects, at first strike the critic as at least coarse, if not altogether free from objectionable associations.

January 10, 1790. *Frog Hunting.* Published by T. Rowlandson, 50 Poland

Street.—Three Frenchman of quality, adorned in the most modish taste, with their frills, powdered curls, pigtails, ear-rings, ruffles, and dress swords, are plunging knee deep in a pond of water, hunting, with the enthusiasm of true epicures, a party of frightened frogs.   A fashionably clad Frenchwoman is stand-

A BUTCHER.

ing on the bank, holding a parasol in one hand, and a row of frogs, the spoils of the chase, strung on a skewer, in the other.

February 20, 1790.   *Toxophilites* (large plate).   Published by E. Harding, 132 Fleet Street.

February 20, 1790.   *Repeal of the Test Act.*   Published by S. W. Fores, 3 Piccadilly.

REPEAL OF THE TEST ACT.

> Bell and the Dragon's chaplains were
> More moderate than those by far ;
> For they, poor knaves, were glad to cheat,
> To get their wives and children meat.
> But these will not be fobb'd off so ;
> They must have wealth and power too.

An exaggerated, view from a Conservative point of observation, of the results which were to be anticipated if the repeal of the Test Act was allowed to be carried.

This caricature was put forth at the time Doctors Priestley and Price—those *revolution sinners*, as their opponents styled them—were lecturing and spreading broadcast principles of religious equality, reforms, which, as the Ministers industriously circulated, if carried into effect, would prove subversive of everything. A portly Bishop, with his *Refutation of Dr. Price* by his side, is left to the tender mercies of the Reformers—'And when they had smote the shepherd, the sheep were scattered.' The work of revision is carried on by main force, two of the 'new lights,' aided by stout cudgels, are converting the overgrown Shepherd : 'Make room for the Apostle of Liberty ;' and 'God assisting us, nothing is to be feared.' Doctor Priestley is superintending the demolition of the venerated edifice : 'Make haste to pull down that, and we'll build a new one in its place.' Two of the Reformers are displaying their 'brotherly love' by fighting for the possession of the Chancellor's purse and mace. The *Thirty-nine Articles* are sent to feed a bonfire. A leader of the movement, inspired by 'love of our country,' has climbed up where the insignia of church and state are seen swinging upon a sign-post. He is provided with a flaming *Torch of Liberty*, with which he is threatening their destruction.

Fox is shown as the arch-director of this innovating agitation :—'day next, a charity sermon by the Rev. Charles Fox.' The Whig chief is drawn at a window, armed with a speaking-trumpet, and advertising '*Places under Government to be disposed of. N.B. Several Faro and E. O. Tables in good condition.*' Dissenting preachers are hurrying up, furnished with well-filled money-bags, to secure the political influence which Fox is openly holding out for purchase, without any attempt at disguise.

1790. *Dressing for a Masquerade.* (Cyprians.)

1790. *Dressing for a Masquerade.* (Ladies.)

1790. *A French Family.* T. Rowlandson, del. S. Alken, fecit. Published by S. W. Fores, 3 Piccadilly.—One of the two subjects highly commended by H. Angelo in his 'Reminiscences.' The companion, *An Italian Family*, will be given under the head of caricatures published in 1792. Both impressions are scarce, and very seldom met with. These prints are supposed to represent the domestic and interior lives of foreign artists, as studied from observations founded, it is presumed, on the everyday habits of the aliens domiciled in England. Monsieur and his family are probably professional dancers, and the picture introduces us to their more intimate hours of practising; at all events, we find nearly the entire generation giving up their energies—somewhat to the neglect of the proprieties, it is true—to the practice of the one accomplishment in which the politest of nations was supposed to enjoy pre-eminence. The grandfather, in a cotton nightcap, is supplying the music from his fiddle, but the contagion of motion is affecting his aged limbs, and he is skipping about with the animation of old Vestris; by his side is the youngest child, who, still in her night-clothes, is practising the first positions. It will be noticed that, in spite of somewhat squalid surroundings, the whole generation excel in personal finery: a profusion of hair, dressed in the extreme of fashion, ruffles, furbelows, frills, bows, ear-rings, and elegant slippers, are displayed by the various members.

The son and daughter are gracefully executing a *pas de deux*. The person of Madame is charmingly rendered; an elaborately constructed tower of fair hair, and a nodding plume of feathers, add height and distinction to her figure, to which the designer has lent a grace and ease of motion peculiarly French. Monsieur is truly magnificent in the item of wig; his pink satin coat is hung on the top of the turn-up bedstead, and he is disporting himself in a sleeved vest; the lower limbs of the gentleman give room for conjecture. Whether he has taken the liberty of appearing in *sans-culotte* negligence out of respect to the principles of the Revolution, then in its fury, or whether his nether garments and stockings have been pledged to satisfy the necessities of the hour, is not clear. Perhaps the artist drew the Frenchman in this guise as a concession to English prejudices at the period when it was a pretty universally received theory that his compatriots lived on frogs exclusively, and had thrown away their *culottes* for good; the last supposition being to a large degree warranted by the maniacal excesses of the Jacobin, Poissarde, and other sections in Paris. In the left-hand corner of the picture is a cleverly designed group, somewhat independent of the main action. A French child, dressed in the burlesque of miniature manhood, as then adopted by our tasteful neighbours, is playing a pipe and tambourine and training a pair of performing poodles to dance a minuet on their hind legs. A lean cat is vainly trying to find something to satisfy her hunger in the cupboard. The only decent article of furniture in the chamber—which is dirty, patched, and poor—is a concession to vanity in the form of a large mirror.

March, 1790. *A Kick-up at a Hazard Table.* Published by Wm. Holland, Oxford Street.—A large plate, executed in bold outline with a little mezzo work, introduced in the darker parts. The *Kick-up* is of a serious character; the gamblers who lately occupied the front of the table are upset in the confusion, and others are endeavouring to get out of the way of the danger. A stout old buck in the King's uniform—a loser, it would seem, from his empty pocket-book —has drawn his pistol on a player opposite, who has presumably won the irate gentleman's gold, since he is covering the pile with one hand, and with the other is aiming, in his turn, a pistol full at his adversary's person. Great excitement prevails around; one man is dashing a chair at the officer's outstretched firearm, and a brother officer is striking with a bottle and a candlestick at the other weapon; bludgeons are flourished, and swords are drawn by some of the gamblers, while others are endeavouring to stand clear before the bullets begin to fly.

A party of gentlemen assembled on the evening of a Court Drawing-room at the Royal Chocolate-house in St. James's Street, where disputes at hazard produced a quarrel, which became general throughout the room. Three gentlemen were mortally wounded, and the affray was at length concluded by the interposition of the Royal Guards, who were compelled to knock the parties down with the butt ends of their muskets indiscriminately, as entreaties and commands were of no avail. A footman of Colonel Cunningham's, greatly attached to his master, rushed through the swords, seized, and literally carried him out by force without injury.

May 29, 1790. *Who kills first for a Crown.* In two compartments. —The objects of the chase being the respective crowns of two kingdoms, both of which were disturbed at the date of this publication, by the ambitious views of the advanced parties; headed by the Heir-Apparent in the one case, and the Duke of Orleans in the other.

The Crown of England is threatened in the upper compartment, and the situation is typified as a Stag Hunt in the Park at Windsor. The Prince of Wales, on horseback, is performing the part of huntsman, and his followers are travestied as the Prince's pack of hounds—a favourite figure with the pictorial satirists. Sheridan is the leading dog; the faces of Mrs. Fitzherbert, Burke, a Bishop, and others, are distinguishable among the pack, which is harassing the royal quarry.

The Crown of France is endangered in a similar fashion. It will be remembered that the stability of the government of Louis the Sixteenth received its first shock from the Duke of Orleans, who, imitating the factious conduct of the Prince of Wales at home, was in alliance with the enemies of the throne; in the case of the Duke, with the Revolutionary parties of France.

The royal French Stag is run down at Versailles. The Duke of Orleans, first Prince of the blood, is acting as whipper-in. He is dressed in a fantastic habit of *le sport*, a compromise between a French postilion and a huntsman; he is winding on his pack with *une corne de chasse.* The individuals constituting the aristocratic French pack are described below the print, the names giving some indication of the members of that Palais Royale clique of intriguers which wrought so much evil to the reigning branch. Certain members of the Orleans pack were destined to become notorious on the theatre of events which were then impending over France.

1. *Madame La C'tesse de Buffon.* 2. *Madme. La C'tesse de Blot.* 3. *Le Cte. de Touche.* 4. *Le Mqis. de Sillery.* 5. *Le Cte. de Vauban.* 6. *Le Bn. de Talleyrand* (who, in the hunt, has seized the royal stag with his teeth). 7. *M. de Simon.*

1790. *Philip Quarrel, the English Hermit, and Beau Fidelle, the mischievous She-Monkey, famous for her skill on the viol de gamba.*—Philip Thicknesse, leaving his hermitage in the background (see *Public Characters*, 1806), is journeying along one mile from Bath ; the ex-Governor of Languard Fort is in regimentals, but instead of a hat the artist has drawn a boar's head, the present of Lord Jersey, above that of the *Hermit.* More particular reference to this boar's head is made in the *Gentleman's Magazine,* 1761, pp. 34, 79.

Across Philip's back is slung his wooden gun ;[1] under his left arm are held his writings, which gained him but equivocal fame ; a bare axe, marked ' *Gratitude,*' is in his right hand ; the Duke of *Marlboro's pistols* are in his belt ; he has a *Subscription Scheme, Gunpowder,* as a cartouche-box, and his foot is resting on the *Vagrant Act.* Miss Ford (Mrs. Thicknesse), as *Beau Fidelle,* is following *Quarrel's* wanderings ; her *viol de gamba* is strapped across her back.

(Handbill.)

STRAYED FROM KENSINGTON GORE

A VICIOUS OLD DOG ;

A mongrel, with a large mark on the left side of his head, resembling a tarnished cockade ; on his collar is marked *P. T.*, but answers to the name of GALLSTONE ; has got a sore tail, occasioned by a *copper platter*, cruelly tied to it some time since—the fright arising from which caused him to run away from London. He has a great aversion to the smell of gunpowder ; is extremely mischievous, and very apt to snap and bite those who let him into their houses ; but, though very noisy, is easily quieted by the slightest threat. He has been heard of at Farthingoe, in Northamptonshire, where he attempted to bite the churchwardens ; but being whipped from thence, has since been discovered lurking near the Royal Hotel, at Dover, and is supposed to be now hid among the rocks on the Kentish coast.

Whoever will trace him and give intelligence by the post to J. G. (James Gillray), at No. 18 Old Bond Street, London, so that he may be found and muzzled, will be gratefully thanked !

[1] Wooden Gun. See *Public Characters*, 1806, p. 99.

THE MONSTER.

B. Argensteen takes the earliest opportunity of informing the nobility and the public of
the *Monster's* reappearance in town on Friday last, 4th.   He is dressed in a scarlet
coat, wears a prodigious cockade, and bears in every respect a striking likeness to that
much-respected character, PHILIP THICKNESSE, Esq.

He has already frightened a number of women and children, made several desperate
attempts upon different noblemen, and has attempted to cut up his own children.

SALOON AT THE PAVILION, BRIGHTON.

Since his last arrival in London he has assumed the name of *Lieut.-Gov. Gallstone;*
and it is strongly suspected that his present journey to town is in order to devour
all editors of newspapers, engravers, and publishers of satiric prints, and every other
person who has dared to arraign his conduct.   The public are cautioned to be on their
guard.

N.B.—The reward for his apprehension still remains in full force.

1790.   *An Excursion to Brighthelmstone, made in the year* 1789, *by Henry
Wigstead and Thomas Rowlandson.   Dedicated (by permission) to His Royal
Highness the Prince of Wales.   Embellished with eight engravings in aquatinta,*

from views taken on the road to and at that place.   London : Printed for C. G. J. and I. Robinson, Paternoster Row.   Oblong folio.   June 1, 1790.

Introduction.—' The following descriptive account of an excursion to Brighthelmstone is intended to give those who have not visited that delightfully situated town and its environs an idea of the pleasures with which a lively and feeling mind will be impressed on viewing those scenes which the Authors have endeavoured to illustrate. . . . Of the roads which lead to Brighthelmstone,

WAITING FOR DINNER.

that immediately from London being most frequented, the Authors have endeavoured to familiarise it to the traveller by pencil and pen.

'The various scenes which are introduced are slightly represented, and intended merely to impress the mind with the general effects of nature. It is, in short, a conversation narrative, illustrated occasionally with sketches of scenes and incidents which seemed most worthy of notice.'

The plates were all drawn and etched by Rowlandson, and aquatinted by Alken.

> *Sutton.*   (' The Cock.')
> *Reigate.*   (' The White Hart' posting house.)
> .   *Crawley.*   (Sale of a horse by auction outside the ' George Inn.')
> *Cuckfield.*   (Market Day—a recruiting party, &c.)
> *Saloon at the Marine Pavilion.*

' The Marine Pavilion of H.R.H. the Prince of Wales, on the west side
of the Steine, is a striking object, and admirably calculated for the summer
residence of a royal personage. . . . This Pavilion, correctly designed and

AT DINNER.

elegantly executed, was begun and completed in five months.   The furniture
is adapted with great taste to the style of the building.   The Grand Saloon is
beautifully decorated with paintings by *Rebecca*, executed in his best manner.
The *tout ensemble* of the building is, in short, perfect harmony.   The whole
was executed by Mr. Holland, under the immediate inspection and direction of
Mr. Weltjé, the Prince's German cook, who leased the property to his royal
master.'

Bathing Machines.

The Steine (and promenaders).

Race Ground. The Course, the Stand, &c., with a race being run.

June 1, 1790. *Saloon at the Pavilion, Brighton.* Aquatinted by T. Alken. Published by Messrs. Robinson.—One of a series of drawings made from the Regent's fantastic seaside residence, and published in aquatint. See *An Excursion to Brighthelmstone, made in the year* 1789, *by Henry Wigstead and Thomas Rowlandson.* (1790.)

AFTER DINNER.

1790 (?). *Waiting for Dinner.* 1790 (?). *At Dinner.*

1790 (?). *After Dinner.*   1790 (?). *Preparing for Supper.*

1790 (?). *Fox-hunters Relaxing.*

About 1790. *Evening.*—A small etching. A stout sportsman, lolling on his pony, and followed by a miscellaneous tribe of dogs, has evidently been out shooting, and on his homeward way he has fallen in with an encampment of gipsies, who have pitched their tent beside a wood ; three brawny nymphs are sitting about in easy attitudes, and a fourth, leaning on the stranger's horse, is beguiling the Nimrod with her wiles ; it seems probable, from the foolish expression thrown into the rider's face, that he is likely to fall an easy victim into mischievous hands.

August 6, 1790.   Cattle at the River.   The Horse Race.   A View in Cornwall.   The River ; towing barges, &c.   Rustic Refreshment.   Winter Pastime : Skating on a Frozen River.

September 1790.   A Dressing Room at Brighton.   Published by I. Brown,

PREPARING FOR SUPPER.

6 Crown Street, Soho.—As the title expresses, this plate represents the interior of a chamber at the fashionable marine resort.   Three gentlemen are seated in their combing-chairs ; their hair is being curled and powdered by three hairdressers.

October 20, 1790.   Four o'clock in Town.   Designed and etched by Thomas Rowlandson.   Published by J. Jones.—This plate, which is entirely due to Rowlandson's hand, is etched in outline, and filled in with aquatint, in imitation of a faint drawing in Indian ink.   A young and well-favoured military buck

has returned to his house at the advanced and disreputable hour of four o'clock
in the morning, as indicated in the title ; he has evidently been 'making a night
of it,' and is considerably the worse for his potations.   His young and pretty
wife, who is in bed, is thrown into a mixed condition between consternation, fear,
and resentment at the condition of her gallant spouse ; the husband is propped
up in an armchair, and left to the care of two comely housemaids, who are
making efforts to assist this hopeless rake to divest himself of his clothes—an
essential preliminary towards going to bed which he is signally unable to perform for himself.   He is perfectly helpless in the hands of these wenches, and
is contemplating with an imbecile air an empty purse, the result of his evening's
recreations.   In spite of the somewhat suggestive nature of this subject, all the

FOX-HUNTERS RELAXING.

figures are graceful and pleasingly expressed, and the faces are delicate and
attractive.

October 20, 1790.   *Four o'clock in the Country.*   Designed and etched by
T. Rowlandson.   Published by S. W. Fores, 3 Piccadilly.—The episode presented in this picture is the complete reverse of that shown in the companion
plate, *Four o'clock in Town.*   While the London rake is being assisted to his
late bed the country Nimrod is rising with the dawn.   The enthusiast for the
chase has tumbled out of his early couch ; his clothes are hastily thrown on in
the partial light of daybreak, and he is, while still half-asleep, making terrific
exertions to draw on his boots.   His wife, who has not had time to commence
her toilette, and who, evidently, will resume her interrupted repose on the

departure of the hunting party, is standing, exactly as she has left her bed, with a bottle of cordial and a glass, pouring out a nip of comfort to keep out the cold, for the benefit of her sporting spouse. The chamber is alive with motion, and it is evidently the accustomed method of departure; pairs of dogs are rushing about, huntsmen and grooms are carrying saddles on their heads and making preparations for the start. The remains of last night's relaxations, in the shape of pipes and mugs of ale, are still uncleared ; and the articles scattered around, guns, saddles, whips, hunting-horns, and fox-skins, attest the pronounced sporting tastes of the country squire. A pretty child is tranquilly sleeping, in its cradle, undisturbed by the bustle of the hunter's early start.

1790.   *John Nichols.*

> With anger foaming and of vengeance full,
> Why belloweth John Nichols like a bull ?

—John Nichols is seated at a rustic table ; the *Gentleman's Magazine* is at his feet; his literary productions—*rebus, conundrum, riddle, charade,* &c.—are scattered about. In the background is shown an allegory of the Temple of Fame, at the summit of Mount Parnassus, towards which the author is vainly stumping on stilts, propped up on books, with his *Essay on Old Maids* under his arm, as the certificate which is to serve as his passport to immortality; his exertions are parodied by a monkey at his side, who has ascended to the top of a ladder and can get no higher.

1790.   *A Series of Miniature Groups and Scenes.* Published by M. L., Brighthelmstone ; and H. Brookes, Coventry Street, London.

1790. *A Christening.*

1790. *The Duenna and Little Isaac.* Engraved by W. P. Carey.

January 13, 1791. *The Prospect before us. No.* 1. *Humanely inscribed to all those Professors of Music and Dancing whom the cap may fit.* Published by S. W. Fores, Piccadilly.—The possible future condition of the foreign artists located within our shores, the performers at the Italian Opera, seems to have provoked three large cartoons from Rowlandson's graver at the beginning of 1791. The straits to which these fashionable exotics, it was suggested, might be reduced by the decaying state of the theatre in which they had been playing are more particularly dwelt on in this and a later caricature. It appears it was found necessary to close their house for restorations, which, if the state of things hinted in *Chaos is Come Again* (February 4, 1791), may be considered in any way prophetic, was resolved on none too soon. *The Prospect before us* evidently offers the choice of two conditions. The first seems to have been an appeal to the charitable, pending the construction of a new Opera House ; the second, which was accepted, being the conversion of the Pantheon into a theatre ; a substitute which in the end accidentally proved equally deplorable.

We first find the professors of music, singing, and dancing thrown on the vicarious exercise of their talents as a wandering troupe round the town. The model of the new house is borne as a plea to the benevolent, much on the principle of the disabled sailors who, tramping the streets, singing and begging, carried the model of their ship, to tempt the liberality of the almsgiving public.

A sweeper-lad is dropping a copper into the laced hat of one of the French dancers, whose figure is probably intended for that of Didelot, one of the highest paid and most popular performers in his walk on our stage. A butcher, with evident sympathies for imported art, is compassionately dropping a bullock's heart into the hat of an elderly artist, whose figure may possibly be intended for that of old Vestris.

The tattered and reduced regiment of foreign performers are evidently not prospering on their street perambulating campaign, since, judging from the surroundings, they are reduced to solicit the patronage of the denizens of the most squalid neighbourhoods. Their graces are displayed outside the premises of one *Michael Nincompoop*, who, according to his notice-board, is engaged in a

THE PROSPECT BEFORE US. NO. I.

THE PROSPECT BEFORE US.   NO. 2.

somewhat miscellaneous line of trading, '*purveying, brickmaking, breeches, brandy-balls, and all other kinds of sweetmeats.*' The circumstances of the Italian Opera are more distinctly alluded to in a poster stuck on the wall, announcing : '*A new Fantoccini this evening, called " Humbugallo in the Dumps." A dance called " The Battle of the Brickbats ;" to conclude with a grand crush by all the performers.*'

January 13, 1791. *The Prospect before us. No. 2. Respectfully dedicated to those Singers, Dancers, and Musical Professors who are fortunately engaged with the Proprietor of the King's Theatre, at the Pantheon.* Published by S. W. Fores. —Dismissing the less fortunate artists whose services were not retained for the new enterprise, we return to the subject of the opening of the Pantheon. In anticipation of the success of this new Opera House, Rowlandson issued a large cartoon representing a *coup d'œil* of the interior of the theatre, as seen from the stage during the performance of a ballet. The Royal box, in the centre, is tenanted by the King and Queen, and the boxes around are occupied by the nobility and leaders of fashion. On the stage are Didelot and Madame Theodore, dancing in the ballet of *Amphion and Thalia.* O'Reilly, in the orchestra, is presiding over the band. The dancers, at this period, were the highest paid performers in the company ; with the leading artistes of the ballet were engaged the vocalists Mara, Pacchierotti, Lazzarini, &c., for the performance of operas.

The *Gentleman's Magazine* thus notices the privileged rehearsal which preceded the regular season :—

'Thursday, February 10, 1791.—This evening the Opera at the Pantheon was opened to the subscribers, and a very elegant audience attended at the rehearsal of the performance of *Armida.* Though none of the Royal Family were present, a crowd of fashionable visitors exhibited patronage adequate to the support of any undertaking.'

European Magazine :—'February 17, 1791.—The new Opera House in the Pantheon was opened with *Armida*, in which Pacchierotti, Mara, Lazzarini, &c., distinguished themselves. Afterwards the ballet of *Amphion and Thalia* was performed, with applause, by Didelot, Theodore, &c.'

Another paragraph from the *Gentleman's Magazine* briefly relates the end of this prosperous undertaking a year later :—

'Saturday, January 14, 1792.—This morning, between one and two o'clock, the painter's room in one of the new buildings which had been added to the Pantheon, to enlarge it sufficiently for the performance of operas, was discovered to be on fire. Before any engines were brought to the spot the fire had got to such a height that all attempts to save the building were in vain. The fire kept burning with great fury for about ten hours, by which time, the roof and part of the walls having fallen in, it was so much subdued that all fears for the safety of the surrounding houses were quieted.

' The performers, next to the insurance offices, will be the greatest sufferers, for they have put themselves, as usual, to great expense in preparing for the season; many of them were obliged to do this upon credit; but their salaries ending with the existence of the house, and before any of them had their benefit nights, they have now no means of extricating themselves from their difficulties.'

We learn from the *Memoirs of Henry Angelo* that the author's father was Master of the Ceremonies when the building was first opened for balls, &c. We quote a paragraph which well describes the final calamity:—

' The Pantheon was certainly the most elegant and beautiful structure that had been erected in the British metropolis. Shortly after the conflagration of the Opera House in the Haymarket, in the year 1789, the proprietors of the Pantheon, which had been deserted of late for Madame Corneilly's, in Soho, were all put into high spirits, as proposals were made to construct a theatre in the grand saloon there, and to transfer the performance of the Italian ballet and opera to its stage. No theatre ever, perhaps, opened with greater *éclat*. The pit, boxes, and gallery were spacious, and magnificently fitted for the reception of an audience. The stage was of vast extent, and no expense was spared to render the scenic and the wardrobe department splendid and grand in proportion to the spectacles announced. Their Majesties frequently visited this new theatre, and everything was proceeding with advantage to all concerned, when within a few months, one unfortunate night, this noble monument of the genius of Wyatt was consumed by the same destructive element, and that great architect beheld on the morrow, with indescribable grief, the entire ruin of that fond monument of his youthful genius. The rising architects, too, were deprived of the most beautiful model that modern art had yet produced for their study.'

February 4, 1791. *Chaos is Come Again. Qui capit inven., ille habet fec.* Published by S. W. Fores, Piccadilly.

> Music hath charms to soothe the savage breast,
> To soften bricks and bend the knotted oak.

The end of the Italian Opera performances, when the surveyors of Drury Lane Theatre had come to the conclusion that the old building required to be pulled down, is pictorially set forth by the artist in one scene of general collapse and ruin. This print, for some undiscovered reason, is sometimes met without the lettering; it was probably issued at the beginning of 1791 in that condition, and then published later with a date, which rather interferes with its purpose or intention, if it had not appeared earlier, since the prospects of the Opera company were reassured by the conversion of Wyatt's famous Pantheon into a theatre for their future use.

We learn from a later paragraph (*Gentleman's Magazine*, September 1791) that the house in the Haymarket was completed and opened for performances

CHAOS IS COME AGAIN.

in the autumn of the year—a rival speculation to the successful season which inaugurated the adaptation of the magnificent and unfortunate monument in Oxford Street as a theatre.

'Thursday, September 22, 1791.—The Drury Lane company performed in the Opera House in the Haymarket. There was much clamour and some disturbance at first, owing to some inconveniences attending the alterations in the house, and chiefly the entrances, which, being soon got over, a scene was introduced of Parnassus, which was painted and contrived in a very grand style; and Messrs. Dignum and Sedgwick sung the air. The *Haunted Tower* then began; and the audience, restored to good humour, honoured the performance with the loudest plaudits.'

January 31, 1791. Sheets of picturesque etchings:—*A Four-in-Hand. The Village Dance. The Woodman Returning. River Scene. A Water Mill. Shipping, &c.*

January 31, 1791. *Huntsmen Visiting the Kennels. The Haymaker's Return. Deer in a Park. Cattle. Shepherds. Horses in a Paddock. Cattle Watering at a Pond. A Piggery.* Published by S. W. Fores, Piccadilly.

1791. *Traffic* (old Jew clothesmen). Published by S. W. Fores, 3 Piccadilly.

January 30, 1791. *Toxophilites.* (See 1794.) Published by E. Harding.

March 1, 1791. *The Attack.* Published by S. W. Fores, 3 Piccadilly.—A gentleman, who is driving four horses harnessed to a sort of curricle, with an elegant and fashionably-dressed female by his side, is thrown into consternation by the sudden apparition of a mounted knight of the road, who, seated on a high-mettled steed, is presenting a pistol full at the driver. The traveller's servant, dressed in his livery, and mounted on a cob, is brought up suddenly by the stopping of his master's vehicle; his face indicates the greatest astonishment at the demeanour of the highwayman and alarm at the unforeseen danger to which his patron is exposed; it does not, however, occur to him to render any assistance.

March 22, 1791. *Bardolph Badger'd, or the Portland Hunt.*—Sheridan, with G. P. on his collar, is, in this instance, represented as the hunted cur; he has certain plans tied to his tail, and he is tearing off from the Duke of Portland's mansion (the great rallying-place among the leaders of the Whig party); 'Sherry' is escaping towards Carlton House, to take refuge with his new master; Fox is clapping his hands to accelerate *Bardolph's* speed; the Duke of Portland is throwing bundles of papers after the badgered fugitive; Burke is threatening him with his *shelairy*; Lord Holland is aiming a stick at him, and a crowd of other political celebrities belonging to the party are assisting to drive out the frightened cur from their midst. In spite of his brilliant abilities Sheridan did not reflect much credit on the party with which he had been allowed to ally himself. The

Prince of Wales, the good faith of whose allegiance was no less equivocal, finally turned his back on his friends, while retaining the services of the *Bardolph* of the picture. 'Sherry's' party had good cause to regard him with distrust.

April 12, 1791. *European Powers. An Imperial Stride.* Published by William Holland, 50 Oxford Street.—Some doubt exists as to the authorship of this and the following political satires; there are several similar plates by Kingsbury, who was working for W. Holland at this date, but, from certain points in their execution, we are inclined to include one or two of these prints with the series by Rowlandson. The Empress Catherine, in her 'Imperial Stride,' has one foot resting on Russia, and the other touching the crescent above the dome of St. Sophia, in Constantinople. The various sovereigns of Europe are regarding this acrobatic performance with wonderment. Stanislaus the Second is reflecting on the 'length to which power may be carried;' Pope Pius the Sixth is declaring that 'he shall never forget it;' Charles the Fourth of Spain is threatening that he will 'despoil the spoiler!' Louis the Sixteenth 'never saw anything like it!' George the Third is saying, 'What, what, what a prodigious expansion!' the Emperor Leopold the Second, is remarking that it is a 'wonderful elevation!' and the Sultan, Selim the Third, is expressing his belief that 'all Turkey would not satisfy the ambition of the Empress.'

April 25, 1791. *The Grand Battle between the famous English Cock and Russian Hen.*—As we remarked, in treating of the previous print, some doubt, may exist as to the authorship of these plates ; we have included a reduction of this engraving among our illustrations, so that our readers may be enabled to form their own impressions.

These cartoons are not without interest, as they offer a fair view of the relative positions of European sovereigns at the period of their publication.

King George the Third and the Empress Catherine of Russia are matched against one another in the great European cockpit for a decisive struggle—such a conflict as has been imminent under nearly similar conditions at various emergencies since 1791. The Great Powers are assembled to witness the encounter, and are backing their respective champions. The Empress, who is game to the last, is declaring, 'I have vanquished many a finer bird than you!' King George is retorting, 'Boo, boo; bluster, bluster! won't leave you a feather!' Queen Charlotte has a pile of money before her, which she is guarding from straggling fingers ; she is holding a laurel wreath—held out on the end of the regal sceptre—over the head of her champion bird, and offering to wager 'a million to ten thousand' on his chances of victory. The Lord Chancellor Thurlow, who, although he was reckoned 'the wisest of men,' perpetually compromised his prospects by his anxiety to make his own future secure, at the sacrifice of consistency, is inclined to put his 'ratting' principles into practice :

THE GRAND BATTLE BETWEEN THE FAMOUS ENGLISH COCK AND RUSSIAN HEN.

' She looks as if she wasn't afraid of any cock in Europe. I won't bet a penny !'
Pitt, seated beside his sovereign, is crying, ' I should like to have a bout with
her, but I'm afraid she'd soon do my business !'   The King of Prussia has every
confidence in his champion : 'Two hundred thousand rix-dollars the cock wins !'
The Prince of Wales is entering into the sport : ' I wish they'd let my bird
encounter her ; he'd soon lower her crest ; ten thousand she turns tail !'   The
Grand Seigneur is striking his Grand Vizier, and declaring to a female favourite

A LITTLE TIGHTER.

who is leaning over his shoulder, ' If the cock wins, by our holy Prophet, I swear
he shall be cherished in our seraglio as long as he lives !'   The King of Spain
is remarking, ' It is easy to see by her spunk Potemkin has been her feeder !'
The Emperor of Austria's pocket-book seems empty.   Catherine's favourite,
Potemkin, full of valorous confidence, is encouraging his Empress : ' A million
roubles she'll win !   At him again, my dear mistress !   Potemkin, your invincible
feeder, will back you to the last.'   Louis the Sixteenth of France, whose crown

has dwindled down to a mere trinket, is falling into raptures of admiration over the Russian hen : ' I would give all that I have left of a crown for such a glorious bird !'

May 16, 1791. *The Volcano of Opposition.* Rowlandson (?).

May 17, 1791. *The Ghost of Mirabeau and Dr. Price Appearing to Old Loyola.* Rowlandson (?).

May 18, 1791. *A Little Tighter.* Published by S. W. Fores, 3 Piccadilly. —The picture tells its own story. A ladies' tailor has brought home a pair of stays for a corpulent dowager. The process of investing her ladyship in her new corsage seems to demand an enormous exertion of muscular vigour.

DAMP SHEETS.

May 18, 1791. *A Little Bigger.* (Companion print.)—The principal figure in this plate is that of a corpulent individual, who is being measured by a meagre whipper-snapper anatomy of a tailor ; the girth of his portly client is giving the knight of the needle no slight difficulty to surround his person with his measuring-tape, and the customer is impressing on his tailor the necessity of leaving ample room for his obese proportions.

1791. *Cold Broth and Calamity.* (See 1792.)

August 1, 1791. *Housebreakers.* (See 1788.) Published by S. W. Fores.

August 1, 1791. *Damp Sheets.* Drawn and etched by T. Rowlandson ;

aquatinta by T. Malton.—A gentleman, who is evidently on his travels, is thrown into a state of the most furious indignation on arriving at the discovery,

as he is retiring to rest, that he and his wife have been put into a bed with damp sheets; the lady is wringing the moisture from the offending linen, and the husband is dancing about, gesticulating in frantic fashion and shaking his fist in the face of a pretty servant-maid, who, replying to the summons of the injured guests, is bustling up with the warming-pan in her hand, believing her services are required in that direction.

August 12, 1791. *English Barracks.* Aquatinted by T. Malton. Published by S. W. Fores.—A view of the interior of a cavalry barracks, reproducing a scene more properly indicative of domestic than of military life, although weapons and accoutrements are scattered about. Drums and guns are piled in one corner; at the window is a trooper *en négligé* employed in brushing his uniform. A woman is nursing a strapping boy, while a soldier at her side, in complete uniform, is adjusting his helmet at the looking-glass. Another trooper has a child in his arms, and is putting a lad, who is playing at soldiers, through his musketry exercise; while a pretty maiden is presiding at the washing-tub. An old grandmother, who is giving a playful infant a ride on her back, is pouring out a glass of cordial for another warrior, whose toilette is far from complete. Guns, sabres, military saddles, pistol-holsters, and other warlike objects are hung on the wall, giving the apartment, which is otherwise blank enough, a certain air of picturesque decoration.

August 12, 1791. *French Barracks.* (Companion to the above.)—The interior of a French barracks offers a perfect contrast to the simplicity and decorous order which mark the occupants of an *English Barracks.* The barrack-room is extensive, and handsomely decorated with trophies of weapons, which, with a suit of mail, are disposed on the walls with a good eye to effect. The officers are rising and dressing for morning parade. An officer, the principal features of whose countenance are absorbed in a pair of huge moustachios, is seated on the regimental drum, while a pretty girl is employed unromantically in trimming the warrior's toenails. A soldier-barber is at the same time dressing the hero's locks and binding up his monstrous pigtail, which reaches over a yard in length— a standard of valour of protracted dimensions. A lad is bringing this well-attended son of Mars his monstrous jack-boots, of a size and weight to displace the great guns of his battery with considerable effect. All these dandy warriors seem to be utterly dependent on the assistance of their factotums; it is difficult to imagine these 'curled darlings' in connection with gunpowder and a field of battle. A second officer is enveloped in his powdering-gown, while his barber-valet is smothering him with volumes of violet-clouds from his puffing apparatus. Another hero appears reluctant to abandon his morning slumbers; he is seated, in his shirt, gaping frightfully, on the side of his bed. One distinguished being has almost completed his elaborate toilette; the due adjustment of his lace fall and cravat is engaging his exclusive attention; he is standing in front of a large mirror to perform this delicate manipulation with proper effect, and a very beautiful girl—whose own toilette is neglected, and whose voluptuous charms are freely exposed—is holding a second glass at the warrior's back, that he may be enabled to contemplate the reflection of his own admired rear in the larger mirror ; meanwhile one of his petty officers is standing on the salute, ready to receive the orders of his chief.   A pretty woman, a young mother, is suckling an infant ; and another child, whose wardrobe is limited to a single garment, is, while eating breakfast, training a poodle to stand at ease with a sword in his paw—a ridiculous parody of the warlike accompaniments around.

SLUGS IN A SAWPIT.

October 28, 1791.   *Slugs in a Sawpit.*   Published by S. W. Fores, 3 Piccadilly.—A brace of heroes, naval and military, are endeavouring to adjust their differences by an appeal to arms ; the combat, for the sake of retirement and convenience, is taking place at the bottom of a sawpit.   It seems that the duel is of a most obstinate nature ; three or four broken swords are strewn around ; and, honour not being yet satisfied, recourse has evidently been had to pistols, several of which (some dismantled), with balls, &c., are also thrown about on the limited field of conflict.   It seems the antagonists are most implacable, as, after exchanging all these inconclusive passes and discharges, they are resorting finally to the use of a pair of huge blunderbusses, about the dimensions of fieldpieces, which would hold some pounds of slugs. The old Commodore is stooping his fat body, and the military buck is resting on one knee, in order to get the monstrous weapons into comfortable positions for firing; both combatants look a trifle nervous, as the results are likely to be tolerably marked at such ranges; the guns of the inveterate duellists are side by side, the stocks resting on their respective shoulders and the muzzles just touching their noses. The consequences likely to ensue on pulling the triggers can be easily imagined. A workman has just arrived at the edge of his sawpit in time to discover the trespasses these ferocious fire-eaters are making on his property.

November 22, 1791. *How to Escape Winning.*—A pictorial satire directed against a famous incident of the turf, which provoked an unusual amount of attention and scandalous comments in proportion; the question never having been satisfactorily disposed of, although it has been generally received that the Prince of Wales, who owned the notorious racehorse *Escape*, was more sinned against than sinning. It is sufficient to mention that the horse in question, from certain circumstances which became a subject of vexed debate long after the occurrence, did *not* win the race, when it was pretty evident, under fair conditions of horse-racing, that he could have distanced every horse on the course. In the print—which is the chief point we have to deal with—the race is being run; the other jockeys are making great efforts to get ahead; the Prince's jockey, Chiffney, on *Escape*, is holding in his mount; the horse is furious at the restraint which is crippling him and preventing his running freely, the animal's near fore-leg being secured to his off hind-leg with the owner's *Order of the Garter, 'Honi soit qui mal y pense.'* The figure of a sporting character, intended either for that of the owner or trainer of this unlucky *Escape*, is standing with his finger to his nose, an action implying that he has made it all right for himself. In the distance the backers of the Prince's horse are either regarding the owner with suspicion or are stamping with rage at the fraud by which they are doomed to lose instead of winning their money.

November 22, 1791. *How to Escape Losing.*—The principal figure is standing in much the same style of 'knowing' attitude as that displayed in the previous plate. The race is still being run; *Escape* is leading, the garter, *Qu'en pensez-vous*, only remains attached to the near fore-leg; but the horse's chances are borne down by heavy impediments; a pair of weights are slung over the jockey's shoulders and other weights are suspended round the horse's neck and in front of and behind his saddle.

1791. *Angelo's Fencing Rooms.* (From *Reminiscences of Henry Angelo, with Memoirs of his Friends, &c.*)—'For some years I had a fencing-room at the Opera House, Haymarket, over the entrance of the pit-door. On the evening of June 17, 1789, about eight o'clock, when in Berkeley Square, I saw a black smoke ascending; and soon hearing that there was a fire in the Haymarket, I directly hastened there, when, to my surprise, I beheld the Opera House in flames. Having the key of my room in my pocket, and the crowd making way for me, I soon got there, at the time the back part was burning. I first secured the portrait of Monsieur Saint George (the famous fencer), which hung over the chimneypiece and removed it to St. Alban's Street, where I then resided. At my return, though I was not absent six minutes, the mob had rushed in and plundered the room of everything. As to the foils, jackets, &c., they were of little value to me compared to what I had in my closet—a portfolio of beautiful drawings, particularly several valuable ones of Cipriani, also of Mortimer, Rowlandson, &c., the loss of which I much regretted; but consoled myself by saving Saint George's picture, which he sat purposely for and offered me, after our fencing together, the second day of his arrival in the country. It was painted by Brown, an American artist, much encouraged here at the time. The last day of his sitting he dined at my father's, when, my mother enquiring of him if it was a good likeness, he smiled and replied (he was a Creole), 'Oh, madame, c'est si ressemblant *que c'est affreux.*' My room, which was in the front, was the only one saved from the flames in the whole house; and fortunately, the engines being placed in it, prevented the fire from communicating to Market Lane.

'Sergeant Leger was an excellent fencer of the *première force,* whose elegant figure and mildness of manners greatly influenced the amateurs of the science. Though he was only in the ranks, his presence in every fencing-room was acceptable, and when Saint George was his antagonist the match never failed to excite attention.

Fencing.—'In 1785 Monsieur Le Brun, a celebrated fencing-master now at Paris, visited England. My academy in the Haymarket being then the general rendezvous for all the foreigners who were either masters or amateurs of the science, and near the coffee-house, their usual resort, he paid me a visit. I was his first antagonist. I soon found out, as the pugilists call it, that he was a "good customer" (a queer one to deal with); so much so, that, however I might have distinguished myself before my scholars with the number of fencing-masters, &c. whom I have opposed, here I had nothing to boast of.

'I should observe that he was a left-handed fencer, and in full exercise in Paris, and of course he must have been daily in the habit of fencing with many, while in the course of years I might not meet with six of superior force. Finding such an excellent competitor, and as I thought that it would be beneficial to my scholars to accustom themselves to practise against a left-handed fencer, I told him he would be welcome to us all.'

Henry Angelo, who held the highest opinion of St. George, has drawn up the following account of his accomplishments :—

'The Chevalier de St. George was born at Gaudaloupe. He was the son of M. de Boulogne, a rich planter in the colony. His mother was a negress, and was known under the name of the "handsome Nanon;" she was justly considered one of the finest women that Africa had ever sent to the plantations. The Chevalier de St. George united in his own person the grace and the features of his mother with the strength and firmness of M. de Boulogne. No man ever united so much suppleness to so much strength. He excelled in all the bodily exercises in which he engaged; an excellent swimmer and skater, he has been frequently known to swim over the Seine with one arm, and to surpass others by his agility upon its surface in the winter. He was a skilful horseman and a remarkable shot—he rarely missed his aim, when his pistol was once before the mark ; his talents in music unfolded themselves rapidly : his concertos, symphonies, quartettos, and some comic operas are the best proofs of his extraordinary progress in music. Though he was very young he was at the head of the concert of amateurs : he conducted the orchestras of Madame de Montesson and the Marquis de Montalembert.

'But the art in which he surpassed all his contemporaries and predecessors was fencing ; no professor or amateur ever showed so much accuracy, such strength, such length of lunge, and such quickness ; his attacks were a perpetual series of hits—his parade so close that it was in vain to attempt to touch him ; in short, he was all nerve.

'In the summer of the year 1787, on returning to my residence in St. Alban's Street, I was surprised at the appearance of lights and a crowd of people entering Mr. Rheda's fencing academy; on enquiry I was informed that the Chevalier St. George had arrived in England, and was about to exhibit his great talents at that place. I immediately went in and renewed my acquaintance with him ; and as it is customary for fencing-masters of celebrity to engage with each other at such meetings, I proposed myself, and was accepted as the first professor who engaged with him in this country.

'It may not be unworthy to remark that, from his being much taller, and consequently possessing a greater length of lunge, I found I could not depend upon my attacks with sufficient confidence unless I closed with him ; the consequence was, upon my adopting that measure, the hit which I gave was so "palpable," that it "threw open his waistcoat," which so enraged him that, in his fury, I received a blow from the *pommel* of the foil on my chin, the mark of which I still retain as a *souvenir* of having engaged with the first fencer in Europe.

'It may be remarked of this celebrated man, that although he might be considered as a lion with a foil in his hand, yet, the contest over, he was as docile as a lamb; for soon after the engagement, when seated to rest himself, he said to me, "*Mon cher ami, donnez-moi votre main, nous tirons tous les jours ensemble.*" '

On leaving this country the Chevalier St. George presented Mr. Angelo with his portrait by Mather Brown, his fencing-foil, glove, and jacket, which were hung up in the rooms rented by Angelo over the Opera portico (Haymarket).

Among the competitors in these fencing assaults, which were patronised by the Prince of Wales, and were sometimes held at Carlton House, are mentioned the names of D'Eon, M. Fabian, M. Magé (who was reckoned second to M. St. George among the amateurs of Paris), M. Sainville, Mr. Rheda, Mr. Mola, and Mr. Angelo, Sen.

1791. *A Four-in-Hand.*

1791. *The Inn Yard on Fire.* Drawn and etched by T. Rowlandson; aquatinted by T. Malton.—*Dover, Deal, Margate, and Canterbury Coaches.*—Fires at inns were by no means exceptional occurrences, if we may trust contemporary novelists; and who could have seized the changeful scenes of life flitting around them with such humour and fidelity as Fielding and the followers of his genial, life-like school have arrived at? Their fictitious personages, as Thackeray has argued, have often more vitality than those of actual history.

Everyone who was not content to live and die in one spot—the little space whereon they were born—must, at one time or another, have given way to the incentive of travel; all the world, high and low, aristocratic or mercantile, must, in the course of journeys in the pursuit of pleasure, variety, scenery, health, gain, or from necessity, from spot to spot, have encountered the humours of an inn; since the slow-going waggon, or the inevitable 'machine,' which, in a later generation, was supplanted by the flying stage-coach (itself, as judged by the present system of transport, a very tedious, insupportable affair, according to modern ideas—a serious and solitary means of travelling), and the various eccentric methods of locomotion indulged in a century back, rendered frequent 'puttings up' at posting-houses in a measure unavoidable. A traveller in the good old days when Fielding and Smollett noted down their pictures of life was almost bound to meet adventures of one sort or another. There was the excitement of the start, the difficulty of securing comfort in the article of seats, and sociability in the way of companionship; the dangers of the environs of London—the heaths, where the mail was always liable to be arrested at the wayward will of the pleasant and popular Mr. Richard Turpin, on his equally well-bred 'Black Bess,' or at the hands and holsters of less famous and ruder professional contemporaries; the risk of the roads; the digging of the great lumbering Noah's

Ark from soft ways and quagmires ; capsizing, or being snowed up, and such even.
tualities. Bad roads, disagreeable comrades, a stuffy inside place, or a moist
outside 'shake-down,' were at intervals relieved by the arrival of the *cortège* at
some hospitable hostelry, with its vast rambling galleries and its commodious
courtyard, where further adventures were not unlikely to attend the voyager.

> Who'er has travell'd life's dull round,
>   Through all its various paths hath been,
> Must oft have wondered to have found
>   His warmest welcome at an inn !

INN YARD ON FIRE.

The ardent house-warming prepared for the passengers at the *Inn Yard on
Fire* barely justifies the rapture of the rhymer. From the notice-board we find
the *Dover, Deal, Margate, and Canterbury Coaches* are advertised to set out
from the caravansary in question. The strangers are rudely disturbed, while the
flames are lapping the old building and serpentining their way round the inflammable wooden balconies, as the suddenly awakened inmates take to flight
with such solitary articles as come first to hand. Peregrine is rescuing Emilia
much as Rowlandson has drawn that worthy in his illustration to the exciting
situation of the fire at an inn yard. (See *The Adventures of Peregrine Pickle*,

chapter xxvii.)   A sufferer from gout is being conveyed in a wheelbarrow out of imminent danger of roasting; an old dowager has appeared on the scene with a pair of leather breeches to cover her shoulders, recalling similar episodes in La Fontaine, Boccaccio, &c.; while a corpulent old boy has simply thrown a lady's quilted petticoat round his neck.   A waggon and horses are being dragged out of the dangerous vicinity.   From its contiguity to the French route between Dover and Calais the house is evidently frequented by foreigners lately landed on our shores, and the unexpected warmth of their reception is too much for the excitable Gauls.   One Frenchman, an officer, is making good his escape; his personal wardrobe is sacrificed, but he has secured his most precious belongings, an umbrella, a sword, his jack-boots, and his wig and solitaire—wigs being in those days somewhat costly appendages.   A compatriot by his side is endeavouring to make off with his worldly possessions, and is dragging a heavy portmanteau at his heels; this salvage is endangered by the suspicions of a bulldog, who is not to be shaken off; the animal is first stopping the box, and finally arresting the fugitive by seizing his long *queue* in his mouth, a mode of arrest against which the terrified *Parlez-vous* is unequal and unable to defend himself.   An antiquated husband is holding a ladder for the escape of his pretty wife; the curmudgeon is furious that the personal attractions of his better half should be thus displayed to the less privileged males around, who are assisting her delicate descent. The dangers of the fire are increased by the reckless impulse characteristic of similar casualties, in which blazing objects are hurled out of window, spreading the flames to places which have hitherto escaped ignition.   Mirrors and tables, sheets and other objects, are sent flying from the upper galleries on to the heads of the scared travellers below.   If the *Squall in Hyde Park* may be accepted as an ordeal by water, the *Inn Yard on Fire* must be acknowledged a most appropriate pendant.   These plates were, it is believed, issued as a pair.   Both are of one size, etched by Rowlandson, and aquatinted by T. Malton; the execution is spirited as regards outline, and the tinting is most successfully and delicately carried out.   The second print, *A Squall in Hyde Park*, is, the Editor has reason to believe, the scarcer of the two; a copy (proof) in the National Library, Paris, and the one in his own collection, are the solitary examples with which he is acquainted.   The *Inn Yard on Fire* is more familiarly known; and, although original impressions command prices which are seemingly fabulous, several impressions, of varying excellence, have come under the writer's attention.

1791.   *A Squall in Hyde Park.*   Drawn and etched by T. Rowlandson; aquatinted by T. Malton.—The fashionable throngs which Rowlandson, with his marvellously faithful pencil, has so often drawn, disporting themselves in the paths of frivolity amidst the haunts of *the ton*, are viewed by him under a more excited aspect.   The promenaders, in a state of *sauve qui peut*, are rushing off pell-mell in an attempt to preserve their dripping finery from the effects of a sudden thunderstorm. Doubtless *A Squall in Hyde Park* may occur frequently enough in our day, but the artist who proposes to lend his graphic powers to delineate the episodes of such a stampede in the present generation would not have his eye for the picturesque gratified by the discovery of such grotesque elements as gratuitously lent themselves to the appreciative caricaturist a century back. Rowlandson's animated cartoon successfully includes all the diversities of the situation. The park-gates are crowded by the sudden *exeunt omnes*—pedestrians, horses, and carriages are mixed in one confused mass in the struggle to escape from a miniature tempest. Peers and pedagogues, the man of fashion in search of gallant adventures, and the hypochondriac, limping parkwards to take the air; the ignorant, new-fledged squire, the rustic dandy, whose head-dressing does not extend beyond the powdered and frizzed peruke, and the man of knowledge and philosophy, are thrown into violent contact, and unexpectedly realise whose cranium is the hardest. The storm breaks, the black clouds gather and meet, down pours a very torrent, and the wind suddenly takes to blowing 'big guns;' hats, caps, and bonnets, wigs and head-gear generally, are sent flying off on independent excursions; the sport of the sudden squall, to the dismay of the bereaved owners; umbrellas of the period—still popular novelties, in substantiality very different to their genteel descendants—are without exception blown insideout; feathers, which were worn of great height, splendour, and profusion, are moistened and dripping like weeping willows. The Prince of Wales, in ' blue and buff,' on horseback, followed by his groom, is pushing forward for Carlton House; Lord Barrymore, in his lofty phaeton,[1] has to exert all his charioteering skill to restrain his terrified and plunging high-mettled steeds; while the fair companion perched by his side, high over the heads of the humbler stream of struggling humanity, is complacently enjoying the spectacle of the dilemmas around her. Footmen are dripping; naval and military heroes are retreating; such hats as have not been violently carried off are secured by handkerchiefs tied under the chin, or held on by main force; petticoats are turned over shoulders. The spectacle of confusion is fairly completed by an unfortunate slip, which has left the person of the unhappy victim a stumbling-block for the general capsizing of the hurried file which is following in his footsteps. A sturdy old admiral, in an advanced stage of corpulence, is rather enjoying the opportunity, to which the ruffling winds are contributing, of viewing the points of the dishevelled fair, and, spyglass in eye, like his Grace the notorious Peer of Piccadilly, he is quizzing the

---

[1] 'Lord Barrymore's phaeton was a very high one; and after our midnight revels in town I have often travelled in it with him to Wargrave. One very dark night, going through Colnbrook, in the long street called Featherbed Lane, he kept whipping right and left, breaking the windows, delighted with the noise as he heard them crack—this he called *fanning the daylights.'—Angelo's Memoirs.*

ankles and criticising the symmetry of the dainty belles before him; the long, gauze-like, and limp drapery in multitudinous folds then in vogue being exceptionally liable to come to grief under all such sinister emergencies. To add to the terrors of the flight, a fierce bulldog, irritated with the general condition of things, is taking exception to this universal attempt at escape, as indicating suspicion to his faithful mind; he is making darts at the passengers, and it will go hard with the fugitives he may take it into his head to arrest by the tension of his formidable teeth.

Plates dated 1791–93 *and* 1795–96. *The History of Tom Jones, a Foundling, by Henry Fielding, Esq. With prints by Rowlandson.* Edinburgh and London (Longman & Co.), republished 1805.

Volume I.

Frontispiece, book I. c. iii. The Infant Jones found in the bed of Mr. Allworthy.

Book II. c. iv. The astonished Partridge meets the vengeance of the whole sex (Partridge cruelly accused and maltreated by his wife).

Book IV. c. v. Tom Jones discovers the Philosopher Square in the Chamber of Moll Seagrim.

Book V. c. x. The constancy of Tom Jones subdued by meeting Molly Seagrim in the wood.

Volume II.

Book VIII. c. xiv. Terror of the Sentinel on seeing Jones issue from the Chamber in search of Northerton.

Book IX. c. ii. Tom Jones rescues Mrs. Waters from the violence of Northerton.

Book IX. c. iii. Battle of Upton; Tom Jones and the Landlord, Partridge and Susan, Mrs. Waters and the Landlady.

Book XI. c. ii. Sophia's modesty shocked by a fall from her horse.

Volume III.

Book XIII. c. ii. Tom Jones refused admittance by the porter at the door of an Irish peer.

Book XIII. c. ii. Jones and Sophia interrupted in a *tête-à-tête* by Lady Bellaston.

Book XIV. c.ii. Partridge interrupts Tom Jones in his protestations to Lady Bellaston.

Book XV. c. 5. Lord Fellamar rudely dismissed by Squire Western.

1791–93, 1795–96. *The Adventures of Peregrine Pickle; in which are included Memoirs of a Lady of Quality. By T. Smollett, M.D. With plates by Rowlandson.* Edinburgh and London (Longman): 1805.

Chap. xxvii. *Fire at the Inn. Peregrine Rescues Emilia, &c.*
Chap. xliv. *Feast after the Manner of the Ancients.*

1791. *Délices de la Grande-Bretagne.* Engraved and published by William Birch, enamel painter, Hampstead Heath. Two illustrations by Rowlandson.

Dover Castle; with the setting off of the Balloon to Calais, in January 1785.
Market Day at Blandford, Dorsetshire.

1792.

January 1792. *St. James's—St. Giles's.* H. Wigstead, invt. Published by T. Rowlandson, Strand; and republished (1794) by S. W. Fores, 3 Piccadilly. —The parish of *St. James's* is represented by two modish frail nymphs, elegantly decked out in the Frenchified fashion of the period; their profuse locks spread forth, frizzed and powdered, in the style imported from Paris by Mrs. Fitzherbert; the refinement of their appearance ill accords with a bowl of punch which they are convivially sharing. The ruder precincts of *St. Giles's* are pictured in the persons of two coarse, overgrown females of the ' fishfag' and 'street ballad singing' order, swaggering with sufficient impudence to set the universe at defiance.

January 1792. *Oddities.* Henry Wigstead, invt., January 1792. Published by T. Rowlandson, Strand. Republished 1794, by S. W. Fores, 3 Piccadilly.—A group of caricatured heads, types of expression and burlesqued peculiarities, in two prints, designed by Henry Wigstead, and engraved and published by Thomas Rowlandson.

February 22, 1792. *The Bank.* Published by T. Rowlandson, Strand.

February 22, 1792. *Work for Doctors' Commons.* Published by T. Rowlandson, Strand.—There is no evidence to prove this print directly proceeds from the pencil of Rowlandson, but there are indications of his style, both in the subject and in the execution; it is also in points suggestive of the early style of Morland. A lady and a captain—a pretty pair—are dallying on a sofa, while the superannuated lawful spouse of the frivolous fair one is ensconced behind a screen, standing on a chair, and surveying the situation over the top of this ambuscade; his footman is watching by his side, impressed as a witness, and is struck with horror at the spectacle of domestic faithlessness, of which he is taking observations through a peephole made through the screen for the purpose of spying.

From a MS. note to an impression which has come under the Editor's notice it appears that the contemporary scandal relates to a certain Mrs. Walsh and General Upton.

March 1792. *A Dutch Academy.* Published by T. Rowlandson, 52 Strand, 1792.—The caricature represents, as the title describes, the interior of a drawing school in Holland ; just such a one as may be found there to this day. A corpulent *vrow* is sitting as a model to the painters, in an attitude more easy than graceful. The Mynheers are clustered around, some of the students, most of whom are advanced in life, and of clumsy, corpulently developed figures, are seated on tubs, others are squatting on the floor, and nearly all are smoking. The Dutchmen, who are of the conventional type—much as we find them pictured in the veracious Knickerbocker's famous *History of New York*, closely encased in buttoned-up jackets, and roomy nether garments—are plodding away at their studies ; some few are too interested to do anything beyond indulging in a stolid contemplation of the charms of their material Venus.

April 1, 1792. *A Lying-in Visit, or a Short-sighted Mistake.* Published by S. W. Fores.—There are various versions of this subject, which it seems was originally suggested by Newton. Several of his contemporaries have tried their hand on it. A small version of the print is due to Rowlandson, and it evidently found favour in its day. A purblind and antiquated spinster, decked out in the very height of the fashion of the day—recalling the artist's suggestive *Old Ewe dressed Lamb Fashion*—is supposed to have called on a visit of congratulation to a young wife who has recently been deserving well of her country, by increasing its population. An old footman, with a powdered head, is bringing in a scuttle of coals ; the gushing visitor, who was prepared to go into promiscuous raptures in anticipation, is advancing to embrace the scuttle, which she imperfectly distinguishes, fulsomely exclaiming to the consternation of John Thomas, who is lost in confusion :—' O you pretty creature ! Bless the dear baby, how it smiles ! Give it to me, Nurse ! It has exactly its Papa's nose and Mama's eyes ! Oh, it is a delightful little creature !'

May 29, 1791–2. *Six Stages of Marring a Face—dedicated with respect to the Duke of Hamilton.* A companion to the *Six Stages of mending a Face.*— Stage the first represents the prize fighter (in the days when pugilistic exhibitions were specially given under the patronage of noblemen such as the Duke of Hamilton), in all his muscular force, stripped for the contest, his face undisfigured and manly, as left by nature ; in stage the second, one eye is closed ; in stage the third he is much disfigured ; in the latter stages the shape is entirely beaten out of his features, until the champion is left, in stage the sixth, a hideous mass of bruises, cuts, and bleeding wounds, hammered out of all resemblance to his former self—a spectacle sufficiently revolting to act as an antidote to the morbid excitement and attractiveness of the prize ring. It is worthy of remark that the artist must have drawn this print, exposing the barbarity of the ring, from sheer conviction founded on his own observations, and not from any squeamish distaste for the sport ; Rowlandson had enjoyed a wide experience of athletic exercises, in which he was understood to excel, and attended numerous pugilistic encounters, amateur and professional, in his time ; his pleasure in drawing well-built figures, with the play of muscle which would be exhibited in the course of ' bouts at fisticuffs ' such as he had both the power and skill to delineate, proves that he had a decided predilection for the science, apart from its reprehensible brutalities.   It further appears that the artist was somewhat of a boxer.

May 29, 1791–2. *Six Stages of Mending a Face. Dedicated with respect to the Right Honorable Lady Archer.* Published by S. W. Fores, 3 Piccadilly. —This plate traces the progress of manufacturing a beauty *à la mode.*   The first stage introduces the fair one in a very dilapidated condition, and the materials from which the lady is to be reconstructed do not seem promising.   A handkerchief is tied over her head to remedy the scarcity of hair ; one eye is absent, and the gums are toothless.   A handsome glass eye is being adjusted in *stage the second. Stage the third* represents the crowning of the shaven pate with a luxuriant and fashionably dressed head of hair.   An artificial set of teeth are being placed in the lady's mouth in the next stage.   The lady now approaches an appearance of youth and beauty.   In *stage five* she supplies the roses, hitherto absent from her cheeks, with a hare's foot and rouge. *Stage six* pictures the completed work, a dashing and captivating belle, with fine eyes (not necessarily a perfect pair it is true), flowing, profuse, and becoming locks of hair, perfect teeth, blooming complexion, and a carriage of conscious grace and coquetry.

June, 1792. *Ruins of the Pantheon—after the Fire which happened January* 14, 1792.   Sketched by Rowlandson and Wigstead.   Published by T. Rowlandson, Strand. *Pantheon.*—' Persons who witnessed the progress of this tremendous fire declare that the appearances exhibited through the windows, the lofty scagliola pillars enveloped in flames and smoke, the costly damask curtains waving from the rarefaction of the air, and the superb chandeliers turning round from the same circumstance, together with the successive crashing and falling in of different portions of the building, furnished to their minds a more lively representation of Pandemonium than the imagination alone can possibly supply.   The effects too of the intense frost which then prevailed, on the water poured from the engines upon the blazing pile, are described as equally singular and magnificent.'   J. B. Papworth.

1792. *The Chairman's Terror: Leaving a Levée,* St. James's Palace. Published by T. Rowlandson, 52 Strand.

The Adventures of Roderick Random. Roderick Random is conducted by his uncle Tom Bowling on a visit to his grandfather, the judge.—' After a few minutes' pause we were admitted, and conducted to my grandfather's chamber through a lane of my relations, who honoured me with very significant looks as I passed along.   When we came into the judge's presence, my uncle, after two or three sea-bows, expressed himself in this manner.   "Your servant—

your servant. What cheer father ? what cheer ? I suppose you don't know me—
mayhap you don't. My name is Tom Bowling ; and this here boy—you look
as if you did not know him neither—'tis like you mayn't. He's new rigged,
i' faith ; his cloth don't shake in the wind so much as it wont to do. 'Tis my
nephew, d'ye see, Roderick Random—your own flesh and blood, old gentleman.
Don't lay astarn, you dog " (pulling me forward). My grandfather, who was
laid up with the gout, received his relation after his long absence with a coldness
of civility which was peculiar to him ; told him he was glad to see him, and

LIEUTENANT BOWLING PLEADING THE CAUSE OF YOUNG ROY TO HIS GRANDFATHER.

desired him to sit down. " Thank ye, thank ye, sir, I had as lief stand," said
my uncle. " For my own part I desire nothing of you ; but if you have any
conscience at all, do something for this poor boy, who has been used at a very
unchristian rate. Unchristian, do you call it ? I am sure the Moors in Barbary
have more humanity than to leave their little ones to want. I would fain know
why my sister's son is more neglected than that there fair-weather Jack " (pointing to the young squire, who, with the rest of my cousins, had followed us into
the room). " Is not he as near akin to you as the other ? Is not he much

handsomer, and better built than that great chucklehead? Come, come—consider, old gentleman, you are going in a short time to give an account of your evil actions. Remember the wrongs you did his father, and make all the satisfaction in your power before it is too late. The least thing you can do is to settle his father's portion on him." The young ladies who thought themselves too much concerned to contain themselves any longer, set up their throats altogether against my protector, "Scurvy companion—saucy tarpaulin—rude, impertinent fellow—did he think he was going to prescribe to grandpapa? His

THE PASSENGERS FROM THE WAGGON ARRIVING AT THE INN.

sister's brat had been too well taken care of; grandpapa was too just not to make a difference between an unnatural, rebellious son and his dutiful loving children, who took his advice in all things"—and such expressions were vented against him with great violence, until the judge at length commanded silence.

The Adventures of Roderick Random. Chap. XI.—Roderick Random, and his companion Strap, having alighted from the waggon, are standing a little back in the best room of the Inn, where the landlord, candle in hand, is receiving the rest of the guests, who are entering from the conveyance; Joey, the honest driver of the waggon, is standing behind the obsequious Boniface. Roderick Random thus pursues his narrative :—

'Here I had an opportunity of viewing the passengers in order as they entered. The first who appeared was a brisk airy girl about twenty years old, with a silver laced hat on her head instead of a cap, a blue stuff riding-suit trimmed with silver, very much tarnished, and a whip in her hand. After her came limping an old man, with a worsted nightcap buttoned under his chin, and a broad brimmed hat slouched over it, and an old rusty blue cloak tied about his neck, under which appeared a brown surtout that covered a threadbare coat and waistcoat, and, as we afterwards discerned, a dirty flannel jacket. His eyes were hollow and bleared, his face was shrivelled into a thousand wrinkles, his gums were destitute of teeth, his nose sharp and drooping, his chin peaked and prominent, so that when he mumped or spoke, they approached one another like a pair of nutcrackers; he supported himself on an ivory headed cane, and his whole figure was a just emblem of winter, famine, and avarice. But how was I surprised when I beheld the formidable captain in the shape of a little thin creature, about the age of forty, with a long withered visage very much resembling that of a baboon, through the upper part of which two little grey eyes peeped : he wore his own hair in a queue that reached to his rump, which immoderate length I suppose was the occasion of a baldness that appeared on the crown of his head, when he deigned to take off his hat, which was very much of the size and cock of Pistol's. Having laid aside his great coat, I could not help admiring the extraordinary make of this man of war: he was about five feet and three inches high, sixteen inches of which went to his face and long scraggy neck; his thighs were about six inches in length, his legs resembling spindles or drumsticks, two feet and a half, and his body, which put me in mind of extension without substance, engrossed the remainder, so that on the whole he appeared like a spider or grasshopper erect, and was almost a *vox et præterea nihil.* His dress consisted of a frock of what is called bear-skin, the skirts of which were about half a foot long, an hussar waistcoat, scarlet breeches reaching halfway down his thighs, worsted stockings rolled up almost to his groin, and shoes with wooden heels at least two inches high ; he carried a sword very near as long as himself in one hand, and with the other conducted his lady, who seemed to be a woman of his own age, and still retained some remains of a handsome person ; but so ridiculously affected that, had I not been a novice in the world, I might have easily perceived in her the deplorable vanity and second-hand airs of a lady's woman.'

October 1, 1792. *On Her Last Legs.* Published by S. W. Fores, 3 Piccadilly.

November 5, 1792. *English Travelling, or the First Stage from Dover.* (See December, 1785.)

November 5, 1792. *French Travelling, or the First Stage from London.* (See December, 1785.)

November 5, 1792. *Studious Gluttons.* Published by S. W. Fores, 3 Piccadilly.

Adventures of Joseph Andrews and his friend, Mr. A. Adams. By Henry Fielding. Illustrated by Rowlandson, 8vo.

November 5, 1792. *The Convocation.* (See 1785.) Published by S. W. Fores, Piccadilly.

1792. *Philosophy run Mad, or a stupendous Monument of Human Wisdom.*

ON HER LAST LEGS.

Signed G. L. S.—As this print exhibits various indications of Rowlandson's handiwork, it has been thought advisable to include it amongst the present selection. The plate represents the general upset of affairs in France. On the wreck of a number of columns marked *Humanity, Social Happiness, Security, Tranquillity, Domestic Peace, Laws, Order, Religion, Urbanity,* &c., is balanced the seat of the republic of France, or rather that of Paris. A Fury yelling *ça ira* represents *La République*; in her hand is a picture of *Religious Indifference* graphically set forth as an *auto da fè* of Papish Bishops and Cardinals. *Plenty* is represented by a Fury extending her cornucopia of ' Assignats' to a group of hungry-looking half-starved Frenchmen. *Peace* is displayed firing a bomb marked *Abolition of Offensive War*; the gun carriage

is inscribed *Universal Benevolence*; the Goddess of Order is blowing through a
trumpet the tidings, *Peace of Europe established.*

Equality is travestied as an aristocrat kneeling in the dust, while a half-naked
sansculotte is treading on his neck and beating his head with a club. *Liberty*
is shown as a Jacobin, trampling on the Law, and holding the head of a Con-
ventionalist on a dagger, to which the rulers of the state are compelled to bow

STUDIOUS GLUTTONS.

their obeisance.   *Humanity* is parodied by a female monster holding up the
heart of a martyr to the new religion.

1792.   *The Grandpapa.* Designed by H. Wigstead. (See January 1,
1784.)

1792.   *Cold Broth and Calamity.*—This print has the reputation of being
an unusually successful example of the artist's humorous powers of delineation, and the writer has seen several original designs on the same subject by
Rowlandson's hand ; in some cases the drawings are larger and more important

in character than the etching of *Cold Broth and Calamity*; the subject seems to have been a favourite one.

The scene represents the waters of one of the parks, or of a frozen river; in the foreground is a scene of grotesque confusion, the ice has given way, and a party of skaters have fallen through; heads, arms, and skate-bound feet are waving over the hole, through which a group of unfortunates are engulphed. A little distance off the face of another unfortunate is thrust through a hole in the ice, wigless, and wearing the sort of alarm one could conceive under the circumstances; while further on half a face, with a wig and pig-tail attached, is visible, the owner of which is evidently shouting for assistance. Other skaters are disporting themselves in the distance; they, too, are getting themselves into difficulties. A stout parsonic-looking personage, in a full-bottomed wig, is falling forward, with the certainty of his body breaking through the ice : the upset of this capacious individual will involve a skater who is following him closely, whose hat and wig have already flown away from him. A party of snug old gentlemen in top-boots and ample great-coats are enjoying the sufferings of their fellow-creatures, comfortably on the banks, and in the distance is seen a large tent for the accommodation of visitors.

1792. *An Italian Family.* (See *A French Family*, 1790.) Drawing exhibited at the Royal Academy, 1784.

November 5, 1792. *The Hypochondriac.* Designed by James Dunthorne; etched by T. Rowlandson; published by S. W. Fores, 3 Piccadilly.

> The Mind distemper'd—say, what potent charm,
> Can Fancy's spectre—brooding rage disarm ?
> Physic's prescriptive art assails in vain
> The dreadful phantoms floating 'cross the brain !
> Until, with Esculapian skill, the sage M.D.
> Finds out at length by self-taught palmistry
> The hopeless case, in the reluctant fee :
> Then, not in torture such a wretch to keep,
> One pitying bolus lays him sound asleep.

The *Hypochondriac*, forming a companion to *Ague and Fever* (See March 29, 1788), is another instance of the difficulty of attempting to express mental and physical maladies by pictorial embodiments, the designer being one of the ingenious amateurs of the period, who had recourse to more experienced professional hands to work their conceptions into presentable shape, with, at least, some regard for the accepted ideas of form, and a certain respect for the technicalities of execution. The *Hypochondriac* is seated in his arm-chair, in night-cap and slippers, and wrapped in a flannel dressing-gown, his arms are folded, and his head droops, in melancholy meditation, on his chest; the expression

AN ITALIAN FAMILY.

of his features is moody in the extreme.   By his side is an iron-clamped chest,
to hint that the sufferer is somewhat tenacious of his wealth, although his life has
otherwise become insupportably burdensome.   Phantoms, and figurative horrors
of various descriptions, are haunting the invalid's diseased mind.   There is a
dagger, like the sword of Damocles, trembling above his head.   A grim skeleton
of Death is, with grotesque energy, threatening to hurl his dart, as a release
from life's fretful calamities.   A corpse, with grave-clothes clinging to its ghastly

BENEVOLENCE.

frame, is proffering the means of making an untimely exit, by a rope or a pistol
at choice; another phantom figure is setting the example of plunging headlong
down to destruction; a goblin is offering a cup of poison; while a spectre, wearing
the sufferer's own image, is suggesting on his fictitious person the ease of cutting
his throat.   A hand with a drawn sword, a ghostly hearse, and heads of
Medusa-like description, with furies, fates, &c., appear for the purpose of
daunting the unsettled brain of the haunted *Hypochondriac.*   A table is covered
with *Doctor's Stuff,* and a well-fed and prosperous charlatan, in attendance on

the distempered patient, is in consultation with a pretty waiting-maid, whose face and person give indications of the most flourishing health—a palpable contrast to the sufferer on whom she is retained to attend.

November 25, 1792. *Benevolence.* Published by S. W. Fores.

1792. *Botheration; dedicated to the Gentlemen of the Bar.* (See 1785.)

December, 1792. *The Contrast,* 1792. *Which is best ? British Liberty, Religion, Morality, Loyalty, Obedience to the Laws, Independence, Personal Security, Justice, Inheritance, Protection, Property, Industry, National Prosperity, Happiness; or*

BEAUTIES.

French Liberty, Atheism, Perjury, Rebellion, Treason, Anarchy, Murder, Equality, Madness, Cruelty, Injustice, Treachery, Ingratitude, Idleness, Famine, National and Private Ruin, Misery ?

A pair of medallions, designed by Lord George Murray, and sent by him to the *Crown and Anchor,* from whence they were freely distributed; the style of the execution bears the strongest resemblance to Rowlandson's handiwork.

British Liberty is peaceful and flourishing; Britannia is seated under an oak, her arm resting on her shield; in one hand is the cap of *Liberty,* and *Magna Charta,* in the other the scales of Justice evenly balanced. The British Lion is at her feet; seen in the rear is the wide ocean, with British ships riding trium-

phant.   The contrast to this prospect is *French Liberty*; the genius of France is
a fury, serpents are twined round her head and waist, she is carrying flames and
destruction in her progress ; she is holding a dagger in one hand ; in the other is
a pike, on which two human hearts and a head are impaled ; her foot is trampling
on the decapitated trunk of one of the victims to revolutionary frenzy.   An
aristocrat is shown in the background, hanging by the neck to a street lamp.

Sold by S. W. Fores (January 1, 1793), twenty-one shillings per hundred
plain, two guineas coloured.

December 1, 1792.   *Beauties.*   Published by S. W. Fores, 3 Piccadilly.

1793.

January 1, 1793. *The Old Angel Inn at Islington.* Published by S. W. Fores, 3 Piccadilly.

January 8, 1793. *Reform Advised: Reform Begun: Reform Complete.* Published by J. Brown, 2 Adelphi.—*Reform Advised:* John Bull, in his comfortable easy chair, and wearing the homely and decent clothes of a well-to-do citizen, is seated beside his substantial fare of good roast beef and plum pudding, with his mug of 'home-brewed.' Three of the French reformers are taking compassion upon his peaceful ignorance; they have come over from Paris expressly to convert him to the advantages of the new order of things. These tatterdemalions are hungry, ragged, and by no means prepossessing as regards their exteriors; and, while John Bull is attributing his comforts to 'the blessed effects of a good constitution,' the sansculottes are taking considerable pains to bring him to a contrary conviction. The leader is offering him the cup of liberty and tricolor, and asserting: 'I am your friend, John Bull : you want a reform;' his followers declare, 'My honourable friend speaks my sentiments;' and 'John Bull, you are too fat!'

Reform Begun discovers John Bull under altered circumstances; his broadcloth is all in tatters, he has a wooden leg, and is shoeless; in his hand is a frog, which he despairs of relishing: 'A pretty Reform, indeed; you have deprived me of my leg, and given me nothing but frogs to eat; I shall be starved; I am no Frenchman!' His three philosopher friends now wear a more threatening aspect, and are menacing John Bull with bludgeons and daggers; one is crying: 'Eat it, you dog, and hold your tongue: you are very happy.' The others are adding: 'That's right, my friend, we will make him happier still!' and 'He is a little leaner now!'

Reform Complete shows the national prototype thrown to the ground, and quite powerless under the results of the new *régime*: 'Oh, oh! French fraternity!' he is groaning, while the Reformers, flourishing their flaming incendiary torches, are dancing on his prostrate body: 'Oh, delightful! you may thank me, you dog, for sparing your life—thank me, I say!' 'Now he is quite happy—I will have a jump!'

1793. *New Shoes.* Published by S. W. Fores, Piccadilly. (Republished 1804.)—The interior of a cottage, a pretty buxom country maiden is artlessly exhibiting a pair of new shoes to a smart young collegian, who is stooping, cap in hand, to admire the effect. The father, looking in at the window, has taken in the situation at a glance, and his face does not express approval. A cat is taking advantage of the general attention being fully engaged, to help herself liberally from a pan of milk.

1793. *Major Topham* (of the 'World,') *endeavouring with his squirt to extinguish the Rising Genius of Holman.* Republished (see 1785, &c.).

1793. *Illustrations to Smollett's Novels.* Published by J. Siebbald, Edinbrough. Republished 1805, Longman and Co. (See 1791.)

May 25, 1793. *A Tit Bit for the Bugs.* Published by S. W. Fores, 3 Piccadilly.—A stout victim disturbed in the night, by the plague of insects, is sleepily trying to free himself from his tormentors.

> Alas! what avails all thy scrubbings and shrugs :
> Thou hadst better return to thy sheets ;
> Heap mountains of clothes over thee and thy bugs,
> And smother the hive in the streets.

September 25. 1794. *An Old Maid in Search of a Flea.* Published by S. W. Fores. G. M. Woodward invt., Rowlandson sculp. Companion to the above.

1792-93. Two illustrations, published by J. Siebbald, 1792. One illustration, *Soldiers on March, making a feast with Filles de Joie,* 1793, vol. ii. p. 44.

1793. *Narrative of the War.*

October 17, 1793. *Amputation.* Published by S. W. Fores. (See 1783.)

Illustrations to Fielding, *Tom Jones,* &c. (see 1791); T. Smollett. *Expedition of Humphrey Clinker,* ten plates by T. Rowlandson, republished 1805, Longman & Co.

<h1 style="text-align:center">1794.</h1>

THE GRANDPAPA.

is due to Henry Wigstead, the Bow Street magistrate, to whom as a friend and travelling companion of Rowlandson, a merry wit, and one of the congenial spirits of his day, several references have been made in the course of this work. The grandpapa is evidently enraptured with his infantine descendant, for whose diversion he is going through certain ludicrous antics; the venerable gentleman's tongue is not, as at first glance it would appear, lolling out in idiotic contortions : it is a lump of sugar which he is holding between his teeth to divert the infant ;

ENGLISH CURIOSITY, OR THE FOREIGNER STARED OUT OF COUNTENANCE.

and his performances are so far crowned with success, that his little favourite
seems delighted with his exertions.

1794.   *Grog on Board.*   (See 1785.)

1794.   *Tea on Shore.*   (See 1784.)

January 1, 1794.   *English Curiosity, or the Foreigner stared out of Countenance.*   (See 1784.)—This print, republished by S. W. Fores, and bearing
the date of 1794, seems to have made its appearance as appropriate to the time,
the caricatures of this year making capital out of the arrival of a distinguished
stranger in this country, the great *Plenipo*, whose title appears in numerous
satires and ballads :—

TRAFFIC.

When he came to the Court, oh, what giggle and sport,
    Such squinting and squeezing to view him !
What envy and spleen in the women were seen,
    All happy and pleased to get to him.
They vow'd in their hearts if men of such parts
    Were found on the coast of Barbary,
'Twas a shame not to bring a whole guard for the king,
    Like the great plenipotentiary.

January 1, 1794.   *Arrival of a Balloon.*   Aquatinted.

January 1, 1794. *A Series of small Landscapes.* Aquatinted.

January 17, 1794. *St. James's and St. Giles's.* (See 1792.)

September 25, 1794. *An Old Maid in Search of a Flea.* S. M. U. invt., Rowlandson fecit.

New Shoes. Published by S. W. Fores. (See 1793.)

December 16, 1794. *Traffic.* Republished by S. W. Fores. (See 1791.)—Two Jew clothesmen are securing a parcel of cast-off garments at the door of a highly respectable mansion, whereat a buxom housemaid is disposing of her master's old apparel. In the street beyond is shown the milkman adding up his score—a mode of calculation prevalent in the artist's day, although it has become obsolete long enough ago in the metropolis.

December 16, 1794. *The Comforts of High Living.* Published by S. W. Fores.

December 18, 1794. *Village Cavalry practising in a Farm Yard.* G. M. Woodward invt. Rowlandson sculp. Published by S. W. Fores, 3 Piccadilly. —The volunteer and militia movements were pushed forward with enthusiasm in 1794, it being generally believed that the French might attempt a descent on our shores at any moment, and the loyally disposed were determined that they would not be taken either unawares or unprepared. Abundant materials were offered for the sallies of the satirists : the training and equipment of this new army of defence presented a sufficiency of comic incidents ; we find Bunbury, Gillray, Woodward, and Rowlandson, burlesquing the rustic cavalry; in the present plate a number of farmers and helpers, mounted on cart horses and armed with blunderbusses, flails, pitchforks, &c., are horrifying their officer by executing an impromptu charge upon a peaceful farmyard, knocking down old ladies, scattering the poultry, shooting the pigeons, capsizing labourers into wells, and producing an effect of universal confusion and dismay.

December 20, 1794. *A Visit to the Uncle.* Published by S. W. Fores.—The Uncle, who is a sufferer from gout, is evidently a well-to-do personage ; and the attentions of his relatives, who are favouring the sufferer with a visit of condolence, are, it appears, suggested by self-interest. One of the highly considerate relations seems good-naturedly assisting the invalid by making his will, while a pretty young damsel is embarrassing their interesting connection with a tender embrace, and altogether the members of the party are evidently set upon promoting their own prospects with a view to a division of the estate.

This print, which is aquatinted by F. Jukes, has been described as Hogarthian in type; it was issued with a companion plate executed under similar auspices, and entitled *A Visit to the Aunt.*

1794 (?). *Jews at a Luncheon, or a peep into Duke's Place.*—Three long-bearded Jews seated at table, on the eve of a feast. The joint is a sucking pig, into which the carver has put knife and fork ; the faces of the epicures express the most greedy avidity. The appearance of white wigs above their black locks and goat-like beards gives an unusually grotesque effect to Rowlandson's delineation of the Hebrew race, always marked by the exaggerations of his fantastic humour.

1794. *Luxury and Misery.* Published by S. W. Fores. (See 1786.)

December 25, 1794. An Early Lesson of Marching. Woodward del. Etched by T. Rowlandson. Published by S. W. Fores, 3 Piccadilly.

December 28, 1794. Bad News upon the Stock Exchange. Published by S. W. Fores, 3 Piccadilly. Woodward del., Rowlandson sculp.—A meeting of the various merchants and brokers upon the old Exchange. Sinister informa-

A VISIT TO THE UNCLE.

tion is supposed to have upset the market; the countenances and actions of the various representative pillars of commerce present are expressive of profound depression and distress. The individual oddities of such an assemblage are characteristically dealt with ; the grouping is good, and the faces, costumes, and movements of the figures are hit off with the felicity which more particularly belonged to Rowlandson's graver.

1795.

1795.   *Harmony—Love.*   Republished.   (See 1785.)
1795.   *Effects of Harmony—Discord.*   (See 1785.)

A MASTER OF THE CEREMONIES INTRODUCING A PARTNER.

November 24, 1795.   *A Master of the Ceremonies introducing a Partner.*—
Bath, 1785.   'Mr. Tynson was unanimously elected for the New Rooms, and
Mr. King for the Lower Rooms; they reigned till 1805, when Tynson resigned.
Gainsborough painted King; the portrait is now in the Assembly Rooms at
Bath.'

1796. *Sir Alan Gardiner, Covent Garden.—' Weeds carefully Eradicated and Venomous Reptiles destroyed—By Royal patent. God save the King!'*—This print bears the name of Kingsbury, and it may be considered out of place in a work treating of Rowlandson's productions ; as, however, the traces of the latter artist's handiwork are easily distinguishable, while the resemblance the plate offers to the known etchings after Kingsbury are less distinctive, it is probable that the execution, at least, is due to the skill of our caricaturist.

Sir Alan Gardiner was elected Member of Parliament for Westminster, June 1796. The naval hero, as represented in the engraving, is dressed in his uniform, supplemented with a gardener's apron ; he is reaping the Republican crop with his ' Sickle of Loyalty,' while protesting his patriotism : ' My life and services are ever devoted to my King and country.' Britannia with her buckler is encouraging the admiral, and crowning her gallant son with a laurel wreath— ' Go on, Britannia approves, and will protect you!' In the distance is shown Gardiner's ship *The Queen* with the words, *First of June*, inscribed on her flag. The admiral is slicing off the head of the Whigs ; Fox is declaring : ' I was always a staunch friend to the crops and *sansculottes*, but this damned crop is quite unexpected.'

John Horne Tooke, represented as a reptile, is being swept up by the rake of the Fiend in person ; he is crying, ' Now will no prospering virtue gall my jaundiced eye, nor people fostered by a beloved sovereign and defended by the wisdom of his counsellors. To anarchy and confusion I will blow my *Horne*, and wallow in everything that's damnable !'

The Evil One has already secured the head of Thelwall in his clutches— ' This will not *Tell well*.' Hardy is groaning, ' I was always Fool-*Hardy*.' The Devil is congratulating the captured Horne Tooke—' Long looked for come at last, and welcome, thou staunch friend and faithful servant, enter thou into the hot bed prepared for thee !'

We find a drawing by Rowlandson dated November, 1796, caricaturing the figures of three very eminent personages in conference, the Lord Chamberlain (Lord Salisbury), the King of Würtemburg—who had come over to this country on a high matrimonial mission, to marry the Princess Royal—and the Duke of Gloucester, playfully described by the satirists, on account of his slimness, as a 'slice of single Gloucester.' These portraits, which are very spirited, and full of character, are drawn on the back of another sketch, the first suggestions, in Rowlandson's clear and effective outline, for the cartoons of 'John Bull going to the wars' and 'John Bull's victorious return,' the best known version of which was issued by Gillray. (*John Bull's Progress.* Published June 3, 1793.)

May 5, 1796. *General Complaint.* Published by S. W. Fores.—The credit of this invention is due to Isaac Cruikshank, the father of the great caricaturist, but Rowlandson certainly had a hand in the execution of one version. The print represents a dissatisfied hero, whose dolorous portrait is described by the title ; his head occupies the major part of his trunk, and he is not in that respect unlike the figurative impersonations of the potent and universally familiar *Nobody.* In one hand he is holding out his empty purse ; in the other is the *London Gazette* ; one sheet is filled with *Bankruptcies,* and the rest is devoted to fresh unpopular exactions to meet the requirements of the Budget. The people were generally weary of the war, and dissatisfied with the high prices and the decline of commerce brought in its wake. The ministers in power were not liked, and the generals, officers, and those who had the conduct of military affairs, were regarded with undisguised distrust ; suspicions and grumblings against the administration were rife and outspoken, and in short the conduct of affairs was pretty unanimously voted disastrous for England, and discouraging as to her future. There was, according to the critics and satirists, but one popular headpiece, and he was easily to be recognised as *General Complaint.*

> Don't tell me of Generals rais'd from mere boys,
>   Though, believe me, I mean not their laurels to taint ;
> But the General sure that will make the most noise—
>   If the war still goes on—will be GENERAL COMPLAINT !

1796. *Love.*

June 15, 1796. *A Brace of Public Guardians—A Court of Justice—A Watchman.*

June 15, 1796. *The Detection.* Designed by H. Wigstead. Executed by T. Rowlandson. Published by S. W. Fores.

The credit of having executed the following engravings from the designs of an amateur has been assigned to Rowlandson ; we are not satisfied that the plates are entirely due to his hand, but it seems likely that he has had some share in the work, at least as far as the frontispieces are concerned.

An accurate and impartial Narrative of the War.—By an officer in the Guards. In two volumes, containing a Poetical Sketch of the Campaign of 1793. Also a similar sketch of the Campaign of 1794. To which is added a Narrative of the Retreat of 1795, memorable for its miseries, with copious notes throughout. Embellished with engravings taken from drawings made on the spot, descriptive of the different scenes introduced in the poem.

' Per varias casùs, per tot discrimina rerum.'—VIRG.

London : Published by Cadell and Davies, Strand.

Illustrations.

VOLUME I.

An Austrian Foot Soldier. (Hungarian battalion.)
Favourite Amusement at Head-quarters.
Council of war interrupted.

VOLUME II.

An Austrian Foot Soldier. (Back figure.)
How to throw an army into confusion.
Perils by Sea.

1797.

January 1, 1797. *Spiritual Lovers.* Published by Hooper and Wigstead, 12 High Holborn.

1797. *A Theatrical Candidate.* (*Vide Kelley's Memoirs.*)—Sheridan, in his managerial chair, is seated before his business table, on which is spread a long and discouraging statement, setting forth those bugbears of 'Sherry's' tranquillity —a list of 'unpaid salaries,' 'proprietor's demands,' 'Chancery proceedings,' and other applications for money. Letters from authors: *Sir, do you ever mean to pay me for my Tragedy? &c.* Beneath the sly manager's seat is perceived, 'pit money,' 'renter's shares,' and his own particular *Art of Humbug.* A most unpresentable candidate for dramatic honours is standing confronting the great man; according to a placard on the wall, this quotation from *Hamlet* is applied to the ungainly applicant, 'Oh, there be players that I have seen play, and heard others praise—and that highly (not to speak it profanely)—that neither having the accent of Christian, nor the gait of Christian, Pagan, nor man, have so strutted and bellowed, that I have thought some of nature's journeymen had made men, and not made them well : they imitated humanity so abominably.'

" A candidate for the stage lately applied to the manager of Drury Lane Theatre for an engagement. After he had exhibited specimens of his various talents, the following dialogue took place :—'Sir, you stutter;' 'So did Mrs. Inchbald.' 'You are lame of a leg ;' 'So was Toote.' 'You are knock-kneed ; ' 'So is Wroughton.' 'You have a d——d ugly face;' 'So had Weston.' 'You are very short ;' 'So was Garrick.' 'You squint abominably;' 'So does Lewis.' 'You are a mere monotonous mannerist;' 'So is Kemble.' 'You are but a miserable copy of Kemble;' 'So is Barrymore.' 'You have a perpetual whine;' 'So has Pope.' 'In comedy you are quite a buffoon;' 'So is Bannister.' 'You sing as ill as you act;' 'So does Kelly.' 'But you have all those defects combined;' 'So much the more singular.' "

August 1, 1797. *Feyge Dam, with part of the Fish Market at Amsterdam.* Rowlandson del., Wright and Schultz sculp. Published by R. Ackermann, Strand.—A large and important plate presenting boats, canals, and the quaint buildings; the appearance of these edifices, a hundred years ago, differed but slightly from their present aspects; the view is enlivened with crowds of Dutchmen, Jews, vrows, &c., variously occupied: all the humours and activities of the scene have been seized and improved on by the artist with his characteristic vigour and animation. The architectural portions of Rowlandson's Dutch and Flemish views are worked out with care and attention, and with an easy skill, strongly suggesting Prout's studies from similar picturesque materials.

Stadthouse, Amsterdam. Rowlandson del., Wright and Schultz sculp. Published by R. Ackermann.

Place de Mer. Antwerp. Rowlandson del., Wright and Schultz sculp. Published by R. Ackermann.

'From the Lion d'Or at Antwerp,' writes Angelo in his *Reminiscences,* 'I rambled about the town; the next day I saw the grand church, where the curious representation of Purgatory is exhibited, and the Place de Mer, which, as well as the view of the Stadthouse at Amsterdam, has been so accurately designed by Rowlandson (published by Ackermann) when on a tour in Holland with Mr. Mitchell, late partner in Hodsoll's (the banker's) house.'

1797. *Dutch Merchants, sketched at Amsterdam.*

August 1797. *Tiens bien ton Bonnet, et toi, defends ta Queue. Rollandson inv.* P. W. Tomkins sculp.—The plate which bears this title is somewhat of an enigma, especially as regards the orthography of the artist's name, which must have been generally familiar in 1797. The style of engraving, more pretty than powerful, a combination of delicate line and stipple, removes it still further from the recognised characteristics of Rowlandson's works; and the extreme finish and smallness of the method employed have produced a somewhat hard and laboured result, such as one does not expect to find in engravings by or after this artist.

The subject is revolutionary; an aristocrat, one of the *jeunesse dorée* order, and one of the mob, a *bonnet rouge,* are in active conflict. The two estates have come into collision; the representative of social refinement is tall, elegant, well-favoured, and scrupulously attired, in the advanced fashion of the hour; his opponent is shambling, misshapen, uncombed, wretchedly clad, and with his ragged shirt open at the front and exposing his chest. The hero of the curled and scented locks has had the temerity to seize the red bonnet of Liberty, which is the only pretension to finery indulged in by the ruffian; in return, the strong hand of the latter is entwined in the clubbed tail of the dandy, and a significant warning is given him to take off that cherished appendage—shaving a *queue* and cutting off a head by Mère Guillotine, the barber of the aristocrats, being sometimes synonymous terms during the reign of the Jacobins.

It was in the spring of this year (1797) that a duty was proposed in England on hats, an impost the people avoided by wearing caps: the satirists intimated the danger that similar taxes would end in driving John Bull to adopt the republican habits of our neighbours, and, among other allusions, Gillray published a plate (April 5th, 1797) under the title of *Le Bonnet Rouge, or John Bull evading the Hat Tax*, in which the national prototype is shown trying on the famous red bonnet of the Jacobin section.

1797. *Cupid's Magic Lanthorn.*—Rowlandson, engraved after Woodward.

Waggon and Horses outside 'The Feathers,' published by Laurie and Whittle (see 1787), republished 1803.

1798.

January 12, 1798. *The Dinner.* Published by J. Harris, Sweeting's Alley, Cornhill, and 8 Broad Street.—This plate forms one of a series of important size (21 × 17) executed by Rowlandson in a bold and spirited manner; the plate is dated 1787, and was issued in 1798.

The set, it is certain, was deservedly popular in those famous fox-hunting days, and doubtless the five best known subjects have graced the walls of many fine mansions, the owners of which inclined to the sports of the chase; indeed, this hunting series may be found in grand old country houses, much prized, and preserved to the present day, although too frequently the prints are found discoloured by time from the effects of having been varnished.

The *Hunt Dinner* pictures the wind-up of a successful day's sport. The table has been cleared, punch bowls are introduced, the run has been recorded and canvassed, and the venerable ancestral hall, hung with the armour of an earlier generation of the occupant's progenitors, is ringing with the sounds of hilarity. The young squire, a man of mettle, has mounted a chair in front of the portrait of his sire, who it seems was a Nimrod in his day: field sports are obviously the family taste; the owner of the estate, standing at the head of the table to pledge a toast, and holding a huge prize cup, in which Reynard's brush is dipped, is waving his cap, and giving a 'View Halloo!' which is inspiring his guests, the bold hunters gathered round his mahogany, who are acknowledging his lead with an enthusiasm and *entraînement* which correspond to the ardour of their host; the bumpers are lifted on high with reckless hands, and numerous pairs of stentorian lungs are echoing the challenge with boundless goodwill; in some instances the good cheer is a trifle overwhelming, and one hero, though capsized in his chair, is still doing honour, with undiminished rapture, to the toast of the evening: even the privileged hounds are adding their voices to the general hilarity.

January 6, 1798. *Comforts of Bath.* Published by S. W. Fores, Piccadilly.

THE NEW BATH GUIDE;

OR MEMOIRS OF THE BLUNDERHEAD FAMILY.

IN A SERIES OF POETICAL EPISTLES

By CHRISTOPHER ANSTEY, ESQ.

I'll hasten, O Bath, to thy springs, Thy seats of the wealthy and gay,	Where the hungry are fed with good things, And the rich are sent empty away.

I'm certain none of Hogarth's sketches
E'er formed a set of stranger wretches.

COMFORTS OF BATH.   I.

Plate I.

We all are a wonderful distance from home !
Two hundred and sixty long miles are we come !
'Tis a plaguy long way ! but I ne'er can repine,
As my stomach is weak and my spirits decline :
For the people cry here, be whatever your case,
You are sure to get well if you come to this place.
As we all came for health (as a body may say),
I sent for the doctor the very next day ;
And the doctor was pleased, though so short was the warning,
To come to our lodging betimes in the morning :

He looked very thoughtful and grave, to be sure,
And I said to myself, There's no hopes of a cure !
But I thought I should faint when I saw him, dear Mother,
Feel my pulse with one hand, and a watch in the other :
No token of death that is heard in the night
Could ever have put me so much in a fright :
Thinks I, 'tis all over, my sentence is past,
And now he is counting how long I may last.

And so, as I grew every day worse and worse,
The doctor advised me to send for a nurse.

COMFORTS OF BATH.   II.

And the nurse was so willing my health to restore,
She begged me to send for a few doctors more ;
For when any difficult work's to be done,
Many heads can despatch it much sooner than one ;
And I find there are doctors enough at this place,
If you want to consult in a dangerous case !

Plate II.

Why, Peter's a critic —with true Attic salt
Can damn the performers, can hiss, and find fault,

And tell when we ought to express approbation,
By thumping, and clapping, and vociferation ;
But Jack Dilettante despises the play'rs—
To concerts and musical parties repairs,
With benefit-tickets his pockets he fills,
Like a mountebank doctor distributes his bills ;
And thus his importance and interest shows,
By conferring his favours wherever he goes ;
He's extremely polite both to me and my cousin,
For he often desires us to take off a dozen ;
He has taste, without doubt, and a delicate ear,
No vile *oratorios* ever could bear ;
But talks of the *op'ras* and his *signora*,
Cries *Bravo, benissimo, bravo, encora !*
And oft is so kind as to thrust in a note
While old Lady Cuckow is straining her throat,
Or little Miss Wren, who's an excellent singer ;
Then he points to the notes with a ring on his finger,
And shows her the crotchet, the quaver, and bar,
All the time that she warbles and plays the guitar ;
Yet I think, though she's at it from morning till noon,
The queer little thingumbob's never in tune.

Plate III.

One thing, though I wonder at much, I confess, is
The appearance they make in their different dresses ;
For, indeed, they look very much like apparitions
When they come in the morning to hear the musicians ;
And some I am apt to mistake, at first sight,
For the mothers of those I have seen over night.
It shocks me to see them look paler than ashes,
And as dead in the eye as the busto of Nash is,
Who the evening before were so blooming and plump,
I'm grieved to the heart when I go to the pump ;
For I take every morning a sup of the water,
Just to hear what is passing and see what they're a'ter ;
For I'm told the discov'ries of persons refined
Are better than books for improving the mind.
But a great deal of judgment's required in the skimming
The polite conversation of sensible women,
For they come to the pump, as before I was saying,
And talk all at once while the music is playing !
'Your servant, Miss Fitchet.'   'Good morning, Miss Stote.'
'My dear Lady Riggledum, how is your throat ?
Your ladyship knows that I sent you a scrawl
But I hear that your ladyship went to the ball.'

' Oh, Fitchet, don't ask me—good heavens, preserve ——
I wish there were no such a thing as a nerve ;
Half dead all the night, I protest and declare ——
My dear little Fitchet, who dresses your hair ?
You'll come to the rooms—all the world will be there.
Sir Toby Mac Negus is going to settle
His tea-drinking night with Sir Philip O'Kettle :
I hear that they both have appointed the same ;
The majority think that Sir Philip's to blame ;
I hope they won't quarrel, they're both in a flame :

COMFORTS OF BATH.   III.

Sir Toby Mac Negus much spirit has got,
And Sir Philip O'Kettle is apt to be hot.'
' Have you read the " Bath Guide," that ridiculous poem ?
What a scurrilous author !   Does nobody know him ?'
' You know I'm engaged, my dear creature, with you
And Mrs. Pantickle this morning at loo ;
Poor thing ! tho' she hobbled last night to the ball,
To-day she's so lame that she hardly can crawl—
Major Lignum has trod on the first joint of her toe ;—
That thing they played last was a charming concerto,
I don't recollect I have heard it before ;

The minuet's good, but the jig I adore ;
Pray speak to Sir Toby to cry out *encore.*'

Plate IV.

Jen declar'd she was shocked that so many should come
To be doctored to death such a distance from home,
At a place where they tell you that water alone
Can cure all distempers that ever were known.
But, what is the pleasantest part of the story,
Jen has ordered for dinner a piper and dory ;

COMFORTS OF BATH.   IV.

For to-day Captain Cormorant's coming to dine,
That worthy acquaintance of Jenny's and mine.
'Tis a shame to the army that men of such spirit
Should never obtain the reward of their merit ;
And after so many hardships and dangers incurred,
He himself thinks he ought to be better preferred.
And Roger, or, what is his name ? Nicodemus,
Appears full as kind, and as much to esteem us ;
Our Prudence declares he's an excellent preacher,
And by night and by day he is so good to teach her ;
I told you before that he's often so kind
To go out a riding with Prudence behind,

So frequently dines here without any pressing—
And now to the fish he is giving his blessing ;
And as that is the case, though I've taken a griper,
I'll venture to peck at the dory and piper.

Plate V.

But my cousin Jenny's as fresh as a rose,
And the Captain attends her wherever she goes.
The Captain's a worthy good sort of a man,
For he calls in upon us whenever he can,

COMFORTS OF BATH.   V.

And often a dinner or supper he takes here,
And Jenny and he talk of Milton and Shakspeare ;
For the life of me now I can't think of his name,
But we all got acquainted as soon as we came.

Plate VI.

But come, Calliope, and say
How pleasure wastes the various day :
Wheresoever be thy path,
Tell, O tell, the joys of Bath.

X X 2

Every morning, every night,
Gayest scenes of fresh delight.
O ye guardian spirits fair,
All who make true love your care,
May I oft my Romeo meet,
Oft enjoy his converse sweet ;
Lo! where all the jocund throng
From the pump-room hastes along,
See with joy my Romeo comes!
He conducts me to the Rooms ;

COMFORTS OF BATH.   VI.

There he whispers, not unseen,
Tender tales behind the screen ;
While his eyes are fixed on mine,
See each nymph with envy pine.
O the charming parties made!
Some to walk the South Parade,
Some to Lincomb's shady groves,
Or to Simpson's proud alcoves ;
Some to chapel trip away,
Then take places for the play ;
Or to the painter's we repair,
Meet Sir Peregrine Hatchet there,

Pleased the artist's skill to trace
In his dear Miss Gorgon's face.
Happy pair! who fixed as fate
For the sweet connubial state,
Smile in canvas *tête-à-tête!*

Plate VII.

' And if you've a mind for a frolic, i' faith,
I'll just step and see you jump into the bath.'
Thinks I to myself, they are after some fun,
And I'll see what they're doing, as sure as a gun :

COMFORTS OF BATH. VII.

Oh ! 'twas pretty to see them all put on their flannels,
And then take the water like so many spaniels ;
And though all the while it grew hotter and hotter,
They swam just as if they were hunting an otter.
'Twas a glorious sight to behold the fair sex
All wading with gentlemen up to their necks,
And view them so prettily tumble and sprawl
In a great smoking kettle as big as our hall ;
And to-day many persons of rank and condition
Were boil'd by command of an able physician.

You cannot conceive what a number of ladies
Were stewed in the water the same as our maid is :
So Tabby, you see, had the honour of washing
With folks of distinction and very high fashion ;
But in spite of good company, poor little soul,
She shook both her ears like a mouse in a bowl.
But what is surprising, no mortal e'er view'd
Any one of the physical gentlemen stew'd ;
Since the day that King Bladud first found out these bogs,
And thought them so good for himself and his hogs,
Not one of the faculty ever has try'd
These excellent waters to cure his own hide ;
Tho' many a skilful and learned physician,
With candour, good sense, and profound erudition,
Obliges the world with the fruits of his brain,
Their nature and hidden effects to explain.

Plate VIII.

Our trade is encouraged as much, if not more,
By the tender soft sex I shall ever adore ;
But their husbands, those brutes, have been known to complain,
And swear they will never set foot here again.
Ye wretches ingrate !   To find fault with your wives,
The comfort, the solace, and joy of your lives ;
Oh ! that women, whose price is so far above rubies,
Should fall to the lot of such ignorant boobies !
Doesn't Solomon speak of such women with rapture,
In verse the eleventh and thirty-first chapter ?
And surely that wise King of Israel knew
What belonged to a woman much better than you !
He says, ' If you find out a virtuous wife,
She will do a man good all the days of her life ;
She deals like a merchant, she sitteth up late.'
And you'll find it is written in verse twenty-eight,
Her husband is sure to be known at the gate :
He never hath need or occasion for spoil,
When his wife is much better employ'd all the while ;
She seeketh fine wool, and fine linen she buys,
And is clothed in purple and scarlet likewise.
Now, pray, don't your wives do the very same thing,
And follow th' advice of that worthy old king ?
Do they spare for expenses themselves in adorning ?
Don't they go about buying fine things all the morning ?
And at cards all the night take the trouble to play,
To get back the money they spent in the day ?
But these to their husbands more profit can yield,
And are much like a lily that grows in the field ;

They toil not, indeed, nor, indeed, do they spin,
Yet they never are idle when once they begin,
But are very intent on increasing their store,
And always keep shuffling and cutting for more.
Industrious creatures! that make it a rule
To secure half the fish, while they *manage* the pool;
Methinks I should like to excel in a trade
By which such a number their fortunes have made.
I've heard of a wise, philosophical Jew,
That shuffles the cards in a manner that's new;

COMFORTS OF BATH.   VIII.

One Jonas, I think; and could wish for the future
To have that illustrious sage for my tutor;
And the Captain, whose kindness I ne'er can forget,
Will teach me a game that he calls *lansquenet*.

Plate IX.

SONG, WRITTEN AT MR. GILL'S, AN EMINENT COOK AT BATH.

Of all the cooks the world can boast,
    However great their skill,
To bake or fry, to boil or roast,
    There's none like Master Gill.

Sweet rhyming troop, no longer stoop
    To drink Castalia's rill ;
Whene'er ye droop O taste the soup
    That's made by Master Gill.

'Tis this that makes my Chloe's lips
    Ambrosial sweets distil ;
For leeks and cabbage oft she sips
    In soup that's made by Gill.

Immortal bards, view here your wit,
    The labours of your quill,

COMFORTS OF BATH. IX.

To singe the fowl upon the spit
    Condemned by Master Gill.

My humble verse that fate shall meet,
    Nor shall I take it ill ;
But grant, ye gods ! that I may eat
    That fowl, when drest by Gill.

These are your true poetic fires
    That drest this savoury grill ;
Even while I eat the Muse inspires,
    And tunes my voice to Gill.

When Chloe strikes the vocal lyre,
　　Sweet Lydian measures thrill ;
But I the gridiron more admire,
　　When tuned by Master Gill.

' Come, take my sage of ancient use,'
　　Cries learned Doctor Hill ;
' But what's the sage without the goose ? '
　　Replies my Master Gill.

He who would fortify his mind,
　　His belly first should fill ;
Roast beef 'gainst terrors best you'll find ;
　　' The Greeks knew this,' says Gill.

Your spirits and your blood to stir,
　　Old Galen gives a pill ;
But I the forced-meat ball prefer,
　　Prepared by Master Gill.

Plate X.

What joy at the ball, what delight have I found,
By all the bright circle encompassed around !
Each moment with transport my bosom felt warm,
For what, my dear mother, like beauty can charm !
E'en the Goddess of Love, and the Graces, and all
Must yield to the beauties I've seen at the ball ;
For Jove never felt such a joy at his heart,
Such a heat as these charming sweet creatures impart.
In short, there is something in very fine women,
When they meet all together, that's quite overcoming.

　　　.　　　　.　　　　.　　　　.　　　　.

But hark ! now they strike the melodious string,
The vaulted roof echoes, the mansions all ring ;
At the sound of the hautboy, the bass, and the fiddle,
Sir Boreas Blubber steps forth in the middle.
Now why should I mention a hundred or more,
Who went the same circle as others before,
To a tune that they play'd us a hundred times o'er ?
And who at the ball on that night did appear,
Who danc'd in the van and who limp'd in the rear,
What dukes and what drapers, what barbers and peers,
What marquises, earls, and what knights of the *shears*,
What cook and what countess, what nymphs of the brooms,
What mop-sceptred queens came that night to the Rooms.
But at what time they heard the horn's echoing bellow,
The hautboy's shrill twang, the brisk fiddle, the mellow
Bassoon, and the sweet grumbling violoncello.

At what time they heard the men puff and belabour
With mouth, stick, and fist the gay pipe and the tabour,
At once they did scuttle, did flutter and run,
And take wing like wild-geese alarm'd with a gun,
In a moment came bustling and rustling between one ;
Some coupled like rabbits, a fat and a lean one,
Some pranc'd up before, some did backward rebound,
While some more in earnest, with looks more profound,
And sweat-bedew'd foretops, did lard the lean ground ;
But others more neat on the pastern arose,
Like the figure of Pan, whom you've seen, I suppose,
Just saluting the turf with the tips of his toes ;

COMFORTS OF BATH. X.

And as nothing, I think, can more please and engage
Than a contrast of stature, complexion, and age,
Miss CURD with a partner as black as Omiah,
KITTY TIT shook her heels with old Doctor GOLIAH,
And little JOHN CROP, like a pony just nick't,
With long DOLLY LOADERHEAD scamper'd and kick't.
As for MADGE, tho' young SQUIRT had been promised the honour,
BILLY DASHER stept forth and at once seized upon her ;
While with flames that keen jealousy's rage did improve,
Poor SQUIRT felt the heart-rending passion of love.

Plate XI.

For persons of taste and true spirit, I find,
Are fond of attracting the eyes of mankind :
What numbers one sees, who, for that very reason,
Come to make such a figure at Bath ev'ry season !
'Tis this that provokes Mrs. Shenkin Ap-Leek
To dine at the ord'nary twice in a week,
Though at home she might eat a good dinner in comfort,
Nor pay such a cursed extravagant sum for't ;
But then her acquaintance would never have known
Mrs. Shenkin Ap-Leek had acquired the *bon ton ;*

COMFORTS OF BATH. XI.

Ne'er show how in taste the Ap-Leeks can excel
The Duchess of Truffles and Lady Morell ;
Had ne'er been ador'd by Sir Pye Macaroni,
And Count Vermicelli, his intimate crony ;
Both men of such *taste,* their opinions are taken
From an ortolan down to a rasher of bacon.

 . . . . .

The company made a most brilliant appearance,
And ate bread and butter with great perseverance
All the chocalate, too, that my lord set before 'em,
The ladies despatched with the utmost decorum.

The peer was quite ravished, while close to his side
Sat Lady Bunbutter, in beautiful pride!
Oft turning his eyes, he with rapture surveyed
All the powerful charms she so nobly displayed.
Oh had I a voice that was stronger than steel,
With twice fifty tongues to express what I feel,
And as many good mouths, yet I never could utter
All the speeches my Lord made to Lady Bunbutter!
So polite all the time that he ne'er touched a bit,
While she ate up his rolls and applauded his wit:

COMFORTS OF BATH. XII.

For they tell me that men of *true taste*, when they treat,
Should talk a great deal, but they never should eat;
I freely will own, I the muffins preferred
To all the genteel conversation I heard.

Plate XII.

I never as yet could the reason explain,
Why we all sallied forth in the wind and the rain;
For sure such confusion was never yet known;
Here a cap and a hat, there a cardinal blown!

How the Misses did huddle, and scuddle, and run !
One would think to be wet must be very good fun ;
For by waggling their tails, they all seemed to take pains
To moisten their pinions, like ducks when it rains.
I saw, all at once, a prodigious great throng
Come bustling, and rustling, and jostling along ;
As home we came—'tis with sorrow you'll hear
What a dreadful disaster attended the peer.

April 1, 1798. *Views of London.* No. 3.—Entrance of Tottenham Court Road Turnpike, with a view of St. James's Chapel. Rowlandson delin., Schultz sculp. Published April 1, 1798, Ackermann's Gallery, Strand.

April 1, 1798. *Views of London.* No. 4.—Entrance of Oxford Street or Tyburn Turnpike, with a view of Park Lane. Rowlandson delin., Schultz sculp. Published April 1, 1798, Ackermann's Gallery, Strand.

June 1, 1798. *Views of London.* No. 5.—Entrance from Mile End or Whitechapel Turnpike. Rowlandson delin., Schultz sculp. Published June 1, 1798. Ackermann's Gallery, Strand.

June 1, 1798. *Views of London.* No. 6.—Entrance from Hackney or Cambridge Heath Turnpike, with a distant view of St. Paul's Rowlandson delin., Schultz sculp. Published June 1, 1798. Ackermann's Gallery, Strand.

May 1, 1798. *He won't be a Soldier.* Schultz sculp. Published by R. Ackermann.

May 1, 1798. *She will be a Soldier.* Schultz sculp. Published by R. Ackermann.

1798. *An extraordinary scene on the road from London to Portsmouth, or an instance of unexampled speed used by a body of Guards, consisting of* 1,920 *rank and file, besides officers ; who on June* 10, 1798, *left London in the morning, and actually began to embark for Ireland at Portsmouth at* 4 *o'clock in the afternoon, having travelled seventy-four miles in ten hours.* Rowlandson del., Schultz sculpt.

July 18, 1798. *Light Horse Volunteers of London and Westminster, Reviewed by His Majesty on Wimbledon Common.* July 5, 1798.

August 1, 1798. *Soldiers Recruiting,* 1. Rowlandson del., Schultz sculp. Published by R. Ackermann.

August 1, 1798. *The Cottage Door.* Rowlandson del., Schultz sculp. Published by R. Ackermann.

August 1, 1798. *Private Drilling,* 5. Rowlandson del., Schultz sculpt. Published by R. Ackermann.

September 1, 1798. *The Consequence of not Shifting the Leg.* Published by H. Angelo, Curzon Street, Mayfair.

September 1, 1798. *The Advantage of Shifting the Leg.* Published by H. Angelo, Curzon Street, Mayfair.

October 15, 1798.   The glorious victory obtained over the French fleet off the Nile on August 1, 1798, by the gallant Admiral Lord Nelson of the Nile.— Showing the distressed situation of the French frigate *La Serieuse*, of 36 guns and 250 men, which, after having been dismasted, sank.   *L'Orient* of 120 guns, and 1,010 men, commanded by the French Admiral Brueys, is seen in the background blowing up, by which she considerably damaged *The Majestic*, of 74 guns, 590 men, commanded by Captain Westcott, who fell early in the action. *The Majestic* was, after his death, fought with the utmost bravery by her first

THE CONSEQUENCE OF NOT SHIFTING THE LEG.

lieutenant, Mr. Cuthbert, during the remainder of the action.   London : published October 15, 1798, at Ackermann's Gallery, 101 Strand.   Rowlandson del.

October 20, 1798.   Admiral Nelson recruiting with his brave tars after the glorious Battle of the Nile.   Rowlandson del. and sculp.   Published at Ackermann's Gallery, Strand.—The gallant admiral and his chosen captains are raised above the crowd on deck; they are, like true British tars of the old school, encouraging the *esprit de corps* which the hero perfectly understood, since he was able, so far as the sea-lions who served under him were concerned, to cultivate it to such unmeasurable advantage for the honour of his country.

The brave tars, of all denominations, are thoroughly enjoying themselves after their own hearts, while commemorating the immortal victory of Aboukir Bay, and with each successive bumper are toasting their idol, who is set in their midst, and drinking success and glory to the navy of Old England, and confusion to her enemies—patriotic sentiments to which one and all were prepared to give practical effect in the hour of action.

> Dammy Jack, what a gig, what a true British whim,
>   Let the fiddles strike up on the main :

THE ADVANTAGE OF SHIFTING THE LEG.

> What seaman would care for an eye or a limb
>   To fight o'er the battle again ?
>   Put the bumpers about and be gay,
>   To hear how our doxies will smile.
>   Here's to Nelson for ever, huzza,
>   And King George on the banks of the Nile.
> See their tricolor'd rags how they're doft,
>   To show that we're lords of the sea,
> While the standard of England is flying aloft,
>   Come, my lads, let us cheer it with three !

1798. *A Mahomedan Paradise.*—A Turk embracing an elegantly dressed and highly presentable female.

November 12, 1798. *High Fun for John Bull, or the Republicans put to their last shift.* Published by R. Ackermann, 101 Strand.—The victory gained by Nelson at Aboukir Bay, over the combined fleets, disconcerted the French enthusiasts and restored confidence at home; it was recognised that while English admirals could sweep their enemies from the seas, neither the dangers of invasion, nor the difficulties of contending with France, need be ranked of much consequence. In the print, John Bull is enjoying the *High Fun* of setting his opponents to equip fresh fleets, in order that his sailors may carry them off captive as trophies. A *Dutch Oven* is serving as the bakery, Mynheer is pushing in a fresh batch of war frigates; 'Donder and Blaxan to dis fraternisation, instead of smoking mine pipes, and sacking de gold, dis French broders make me build ships, dat Mynheer Jan Bull may have the fun to take dem.' The Spaniard, with a tray of big guns, is faring no better under fraternisation. 'How! that Nelson wit one arm and eye can take our ships by dozens, then vat shall we do against the autres, wid two arms and eyes? day will have two dozen at a time.' The Frenchmen are excited over their prospects; the head baker has a fine batch ready for the oven: 'Sacredieu, Citoyens, make a haste wit one autre fleet, den we will show you how to make one grande Invasion;' the journeyman is working at his kneading tub, which contains such ingredients for fresh fleets as, *Ruination, Botheration, Confiscation, Requisition, Plunderation, Limitation, Execution, Constitution, Fraternisation, Naturalisation, Expedition, Abolition, Cut-throatation, and Damnation.* The assistant is not hopeful: 'By Gat, well you may talk, make haste, when that English Nelson take our ships by the douzaine!' John Bull, whip in hand, is laughing with satisfaction: 'What! you could not find that out before, you stupid dupes, but since you began the fun you shall keep on—so work away, dam ye, else Jack Tar will soon be idle.' Jack Tar is seen hopping off with a full load of ships; his spirits are excellent: 'Push on, keep moving, I'll soon come for another cargo; Old England for ever, huzza!'

1798. *The Discovery.* Republished 1800, 1808–9, &c.—A bed-chamber is the scene of the discovery; a young couple have been surprised by a corpulent old gentleman, who is threatening a kneeling and simple-looking youth with a red-hot poker; the detected swain, who has been disclosed in a cupboard, is entreating forgiveness with clasped hands, and the lady is dissolved in tears.

Published 1798. Lately published by William Wigstead, 40 Charing Cross. Printed September, 1799.

Published 1798. *Annals of Horsemanship.—Containing accounts of accidental experiments, and experimental accidents, both successful and unsuccess-*

ful, communicated by various correspondents to Geoffrey Gambado, Esq. Illustrated with seventeen copper plates. Printed on a super-royal paper. Price in boards, 15s. 3d.

Published 1798. *The Academy of Grown Horsemen.—Containing complete instructions for walking, trotting, cantering, galloping, stumbling, and tumbling.* Printed on a super-royal paper, and illustrated with twelve copper plates. Price in boards, 15s. 3d.

Published 1798. *Love in Caricature.* On eleven plates, etched by Rowlandson; with a humorous frontispiece. The plates consist of—Spiritual Lovers, Aged Lovers, Sympathetic Lovers, Quarrelsome Lovers, Duke's Place Lovers, Avaricious Lovers, Country Lovers, Forgiving Lovers, Bashful Lovers, Platonic Lovers, and Drunken Lovers. Published in two numbers, 5s. each.

1799.

January 1, 1799. *Cries of London. No.* 1. *Buy a Trap, a Rat-Trap, buy my Trap.* Published by R. Ackermann, 101 Strand.—The vendor of rat-traps is pausing before a shop decorated with such live stock as a rabbit in a hutch, and a jackdaw in a cage; he is offering his traps to a spectacled old gentleman, who is considering his ware with curiosity. The rats in a trap, carried on the trap-seller's arm, are exciting the interest of a dog.

January 1, 1799. *Cries of London. No.* 2. *Buy my Goose, my Fat Goose.* Published by R. Ackermann, 101 Strand.—A fat countrified-looking dealer is offering some fine fat geese for sale at the door of an apothecary, who, with his wife, is examining the birds with unnecessary closeness.

February 20, 1799. *Cries of London. No.* 3. *Last Dying Speech and Confession.* Published by R. Ackermann, 101 Strand.—A street ballad singer, of the St. Giles' order, is crying the last speech of ' the unfortunate malefactors who were executed this morning:' a common enough announcement when the extreme punishment of hanging visited small offences, and executions were of more frequent occurrence. That the fear of capital punishment did not act as a corrective to theft is illustrated in the background of the print, where a mere infant is drawn in the act of picking the pocket of a passing pedestrian.

February 20, 1799. *Cries of London. No.* 4. *Do you want any brick-dust?* Published by R. Ackermann, 101 Strand.—From this plate it seems that brick-dust, in the artist's days, was sold like sand. A patient donkey is saddled with an enormous pannier of brick-dust, and the vendor is pouring the contents of a measure into a bowl, held at the door of a highly respectable residence, by a pretty maid, to whose personal captivations the attentions of the brick-dust dealer are most particularly addressed.

March 1, 1799. *Cries of London. No.* 5. *Water-cresses, come buy my Water-cresses.*—An old shylock-like person is knocking at a door in Portland Street (Mrs. Burke's), and is solicited to buy water-cresses by a neat maiden with a pretty face and a tall shapely form; the old reprobate is leering at the water-cress girl, and is disregarding a further offer of cresses from a more

CRIES OF LONDON.   NO. 1, 'BUY A TRAP, A RAT TRAP, BUY MY TRAP.'

ragged and juvenile seller. A pair of highly-coloured damsels, redundant in charms and florid finery, are peering out of an upper window at the aged visitor.

1799. *Cries of London. No. 6. All a growing, a-growing; here's flowers for your gardens.*—A smart young gardener, with a substantial cart, drawn by a donkey, has a handsome selection of various evergreens and flowers for sale; he is standing at the door of a mansion, where a lady and little girl are choosing

CRIES OF LONDON. NO. 5, 'WATER-CRESSES, COME BUY MY WATER CRESSES.'

from his stock of geraniums in pots.

May 4, 1799. *Cries of London. No. 8. Hot cross buns, two a penny buns.* —A decent woman, wearing a white apron, and with a cloth over her basket, is supplying a patroness with a plateful of hot cross buns. A pretty woman, in a neat morning dress, is buying buns, and her children by her side are tasting the same without any loss of time. Outside a church, in the background, is a stout dignitary, with flowing gown, sleeves, and full wig, who is sweeping away from an appeal for charity addressed to him by a beggar woman and her offspring.

February 1, 1799. *A Charm for a Democracy, Reviewed, Analysed, and Destroyed, January* 1, 1799, *to the confusion of its Affiliated Friends.* Published for the *Anti-Jacobin Review,* by T. Whittle, Peterborough Court, Fleet Street. —The Tory party at the beginning of 1799 (the parliamentary session had opened at the end of November 1788) endeavoured to stifle the Opposition by raising outcries against sedition, and by denouncing publications of a revolutionary tendency, with which they pretended to implicate the Whigs. On the strength of certain alarmist tracts, extraordinary measures were taken to restrain the liberty of the press, and a few months later, in July, the Ministry went so far as to put into effect the extreme measure of subjecting printing presses to a licence. The organs of the Tories, exulting in the discomfiture of their opponents, were continually urging increased and severer political persecutions, while they pretended that the members of the Opposition were, in despair of succeeding in preserving their party by fair means, identifying themselves with the more treasonable writers, and were laying secret trains for the destruction of the Constitution. The King's Bench, Newgate, and Coldbath Fields began to be crowded with political prisoners, the last-mentioned receiving the popular nickname of *the Bastille.* The *Anti-Jacobin Review* was, as usual, peculiarly smart at the expense of the malcontents, and Rowlandson's assistance was enlisted to prepare a cartoon which, it was supposed, would expose the Whigs in their true colours, and hold up the abettors of sedition to the execration of all loyal subjects.

There are four elements displayed in this general view of the fancied emergency : the supernatural department, headed by the arch-fiend in person ; the Radical pamphleteers and so-called workers of treason ; the prominent members of the disconcerted Opposition and their followers; and the King and his ministers displayed, as Olympians, in the clouds. The Infernal Influence is superintending the preparation of the charm, which Horne Tooke and his friends, as the witches in Macbeth, are working at a boiling cauldron ; the nature of the component parts of the conjuration are thus set forth :—

> Eye of STRAW and toe of CADE,
> TYLER'S bow, KOSCIUSKO'S blade,
> RUSSELL'S liver, tongue of cur,
> NORFOLK'S boldness, FOX'S fur ;
> Add thereto a tiger's chauldron,
> For the ingredients of our cauldron !

One of Horne Tooke's colleagues is working the incantation from a breviary of his own, 'Lying, False Swearing, &c.,' and is flourishing a witch's besom, 'Thrice

A CHARM FOR A DEMOCRACY, REVIEWED, ANALYSED, AND DESTROYED, JANUARY 1ST, 1799, TO THE CONFUSION OF ITS AFFILIATED FRIENDS.

the Gallic wolves have bayed!'   Another of the weird sisterhood is stirring the
unholy mixture, crying: 'Thrice! and twice King's Heads have fallen!'
Horne Tooke is attending to the fuel department; he is muttering: ''Tis time,
'tis time, 'tis time!'   The witches' familiars are whirling above their heads, and in
the midst of the flames from the cauldron, in the shape of wild cats, with wings; a
flying monkey, with 'Voltaire' on his collar; a tiger with vulture wings, marked
Robespierre; and Dr. Price's little dog, which is even more remarkable than the
animal associated with the early magicians, are the ministering imps.   The
fiend, with his pitch-fork, and attended by dragons, serpents, Cerberus, and
other terrific monsters of an imaginative construction, suggestive of Callot's
grotesques, is directing as head cook the Democratic philter-workers to

> Pour in streams of Regal Blood,
> Then the charm is firm and good.

The inflammable materials, which are piled up to make the pot boil, and fanned
into flames by a diabolical news-boy, from the *Courier*, consist of such com-
bustibles as *O'Connor's Manifesto; Oakley's Pyrology; Belsham's History;
Rights of Nature; Quigley's Dying Speech; Frend's Atheism; Whig Club;
Universal Equality; Darwin's topsey-turvey Plants and Animals' Destruction;
Sedition; French Freedom; Political Liberty; Duty of Insurrection; Equality;
Fraud; Sophisms; Blasphemy; Heresy; Deism*, together with such fiery sentiments as *Kings can do no good; Joel Barlow; Resistance is Prudence; The
Vipers of Monarchy and Aristocracy will soon be strangled by the infant Demo-
cracy; Kings are Servants, &c.;* with the *Analytical Review*, a rival publication,
thrown in as *Fallen never to rise again*.

The Duke of Bedford is at the head of the Opposition; the members seem
to fare badly between the two extremes of Pittites and Radicals, the leader is
demanding: 'Where are they! Gone.   Pocketed the Church and Poorlands!
The Tythes next!'   The Duke of Norfolk is deploring the 'Fallen Sovereignty
(of the People).   Degraded Counsellor!' having been deprived of some of his
offices as a punishment for the famous toast.   Lord Derby is equally hopeless:
'Poor Joe is done.   No Test, no Corporation Acts.'   Fox, who had kept his
word and absented himself from the debates, is reduced to a tattered state, and
enquires: 'Where can I hide my secluded head?'   Erskine, in legal trim, as
'Counsellor Ego,' is deploring: 'Ah, woe is me—poor I!'   Tierney is regretting
his past activity: 'Would I had never spoke of the licentiousness of the press!'
Sir Francis Burdett, who had brought an investigation into the abuses practised
on the unfortunates in the New State prison, before the House, a motion founded
on his own observations, is enquiring: 'What can I report to my friends at the
Bastille?'   Thelwall, with his lectures under his arm, is 'Off to Monmouthshire;'

and the followers of the dispirited 'party' are wandering blindly, lost in the 'Cave of Despair.'

Above the clouds is the King as Jupiter, with his supporters; light is being poured down in streams, upon the machinations of the disaffected patriots, from a symbolical source: *Afflavit Deus et Dissipantur.* 'Your Destruction cometh as a whirlwind!' 'Vengeance is ripe!' The monarch is strangling a brace of serpents, and asserting, 'Our enemies are confounded!' One minister is offering congratulations on a 'Great Victory!' while Pitt, behind the Crown, is insinuating an expeditious method of disposing of his adversaries: 'Suspend their bodies.' The Lord Chancellor, careful of the forms of law, is suggesting a more formal mode of procedure: 'Take them to the King's Bench and Coldbath Fields!'

February 10, 1799. *An Artist Traveling in Wales.* Rowlandson delin., Mereke sculp. Published by R. Ackermann, 101 Strand.—The caricaturist— in company with his friend, Henry Wigstead, himself a bit of an artist, further given to sportive flirtation with the Muses—visited North and South Wales in August 1797, for the purpose of carrying out a picturesque tour, to which the two travellers furnished the accompaniments of descriptive sketches and sketchy descriptions. The journey was undertaken solely as a pleasure trip, and not carried out with the intention of 'making a book.' It seems, however, that the interest which partial friends took in the notes of scenery, as found in Rowlandson's sketch-books, and in the minutes of travel, as jotted down in Wigstead's journal, finally prevailed over the travellers' reluctance to make much of a little; and accordingly, some two years later, the *Remarks on a Tour to North and South Wales* were submitted to the public, in the form of an octavo book, with some additional views by the hands of Pugh, Howitt, &c. (See 1800.)

Rowlandson appears both to have enjoyed this excursion, and to have been able to turn his opportunities to good account. He made several characteristic landscape sketches, and the present writer possesses a few drawings, in various stages of progress, which were evidently commenced on the spot.

A more Rowlandsonian relic of the tour is preserved in the plate, *An Artist Travelling in Wales,* first published soon after the traveller's return to town. Who the artist so represented may be the writer is not prepared to assert; but, as caricaturists have a well-recognised habit of turning not only the figures of their friends, but their own persons, to satiric usages on occasions, it is suggested that the large and gaunt limner, with his strongly-outlined features, and with his long legs slung across a Welch pony, may offer some points of resemblance to the designer; it is evident that more than once (See *The Chamber of Genius,* April 2, 1812) Rowlandson has burlesqued his own figure, or made himself the hero of equivocal situations, much as artists who have lived in our times have, now and again, delighted to introduce their own features amidst the fictitious personages they have thought proper or have been called upon to introduce. Notably in the cases of Thackeray and Cruickshank, this whimsical *penchant* is of such frequent occurrence, that the student, curious in tracing out such eccentricities of genius, will be able to discover at least a dozen characteristic and intentional resemblances of those admirable masters scattered over their illustrations, and relating to various periods of their careers.

It may be that remembrances of his old master at the Academy, Richard Wilson, who held the office of Librarian when the waggish youth, Rowlandson, was a student at the Academy, floated through the artist's mind in the course of his Welsh peregrinations, and tempted him to combine points of personality peculiar to both. It was not the first time Rowley's pencil had taken liberties with the marked traits of ' Red-nosed Dick,' who died, it must be conceded, some fifteen years before the tour in question. At all events, Peter Pindar, the witty and vituperative, was one of Rowlandson's intimates, and his advice to landscape-painters in general and to his friend and chum, Richard Wilson, in particular, whose talents he had the daring to lavishly acknowledge in the face of a generation which treated the artist with cold neglect because, forsooth, his works were ' not fashionable,' should appropriately be engraved below Rowlandson's unflattering presentation :—

> Claude painted in the open air.
> Therefore to Wales at once repair,
>   Where scenes of true magnificence you'll find ;
> Besides this great advantage—if in debt,
> You'll have with creditors no *tête-à-tête ;*
>   So leave the bull-dog bailiffs all behind,
> Who hunt you with what noise they may,
> Must hunt for needles in a stack of hay.

A view in Wales is faithfully pictured ; the unsophisticated natives are struck with astonishment at the figure of the travelling artist, whose profession they are far from comprehending, and whose paraphernalia excite their wonder. Rain, which is not unknown in the Principality, is wrapping landscape and figures in a moist embrace. The artist's very remarkable umbrella is a poor protection ; his hat is limp ; for safety his long clay pipe, a luxury difficult to replace, is thrust through a slit in the flap ; his lank locks are dripping ; the moisture is concentrating, and dropping down his well-defined proboscis. Of course it was necessary, in such an expedition, to bear the baggage and incidental impedimenta. A box contains the artist's larder and wardrobe ; his saddle-bags hold the provisions of the hour ; beside him swing his tea-kettle and coffee-pot ; his goodly sketch-book is slung across his back, much as the observant traveller may have seen canvasses strapped across the shoulders of pedestrian artists during the season, and in the vicinity of Bettews, Conway and the Lluwy in our day. The easel is folded up —and a vastly unwieldy affair it is—on the back of the stumpy pony ; brushes, a palette, knife, flasks of oil of goodly proportions, and a palette of extensive dimensions, are attached to the animal's neck ; and thus equipped, the man of paint and his rough steed are picking a devious way through the saturating moisture, up and down the steep mountains of the country : a pleasant souvenir of past hardships and discomforts by the way.

February 18, 1799. Nautical Characters.

1. Cabin boy.	6. Purser.
2. Sailor.	7. Lieutenant.
3. Marine.	8. Captain.
4. Cook.	9. Admiral.
5. Midshipman.	10. Captain of Marines.

March 1, 1799. An Irish Howl. Published for the *Anti-Jacobin Review* by T. Whittle, Peterborough Court, Fleet Street.—The month following, the Irish patriots, and rebels alike, were favoured with a view of their position, which was hardly more encouraging than the pictorial prospect held out for the enlightenment of the Democrats at home. A National Convention is supposed to have been assembled; the members are thrown into consternation ; and the table, round which they have been deliberating over the concoction of their organ the *United Irishmen*, is upset. A diabolical visitation is sufficient to account for this confusion. A monstrous representative of the Fiend of Evil, with formidable horns and claws, bearing a pitchfork over his shoulder, and with the French cap of Liberty, labelled *Anarchy*, on his brow, is intruding on the scene, with a masterpiece of his own preparation, setting forth the tender fate which the Irish patriots were likely to meet at the hands of their allies the Jacobins. *Le Tableau Parlant* affects to portray an 'Irish Stew, a favourite dish for French Palates.' The sons of Erin are, according to the canvas, thrust into a 'Revolutionary Pot,' which is boiling over a fierce fire; certain Jacobin French cooks, wearing the caps of Liberty, are thrusting their betrayed disciples into the seething cauldron, '*Equality*, all to be stewed *en masse*,' while another apostle of Freedom is clapping on the lid : ' Liberty of being stewed !' The Arch-Deceiver, thrusting out a forked tongue, is imparting his instructions : 'Stew it well ; it cannot be overdone for you and me !'

The United Irishmen are variously affected with despair at the probable end of their plottings. One patriot, intended for Grattan, or O'Connor, is exclaiming, 'My merits with the Republic should have saved me ; but I find we must all stew together !' A ragged Reformer is thrown on his back ; a bundle of pikes

AN IRISH HOWL.

are at his feet ; a case of *Radical Reform*. A papist friar is crying : ' By St. Patrick, a complete Catholic emancipation.' Others of the party are crushed. A legal gentleman is moaning in despair : ' So much for Republicanism and glorious independence! No money! No lawyer !' His neighbour cries : ' I now howl in vain ; we are all gone to pot!' Another patriot is thinking regretfully of Ireland's proper and natural ally : ' Brother John would not have treated us so ! What your own O'Connor, too !' The Map of Ireland is dragged to pieces, and dismantled by flying devils and imps of mischief christened ' Tallien, Barras, Lepaux,' &c. One of the united brethren is turning his eyes on the pitiful end of the Green Isle : ' Poor Erin, how thou'rt torn to pieces by these five harpies !'

1799. *An Etching after Raphael Urbinas.* An example of Rowlandson's powerful renderings of studies after the old masters, executed in a bold and flowing manner.—The nude figure of a man, who has probably been sleeping at the foot of a tree, has suddenly unfolded his cloak and found himself confronted by a hissing serpent, which has raised itself on its tail in readiness to attack the unprepared victim, whose face is made to wear an expression of statuesque horror. A club is on the ground at the feet of the man.

Apollo, Lyra and Daphne. Frontispiece probably to a book of music.— Apollo, with his crook and shepherd's dog by his side, and with sheep at his feet, is seated at the entrance to a wood. Several musical instruments, bound together with ribands, are hung on the branch of a tree over his head. On the other side of the picture is a nymph in classic guise, evidently captivated with his harmonies ; she is resting her hand on the shoulder of a second listening maiden, dressed as a shepherdess.

April 10, 1799. *St. Giles's Courtship.* Published by R. Ackermann, 101 Strand.

> Here vulgar Nature plays her coarser part,
> And eyes speak out the language of the heart,
> While health and vigour swell the youthful vein,
> To die with rapture, but to live again.

April 10, 1799. *St. James's Courtship.* Published by R. Ackermann, 101 Strand.

1799. *View of a Cathedral Town on Market Day (Great Yarmouth)*, Rowlandson del. and sculp.

May 10, 1799. *Borders for Rooms and Screens.* Published by R. Ackermann, 101 Strand. Woodward delin. Etched by Rowlandson. In twenty-four sheets. Republished May 20 and August 1.

June 20, 1799. *Connoisseurs.* Published by T. Rowlandson, 1 James Street, Adelphi.—The interior of a cabinet of choice works of art. On an easel

ST. GILES'S COURTSHIP.

is displayed a florid and somewhat suggestive picture of Venus and Cupid richly framed. An old connoisseur, with a glass to his eye, and his three-cornered hat under his arm, is seated in an easy elbow chair, critically examining the work in question. Three other distinguished *dilettanti* are peering over his back, and stretching their noses as near as contrivable to the object of their gloating admiration. All these amateurs have evidently called in to view the collection, which includes an example after 'Susanna and the Elders,' and kindred subjects.

August 1, 1799. *Horse Accomplishments.* Sketch 1. *A Paviour.* Woodward del., Rowlandson sculp. Published by R. Ackermann.

August 1, 1799. *Horse Accomplishments.* Sketch 2. *An Astronomer.* Woodward del., Rowlandson sculp. Published by R. Ackermann.

August 1, 1799. *Horse Accomplishments.* Sketch 3. *A Civilian.* Woodward del., Rowlandson sculp. Published by R. Ackermann.

August 1, 1799. *Horse Accomplishments.* Sketch 4. *A Devotee.* Woodward del., Rowlandson sculp. Published by R. Ackermann.—The rider is somewhat inconvenienced by the eccentricities of his steed. The horse is travelling in a somnolent condition, of which the equestrian seems unconscious, as he is thus soliloquising over the unusual proclivities of his *Rosinante* :—'This is certainly a very devout animal; always on his knees; five times in a mile ; constantly worshipping something or other. What is he at now ?'

August 1, 1799. *Waddling Out.* Woodward del., Rowlandson sculp. Published by R. Ackermann.

August 10, 1799. *Comforts of the City: A Good Speculation.* No. 5. Woodward del., Rowlandson sculp. Published by R. Ackermann, August 10, 1799.—A stout citizen is rejoicing over a fortunate investment.

August 10, 1799. *Comforts of the City: A Bad Speculation.* No. 6. Woodward del., Rowlandson sculp. Published by R. Ackermann, August 10, 1799.—In this case the dabbler in novel ventures is looking very blank and disconcerted, on the receipt of the information that his very latest and most ingenious ' spec ' does not promise to turn out favourably, according to a communication he holds in his hand :—' I am sorry to inform you that your scheme for manuring London with old wigs will not do.'

August 12, 1799. *Procession of a Country Corporation.* H. Bunbury del. Etched by Rowlandson. Published August 12, 1799, by T. Rowlandson, James's Street, Adelphi.—Bunbury's pencil was never more happily employed than when engaged in perpetuating the comicalities which he noticed in the country ; rustic simplicity, the pretensions of inflated noodles, bumptious nobodies, and kindred absurdities, such as are displayed in ' The procession of a Country Corporation,' wherein the Aldermen and Mace-bearers, his worship the Mayor, with

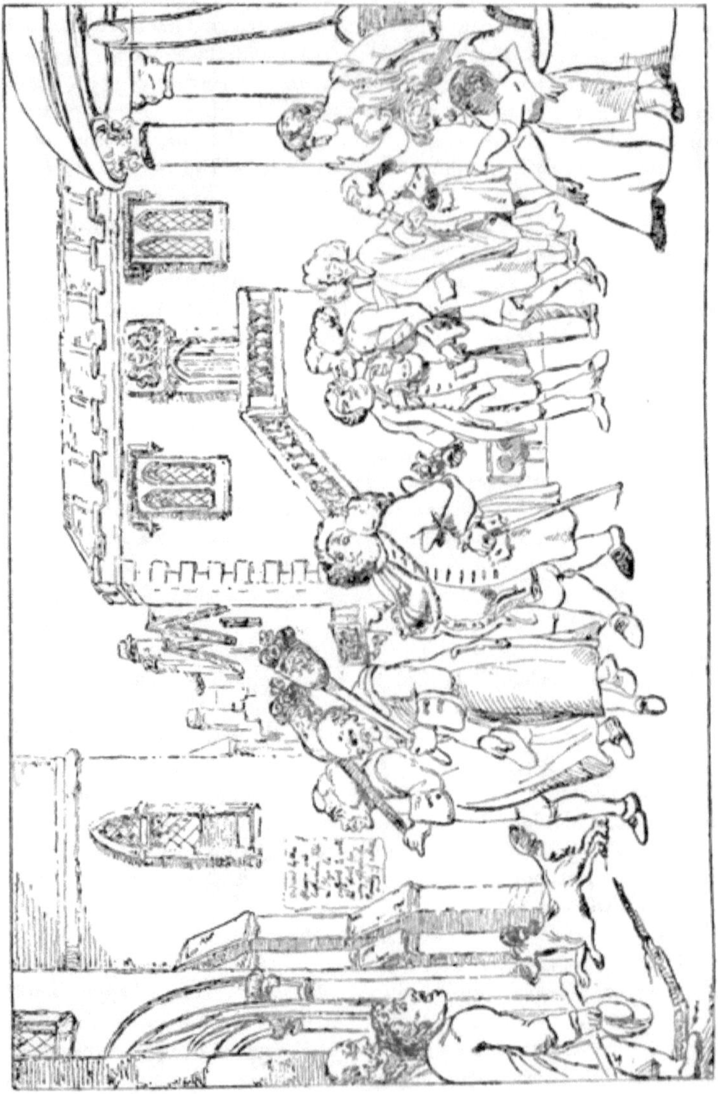

PROCESSION OF A COUNTRY CORPORATION.

his chain, and his dignified deportment, and his following of puffed-up provincial big-wigs are shown filing in solemn state past the pump, the Town-hall, and the stocks, to the Church vestry; the country clodhoppers and honest children of the soil are gazing open-mouthed, over-awed by the impressive nature of the ceremony, and the solemn airs of the performers. Bathos is arrived at in a notice on the wall, past which these 'hogs in harness' are strutting—'Ordered by the Mayor and Corporation that no pigs be suffered to walk the streets. For every offence the penalty of five shillings!'

August 1799. *A Game of Put in a Country Ale House.* G. M. Woodward invt. Etched by T. Rowlandson. Published by R. Ackermann.

1799. *Bay of Biscay.* (See 1789.)

September 3, 1799. *Forget and Forgive, or Honest Jack shaking hands with an old acquaintance.* Published September 3, 1799, by R. Ackermann, 101 Strand.—The troops forming the British Expedition which restored the Prince of Orange to his states are represented landing in the Texel, and delivering the Dutch from the hands of their friends the Sansculottes. Mynheer has become wretched and ragged under the French régime; he is shaking a British tar by the hand, heartily delighted to see a chance of recovering his freedom :—'Ah, Mynheer Bull, these cursed French rats have gnawed us to the backbone; they have barely left us a pipe, a drop of Hollands, or a red herring; oh, what a pretty pickle have we brought ourselves into!' 'Well, Mynheer,' responds Jack Tar, 'you seem heartily sick of fraternity: had you stuck to your old friends instead of embracing your ragged relations, you might have kept your gilders, saved your breeches, and preserved both states and stadtholder.' A Dutch vrow is trampling her foot upon an order of the French Convention :—'If any Dutch woman be detected in concealing any part of her husband's private property, she shall be guillotined.' She has secured a trifling comfort, a bottle of 'Hollands gin.' 'I have had great trouble, Mynheer, to smuggle this bottle for you, those French ragamuffins search me so close!' The troops forming the English contingent are landing from their ships, and driving the French legions before them at the point of the bayonet; the apostles of Liberty are losing their requisitions, 'Ducats and gilders for the use of the municipality;' they despair of converting their invaders: 'Here be dese English Bull dog, dey be such stupid brute dat we cannot make them comprehend the joys of Fraternisation!'

September 20, 1799. *The Irish Baronet and his Nurse.* ('Changed at his Birth.') Woodward del. Etched by Rowlandson.

October 1, 1799. *The Gull and the Rook.* Published by Hixon, 155 Strand.

October 1, 1799. *The Crow and the Pigeon.* Published by Hixon, 155 Strand.

October, 1799. *Twopenny Whist.* Designed by G. M. Woodward. Etched by T. Rowlandson. Published by R. Ackermann, 101 Strand.

October 28, 1799. *A Note of Hand.* Designed by G. M. Woodward. Etched by Rowlandson. Published by R. Ackermann.—From Bunbury to Woodward the change is easy. In all these renderings of the designs of less skilful amateurs it must be remembered that Rowlandson's part was not limited to that of a mere copyist of their ideas; he had to put crude conceptions into a presentable shape, and in most instances he has added points which originated in his own invention, and, as far as execution is concerned, he has made the works mainly his own.

In the present caricature there is actually no indication of Woodward's handiwork; a smart sailor of the period, returning to shore with prize money galore, and a watch, chain, and seals in either fob, neat silver shoe-buckles, and a spic-span rig-out, is calling to cash a twenty-pound note on a banker, who is negligently looking at the ceiling. The honest tar, who probably thinks the amount of the draft he has to draw a veritable fortune, is evincing his consideration for the man of finance—'I say, my tight little fellow, I've brought you a Tickler! A draught for twenty pounds, that's all! But don't be downhearted, you shan't stop on my account! I'll give you two days to consider of it.'

1799 (?). *Legerdemain.*—The subject owes its invention to the observant humour of Henry Bunbury, the caricaturist of gentle birth, who was ever a friendly ally of Rowlandson; while the latter has lent his more trained skill to work out the conceptions of the flattered amateur, further regarded, according to the views of his contemporaries, as his distinguished patron. We are introduced in 'Legerdemain,' to the consulting room and operating surgery of certain rustic practitioners, who combine the twin professions of dentists and pedicures; teeth and corns being extracted promiscuously, as the requirements of their patients might necessitate. Strength, rather than skill, is the chief requisition, if we may trust the whimsicalities of 'Legerdemain,' where main force directs the operations of the performers. One sturdy tooth drawer is bringing his knee and all the brute power at his command to bear in the way of leverage on the refractory grinder of an unfortunate and distracted client; a hammer and a pair of coarse pincers do not argue well for the painless dentistry of the establishment. A squire, judging from the liveried servant in attendance, is submitting his foot to another professor, for the removal of an obstinate corn; the victim is thrown into paroxysms of agony by the forcible mode of procedure adopted: the rude chiropodist has seized the sufferer's foot securely under his arm, and is dragging away with such vigour that, if the corn will not be persuaded to come off decently, the toe will be dragged out by the roots—the latter a most undeniable method of permanent cure so far as corns are concerned.

November 1, 1799.   *March to the Camp.*   Published by T. Rowlandson, 1 James Street, Adelphi.

November 1, 1799.   *Good Night.*   Woodward del.   Etched by Rowlandson. Published by R. Ackermann, 101 Strand.—A gentleman in the last stage of sleepiness with his nightcap on his head, and his chamber-candlestick flaring away—he is yawning like a cavern, and stretching his arms as if heavy with slumber.   The expression is realistically conveyed.

November 5, 1799.   *A Bankrupt Cart, or the Road to Ruin in the East.* Woodward del.   Etched by Rowlandson.   Published by R. Ackermann, 101 Strand.—The fortunate possessor of that dubious vehicle, 'a Bankrupt cart,' is proceeding in state past his own premises with his chin in the air; the showy

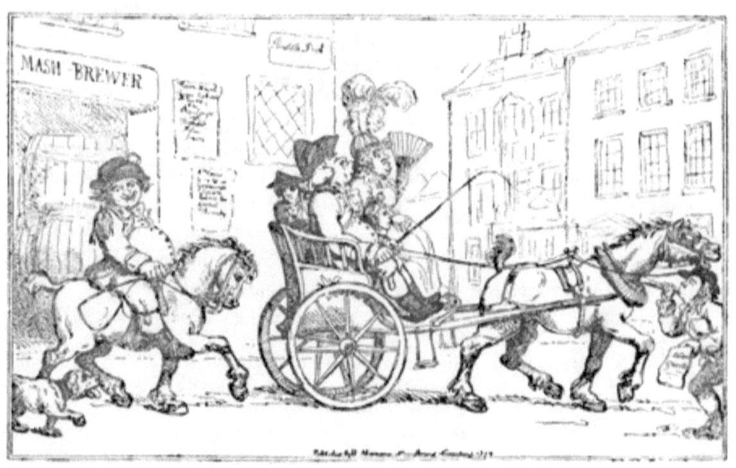

A BANKRUPT CART, OR THE ROAD TO RUIN IN THE EAST.

wife of his bosom in feathers and finery is riding by his side, and their children are packed in sandwich fashion.   A follower, who is probably a drayman, put into livery for the occasion, and mounted on one of the horses used in the business, is grinning at the high and mighty dignity assumed by his employers. A news boy is blowing his horn in the averted faces of the party, offering the *London Gazette*, which contains the objectionable black list of bankruptcies, wherein, it is hinted, the name of ' Mash, Brewer,' figures conspicuously.   Puddle Dock is the scene of this exposure, and the brewery is posted with advertisements, which indicate the sudden downfall of fashionable ambition : ' A house to be let in Grosvenor Square, suitable for a genteel family,' and ' Theatre Royal, Covent Garden, *The Comedy of the Bankrupt*, with *High Life Below Stairs.*'

November 5, 1799. *A Dasher, or the Road to Ruin in the West.* G. M. Woodward del. Etched by T. Rowlandson. Published by R. Ackermann.

1799 (?). *Loose Thoughts.*—A reclining female figure, lightly attired, and gracefully posed, buried in romantic creations of the imagination.

The Bookbinder's Wife.— Somewhat similar to the taste of the preceding. The nude figure of a lady toying with her infant: these subjects, which are avowedly of a slightly suggestive character, are handled with a grace and refinement which goes a long way to redeem the free nature of the subjects.

1799 (?). *The Nursery.*—A domestic subject; a gracefully posed female figure and two infants.

1799 (?). *A Freshwater Salute.*—The occupants of two waterside crafts are exchanging courtesies on the river, a more frequent occurrence at the beginning of the century, when figures of speech, especially among 'waterside loafers,' were more forcible than refined. The boatmen in the respective wherries are bawling at one another, and a stout damsel is extending, in expressive pantomime, an invitation which has shocked the proprieties of the occupants of the other craft, a lady of *ton* in a gay hat and feathers, and a very prim old gentleman, who is looking perfectly rigid with horror and indignation.

1799 (?). *Ride to Rumford.*—'Let the gall'd jade wince.' A stout equestrienne has put up her steed at the shop of an apothecary, who combines the profession of veterinary surgeon: the venerable practitioner, with spectacles on nose, is preparing a diaculum plaister for the scarified horsewoman.

1799 (?). *City Fowlers—mark.* H. Bunbury del., Rowlandson sculp.

> Against the wind he takes his prudent way,
> Whilst the strong gale directs him to the prey;
> Now the warm scent assures the covey near,
> He treads with caution and he points with fear.—GAY.

1799 (?). *The City Hunt.* H. Bunbury del., Rowlandson sculp.—This scene of cockney horsemanship is suggestive of the learned lectures of Geoffrey Gambado, Esq., Riding Master to that authority on equestrianism, the Doge of Venice. It is a question which are the more extraordinary animals, the mounted citizens or their horses; all is grotesque and burlesque. Of course fat men are shown tumbling off and over their steeds; and with equal propriety, a brook is introduced, in which to deposit the unfortunate leapers. Various curs have come out to share the run, and among the most spirited riders may be distinguished a brace of black chimney-sweeps, fraternally perched astride the single donkey possessed by the firm.

1799 (?). *Une Bonne Bouche.*—A stout gourmand impaling an entire sucking-pig on a fork.

1799 (?). *Cits airing themselves on Sunday.* H. Bunbury del., Rowlandson sculp.—A lady and gentleman are enjoying an equestrian promenade, too busily engaged in flirting to notice that their horses are riding over some wandering pigs. A Jew is in a chaise, taking his pleasure in the air; the fair Jewess, his wife, is driving, the rest of their family are by their side. A stout elderly volunteer in his uniform is out for exercise and relaxation, mounted on a heavy horse from the cart, ridden with blinkers.

1799 (?). *A Militia Meeting.*—The original suggestion for this subject, which bears Rowlandson's name, is, with several other small etchings, belonging to the same series, due to Henry Bunbury; it represents a 'justice's parlour,' filled with local magnates, who are seated in council on the momentous militia question. The characteristics of the various personages are individualised with the sense of humour and that power of hitting off quaint expressions with which both Bunbury and Rowlandson were gifted in the highest degree.

1799 (?). *A Grinning Match.*—The companion print to *A Militia Meeting,* executed under the same auspices. A party of rustics, whose rude features are more rudely burlesqued, are grouped around a barrel to assist at a competitive exhibition of 'face-making.' The challenge runs thus : 'A gold ring to be grinned for ; the frightfullest grinner to be the winner.' Mounted on a tub is one of the champions, round his head is the traditional setting of a horse collar, and he is succeeding in making the most fearful grimaces, to the consequent delight of the spectators.

1799 (?). *Distress,* (18 inches by 12⅝,) *from an Original Drawing by Thomas Rowlandson.*—Published by Thomas Palser, Surrey side, Westminster Bridge. —That Rowlandson possessed a remarkable power of grasping the humorous side of life was generally acknowledged in his own day, and is now well established, time having confirmed the justness of his title to a lasting reputation ; indeed, his works in this order have long received a recognition which is more assured than has been accorded to those of his contemporaries. It may, however, be pointed out, with equal sincerity, that his conception of the terrible is even more remarkable than his facility for expressing the whimsical frivolities of society. It would be difficult to find a more realistic representation of the horrors of shipwreck than the appalling scene pictured under the title of ' Distress.' The fearful sufferings of the survivors, exposed without sustenance to the dangers of the deep, and the hopelessness of any chance of rescue, are all simply set forth with intense feeling, and a faithful perception of the horrors of the situation which is harrowing to examine, although it is evident that the terrors of the subject must have exercised a certain fascination over the mind of the delineator. It seems clear that portions of a crew have escaped the loss of their vessel only to become the powerless victims of more insupportable sufferings. A solitary

DISTRESS.

officer and several of the crew are crowded into a boat, which they have no means
of properly navigating. Provisions and water are evidently wanting; the horizon
is a blank, the sea is still running high, and the sky threatens further tempests.
Hunger, thirst, and exposure, are reducing the ocean waifs to madmen; while
some are in paroxysms, others are stiffening corpses, and the body of one
sufferer is about to be cast into the waters to lighten the freight; some are sunk
in blank indifference or imbecile despair; others are furious, one or two are
looking for help from above, and a few, among them the young officer and the
boatswain, are doing their best to steer the open and over-laden boat towards a
likely course. The cabin boy's distress is rendered with peculiar pathos.

1799. *Hungarian and Highland Broadsword Exercise.* Twenty-four plates,
designed and etched by Thomas Rowlandson, under the direction of Messrs. H.
Angelo and Son, Fencing-masters to the Light Horse Volunteers of London
and Westminster. Dedicated to Colonel Herries. Oblong folio. London.
Published, as the Act directs, February 12, 1799, by H. Angelo, Curzon Street,
Mayfair.—Engraved Title and Frontispiece. A tablet topped by the figure
of Fame and supported by a relievo representing Guards on the march; below
it a trophy, and the escutcheon of the corps. On either side an archway or
portico, with relievo tablets above, representing military scenes. On guard and
saluting, on the left, is a Light Horse Volunteer of London and Westminster;
on the right is one of the same corps dismounted, presenting arms. The
etchings are dated September 1, 1798. The subjects are executed with considerable dash and spirit. The major part of the plates represent movements of
cavalry, depicted with knowledge and power; instead of being, as the titles of
the illustrations would indicate, mere definitions of the positions assumed in the
exercises, the artist has, with superior ingenuity and ability, managed to produce
a lively series of military tableaux filled with appropriate actions, in which bodies
of troops, reviews, incidents of war, engagements of large parties, assaults,
repulses, and other military demonstrations, make up the backgrounds, and
convert a set of plates of mere broadsword exercises into an animated and interesting collection of warlike pictures. Judging from the lengthy subscription list
appended to the folio, these plates must have enjoyed a wide popularity, secured
under the auspices of the Angelos, whose acquaintances amongst the fashionable
world enabled them to obtain a satisfactory array of patrons and subscribers.

The subjects are as follows :---

     Prepare to guard.
     Guard.
     Horse's head, near side, protect.
     Off side protect, new guard.

Left protect.
Right protect.
Bridle arm protect.
Sword arm protect.
St. George's guard.
Thigh protect, new guard.
Give point, and left parry.
Cut one, and bridle arm protect.
Cut two, and right protect.
Cut one, and horse's head, near side, protect.
Cut six, and sword arm protect.
Cut two, and horse's off side protect, new guard.
Cut one, and thigh protect, new guard.
On the right to the front, parry against infantry.

Infantry.

Outside guard ; St. George's guard.   Inside guard.
Outside half hanger.   Hanging guard.   Inside half hanger.
Half-circle guard.   Medium guard.
The consequence of not shifting the leg.
The advantage of shifting the leg.

1799. *Loyal Volunteers of London and Environs.*—Infantry and cavalry in their respective uniforms.   Representing the whole of the Manual, Platoon, and Funeral exercises in eighty-seven plates.   Designed and etched by Thomas Rowlandson.   Dedicated by permission to His Royal Highness the Duke of Gloucester.   Engraved title-page ; inscription in a lozenge ; head of Mars above ; Mercury's caduceus and branches of laurel ; Cupid-warrior, and Cupid-justice with scales and sword, supported by a trophy of arms, accoutrements, &c. Dedicatory title.—This illuminated School of Mars, or review of the Light Volunteer corps of London and its vicinity, is dedicated by permission to His Royal Highness the Duke of Gloucester by his most obliged and very humble servant, R. Ackermann, 101 Strand.   August 12, 1799.

List of Subjects.

Infantry.

PLATE.	POSITION.
1. St. James's Volunteers . . .	. *Stand at ease.*
2. The Royal Westminster Volunteers	. *Attention.*
3. Broad Street Ward Volunteers .	. *Fix bayonets, 1st motion.*
4. St. Mary, Islington, Volunteers .	. „ *2nd* „

PLATE.	POSITION.
5. St. Mary-le-Strand and Somerset House Volunteers	*Fix bayonets, 3rd motion.*
6. London and Westminster Light Horse Volunteers (Dismounted)	*Shoulder arms, 1st motion.*
7. St. Clement Danes Volunteers	*„ 2nd „*
8. Bloomsbury and Inns of Court Volunteers	*Recover arms.*
9. St. George's, Hanover Square, Light Infantry	*Shoulder arms (from recover), 1st motion.*
10. St. George's, Hanover Square, Volunteers	*Charge bayonet, 2nd motion.*
11. St. Martin's in the Fields Volunteers	*„ 1st „*
12. Temple Bar and St. Paul's Volunteers (Loyal London Volunteers)	*Present arms, 1st motion.*
13. Cornhill Association Volunteers	*„ 2nd „*
14. Temple Association Volunteers	*„ 3rd „*
15. Bethnal Green Volunteers, Light Infantry (Mile End Volunteers)	*Support arms, 1st motion.*
16. Bethnal Green Battalion Volunteers	*„ 2nd „*
17. Hans Town Association Volunteers	*Stand at ease, supporting arms.*
18. Deptford Volunteer Infantry	*Slope arms.*
19. Loyal Westminster Light Infantry	*Order arms, 1st motion.*
20. The Hon. Artillery Company of London	*„ 2nd „*
21. Pimlico Volunteer Association	*Unfix bayonets, 1st motion.*
22. Richmond Volunteers	*„ 2nd „*
23. Covent Garden Volunteers	*„ 3rd „*
24. Three Regiments of Royal East India Volunteers	*An officer saluting.*
25. Bishopsgate Volunteers	*Handle arms.*
26. Brentford Association	*Ground arms, 1st motion.*
27. Fulham Association	*„ 2nd „*
28. St. Andrew, Holborn, and St. George the Martyr Military Association	*„ 3rd „*
29. Castle Baynard Ward Association Volunteers	*Secure arms, 1st motion.*
30. Finsbury Volunteers	*„ 2nd „*
31. Newington, Surrey, Volunteer Association	*„ 3rd „*
32. Knight Marshal's Volunteers	*Prime and load, 1st priming motion, front rank.*
33. Guildhall Volunteer Association, Light Infantry	*„ 2nd „ „ „*
34. Cheap Ward Association	*„ 3rd „ „ „*
35. Armed Association of St. Luke, Chelsea	*„ 4th „ „ „*
36. Marylebone Volunteers	*„ 5th „ „ „*

<table>
<tr><td>PLATE.</td><td>POSITION.</td></tr>
<tr><td>37. Coleman Street Ward Military Association</td><td>Prime and load, 6th priming motion, front rank.</td></tr>
<tr><td>38. St. Pancras Volunteers</td><td>,,   7th   ,,   ,,</td></tr>
<tr><td>39. Cordwainers' Ward Volunteers</td><td>,,   1st loading motion.</td></tr>
<tr><td>40. St. Margaret and St. John, Westminster, Volunteer Associations</td><td>,,   2nd   ,,</td></tr>
<tr><td>41. Lambeth Loyal Volunteers</td><td>,,   3rd   ,,</td></tr>
<tr><td>42. St. George's, Southwark, Loyal Volunteers</td><td>,,   4th   ,,</td></tr>
<tr><td>43. St. Saviour's, Southwark, Association</td><td>,,   5th   ,,</td></tr>
<tr><td>44. St. Olave's, Southwark, Volunteers</td><td>,,   6th   ,,</td></tr>
<tr><td>45. Poplar and Blackwall Volunteers</td><td>,,   last motion.</td></tr>
<tr><td>46. Sadler's Sharpshooters</td><td>A Light Infantry Man defending himself with Sadler's patent gun and long, cutting bayonet.</td></tr>
<tr><td>47. Radcliff Volunteers</td><td>Make ready, front rank.</td></tr>
<tr><td>48. Union, Wapping, Volunteers</td><td>Present   ,,</td></tr>
<tr><td>49. Loyal Hackney Volunteers</td><td>Fire   ,,</td></tr>
<tr><td>50. Bermondsey Volunteers</td><td>Front rank kneeling, make ready.</td></tr>
<tr><td>51. Loyal Volunteers, St. John's, Southwark</td><td>Present (as front rank kneeling).</td></tr>
<tr><td>52. Langbourn Ward Volunteers</td><td>Prime and load (as a centre rank).</td></tr>
<tr><td>53. St. George's, Hanover Square, Armed Association</td><td>Make ready (as a centre rank).</td></tr>
<tr><td>54. St. Sepulchre (Middlesex) Volunteers</td><td>Present   ,,</td></tr>
<tr><td>55. Farringdon Ward Within Volunteers</td><td>Prime and load (as a rear rank).</td></tr>
<tr><td>56. Aldgate Ward Association</td><td>Make ready   ,,</td></tr>
<tr><td>57. Walbrook Ward Association</td><td>Present   ,,</td></tr>
<tr><td>58. Clerkenwell Association</td><td>Advance arms.</td></tr>
<tr><td>59. Royal Westminster Grenadiers</td><td>,,   4th motion.</td></tr>
<tr><td>60. Bread Street Ward Volunteers</td><td>Shoulder arms, from advance 1st motion.</td></tr>
<tr><td>61. Vintry Ward Volunteers</td><td>Club arms, 1st motion.</td></tr>
<tr><td>62. Portsoken Ward Volunteers</td><td>,,   2nd ,,</td></tr>
<tr><td>63. St. Catherine's Association</td><td>,,   3rd ,,</td></tr>
<tr><td>64. Farringdon Ward (Without) Volunteers</td><td>,,   4th ,,</td></tr>
<tr><td>65. Bridge Ward Association</td><td>Mourn arms, 1st motion.</td></tr>
<tr><td>66. Tower Ward Association</td><td>,,   2nd ,,</td></tr>
<tr><td>67. Christ Church (Surrey) Association</td><td>,,   3rd ,,</td></tr>
<tr><td>68. Loyal Bermondsey Volunteers</td><td>Present arms, 1st motion from mourn arms.</td></tr>
<tr><td>69. Billingsgate Association</td><td>,,   2nd ,,   ,,</td></tr>
<tr><td>70. Highland Armed Association</td><td>An officer.</td></tr>
<tr><td>71. The Armed Association of St. Mary, Whitechapel</td><td>Present arms, 2nd flugel motion.</td></tr>
<tr><td>72. Bank of England Volunteers, Light Infantry</td><td>Order   ,,   ,,</td></tr>
<tr><td>73. Candlewick Ward Association</td><td>Support arms, 1st   ,,</td></tr>
<tr><td>74. Queenhythe Ward Volunteers</td><td>A sergeant with arms advanced.</td></tr>
</table>

<table>
<tr><td>PLATE.</td><td>POSITION.</td></tr>
<tr><td>75. Ward of Cripplegate (Without) Volunteers . . .</td><td>*Order arms.*</td></tr>
<tr><td>76. Dowgate Ward Volunteers</td><td>„</td></tr>
<tr><td>77. Mile End Volunteers</td><td>*Pile arms.*</td></tr>
<tr><td>78. St. Leonard, Shoreditch, Volunteers</td><td>„</td></tr>
<tr><td>79. Trinity, Minories, Association .</td><td>„</td></tr>
</table>

Cavalry.

1. London and Westminster Light Horse Volunteers.
2. Surrey Yeomanry.
3. Deptford Cavalry.
4. Westminster Cavalry.
5. Middlesex Cavalry.
6. Southwark Cavalry.
7. Clerkenwell Cavalry.
8. Lambeth Loyal Cavalry.
9. Loyal Islington Volunteer Cavalry.

END OF THE FIRST VOLUME.

LONDON: PRINTED BY
SPOTTISWOODE AND CO., NEW-STREET SQUARE
AND PARLIAMENT STREET